Back To The
WORLD

Combat Vets come home to a whole new world

A NOVEL BY

Lawrence R. Chime

Written in 2000
Copyright © March 12, 2013 Lawrence R. Chime
All rights reserved.

ISBN: 1484190947
ISBN 13: 9781484190944

Library of Congress Control Number: 2013908315
CreateSpace Independent Publishing Platform
North Charleston, South Carolina

This book is dedicated to my wife, Patti

ACKNOWLEDGEMENTS

I would like to acknowledge everyone who, in one way or another, helped me bring this book to fruition. My wife, Patti, with her patience, encouragement and enthusiasm throughout the process. My sons Jason, Jonathan, Andrew, and Christopher who initially inspired me to write them a story and then provided insight to todays modern Navy and the younger generation. My friends Les Anderson, and Bill Bryant for technical assistance. Nancy Wilson and Sue Ellen Woodward who provided feedback from the woman / wife perspective. Military men Woody Woodward (EOD), Bill Garnett (SEAL/UDT) and Tom Keith (SEAL/EOD) who provided brutally honest but caring feedback. My old Okinawa (LPH-3) shipmate Brian Smith for hooking me up with Ken Levin who provided the final spark to getting this story out there. Thanks all.

PROLOGUE

Southeast Asia, 1960's; the escalating conflict between the United States and the Northern Communist Government of the Republic of Vietnam.

The Cai Lon River, brown and strewn with vegetation, flows lazily southward and eventually feeds into Vietnam's massive Mekong Delta, south of Saigon and on into the blue-green South China Sea. The Delta is a maze of waterways, swampland, and large and small islands dotted with isolated villages, rice paddies, fishing hoochs, and a million places to hide. Seen from a distance, it is a beautiful place. The *National Geographic World Atlas* identifies a vast region within the general area of the Delta as "the Plain Of Reeds." The people do have a way with words, not unlike our own Native Americans. Life is basic and simple. Most of the Vietnamese who call this place home grow rice, fish, and scratch out subsistence vegetable and fruit gardens. They know little about the threat of Communist world domination and care even less. Their own government is corrupt as hell, and they know about that and about the struggle between their countrymen to the north and these recently arrived Americans. The Americans are difficult to understand. They are rough but talk gently about their families back home; they consume and destroy but are almost unbelievably generous. Why are they here in our rice paddies and on our rivers? What do they want?

The PBR (Patrol Boat, Riverine) Base at Rach Soi had been constructed alongside the Cai Lon River to accommodate one of the navy's river patrol boat squadrons assigned to Task Force 116. The six boats in the squadron were thirty-one feet long and powered by GM 220-horsepower diesel engines that drove a Jacuzzi water-jet pump. The jet pump pushed the boat at just under thirty mph and, because there was no propeller, allowed the boat to operate in fairly shallow water. The mission of these boats was to enforce shipping curfews for the local sampan distribution and transportation system, restrict the infiltration of Viet Cong (commonly identified by the radio letters Victor Charlie or VC) into the area, intercept VC tax collectors, and confiscate money and supplies extorted from South Vietnamese villages. Generally they kept the river system open and available to US forces. To make things a little easier for the crewmen, the boats were heavily armed with an assortment of weaponry. Each boat varied slightly based on crew preference, but the basic weapon configuration consisted of bow-mounted twin .50-caliber machine guns; amidships mounts of either M60 machine guns or Honeywell Mark 18 40 mm grenade launchers, and another 50-caliber machine gun in the rear. The handheld weapons of the crew and passengers augmented this already significant firepower. Overall you didn't screw around with the riverboats for very long. The VC either beat feet into the jungle or got their asses shot off. Of course, that was during the day. At night the playing field was a little more level, and the VC, with their home-field advantage and hit-and-run ambush tactics, often held the upper hand, or at least made it more dangerous to operate. The old saying, "The night belonged to Charlie" was truer than most senior officers were ready to admit. Charlie did his business at night pretty much with impunity.

The early sixties and the deployment of US Navy SEAL teams to Vietnam, however, gave US forces a night fighting element that brought the fight into the heart of VC land. Charlie suddenly had to watch his own ass at night and was no longer exclusively the hunter. Now he was also the hunted, the target of "the men with green faces," as the Seals soon came to be known. Anywhere, anytime, men with green, brown and black greasepaint on their faces would materialize out of the jungle, sometimes without a sound and other times with an explosion of firepower, take what they wanted, then vaporize back into the jungle. Sometimes they captured VC officials or tax collectors for interrogation, gathering intelligence to set up other missions. Other times they simply reduced the number of the enemy. Seals accounted for a very high enemy KIA with a surprisingly low loss of life to the teams, given the dangerous and aggressive nature of their operations. While good kill ratios are great, there were never zeros in the ratio. The fact of the matter was that sometimes Seals did die. This was dangerous work.

Seal Team One, home based in Coronado, California, had deployed three platoons to Vietnam in May 1968, just three months after the enemy's Tet Offensive. Platoon Bravo, with one officer, a platoon chief, and twelve men, was assigned to the Rach Soi Base. Although the Seals had smaller boats of their own and a few confiscated local sampans, they sometimes operated with the "regular" navy's river patrol boats. The boats were big and reliable, and came equipped with ballsy crews and beau coup firepower. The PBRs were mainly utilized for delivery and extraction of the team patrols. The guns on the pickup boat significantly augmented firepower of the patrol during extraction. Usually extraction was a quiet affair, with the patrol brought aboard silently in the predawn darkness. But not always. Not infrequently, the VC would be coming after the patrol with guns and rockets blasting, as the pickup boat came roaring in like a fourth of July fireworks float. Then it was just a matter of scrambling aboard as fast as legs would carry you and letting the grenade launchers and .50s rake the shoreline as the boat wheeled and thundered home. If there were a lot of bad guys following, then Navy Seawolf or Army Huey gunship helicopters or the ever-popular field artillery would be called in to deal out additional discouragement. Even offshore navy destroyers or cruisers could be called upon to deliver incredibly precise HE (high explosive) surprises. The VC were so accustomed to having their way at night that in the beginning, they would give loud and revealing chase to the patrols. They learned to give chase more quietly as time went by. Any way you cut it, it was a lethal environment for everyone, and you paid close attention to what was happening around you. The primary ticket to survival was your training, teamwork, and attention to detail. The professionalism of both the boat crews and the Seals gave rise to mutual respect and a good working relationship. The base was a fairly comfortable place to live and work, reasonably free of bullshit rules and regs, senior brass, and other chickenshit military procedure. Do your job and stay out of trouble (or at least don't get caught), and life would be OK.

The violation of a Christmas ceasefire in January 1968—the North Vietnamese Tet Offensive against US installations throughout the entire country—put to rest any thoughts of US military domination and the "we can beat the crap out of these guys" attitude. They had punched us in the mouth, and we were spitting blood. The problem was not with our troops, it was with the decision makers, the politicians. What precisely do you want us to do? What is our objective? The troops were the best in the world, given a clear goal. Take the hill! Stop the invasion! Sink the enemy fleet! Liberate Paris! Whatever. Communism is political ideology, and it's tough to kill ideas with bullets. Well, for the troops in Vietnam, that's exactly what it was—a war of attrition with the objective to kill as many of the enemy as it would take for them to roll over at the Paris peace talks and give up.

Kill! That's it. Body count.

A mission statement so broadly defined gave many military units in Vietnam the latitude to do damn near anything they wanted. This was especially true for many specialized units, some newly created, to define or redefine their roles and experiment with new technology and new ideas. Often these were smaller groups, not under the scrutiny of senior commanders, political armchair leaders, or the media. Snipers, LRRPS (long-range reconnaissance patrols), PsyOps (psychological operations), Air Cavalry. Hell, even the tactical use of helicopters had to be developed almost from scratch. Of course, navy Seals fell into this window of opportunity. They worked quietly, often secretly, and developed techniques and tactics that were effective. These guys were lean and mean, scared the shit out of the enemy, and probably saved many American lives in the bargain.

The Seals operated almost exclusively at night. Each mission would dictate the number of men needed for a patrol, but seldom were there more than eight-man patrols, six being closer to the norm. Stealth and surprise were the key ingredients of a Seal patrol, and fewer people meant fewer possible mistakes. It takes unusual men to live and function so professionally in such violent and hazardous circumstances. The story that follows is about one of those Seals and his struggle to return home—back to the world. He happens to be coming back from Vietnam. Although Vietnam was perhaps more onerous than other wars in our history, it could have been any war. Under the best of circumstances, returning from war, from combat, to a civilized society is a difficult adjustment. It takes its own kind of courage and strength. Ask any combat veteran. Right after you thank him.

CHAPTER ONE

Rach Soi, Vietnam: 1968

PBR (Patrol Boat, Riverine) Operations Base

Feb. 1968

Operations Base for US Navy Seal Team One; Bravo Platoon.

Memorandum: Confidential.

To: Commanding Officer, US Navy Seal Team One, Bravo Platoon, Rach Soi, Vietnam

From: Commander Navy Seal Teams, Southeast Asia Theater, Saigon, Vietnam

Date: 10 February 1968

Subj: Locate and destroy covert enemy forces operating south of Saigon in the Mekong River delta region. Utilize all resources available to search out and disrupt or destroy enemy activity in above-referenced theater of operations. Recent violation of Tet cease-fire requires swift and direct success to this directive. File after action reports ASAP through XO Seal Team One.

Platoon Bravo's commanding officer, Lieutenant Lou Retino, entered the platoon's administrative office, a medium-size Quonset hut within the Rach Soi compound, at around 1200 hours. He wore camouflage shorts and a green T-shirt. Above his polarized sunglasses was a USS *Missouri* baseball cap. He wore a web belt with a beefy marine KA-BAR knife on the left and a holstered Colt 1911A .45 automatic pistol on the right. Seals seldom, if ever, were unarmed. Retino was dark-skinned to begin with, but was nut brown under the steady beat of the Vietnamese sun. His black hair and very dark eyes underlined a determined countenance that signaled authority and a no-nonsense attitude. Lou Retino was a leader who didn't ask of his men what he hadn't already done many times himself. He was an operator who wanted to be where the action was and recognized this trait in others when he saw it. When orders to deploy platoons to Vietnam came in, Lou pretty much handpicked the men he would take in Bravo Platoon. The unusual problem he dealt with was having too many Seals who wanted to go out on patrol. Although some volunteered for the Seal teams to impress people and boast of the tridents on the uniform, most were eager to mix it up with the enemy. A patrol was not a random, unorganized foray into the night, hoping to run across Charlie and bust a few caps. Each patrol was based on as much intelligence as was available and had a fairly precise objective. Some patrols obviously had more intel than others, and sometimes the intel proved inaccurate. But Retino's platoon would strive to go out on bona fide missions, and the men worked hard at gathering information about the enemy. Any and every possible source, including PBR crews, local Vietnamese, army, navy, marine, and air force intelligence sources (official and unofficial channels), and aerial photoreconnaissance were used. Anything that might give them a mission target. The most productive sources were usually captured VC (Viet Cong) or NVA (North Vietnamese Army) and Vietnamese PRU (provincial reconnaissance units) members. The latter were South Vietnamese allies who fell into one of three groups: VC infiltrators sympathetic to the North, South Vietnamese who didn't care one way or another, and some who were once victimized by the VC and now wanted payback. The first two groups, the vast majority, couldn't be trusted with a box of C-rations. The last group was invaluable.

"Good mornin', Lou." Platoon Chief Petty Officer Bob Friendly greeted the officer informally, as was the norm when the two were alone. He was already sifting through the intelligence data gathered over the past forty-eight hours. After forty-eight hours, the data was usually considered out-of-date but kept around and scrutinized for recurring patterns. Friendly was a nice guy, pretty easygoing. But during a briefing or on a patrol, he was anything but friendly. His philosophy was, "Pay attention now, so we don't have to carry you home later in a body bag." His tendency to maintain order and keep everyone's attention on task had probably saved some Seal lives, and while he was, on occasion, thought to be a pain in the ass, he was respected by the platoon. And when business was done, he could bang down a beer and talk story like your big brother.

Friendly wore blue jeans and a Grand Ole Opry T-shirt that had been washed a hundred times. He was thirty-six years old and had come to the Seals via UDT (underwater demolition teams) of World War II. He was one of the older guys in the platoon, rock steady and reliable. Strapped to the inside of his high-topped jungle boot was a knife sheath and a razor-sharp dive knife. His M-16 leaned against the wall behind the desk. It wasn't locked and loaded, but it held a full magazine.

"We might have something hot here, Lou. Lan brought this in this morning," said Friendly, looking back down at the papers.

Lan was part of the Lin Dai Nui Nai (LDNN) a South Vietnamese counterpart of the Seals. Lan had been at war somewhere with someone for most of his life. Somewhere along the line the VC or NVA had fucked over him, his family, or both pretty good. He never said what, but it must have been bad. Lan was tenacious and ruthless in rooting out the VC and exacting his vengeance. He seemed to know everyone; he had a thousand contacts, and when he told you something, you could put it in the bank. You didn't ask where he got the information; you just nodded and planned to have him along on the patrol. Lan was one of the few Vietnamese "good guys" who was reliable and trustworthy. Often he was invited to join a Seal patrol, partly because of his familiarity with the area, but mostly because he had proved that he could be trusted with Seal lives.

"It seems there's a high-ranking NVA officer who's comin down to tally up local provisions and see what's available for the cause. Lan seems to think he knows the whereabouts of lots of local sympathizers, food and weapons caches, medical supplies. Lots of targets and maybe somethin' about troop movements." Friendly was speaking calmly in his faintly southern accent, but there was an underlying sense of excitement in his voice. Maybe an anticipation of the adrenaline flow that might soon follow.

"When?" asked Retino.

"Tomorrow night sometime. For a couple of days, maybe."

"Where?" Retino looked directly into Friendly's eyes.

Without consciously thinking about it, Retino knew that Lan's information was sound and accompanied with useful details. From what Friendly had just said, the target was hot, the kind you occasionally got lucky with. It remained for him to decide the course of action and put together an operation plan, if all the information held up to scrutiny.

"Downriver about two klicks."

"Can we use the PBRs?"

"No. We'd have to go up a trib, that little stream where we caught that officer with the province map. That's too small for PBRs. We could get a PBR to take us up there and tow a raft (CRRC—combat rubber raiding craft). Then take the raft upstream," Friendly offered as he looked over the maps on the desk.

Once a go-no-go decision was made, the two of them would decide who would participate on the patrol. A briefing would be set up for those selected, including the PBR crew if necessary, and the mission, insertion, operation plan, and extraction plan would be determined. These were no-bullshit briefings that were, for the most part, short and sweet. The platoon had been doing this for a while, and most of it had become routine. More time was spent preparing boats, weapons, and ammunition, and alerting support elements that a patrol was imminent. It was good to be sure that helo gunships, artillery, or offshore navy ships were available and tuned into your action.

Retino sat down at the desk. "OK. What do we have?"

"Well, according to Lan, there's a NVA official that's coming down from the north to inspect the local operation. He'll be lookin' at supply caches, troop counts, that shit. He could know where a lot of shit is hidden away. With Lan doing the interrogation, we could get a whole bunch of targets." Friendly knew that Retino had already figured that out, but since the officer thought more than he spoke, his own analysis sounded better than the silence.

Retino nodded and said, "OK, Chief. Let's check this out with other sources and see if we can get some corroboration. Be careful about using any locals. I don't trust them worth a damn and don't want to blow a good target. Meet me here at 1700. We'll see what we have. Pass the word that we might have something tomorrow. Maybe we can get them to bed early."

"Already taken care of, sir. I'm meeting with Lan again this afternoon. I'll bring him to the meeting." Navy chief petty officers were usually on top of things, and Friendly was no exception. His anticipation of the officer's response was no surprise to Retino.

There were so many VC in virtually all facets of the South Vietnamese government and military that you simply didn't trust them with advanced plans, ambush sites, or anything else you wanted to work. Select individuals like Lan were the exception and made you feel like there were at least a few good reasons for being here.

"Good! I'll go over to ops and see if they have anything," said Retino as he moved to the door of the Quonset hut. The operations office for naval Intelligence in the area was about forty-five minutes away by PBR. Rather than use the radio, Retino preferred to hitch a ride and check out the latest information firsthand. A moment later he was outside, striding toward the PBR office. As he strode across the compound, he observed several Seals cleaning weapons and working on one of the Seal boats' outboard motors. He considered going over to say hello but decided against it.

11

"If this information is good, we'll be busy as hell, and the sooner I know the sooner we can get ready." he thought. His decision to lead the patrol had already been made. He returned a wave from one of the men but continued on toward the PBRs.

Dave Constanza watched Lt. Retino walk across the compound, and he waved casually at the officer. Retino returned the wave but kept on walking toward the PBR office. A minute later, he disappeared into its darkness.

"Retino's got something for sure," said Constanza to the others. Three Seals were working on outdoor benches protected from the sun and rain by a thatched roof. "First Friendly, now Retino with that umbrella-up-the-ass walk. We're goin' out tomorrow. Nooo doubt."

Constanza wore no shirt with his camo fatigues. He was, like most Seals, of medium build with blond hair, blue, mischievous eyes, and a very firm jawline. A Wily E. Coyote tattoo adorned his right bicep. The fourth finger on his right hand was stumped at the first knuckle, the result of a primer cap accident that could have been a lot worse. Dave was more careful now but still had a tendency to rush a little. We learn from our mistakes. He was working the action on his weapon of choice, an M-16/XM-148. This was a combination M-16 rifle with single-shot or full-automatic setting. It also featured a thirty-round magazine coupled with a grenade launcher installed just beneath the rifle barrel. Lots of versatility for close-in work and a definite punch that reached out several hundred meters, depending on how much you practiced with the grenade launcher.

"Old Baby Cakes here is ready to smoke. We want to *kick some ass,*" he shouted as he raised his weapon over his head. The small group laughed.

"You and Baby Cakes and Wily E. are gonna tear up the jungle." laughed John McConnell egging Constanza on. They had all seen Retino and heard Friendly's setting a standby status for the following night and were anxious to get out on patrol. Each man reacts a little differently to impending danger—some quietly; some with jokes and kidding; others with nervous laughter. But they were, after all, a Seal team, and they all depended on one another. However they chose to prepare individually, the team would be ready.

"Damn right! We're goin' to 'ding sow pot' and dump in Charlie's rice bowl," said Constanza. Although Seals had some Vietnamese language classes, he had difficulty with it and often joked with the odd-sounding syllable groups that others picked up more easily. Laughter again.

"Soon as the first RPG round goes off, you'll be dumpin' in those camo drawers a yours," chimed in Al Blackly. Things could get heated in this very violent, aggressive environment, especially among Seals, but everyone was smiling, and no one took offense. Blackly was an M-60 machine gunner. He and Constanza were roomies in the bunkhouse and gave each other a little more shit than they gave others, but they were a rock solid team in the field. Sort of like your brother giving you shit, but God help anyone else who did.

"Let's hope there's enough rice bowls to go around." McConnell spoke softly. Not everyone went out on every mission, but McConnell got out more often than most. He often helped with information gathering just to have a better shot at participating and was genuinely disappointed when nothing happened on patrol. He was a hunter.

John Reilly McConnell was twenty-six years old. He had been a Seal for four years, and was on his third combat tour in Vietnam. He had over a hundred patrols under his belt and a lot of notches on his guns. John had brown, close-cropped hair and fierce, blue-gray eyes. He was a little bigger than the average Seal, six one, about 190 pounds. His muscles were well toned but lacked bulkiness because of all the swimming. He was strong as hell and had smoothness about the way he moved. No matter what he was doing, it looked easy. This grace, or whatever you called it, was a characteristic looked for in a good point man. Point men led the way on patrol, looking for the enemy, booby traps, ambushes, snakes, crocodiles, and anything that might prove troublesome. Usually point men were the smaller guys but John proved to be the exception. His weapon of choice on point was the shotgun, specifically an Ithaca model 37, 12-gauge pump sawed-off shotgun with 00 buck loads. Meaner than a junkyard dog!!!

McConnell was working with Jack Thompson on an outboard motor that could be mounted on a CRRC to transform it into a Zodiac-type boat. They had tuned the engine to where it purred and were now experimenting with various muffling devices. Silence was key to surprise; power was the key to a hasty retreat. The Seals were always trying to improve equipment and find new, better ways of doing things.

"You know, this isn't too bad," McConnell said to Thompson. "We should try it out."

"OK. Let's do it," Thompson replied. Thompson was a radioman and carried an M-16 on patrol. He could fix anything mechanical—one of those knacks you are born with that only keeps getting better.

At 1830 hours, Friendly entered the compound recreation hall and makeshift bar. It had a reefer to hold the beer and ice, a radio to get Armed Forces Radio music, several sawhorse-and-plywood tables, and various photos, pinups, and platoon memorabilia. Most of the platoon was there having a beer and waiting for the go-no-go news. Friendly knew they were waiting for him and the news he carried. He walked over to the cooler, pulled out a cold beer, and dropped a quarter into the beer-fund container. He popped the cap on the beer bottle and took a long swallow. No one had spoken since he entered the room.

"Well?" prompted Constanza. "What's up?" He impatiently voiced the question that was on everyone's mind. "Are we on for tomorrow?"

Friendly smiled and looked around at the faces of the young men whose attention he surely held. He took another swig of his beer. His cheeks puffed out slightly as he enjoyed a quiet burp.

"Come on, Chief. Stop breaking our balls," chided Mako McDaniels, another of the platoon's more colorful characters. He was a grenadier and could put a grenade into a fifty-gallon drum at 150 meters. He had actually done that on the firing range back at Coronado. He claimed supreme skill with a tongue-in-cheek smile, but he did do it and had earned bragging rights.

Friendly smiled again and announced, "It's a snatch. Big NVA officer checking out local supplies. We make the snatch and we have targets for a month."

"Hooyah!" Cheers burst forth from the group, and questions poured out.

It was to be an eight-man patrol. Retino commanding; Friendly, second in command; McConnell on point; Thompson, radioman; Blackly with his M-60; Constanza, grenadier; Paul 'Doc' Weatherby as medic. The stoic Lan would be the eighth member of the patrol.

"Finish your beers and be over to the admin office at 1900 hours. We'll get briefed and start packing up. I'll open the armory after the brief and again at 0700, so don't bug me about that," continued Friendly. He then knocked his beer down, smiled, and left the building.

The eight men met in the compound's administrative office. Lt. Commander Dave Toponce was also present. He was the team's in-country executive officer and in charge of intelligence and operations. The metal roof of the Quonset hut was still hot from the afternoon sun as the men gathered around the map table. Lt. Retino went over the mission's operational plan and reviewed each man's basic field load. It was pretty straightforward. This time out, Friendly would carry a Stoner light machine gun. The 5.56-caliber weapon packed a wallop and would be a welcome asset if the target was accompanied by NVA regular troops. The Lieutenant, Thompson, and Weatherby would use M-16s, with Retino carrying extra ammunition for the Stoner. The lieutenant also carried a silenced Smith & Wesson nine mm pistol, refered to as a hush puppy. Normally the radioman and the medic would carry only .45s, but Seal patrols were big on firepower. In addition to the M-16/XM-148 grenade launcher combo carried by Constanza, hand grenades—including WPs (white phosphorous), concussion, fragmentation, and colored smoke (red, blue, and green)—were allocated among the patrol. Nylon rope for tying the prisoner, waterproof bags for documents, swimmer fins, bug repellent, and more were assigned to various members of the patrol. Radio call signs, frequencies, and passwords were studied, and available support elements noted. Several of the men carried ice picks in homemade sheaths, preferring them to the heavy KA-BARs.

Lt. Retino looked at McConnell and said, "John. You get together with Lan tonight or tomorrow morning and go over the route. Maps, aerials, whatever, but talk about how we'll go in and out. You're point, but he'll be right behind you. He knows the country."

McConnell turned toward Lan and looked into Lan's half-closed black eyes. The two nodded to each other, acknowledging their future meeting. The way would not be easy. Mud, insects, streams, and more mud would be their path. The most difficult routes in and out would be less watched by the VC and offer the safest passage with the greatest surprise. Sometimes these off-the-beaten-path routes were booby-trapped, and sometimes Charlie used them for the same reasons the Seals used them. It was a crapshoot, which meant always be alert, move quiet and slow, be ready.

"Right after the meeting, the chief will open the armory, and we can get our gear. Chief, will you need help linking ammo for the Stoner?" Retino asked as he looked over at Bob Friendly. The Stoner machine gun was a belt-fed weapon with bullets linked together with small metal clips. Ammunition was not readily available in usable, prelinked belts, and the team often sat around bullshitting as they linked the individual cartridges together.

"Yeah, I will have to put some together." Friendly didn't have to ask for help. Every Seal knew the comfort the Stoner brought out on patrol and was happy to pitch in. The very sound of a Stoner going off made everybody put their heads down. Especially VC who were trying to kill you. It was a definite asset to the patrol's arsenal.

The light from the Quonset hut's door darkened as a dark, imposing shape blocked the sunlight and entered the room. Chief Bosun Mate Charles Jackson, skipper of PBR 315, walked over to the table. No one had called him Charles for a very long time.

"Good afternoon, Mr. Retino. I hear we're going downriver tomorrow." Jackson was on his third tour in Vietnam and knew his job and the Con Lai River very well. He often volunteered his boat for duty with the Seals.

Competent people often attracted other competent people to their company. Jackson was six feet five inches with broad shoulders and large hands. If his commanding presence didn't instill quick compliance with his orders, the back of his hand did. He had a good crew, and they were proud to be serving on Jackson's boat.

"Good afternoon, Chief Jackson," said Retino.

"Hello, Boats," echoed Friendly.

"Chief." Jackson nodded to Friendly and to the rest of the patrol.

"So how can I help?" Jackson got straight to the point.

Retino moved to the map table and began to bring the PBR skipper up to date. "The question now is choosing an insertion point that will get us to this general location," said Retino pointing to a coordinate on the map. " We have to plan on being out for seventy-two hours and hope our target comes by sooner. So on the way in, we'll be carrying water and rations. That means heavy packs. The way out will be with a prisoner. The terrain is for shit, and that's OK on the way in. Extraction may be hot, without a lot of time for crawling through the mud."

Chief Jackson examined the map closely. He had probably helped to create the map and was putting images in his mind to the lines on the paper. After a few minutes he looked up. "The insertion can be almost anywhere. We can do the usual dummy drops and get you guys in without flagging the whole place. Once you're fifty feet inland, you know more than I do about movin' around. But I have an idea to help with the extraction. I can only go fifty meters up this trib." He pointed to a thin blue line that ran up through the general target area. "Then my boat starts scrapin' bottom, and I can't turn around. But a couple of Whalers could go up a mile—or more, if they had to. I suggest we extract by sending two Whalers with twin eighties up the trib at your signal. If it's quiet, you come out as far as you can and call. They'll sneak in and out without nobody knowin'. If it's hot, call as soon as you're near the stream, and they'll barrel in, pick you up, and barrel out. My PBR will be at the mouth to provide additional cover as necessary. Sounds like the Seawolves should be on standby, too."

17

"Can you be standing by for seventy-two hours?" Friendly asked.

"If this prisoner is as important as he sounds, I don't think my boss will mind. During the day, we'll route regular patrols around that general area. At night we'll be on board, ready to move when you call. Can do." Since chiefs actually ran things most of the time anyway, Jackson spoke with an authority that could be relied on. Retino would call over to the PBR squadron commander as a courtesy, but the deal was set at that moment.

" Thanks, Chief," said Retino. I think we'll send in a second patrol, maybe two guys, after twenty-four hours to keep an eye on the trib. Can you drop them off?"

"Sure thing, Lieutenant. No problem."

With that the bosun strode to the door. "You'll call the commander, sir?" Jackson reminded Retino.

"I'll give you a chance to talk with him. An hour OK?"

"Yes, sir. Thank you, sir."

"Thank you, Chief." Retino was an officer who listened to anyone he thought could help him do his job better. Bosun Jackson had a good idea and the means to make it happen. It enhanced the probability of a successful mission and reduced possible casualties. Both he and the members of the patrol would see to it that the PBR crew got sufficient beer and liquor to have one hell of a party after this was over. Of course, they would help the crew drink it.

After the PBR skipper left, Bob Friendly brought the group's attention back on track. "Any questions?" he said loudly. "We'll leave the dock around midnight tomorrow. Insertion forty-five minutes later. Ammo, three days' rations, water, and water pills. I know the pills taste like crap, but it's better than the drizzly shits for three days in the field. Use 'em."

There were a few questions about gear and who would run the second patrol. They reviewed extraction routes and would again several times before they left. Lan went over the layout of the target area, a small village about one and a half kilometers from the Cai Lon River and about four hundred meters from the extraction tributary.

"Anything else, sir?" Friendly asked Retino, falling back into more formal military routine.

"That's it. Get ready. We'll get together at 1700 tomorrow for gear check. Chief, get McDaniels and Johnson tuned in for the other patrol. Have them at the meeting tomorrow. Make sure they have call signs and frequencies. Sleep tight. This could be a long one."

"Aye, aye, sir," Friendly responded. And the team moved out to prepare their gear and their emotions.

At midnight the following day, the thin, crescent moon had not yet risen, and starlight cast meager shadows as the PBR throttled away from the Rach Soi dock with a low rumble. The patrol had their gear packed and ready to carry, faces and hands painted green and black, and weapons close at hand. They sat huddled low in the boat so only the boat crew was visible to a hostile observer from the shore. The PBR moved through the current to the middle of the river, which was just less than one hundred meters wide. The river meandered, sometimes with fairly sharp curves, widening and narrowing as sandbars and small islands passed like mines waiting to detonate. It was empty of sampan traffic now that the US-imposed midnight curfew was in effect. Bosun Jackson knew the river well and, as often as he could, guided his boat away from the shoreline and possible ambush. The VC were notorious for opening up on patrol boats with machine guns and rockets for just a minute or two then melting back into the jungle and swamp. Mostly they were ineffective sprays of bullets, glancing off the armor plates, but casual crew members having a smoke or not paying attention were occasionally killed or wounded, and a lucky rocket shot from the shore could blow the whole boat out of the water. As quickly as an ambush began, however, return fire was brought to bear, and it was equally lethal.

The PBR moved downriver at about twelve knots. At that speed it was pretty quiet and the current was helping to push them along. The dull brown-and-gray boat with its deadly cargo was not invisible, but you had to be looking closely to observe it in the dim light.

"About twenty minutes till the first insertion," Jackson informed them softly. Noise was held to a minimum. The first insertion would be a dummy. The boat would move in, touch the shoreline for a few moments, then back out and resume travel down the river. The second insertion would take place about five minutes later. This time the patrol would quietly slip over the side and move about five meters up the shoreline. The PBR would then continue on downriver and make three or four more false insertions. Any observer would be hard pressed to figure out what was happening and, hopefully, the patrol would move inland undetected.

The dummy insertion went by uneventfully.

Jackson nodded to Retino. "OK. Lock and load," the lieutenant whispered. "Packs on."

The patrol fumbled getting the heavy packs on. They helped one another, and the heavy packs quickly settled snugly onto their shoulders. Weapons clicked as cartridges slipped into chambers and safeties were set.

"Everybody OK?"

Each man nodded or gave thumbs-up. They spread out along the side rails, still crouched down, hidden from view. Veteran or cherry, your heart beat a little faster now. Adrenaline pumped just a little harder. Some sweat. Some suppressed involuntary laughter. A combat patrol was about to begin.

The boat slowed as the bow pushed into the mud and outer reaches of mangrove. The high-water vegetation line was about five feet away. Retino slipped over the side and the rest of the team followed suit. In a moment, all eight men were in the water, bellying through the mud into the vegetation. Before they fully disappeared into its cover, the PBR had backed off and faded into the blackness of the river. They were alone. The men crept another ten feet into the green-and-brown brush and formed a rough horseshoe with Retino at the top. All weapons faced outward. It was dead quiet. They would stay like that for a long, motionless twenty minutes, watching for any indication of movement or detection.

"Uuuhh!!!" Constanza grunted sharply. The whole team tensed at the sound.

Finally, after a minute of silent tension, Bob Friendly whispered hoarsely, "What?"

" A fucking snake!" Constanza screamed quietly. "A goddamned snake!"

It was quiet except for Al Blackly's barely audible laughter. McConnell looked over at Blackly, saw his shoulders bouncing and knew Blackly was enjoying his roomie's situation. Someone twenty feet away would have suspected nothing.

Ten minutes later, Retino signaled McConnell to take point and lead the patrol to its target area. As each man rose to a crouch and began moving in a single file, the sucking of the mud made noises that were unavoidable. Lan followed three yards behind McConnell. Retino was next, with Jack Thompson and his radio close at hand. Blackly and the M-60 brought up the rear. He needed to watch that no one came across their trail in the mud and moved in behind them. The patrol would travel about a kilometer and a half in the five hours before dawn. McConnell moved slowly through the mangrove and bunch grass. They avoided trails most of the time, wanting to avoid booby traps and the VC out for a stroll or an ambush of their own. The packs weighed heavily on their shoulders and drove them deeper into the mud. Every hundred feet or so, McConnell stopped for a few minutes and listened. Around 0200 hours, the light from stars and moon disappeared behind thick clouds, and a cool rain began to fall. Retino called a halt, and the men tied string lines to one another. The clouds made it difficult to see more than a few feet and, to avoid getting separated in the dark, string was used to keep everyone together and as a silent signal line to alert the man in front or behind to danger or directions from Retino. This done, McConnell moved out. Hot as it might be during the day in Vietnam, at night in the rain, it was cool. Only the strenuous movement through the mud supplied warmth under the wet clothing. The light patter of the raindrops worked to their advantage and disadvantage. They could make more noise, but they could hear less.

At 0430, the small target village came into sight. None of them knew if the village had a name. It really didn't matter. The team moved to within two hundred meters and spread out in a skirmish line. Friendly and Constanza stayed back about twenty meters to guard against approach from the rear. The patrol was positioned well off any paths used by the villagers but close enough in to rapidly react if the snatch victim appeared. Intelligence said he would visit this location today or tomorrow, possibly tomorrow night. It could be a long vigil. The men took turns sleeping. The strings were kept on, and firm tugs alerted or awoke as needed.

At dawn, the village came awake slowly. Smoke from cook fires wafted skyward, and people appeared moving about. Most headed for small rice paddies or gardens and began to work their crops. Several moved a short distance outside the rough village boundary and relieved themselves. Half the patrol watched carefully for the errant villager who might wander toward them. The other half slept or catnapped. This was not the time to become complacent. Intelligence told them this was a VC village. Weapons would be hidden away but readily available when needed. The NVA official would not be alone. At a minimum he would have a cadre of heavily armed body-guards; at least three, maybe as many as a dozen. These would not be armed peasants but regular NVA troops. Seasoned, combat veterans. Retino would have to decide when, how, or if the patrol would make the snatch, based on the circumstances at the time. Seals were aggressive but not stupid.

John McConnell lay on the damp ground, the drying mud on his clothes smelling like anaerobic, black mud smells. Occasionally he reached down to massage his calves or buttocks. His eyes seldom left the village or any poten-tial route that passed even close to their vigil site. He opened a chocolate bar and slowly ate it, washing the sweet taste down with a few swallows of water from one of his two canteens. One of the team would eventually have to crawl over to the stream and refill canteens. Two quarts of water wouldn't last seventy-two hours. That would have to wait until nightfall, though, when darkness would cover the movement. All of McConnell's movements were made slowly. The team was well camouflaged and difficult to see. But sudden movements were quick to be noticed. Every so often he wiped off his shotgun or his KA-BAR knife with an oil rag he kept in his pocket, not because they needed the cleaning, but out of habit for caring for his weapons. It also helped to pass the time.

As the day wore on, the patrol alternately slept and watched, scratched at the flies and bugs, and wiped the noonday sweat away from their eyes. Heavy discipline now was critical, because of their discomfort and the potential for complacency. They had been trained well. Now was when it paid off. At 2000 hours, it was still light enough to see. At the north end of the village, some commotion could be heard. People were arriving. Strings were tugged, and very quickly the patrol was at full alert. Lt. Retino peered through binoculars trying to ascertain what was happening and who was arriving. Lan and Friendly also watched the village through brown, waterproof binoculars.

A dozen men approached the village along the main trail from the tributary, none in uniform but several with weapons in evidence. Some of the men were dressed in peasant garb and black pajamas. Others were better dressed and wore leather boots. Lan watched intently. He would be the one to identify the NVA official. The village headman approached the group of newcomers. Four of them openly carried Russian AK-47 automatic rifles. The bodyguards' weapons were surely there to protect their charge but were equally important for intimidating the headman and the villagers. At the first sign of disobedience or hesitation, the VC had no compunction whatsoever in killing a villager: man, woman, or child. Village support was necessary, and they were ruthless in their pursuit of it. Everyone knew the rules, and compliance was the way to a longer life for you and your family.

When the two groups were about five feet apart, the village headman stopped and bowed several times to the tallest of the visitors. The new arrivals also stopped, with the exception of the taller man, who stepped forward and returned the bow with a slight nod to the headman. Most of the villagers were squatted in front of their hooch or tucked away inside. Two of the armed guards began to move through the village, obviously looking for any threat.

Lan looked over at Retino and nodded. This was the guy. Now it fell to Retino to quickly devise a plan of action. Since much VC movement was at night, he had to believe the target would be leaving after his inspection, perhaps after a meal. Were there any others waiting outside the village? Retino left Weatherby to keep watch and moved the rest of the team back to Friendly's position. He didn't like the idea of grabbing a hostage by ambush. But the circumstances left that his only option. Only a few bodyguards, a narrow trail and a quickly available extraction said 'Go for it!'

"Time to play ball," Retino said quietly. "We'll set up now. I'm not gonna split up, so we'll assume he's goin' out the same way he came in. Aerials don't show any other regular trails out, so we should be OK. We know they have four guns, probably more, but we'll take out the AK-47s right up front. Take out everyone else in his party next. Don't hit the man. At least, don't kill him. We'll set up an L ambush on the trail, two, three hundred meters out. Pick your targets as usual. Lan and I will make the snatch and start for the river. Thompson, get on the radio. Let the PBR and Whalers know we're comin' out tonight. Maybe soon. Have a Seawolf in the air to pick up the prisoner, if that becomes a possibility. McConnell and Friendly, search the others if there's time and opportunity. They might have documents. Al, you keep that '60 on the village, just in case they get brave. If they don't make trouble, let 'em be. Constanza, set up Claymores to cover our retreat. Keep 'em at bay with your grenade popper. Any questions? "

"PBR and Whalers ready, Mr. Retino," Thompson informed the group.

" Tell the Whalers to bring McDaniels and Johnson in with them, one on each boat. They'll protect on the way in and give us additional cover, if we need it on the way out. Lan, you get to the target ASAP. I'll be right behind you, but you concentrate on immobilizing him. Keep your eyes open! McConnell, get on the point and lead us to the trail. Watch close for booby traps."

"Seawolves and artillery on ready standby, sir," Thompson whispered. "Grid coordinates dead on the village, sir."

John McConnell turned and began literally to crawl off toward the village's entry trail. The patrol was still more than two hundred meters from the village and would move in an arc to the right to intercept the exit trail. Though the distance was probably only 150 meters at most, it would take them a full ninety minutes to cover the ground. If they were spotted prematurely, the target would disappear into the bush, his bodyguards containing the Seals just long enough for him to make good his escape. They needed surprise to remove his armed protection and make the grab. If there were significantly more NVA troops hidden up the trail, then the good guys would be in deep shit. But the officer was trying to move through relatively hostile territory without being noticed, and a large, armed group would be difficult to keep from detection. The odds were good that all the players in the game were on the board.

A dog suddenly began a sharp, excited barking about fifty meters outside the village in the bushes. It continued barking and began to move in the direction of the patrol. All eight men flattened to the ground. Each thumbed the safety off and waited. Several villagers and two armed visitors dashed over to the dog to investigate. There was yelling, and more villagers ran over. Soon most of the villagers, and the newly arrived visitors, were gathered around the barking dog waving sticks and machetes. The crowd was less than fifty meters from the concealed patrol's position. At any moment the patrol's situation could shift from an offensive mission to a defensive, escape-and-evade condition.

"What the hell are they doing?" thought Jack Thompson. "This has gone to shit in a lunchbox in a hurry." His index finger lay flat against his rifle just above the trigger housing. In his mind, he was already replacing a spent magazine with a full one. He listened for the report of a teammate's weapon telling him they had been spotted. His eyes expected to look into the eyes of a Vietnamese holding an AK-47. It was not easy to remain composed.

After several long, tense minutes for the patrol, three village men stood up holding what appeared to be a twelve-to-fifteen-foot-long python. They were laughing, and the others cheered as they held it up for all to see. The large snake still writhed in their arms as they started back to the village with their prize. One end of the snake was a bloody stump. There would be meat in the village cook pots tonight. The NVA officer was beaming and nodding his head to the excited headman. If they stayed for dinner, it would be well after dark before they moved on. This was good. The enemy would be full of food and a little sleepy. A little less alert and a little more vulnerable. The patrol relaxed, and McConnell again took the point, continuing to follow the arc to the trail intersection.

By 2230 hours, the patrol had reached the exit trail. Retino had sent McConnell down the trail in the direction of the river to reconnoiter and find a suitable ambush site. The point man had moved slowly, paralleling the trail, looking for hidden NVA troops. Finding no one, he studied the trail and found what he considered a reasonably good ambush site. Since there were few trees of any size, mostly shrubs and bunch grass, he sought cover and mounds of earth that would afford protection from the AK-47s and whatever else they might have. The ambush would also have to be fairly close to the trail, since the target officer would have to be grabbed quickly. McConnell scouted the ambush site and inspected the area closely for booby traps and potential retreat avenues for both the patrol and the enemy. He then returned to the waiting patrol and reported to Retino.

A little after midnight, the Seal patrol ambush was set up along twenty meters of the trail, and the waiting continued. Al Blackly, with his M-60 machine gun, was situated closest to the village. Lan and Retino were in the middle of the line. Retino would not initiate the attack until the target was abreast of him and Lan. Bodyguards in front and in back would be taken out with the initial fire, and the grab made immediately thereafter. Retino, Lan, Thompson, and Constanza would transport the prisoner toward the river as rapidly as possible. The remainder of the patrol would do a covering retreat, slowly moving back to the river. The PBR and the Boston Whalers were alert and standing by. Even in the darkness, it would take the Whalers no more than fifteen minutes to reach the patrol. There was a danger that the extraction boats would encounter patrolling VC along the stream or a VC sampan perhaps waiting for the man. They would have to break through, hopefully disabling the enemy patrol, make the pickup, and on the way back, with a lot more firepower on board, finish it off.

The Vietnamese sun had beat down on the team all day. Sweat had soaked their clothing. The tension and the stealthy but strenuous movement to the ambush site created more sweat and now, at midnight, the coolness of the night and the wet clothing set the men to shivering. Hell week during BUDS training had prepared each man to endure physical hardship. Now was when that strenuous physical and mental discipline paid off.

John McConnell lay almost flat on his stomach, his shotgun ready, waiting for the pressure that would give it life. John could anticipate the ambush in his mind. He had done this many times before. Thoughts about the rush that accompanied the first sighting of the enemy coming down the trail had already begun to release a flow of adrenaline. The young Seal was calm, but his heart rate was slightly accelerated. He could almost hear the explosion of the guns as the team opened fire and the small, unheralded battle began. He was fascinated by, and proud of, the team's proficiency and effectiveness under fire. Any patrol that you and your mates survived was a success. Killing enemy troops, a good snatch, confusing the enemy—all were icing on the cake. McConnell looked down at his shotgun. It was a part of him: an extension of himself that did his bidding like his arms or legs. The shotgun was comfortable. He waited patiently for the rush to come. The fact that he had worked through the personal repercussions of killing another human being—that's what war was about—made him a very dangerous adversary. He remained calm throughout a battle, thinking clearly and reliably about the mission, the safety of his comrades and, finally, his own safety. A wave of cold passed through him, and he shivered involuntarily. A noise up the trail grabbed his attention, and the cold disappeared. It was two o'clock in the morning.

A line of men, the earlier visitors to the village, moved quietly in the dim moonlight down the trail. They were not especially trying to be quiet, but habit built on necessity allowed them to move without a lot of noise. More of the men had weapons visible, probably because it was uncomfortable to walk with an AK-47 concealed beneath your clothing. The NVA officer was almost exactly in the middle of the line. The leading enemy troops passed Al Blackly, McConnell, and Weatherby, and they were moving past Friendly, when Retino's M-16 opened up. A split second later, McConnell's shotgun barked twice, and the soldier directly behind the officer was blown off his feet into the brush on the far side of the trail. The whole team opened up, and the quiet of the night disappeared in the smoke and muzzle flashes of the gunfire. The formation of enemy soldiers jumped from the noise and impact of the heavy fire. Half were dead within seconds. A concussion grenade thrown by Lan went off at the officer's feet. Everyone flinched at the noisy explosion, but the officer was stunned to the point where he dropped to his knees, his hands holding his head. He was dazed but otherwise unhurt, unless an errant bullet had hit him.

From the front of the enemy line came return fire. It appeared to be random, something someone stunned and frightened would do simply to gain a moment of relief. Constanza popped off a grenade in the general direction of the firing. Following the explosion there was no more shooting and some relief for Retino, who did not want to shoot his way to the river if he could help it. In the stillness of the aftermath, the team began to move cautiously to the trail, weapons at the ready. Blackly had raked the rear element pretty good with the M-60, the waist-high grass offering little protection from the heavy machine gun's bullets. McConnell's shotgun had also been busy contributing six rounds of 00 buckshot into the formation. Reloaded and moving up on the remains of the enemy line, each man's faculties were hypersensitive, the kind of wide-eyed alertness that comes when, if you come in second, you're dead. One of the VC, lying face down on the path, started to roll over. McConnell's shotgun barked once and the man was slammed back down on his face. No one spoke. They were looking for danger.

Without any warning a muffled explosion went off. The body of the VC McConnell had just shot jerked about ten inches off the ground and then dropped back to earth. Blood flowed rapidly from underneath his body, pooling on the hard-packed trail dirt.

"The son of a bitch had a grenade," Chief Friendly observed. No additional words were necessary. What might have been considered by some to be a cold-blooded shooting by McConnell was self-preservation in this war. It had been the right thing to do under the circumstances. But the incident was nerve-racking, and attention to business was continued with even more alertness. Lan had already bound the officer and was searching the man for weapons, documents, itinerary, anything that might be useful. Papers would be placed in watertight bags carried by Retino. Friendly and McConnell were searching the others.

Thompson radioed for the Whalers to initiate the extraction.

Retino picked up the stunned officer, slung him over his shoulders, and said. "Let's go!" Constanza led the way down the trail, followed by Lan and Retino. Thompson brought up the rear. The remainder of the patrol finished their search of the bodies and began moving toward the river, watching for any signs of pursuit. The trail was too heavily used to worry about booby traps, and the first increment of Seals made good time to the river.

Upon reaching the river, Thompson radioed the Whalers for an ETA to their position. They were on their way. No trouble yet. The men could do nothing but wait and be alert for danger.

Blackly's M-60 chattered in the distance. Friendly's Stoner followed suit. A moment later the sound of gunfire from downriver echoed to the waiting patrol.

"Shit!" growled Retino. "Trouble on both ends. Thompson, find out what's going on with the Whalers." No one relished the thought of carrying the prisoner back to the Cai Lon through the mud pursued by hordes of pissed off VC. More gunfire from up the trail.

Weatherby came walking down the trail and joined the others.

"What's happening back there?" inquired Retino.

"A few villagers came down the trail. They didn't fire. I don't know if they were even armed. Al and Friendly put a few rounds over their heads. They're not going to do anything. Where's our extraction?"

"It's coming. There was some gunfire downstream. Thompson, anything?"

"Yeah. They sideswiped a sampan. It fired on them, and they shot it up but sideswiped it coming through. It's OK. They'll be here in a minute," Thompson informed Retino and the rest. With that the sound of powerful motors could be heard, and moments later the two Whalers came into sight.

"Constanza, get the others down here fast," ordered Retino.

Lan and Thompson caught the boats as they bounced against the bank of the stream and held them tightly as the others clambered aboard. Mako McDaniels's mouth was bloody, but he reached over to help Retino lift the prisoner aboard the Whaler.

"What the hell happened to you?" Thompson asked McDaniels.

"I was in the bow when this fucking sampan popped up and started firing at us. I shot the shit out of it, but we were going too fast to avoid it, and we sideswiped the mother. My face bounced off the railing. I'm OK," McDaniels replied.

Friendly and the others came down the trail and jumped into the boats. "Let's go!" shouted Friendly and the Whalers pushed off and started back downstream to the Cai Lon River and the waiting PBR. There was no relaxing yet. All the men were ready for a counterattack or just an errant enemy sniper. The boats moved rapidly. The one Whaler had some damage on its hull and at least one bullet hole in it, but it ran fine. The navy coxswains driving the boats had sunglasses hanging around their necks. Although the starlight made it fairly easy to see, an illumination flare could screw up your night vision real fast. At the first indication a flare had been launched, the drivers would put the sunglasses on. As soon as the flare fizzled out in the water or grass, the glasses would come off, and there was still some semblance of night vision.

"The PBR's waiting for us, Lieutenant," Thompson announced.

What seemed like forever, but what was in reality less than fifteen minutes later, the Whalers entered the deeper water of the Cai Lon and were immediately joined by Chief Jackson's PBR. Retino acknowledged the chief and said, "I want to transfer the prisoner to the PBR. Lan, you and McConnell come with me. Keep in sight!" he commanded the Whaler coxswains. And the three boats headed out, the Whalers providing front and rear protection for the PBR and its prisoner. The rush was still there, but the tiredness that always followed an action would soon fall upon them. They had captured their quarry, and now the deadly trio of boats opened throttles and made upriver for Rach Soi.

CHAPTER TWO

San Francisco, California,

University of San Francisco campus

June 1968

The gymnasium on the University of San Francisco campus was echoing with the thumps and bumps of volleyballs as thirteen girls stood in three loose circles and alternately hit the soft, white-leather ball upward with their fingertips and then again against the inside of their wrists. The girls talked and joked as they practiced hitting the balls to one another and waited for their coach to arrive. They were all athletically built and attractive to look at in their gym shorts and T-shirts. All but two were taller than average, and several were over six feet tall.

"It's almost five o'clock. She'll be here any minute. She's talking to the athletic director about the fall schedule," said one of the young women, a strawberry blonde wearing a USF tank top and no bra. "I hear they've got a team at the University of Hawaii. Wouldn't that be terrific? Hawaii, I mean."

"Good luck, Bonnie. Even the men's team won't get the funding for that game. We'll be lucky to get Cal, UCLA, and Humboldt State with the old school bus," another girl, one of the short ones, a setter, one who's primary job was to set the ball up for the taller teammates to hit, responded with a half smile. Everyone knew that women's volleyball, college or otherwise, seldom drew more than friends, family, and a few diehard fans. Being on the team was more about having fun and participating in the most competitive women's volleyball to be found anywhere. So without actually realizing it, they were blazing the way for women's sports, played hard, and enjoyed the camaraderie. Their coach, Rebecca Saunders, had played at Cal across the Bay and had won second team all-American honors. She still enjoyed playing and made being on the team an enjoyable experience with her enthusiasm and intensity. They all had high expectations for next season. Coach Saunders felt that a big part of the fun was winning games. "Losing builds character," she had once said. "And that's what the basketball team is for." The University of San Francisco women's basketball team was terrible. "We win here." She laughed as she said it, but her twinkling hazel eyes were serious.

A moment later, a young woman in her early twenties strode into the gym, a whistle around her neck and a clipboard in her hand. She was about five foot nine with medium length, light-brown hair that tossed about her broad shoulders as she walked purposefully toward the girls. Her breasts and hips were full beneath her USF T-shirt and black sweatpants. Although she was a bigger-than-average woman, she had the build of an athlete and a very attractive figure.

Coach Saunders waved to the team, most of whom were already moving in her direction, to gather round. "OK! Listen up. We got pretty much what we figured. Cal, UCLA, USC, Humboldt, Stanford. We got Oregon State and the Washington Huskies at Eugene." She paused, smiled slowly and then dropped the big one. "We're in the Thanksgiving tournament down in LA. A round robin that includes Arizona State and Hawaii." The girls burst out cheering. They patted the coach on the back and laughed happily.

"Why don't they have the tournament in Hawaii?" teased one of the girls.

"How many on the travel team, Coach?" asked another.

"They're waiting for the popcorn concession to make the airfare to Hawaii," the coach said. More laughter from the excited girls. "I'll take as many as I can, but I don't have that answer now," she said, answering the more serious question. "It will depend to some extent on how well we do during the regular season. If we're on a streak, I have more leverage. Just play hard every minute, and things will work out. Now three lines! Ten-yard sprints. Forward up the court. Backward down the court. At the whistle! Hustle up!" The whistle blared, and the first line of girls raced across the floor.

By eight thirty, the coach had finished up the practice, showered, and changed into dark linen slacks and a cream silk blouse and was on her way to the faculty parking lot. Even though she was still a graduate student study-ing for her master's degree in education, as a coach she rated a parking spot, albeit at the far end of the lot. The days were getting longer, and it wasn't really dark yet. The soft heels of her black espadrilles muted her footsteps as she walked toward the car, thinking about the team and the schedule she had pushed so hard to get. The tournament was a feather in her cap, and she would work hard to have a good, solid season and a competitive show-ing down south. She slid in behind the wheel of a three-year-old dark-blue Mustang, the bulk of which was a graduation gift from her parents. Her father had cosigned a note for the balance. She was proud of the fact that she hadn't missed any payments.

Her plans for the evening were sort of open. The gang, a roughly even mixture of males and females all somehow involved with the university, spent most of their social hours together. The number varied as new people were absorbed in and others drifted away. Graduation usually saw some move on. Sometimes an argument resulted in one or two saying, "Screw you guys!" On several occasions over the past year, a couple would decide to pair off in a more intimate relationship (like living together), find the group less interesting, and seek their own new road to travel. One would have to say the group was close, but it was held together by the school, the party atmosphere that reigned in San Francisco at the time, and the fact that they had fun without the millstone of commitment hanging around their necks. It wasn't that they were always all together. Pairs would go off to concerts, ball games, quiet drinks, or dinner out. No doubt they occasionally slept together but only in a fit of "good buddy" horniness. We're good friends, so why not?

Tonight those who could would meet for a few cocktails at the Camelot, a popular pub in the Union Street district, and then decide what the plan was for the evening. A possibility was that the Camelot would be "hot" tonight, and the entire evening would be spent there drinking, dancing, and rolling dice with the bartenders. San Francisco on a Friday with a bunch of friends was a wonderful time, and even then they all knew it. These were the future good old days.

Rebecca pushed open the swinging door of the Camelot and looked around for her friends. As could be expected, they had commandeered two tables just off the bar and were in the process of receiving a platter of drinks from the white-aproned cocktail waitress.

"Over here, Rebecca!"

"Hey, Coach!" Bruce Carroll, another graduate student, called a greeting. Then to the waitress, "Could you bring another glass of Chablis, please?" He squeezed over on the wood benches against the wall and made room for Rebecca to join them at the table. She wiggled through the group to the open seat, sat down, took a deep breath, and let it out with a long sigh.

"It's been a long day. It feels good to just get off my feet for a few minutes." She smiled as she basked in the group's attention and looked forward to the evening of fun and friendship. It really didn't matter where they went or what they did. They would be together, laughing and enjoying life. Tomorrow she would drive up to St. Helena, a small town in Northern California's wine country an hour north of San Francisco, to help celebrate her mother's birthday. Traditionally, the whole family would pitch in to prepare the meal and set out the good china, crystal, and silverware. The birthday boy or girl got to choose the menu, which could get pretty elaborate: lobster tails, yorkshire pudding, or roast turkey. Her mom's favorite was veal parmesan. Unfortunately, her mom was the only one in the family certified to cook that dish correctly, so Rebecca would serve as assistant chef and cook in spirit, if not in reality. Birthday dinners were something the whole family enjoyed, and they would not be missed intentionally. Her brother and his wife would drive down from Crescent City for the occasion. The music of "Light My Fire" caught her attention—the Jose Feliciano version, not Jim Morrison and the Doors—and brought her back to Camelot.

"Rebecca. Care to dance?" Scott Markham's voice came from across the table just loud enough for her to hear. He was one of the group and had a crush on Rebecca. He kept it low key for fear of being ostracized by the rest if he came on too strong. He was doing graduate studies in world history and had announced he would be applying for the diplomatic service. He was good-looking and smoothly diplomatic. Good career choice, Scott. "Come on, Baby, light my fire. Come on, Baby, light my fiyyarr." The lyrics spoke for him.

"Let me have just a small sip of my wine first." Rebecca begged off. "This is the first chance I've had to sit down all day. Hey! We got the tournament in LA with Arizona and Hawaii. The girls were delirious," she informed the group. Goals, wishes, and dreams were open topics of group conversation, and everyone knew she had been trying to get this for the team. Cheers went up, and congratulations were extended.

"Way to go, Rebecca. I really think you were the only one who could have gotten it for them. Every woman in San Francisco owes you a debt of gratitude." One of her roommates, Charlene Bascomb, was a little more of a woman's libber than the rest and never missed the opportunity to score a point. In this instance, she was sincere and correct.

Rebecca looked at her roommate and smiled. Recognition, from male or female, for getting the job accomplished, felt good. "God knows women's sports were one step above oral surgery," she thought to herself. "That will change! It has to. It isn't right we get screwed all the time." Her smile, however, was her only acknowledgment to her roommate. She didn't want to provide a soapbox for Charlene tonight. Her wine came, and she picked the glass up by the stem, swirled it around, and brought it up to her nose. Having been born and raised in the wine country, it was her habit to examine the first glass of wine, even though she knew she would be teased about it. It was all in fun, and she was good-natured about it. Actually it was not a bad house wine, and the cool, warming liquid triggered her taste buds as it rolled around inside her mouth.

She swallowed the wine, relaxing as it began to work its magic. She took another deep breath and said to Scott Markham, "I'm ready for that dance now." The music had changed in the interim, and the Four Tops belted out, "I Can't Help Myself." The small dance floor pulsed with waving arms and wiggling bodies. "Sugar pie, honey bunch!" There was no physical contact save the errant elbow or hip of other dancers. It wasn't what Scott had in mind, but at least he had Rebecca to himself, if only for a few, disjointed minutes. He feigned indifference to the change of tempo and got into the music with exaggerated limb movements and body gyrations. "I can't help myself. It's you and nobody else."

At about ten thirty, the decision was made to get a late supper. The Iron Maiden, a downtown steak house with an active weekend bar, was selected as the best combination of good food, a live trio, and the fewest number of Friday night drunks. Jim Howe, who lived off a trust set up by his grandparents, opted for an eighteen-ounce prime rib, but most got one of the less-expensive burger selections. Rebecca went with a six-ounce steak and green salad. Having already decided to get home relatively early tonight, she switched to red Chianti with the beef. Discussion centered on what each would be doing during the summer:; trips, vacations, more school. Rebecca would be working on her education master's thesis and working with the volleyball team. She rationalized the rather mundane summer plan as an opportunity to get a jump on her thesis, sharpen up the team, and be spontaneous in glorious San Francisco. The majority of the group would be going home or traveling, but four or five would hold down the local fort.

Amid encouragement to stick around, Rebecca stuck to her plan and headed home to the Steiner Street apartment she shared with Charlene and Cathy Ventura. Cathy was home and working on fashion sketches, although it was half past midnight. Cathy had graduated the year before and was working as a fashion designer. A showing was coming up faster than anticipated, and she was burning late night candles to keep from falling too far behind.

"How's it going, Cath? Can I get a sneak preview?" Rebecca asked, knowing her roommate would ask for her opinion.

"What do you think?" Cathy asked handing over a fifteen-by-twenty-four inch sketchpad. "The idea is like a sundress. You know, like an afternoon tea party on the lawn. Not something you'd want to spend a lot of money on, but you still want to make a statement. What do you think of the sleeves? Too much puff? Would you wear it?" Ah. Nitty-gritty time. Would you wear it? Cathy respected Rebecca's opinion and knew she would be honest. Honest but gentle.

After a few moments of examination, Rebecca answered. "The sleeves are a little…" There was a pause as she searched for the right words.… "little girlish. These afternoon teas are usually cocktail or wine-tasting parties. You want a mature look that says relaxed and comfortable with who I am. But I really like the rest. Is the longer hemline coming back?" Rebecca pretty much wore what she liked, and the heck with fashion. But she was kept up on the latest by her roommate's work and conversation. She was happy to be in the know and occasionally flaunted her inside knowledge with a little name-dropping. Cathy was a good roommate and a friend.

"You're right about the sleeves! I felt that but wanted to experiment. Yes, the hemline is dropping, I think to counterbalance the miniskirt. You know, I really have a problem showing my crotch to every man in San Francisco. I like showing off my legs, but Christ, you can't even sit down without beaver shooting the whole town."

"Good night, Cathy."

"Good night, Rebecca."

The sun beat down on Highway 101 north. The blue Mustang cruised north along at sixty-five mph, and Rebecca enjoyed the straw-colored hills and oak trees that lined her way. In about forty-five minutes, the first vineyards would appear, and she subconsciously associated the grapevines with home and family. During her years at school, she would often bring the whole gang home for a barbecue and backyard volleyball after they had toured Napa Valley's wineries. Her folks were great and always welcomed the students with open arms. Rebecca knew her father, in particular, always wondered if one of the boys was special, a boyfriend. There were always three or four in the group, and they all seemed to share Rebecca's attention equally. He still wondered about it, curious about the man he knew she would someday bring home. And thank God, her brother finally went into the Marine Corps. He used to give the guys such crap. She almost stopped the barbecues altogether because of his antics and open disdain for them. But she loved him and was proud of him. He had been to Vietnam and had come home safely. Sometimes you don't realize how much you care for someone until you understand that you might lose them. The very distinct possibility of death was a real eye-opener, and she was happy to have him back. She was happy, too, that he was now married and living in Crescent city, two and a half hours north of St. Helena. "Maybe another barbecue before school lets out would be fun," she mused.

The car radio began playing Mick Jagger's Rolling Stones. "I… can't… Get No…. Satisfaction" filled the Mustang, and she turned up the volume to hear over the rush of wind in the car's windows. The power of the base guitar overshadowed the story line of the lyrics, and you had to listen carefully to catch the message tangled within the excitement of the music—if in fact you wanted to catch the message, or if there even was a message to be caught. "Life is pretty good," she thought. "There's so much to do. To enjoy." Tears welled up in her eyes as she thought of her mother. Her family. The music heightened her emotions. "And I try, …and I try, …and I try, …and I try…. … I can't get no-…. … satisfaction."

CHAPTER THREE

Rach Soi, Vietnam

Feb. 1968

PBR 315 thundered upriver toward its base, the two Whalers fore and aft running interference for the larger boat and its newly acquired prisoner. The wakes roiled up the brown water, waves splashing along the banks without consideration. As the boats sped away from the extraction point, the men began to slowly relax, knowing that the more distance between them and the village, the less likely there would be pursuit or trouble. The twin fifties gunner on the PBR looked questioningly at Chief Jackson, and the chief nodded. Retino saw the exchange and smiled. "Go 'head," he thought, "You've earned it. Another patrol on the books. No wounded. No KIAs (killed in action). It's been a good day." The gunner reached over and turned on the boom box tucked in behind his mount. The forthcoming sounds were loud and stimulating to all of the young men, almost like another shot of combat adrenaline. The boats picked up speed, the guns continued to bristle, and the warriors began to laugh and recharge, exhilarated to still be alive and ready to kick ass if the need arose. The base guitar throbbed and Mick Jagger wailed out his complaint. "I can't get no-oo satisfaction..., and I try,... and I try. ...I can't get noooo satisfaction." The cool dawn wind and spray from the river blew into their tired, confident faces.

The meandering Cai Lon River was coming alive with sampans and people along its shoreline. Waves from the boats rushed in, rocking the sampans vigorously against their meager moorings. The turbulence shook the morning cook pots crazily. It rocked the families, knocked over rice bowls, and generally disrupted the flow of life for these simple boat people. Oxen in the near fields shied slightly from their plowline, and skinny dogs barked at the intrusion to this otherwise calm morning. Fishermen and farmers, women and children, young and old looked up and watched the boats race by, engines roaring and old Mick booming out. From their own experience and observations, each of them knew how lethal and dangerous these boats could be. And unpredictable. From heads barely turned in the direction of these intruders, their half-closed eyes watched until the danger passed and faded both in sound and sight. There was no yelling to ', "Slow down." Nothing that would draw attention to themselves. That was trouble they didn't want to deal with. Not now. Not anytime. They turned back to their day's tasks with resignation and resolution. These people of the land didn't pray for peace or deliverance. For over a hundred years, they'd caught shit from every direction: the French, Chinese, Cambodian, or their own countrymen. Now the Americans. It didn't matter. Getting through the day alive was good enough. Their country had been at war for generations.

John McConnell watched the prisoner, arms and legs bound, lying on the deck. The man's head and shoulders were propped partially against the lower gunwale; each bounce of the boat jarred his neck and reminded the man of his uncomfortable situation. A trickle of blood ran from his ear, a result of the concussion grenade. Otherwise uninjured, the stunned NVA officer was toast, and he knew it. The rumbling of the engines, the music, and the presence of the men with green faces told him he was in Shit City. The prisoner looked back at McConnell and at the bore of the 12-gauge shotgun pointed directly at him. The American's unwavering steel-blue eyes were dark and dangerous. The eyes told the prisoner he would get little opportunity for either escape or self-destruction. Certainly not mercy. His knowledge of American interrogation methods with ranking enemy officers told him he would give up information. He would break or die. It was also true that they often tried to turn prisoners into agents. This course of action might hold the only promise of life, and possibly even prosperity, for him. He needed to be shrewd; to give up as little as possible and yet convince his captors of his integrity and worth. It was better than dying. The eyes, almost cruel, continued to scrutinize him, peering through the black-and-green coloring, and he felt a shiver of fear run through his body. And the fear leaked into his eyes, his face no longer inscrutable. How did they find me? These troops were not like the others. Not undisciplined. Or lazy. Where did they come from? The boat pounded against the river, and his head bounced against the gunwale. And the fear shook him again.

The disembarkation took place quickly and quietly. A team of military police, an officer, and two burly sergeants from operations's interrogations branch, took charge of the prisoner at the dock. Lan and Lieutenant-Commander Toponce accompanied them back to operations headquarters. Retino and Friendly would go down later to assist in processing information as it was extracted from the prisoner. If things worked out the way everyone hoped they would, the Seal teams would be very busy for the next few weeks.

Retino gathered the men in the ops office for a patrol debrief. The adrenaline was wearing off. Body and mind sent signals to muscles that the tiredness, the aches and pains that had been kept at bay for the last thirty-six hours, could now call for relief. The men slouched on chairs or sat on the floor with backs leaned against the Quonset hut's walls. Retino kept the debrief short. Things had gone well. There had been few, if any, mistakes. The men had no complaints. No egos had been bruised, save perhaps for Constanza's run-in with the snake early on. He would take a little ribbing for a while, but even he had to laugh. "It was too small for dinner," he explained, "or I would have put it in my pocket and brought it back."

"Without the head, of course," countered Blackly as his body doubled over laughing at the memory of his friend's encounter.

"He would have had every bar girl in Vinh Long wanting to get in his pants with that thing in his pocket!" said Jack Thompson. "A monster trouser mouse." And the group roared with laughter.

Retino stood up. "OK. Anybody have anything else? Update the maps, if you remember any landmark not on there. A good patrol, guys. Stand down. Get some sleep." He ended the debriefing with a caution. "Don't get too fucked-up. We could be going out again real soon. Interrogation will press this mother hard. Be ready." At this moment, another patrol was the last thing any of them wanted to think about. But they understood the caution. It was not pleasant to be on a combat patrol with a hangover. It definitely wasn't safe.

As the men started to leave the Quonset hut, Bob Friendly instructed them to turn in weapons and ammo to the armory. Although each man had one or more firearms readily available or on his person at all times, the navy's weapons were stored in the official armory, to be checked in and out as needed. Each man had his own locker within the armory so he could get the same weapon each time he went out. Each man, therefore, returned his weapons to the armory cleaned and well oiled. The weapons were the tools of their trade and were taken care of accordingly. Unofficial weapons would be retained and ready for instant action. Ammunition was all over the place. Even grenades were stashed, ready in the event of a sudden attack. Carrying a weapon here was like carrying your wallet or wearing a belt back home. They were all items you would probably need before the end of the day.

Weapons cleaned and returned to the armory, the men moved to the mess hall and sat down to a huge breakfast of eggs any style, bacon or ham, hash browns, toast, jam, juice, and coffee. Some of the PBR crew was already eating and greetings were exchanged. Plans for a party were discussed, damage to the Whaler, the prisoner, and what would have happened to any gook stupid enough to show his face to this group of the meanest, toughest sailors in the fleet.

"I'll have three eggs over easy," Constanza began, "and maybe a few slices of boa constrictor. I hear it helps build strong sphincter muscles." The Seals all cracked up, and the riverboat sailors looked on wondering what the hell was so funny. McDaniels and Johnson had heard the story at the dock and were on the inside of this one. Breakfast was relaxed and enjoyable. The hungry young men consumed a great quantity of food.

A full meal on top of the dwindling adrenaline, little sleep, and no good reason to stay awake signaled the eyelids to begin drooping. After an hour or so, the men got up from the table and, despite several cups of coffee, began to drift over to the barracks, a warm shower, and the rack. A few would wander around for another hour as they came down more slowly from the excitement of the patrol. McConnell and Jack Thompson walked slowly across the compound. Although it was only 0830, the sun was already beginning to get uncomfortable, and red dust kicked up slightly as the men walked along on the hard-packed dirt.

"John, how did you know that guy had a grenade?"

"I didn't, Jack. He was rolling over. He could have had a gun, a knife, a grenade. He could have had anything. We were not there to take prisoners, Jack. We grabbed the target and … … it just wasn't his lucky day."

"I know," Thompson answered. "I know it was the right thing. Probably saved a couple of our asses, including mine. Sometimes I wonder about this whole fucking war. I wonder what it makes us."

"It makes us the meanest badasses in the delta, Jack."

A middle-aged Vietnamese woman, who looked older than she was, emerged from the Seal barracks carrying a large bundle of what the men knew to be laundry. The military laundry facility always used too much starch and lost whole bundles, and the laundry never seemed to be returned when you needed it. SingDo had proven to be honest and reliable, and she paid strict attention to individual instructions. For the three dollars a week each man paid, the twice-a-week laundry service was the best deal in Vietnam. It was a touch of home. She had been here when the team arrived and would doubtless be there long after they were gone. The woman bent under her bundle as she shuffled toward the two men. As she approached, she bowed low several times.

"Gud moning, gud moning," she said, looking at the ground. Then she glanced up briefly at McConnell and Thompson to reveal a slight twinkle in her eye and a pleasant smile. "Clothes be ready tomorrow. Clean. Good job."

The men bowed back, several times. "Good morning, SingDo. How is your morning today?" John said with exaggerated but sincere politeness.

"Can we help you with that bag, Mama San?" Jack asked. "It looks bigger than you are."

"Not so heavy. I manage OK." The woman suddenly saw the condition of the men's mud-caked clothes and rolled her eyes skyward. "How you get so dirty? Little boys not so dirty! Need to charge more. Iiieeeeh! Too much work!" She shook her head as she shuffled past, the smile still on her face. The men always left generous tips (by Vietnamese standards), recognizing that their laundry often required heavy-duty maintenance.

"Thank you, SingDo."

"Well, we got clean clothes waitin'. Now we're the cleanest, meanest badasses in the delta!" said McConnell, laughing.

"Hooyah!" responded Thompson, shaking his reflective mood. "Goin' into town tonight? A little wine, women, and song? How about the Tiger's Lair? MyLing will be there."

"What're you, in love? You be careful with these women, Jack. You can screw 'em, give 'em presents, play kissy-face all day long. Just don't get serious. You hear me, you romantic son of a bitch? In four months we're out of here. Back to Coronado. The land of round eyes, pizza, and cold beer. Then you fall in love." The two men laughed.

"Yeah. We'll go to the Tiger's Lair and party, Jack," McConnell agreed. "And if MyLing is there, then go for it. But be advised. There'll be a lot of competition for her. You may win her heart, but she's a working girl." McConnell cautioned.

"I know, John. A little fantasy never hurt anything. It's better than just getting laid."

"Just so long as you remember. For your penance, say three Hail Marys and buy two rounds of beers tonight." They laughed again as they approached the barracks door.

Thirty-five minutes later, after a lukewarm shower, brushed teeth, and a little more banter, the two men crawled into their bunks, M-16 and shotgun tucked beneath, and quickly fell into a deep, well-deserved sleep. For the moment, their work was over.

At 1800 hours that evening, nine Seals waited in the compound for a truck that would take them to Vinh Long, a town in the Saigon suburbs, suburbs being more than fifty miles out. It was a relatively small town, revitalized in recent years by the US military presence in Southeast Asia. Numerous bars and nightclubs now lined the main street. Shops filled with black-market goods were tucked away in less obvious locations but did a thriving business anyway. Local people, dispossessed by one aspect or another of the war or lured in by the immense wealth of the Americans, lived in and around the main drag in small houses, temporary by our standards. Many of these homes were bare subsistence shelters occupied by people who had lost everything. They were usually older people, who retained some honor and little else. Other houses were small but clean and well furnished. These were occupied by families who had younger women with a service they could render to the visiting troops. Some were women who lived with a soldier passing through. The faces of the soldiers changed but the benefits kept rolling in. Musicians, shop owners, wheeler-dealers in the black market, and infiltrators from the north rounded out the population. The town was growing and had a very promising future growth potential as long as the war kept rolling along. The main attraction in Vinh Long was what once had been a large French plantation with tall white columns and long shaded driveways. The French influence was attractive. Even workers' quarters had been spacious and airy with overhead fans, verandas, and large open windows. Everything was painted white, and the buildings shone with a purity and cleanliness out of character with the times. The main plantation house was now a hotel and central meeting place of the area. Old workers' quarters had been turned into higher-class shops or homes for affluent locals. Groups of more than two or three Seals, however, were no longer welcome at the plantation. Too much partying; too much damage. Shopping was OK, but as soon as one of them picked up a beer, the local police were called, and the young men were asked to leave. Oh well. They did have some great parties here.

At 1830, a well-worn, brush-painted brown-and-yellow pickup truck pulled up to the compound gate and beeped its horn. This was their taxi to town. Truck and driver were hired for two days and served as a private chauffeur for the group twenty-four hours a day; from the bar, to a hostel, to the shops, and back to the bar. The driver, of undetermined nationality, was nicknamed Pancho. He would keep track of who was where and help in the rounding up of the group the next afternoon for the ride back to Rach Soi. Pancho knew the town of Vinh Long like the back of his hand. He was their black-market negotiator, pimp, hostel reservationist, and guide. This was his full-time job, and you needed a reservation to insure he would be available. He was worth the money.

"Hey, Pancho! Where the hell you been?"

"Let's go!"

The men rushed through the gate and into the back of the pickup. Half his money was paid in advance, half upon return. Weatherby and McDaniels got into the cab, McDaniels riding shotgun, while the rest piled into the bed. Two M-16s were carried in the cab...just in case. Each of the men had some sort of concealable weapon—a knife or a handgun. The road was through open farmland, mostly rice paddies, and some sniper along the forty-five-minute drive might take a potshot at them. But what the hell. As long as there was return fire, the sniper would haul ass, and that would be that. Vinh Long was a "friendly" town, but you still had to watch yourself. A lot of US military were killed in town having a drink or dallying with the ladies. That's not what it said on the death certificate sent home to the parents and wives. But that's the way it was.

Two cases of beer were brought along for the ride, and the men wasted no time cracking them open while they were still cold. There's something about a cold beer on a hot day—the long, slow swallow rolling the cold fluid past the roof of your mouth, taste buds overwhelmed until the end. Then the hops and malts burst forth, and an equally long, deep breath, possibly a polite belch, brought a wonderful sense of peace and contentment. Jesus, would two cases be enough?

The brown-and-yellow truck cruised along at about thirty-five miles an hour, speeding up when the foot traffic on the road allowed. There were few motor vehicles to contend with. Ox-drawn carts, people with buckets hanging from a stick over their shoulders, and the occasional taxi, military truck, or jeep comprised the main traffic. The bigger trucks, the six-bys, seldom slowed and occasionally bumped a bucket or whacked a cart. The Seals were dressed in civilian clothes, mostly blue jeans or chinos with an open-collared or Hawaiian shirt not tucked in. The loose fitting shirts sometimes hid a holstered .38 in the small of the back. Some wore T-shirts, perhaps with an ankle holster. Technically they should have been in uniform, but Seals did not advertise their presence with insignia. Officers and MPs were usually smart enough to let that slide, given the clandestine nature of the Seal community, and the fact that the Seals' reputations preceded them. These guys didn't back off, and they always seemed to get off the hook anyway. Plus, they were all armed.

As the truck passed two not-bad-looking young ladies walking along the road, Constanza called out, "Hey, ladies! Can we give you a lift? Where you headed?"

The girls smiled and waved. "Vinh Long! You give ride?"

"Hold on, boys," said Constanza in a stage whisper. "I got somethin' goin' here."

"You bet, ladies. Pancho! Stop! Back up." The truck stopped abruptly. The men sat up, ran fingers through their hair, and prepped for the arrival of the girls, as young men everywhere will. No one complained about the brief delay. "Hop in, ladies," Constanza said. He reached his hand down to help them up. McConnell, sitting nearest, helped the other girl into the back of the truck. All the men moved to make room, but the girls sat one on each side of Constanza. Each girl wore loose-fitting black pants with a white pull-over shirt that hung down well below the waist. Each of them carried a tote bag which, as it later turned out, contained miniskirts, makeup, stockings, and other accoutrements a Vinh Long bar girl would need. The luck of the draw put McConnell and Al Blackly on the outside of the trio but next to the girls. The addition of the women changed the dynamic of the group and the course of the conversation. Consciously or unconsciously, each man was on the make, smiling, flirting... hoping he would get lucky with the new arrivals. They all knew someone would.

Constanza was the clear front-runner in the get-lucky department and held court, flaunting his position. He introduced the men, adding some personal anecdote with each introduction. His roomie, Al Blackly, was the odds-on favorite to round out the foursome. But it made the trip interesting, and before they knew it, the truck rolled into Vinh Long.

It was about 1930 hours, and the heat from the day was only just beginning to fade. The sun was still above the horizon, and the sky reflected the coming dusk with a beautiful orange-red display. By prearrangement, Pancho would have them rounded up by the same time the following day for the return trip. Sometimes it was a challenge to find everyone, but one way or another they almost always made it. The group typically split up, depending on who wanted to do what and where. An individual would go off and shack up for the entire stay. Several would hang together, drinking and whoring at a steady pace. This usually formed the nucleus, which the others would drift in and out of, touching base for a beer or two then moving along to shop, cruise, or just get away for some private time. Given the quasi-standby notice Retino had put them on, this would be a relatively quiet trip. The key word here was "relatively." In any event, a liquor run before departing was standard operating procedure. The bar at Rach Soi needed to be regularly replenished.

McConnell, Thompson, and Weatherby opted to shop first and party later. This insured that you would, in fact, shop and not get lost in the partying. It also meant you would have some money with which to shop. Many servicemen seemed to feel obliged to take advantage of incredibly low prices to buy cameras, stereo equipment, china, watches, and cookware—items they would bring home to family or use to set up a comfortable bachelor pad back in the world. Perhaps it was an act of rational behavior in the midst of an irrational time. The three asked to be dropped off by the plantation shops, where they would get warmed up to the negotiating process, then scour the smaller black-market shops back in town to compare prices. It was actually fun, and a beer or two along the way made it even better. Pancho would drive by every so often to pick up packages or ferry them to another shop.

Constanza and Blackly got off with the two girls in front of one of the many neon-emblazoned clubs. McDaniels and Johnson tagged along at the encouragement of the girls. "Many pretty girls. We show you," they promised. "You have good time." Red-and-green neon identified the place as the Orchid Club, and slightly off-key guitar music playing popular back-home songs could be heard inside. "See you later, guys. Don't let the bedbugs bite." Constanza smiled, and the girls waved as the truck moved to its next drop. Al Blackly had his arm around one of the girls and a grin as broad as a crescent moon. Somehow he looked smaller without the M-60's ammunition bandoleers.

The rest got off somewhere along the strip, leaving vague instructions for Pancho as to where they would be the following day. Time to turn off the search-and-destroy mentality and remember how civilized people were expected to behave. Since most laws and morals around here were subjugated to the war and its implementation, it was difficult to find the fine line of acceptable or moral behavior and even more difficult to avoid crossing it. Washing the taste of fear and the pain of hardship away meant crossing the line from time to time. Remembering the way it was supposed to be at home kept you from crossing over too much or too far. McConnell, Thompson, and Weatherby wandered in and out of the shops along Plantation Drive. The shops by local standards were clean and airy, the merchandise displayed with some semblance of showmanship, and there were fewer hustlers or hucksters compared with the in-town experience. The shopkeepers would steal your eyes if they could, but it was done with more subtlety. More aplomb.

"Are you guys looking for anything special?" Weatherby asked. "I'm thinkin' about a stereo system. We can ship it home in the platoon container, right?"

"Righto, Doc," responded Jack Thompson. "They always make room for the important stuff."

"Make sure you keep all the boxes and packing. Try it out. Make sure it works. But put it all back together again and seal it up tight. There's a few assholes at Coronado who wouldn't think twice about rippin' off a stereo or camera if they get the chance," counseled McConnell. "I got a really good stereo system, Pioneer mostly, last tour. Turntable, amplifier, a Sansui reel-to-reel tape deck, and some neat 120 speakers. I want to get two more speakers so I can rig it for two rooms. They had really nice mahogany cases. I'd like to get the same ones."

"What about dishes?" asked Jack. "Seems like everybody gets a set of dishes."

"I know," laughed McConnell. "I guess they're such a good deal we shouldn't pass it up."

Paul Weatherby was also laughing. "A touch of home. We'll make great housewives. A real catch for some babe at home." The three men laughed and moved on with a greater sense of purpose.

Several hours later, the three men had gone through the plantation shops, made their way to the black-market shops in town, and had been in and out of the final shops at least twice. They had haggled and walked out only to come back and start anew, each time feeling closer to a deal. By the end of the shopping spree, they owned three sets of dishes, a stereo set with four speakers, and three chess sets purchased for the original price of one.

"We could get arrested for stealing," Weatherby said with a snicker as they walked off with the chess sets. The shopkeeper congratulated them profusely and tried to sell a hand-carved elephant in a last, desperate effort to make a buck.

Thompson and Weatherby had opted for Mikasa china, with John opting for blue-ringed Noritake stoneware. While the other two watched the parcels in the closest bar, McConnell went in search of Pancho. Within thirty minutes, the packages were loaded onto the truck, and the three sat together to have one more cold one before setting out to find some of the others.

"I'm ready to have me a warm meal, a cold beer, and a hot woman," Weatherby informed them, "and I'm not particular about which order it happens in."

"Well I know where I'm headed. Best-lookin' lady in town is just down the street," said Thompson.

McConnell rolled his eyes and smiled. "Well, you got dishes and music. You can set up house and raise kids."

"Fuck you, John. You know she's got the hots for me. And she is the best lookin'," Thompson retorted with a laugh and a medium-to-hard shot to McConnell's bicep.

Suddenly there was a loud explosion from somewhere outside, not that far away. It was the definitive sound of a bomb blast. Pretty powerful.

"What the hell?"

The comfort zone that had begun to descend on the men—on all the military men in town—collapsed. Eyes hardened and searched for immediate enemy movement. Each of them checked their weapons for easy access. McConnell jacked a round into the chamber of his Parkerized .45 and slipped the weapon back into the shoulder holster under his shirt. The eyes of the three Seals quickly scanned the room. They were on their feet assessing the situation, trying to piece together the little information they had. Thompson finished his beer with a single draft.

"Let's find out what the hell happened," said McConnell as he started for the door.

They emerged from the bar to see billows of smoke to the left about a block and a half. Without saying anything, they began to move in that direction. McConnell, the point man, took the lead by force of habit. Weatherby brought up the rear, automatically watching the sidewalk across the street and their back trail. As they got closer, others curious about the blast were also converging on the scene. A local police Jeep screeched to a halt in front of the adjacent building. Two uniformed police jumped out and cautiously approached the now splintered and shattered entrance of the building. Smoke lingered in the air. The smell of cordite was strong, and there were moans and yelling inside. Half a dozen people, including several servicemen, were in the street bleeding from cuts incurred by flying glass shards. People were emerging from the building in various states of disarray and shock. Clothes were torn and blackened. There was blood.

"Jesus," Thompson murmured. "It's the Tiger's Lair."

Doc Weatherby was already moving up to assist the wounded. Sirens announced the imminent arrival of more police or ambulance. Within minutes both were there. Medical people, American military and local, pushed through the crowd, and police began to set up barricades. A number of local and US military police were moving about the scene with weapons at the ready. Was it over? Would there be more?

Several hours later, the death toll was finalized at six, three of whom were American servicemen. Seven more were taken to the hospital, and another dozen or so were treated at the scene for minor cuts. No Seals were in the bar at the time. The bar girl MyLing was among the dead. Apparently a Viet Cong supporter had left a satchel bomb beneath a barstool. The killing had been purely random but obviously targeted at servicemen and the women sharing their favors with them. Another reminder that the war, even when you were on liberty, was not a cakewalk; you had to watch your ass.

Two hours later, all the Seals except Constanza and Blackly had come together and were drinking in a club not far up the street from where the attack had occurred. The mood was jovial but the evening would not be the fun-filled release they had hoped for. Jack Thompson was well on his way to getting shitfaced, his mood alternating between sadness over the loss of MyLing and rage over the dirty bastards who could kill their own women without a second thought. The bar girls were pouring on the charm and still going upstairs with the soldiers, but everything was different. The girls were more tentative, fearing reprisals from the men and rougher, maybe brutal, sex. The soldiers were fighting the Vietnamese. The girls were Vietnamese. Friendly? There were three Americans down the street who got dead flirting with the friendlies. Angry soldiers in any war, in any country, have taken their anger and frustration out on the women. This is not a good thing. It is reality.

"You gonna be OK, Jack?" McConnell asked his friend.

"Sure, I'm gonna be OK. Who gives a shit about one more dead gook? Jesus, three troopers died. That should bother me more than MyLing. Doesn't that bother you, John?"

"You know what I'm talking about, Jack."

"I was just wondering if anything bothered you. I've never seen you really pissed off. I've seen you go a little nuts out on patrol, shootin' up the whole fucking jungle. But you never look really pissed off. Or sad. Or melancholy." Jack looked up at McConnell and started to smile. "Or happy. Or passed out… or trying to screw a duck." The two men both burst out laughing.

"I don't screw ducks when people are around. The ducks don't like it. They crap on my shoes," John shot back and Thompson looked down at his shoes. The heavy laughter that followed released a lot of tension, and they both enjoyed a few moments of respite.

"You know, John, it's not even about MyLing. It's losing the one thing here that seemed good. Even though she was selling her ass, it was out of necessity for her family. She was really an innocent. Naïve. It's like nothing that has any resemblance to goodness can survive in this shithole. Shoot it. Kill it. Destroy it. Just get rid of it. If we go back to the world after our tour, then what the hell is this place? A bad dream?"

55

McConnell knew that his roomie would be all right. He thought about his words and understood what they meant. Where Jack was coming from. But he himself looked forward to patrols. He anticipated the action eagerly. He volunteered for more patrols than was necessary. Vietnam was not the world. Good and evil existed in both places, but evil sure had the upper hand here. He smiled to himself and thought, "But since I'm the meanest motherfucker in the valley, I fear no evil."

"I tell you what, point man," Jack broke back into his thoughts, "You buy me a beer, and I'll set you up with a goose. All night. Clean. No VD." The two men burst out laughing again.

Weatherby and Mako McDaniels came over to the laughter and joined in. Weatherby looked at McConnell. "Trivia? For a beer."

"Subject?" countered McConnell.

"Navy. Any navy. But navy."

John looked at him, sizing him up. Could Weatherby stump him? Not likely. "You're on."

"OK. Here we go," Weatherby began. "The saying 'Cold enough to freeze the balls off a brass monkey.' Where did that saying originate?" McConnell, Thompson, and McDaniels all looked at him, then at each other. Weatherby smiled. He knew from the looks on their faces they didn't have a clue.

"Holy shit." McConnell confirmed his ignorance on this one. "I could think on this one all day; it wouldn't do squat. Go ahead, you got a beer."

"Well," began Weatherby, "in the days of sailing ships and cannonballs, each cannon had a supply of cannonballs, which were stacked in a wooden square made out of two-by-fours. The square cannonball holder was called a 'monkey.' The cannonballs stacked within the monkey formed a triangle, like a pyramid. Now it was customary for the fleet admiral, the high muck-ety-muck, to have as a symbol of his rank a brass monkey stacked with brass cannonballs. When the weather got freezing cold, the brass, being metal, would contract. If it got really cold, it would contract enough to squeeze against the balls to the point where the top cannonball would roll off the stack. Hence 'cold enough to freeze the balls off a brass monkey.'" The men clapped and whistled. It was a new, very good trivia question; one each of them would use in the future to win back a beer.

"Outstanding, Paul, you son of a bitch. That one deserves a beer. We'll even make it a cold one." McConnell waved at his bar girl and ordered for the table.

McDaniels jumped in. "OK, Paul. My turn. I got one for you. For a beer?"

"Go ahead."

"OK. The origin of the term 'posh.' Like posh accommodations. You know, like first class." Again a silence at the table. Again no clue.

"Where do you guys get this shit?" Thompson asked. "You screwing some Vietnamese librarian, she's looking this shit up for you?" Laughter but no answers.

"Go ahead." Paul Weatherby laughed. "I got the next round. Easy come, easy go."

"Before airplanes, rich Americans traveled back and forth to Europe by boat. Luxury liners like the Queen Mary. Usually they went in the summer to avoid Atlantic storms. Trouble was, on the way over, the sun would beat down on the starboard side, and on the port side on the way home. Way too hot for the rich ladies. Soooo when they made their reservations they would ask for a cabin on the port side on the way over—less sun—and a cabin on the starboard side on the way home. Again the good side. So the reservation read port over, starboard home. Abbreviation... POSH." Again rounds of applause and laughter. The trivia game would go on, some tough questions, some not so tough. It would pass the time for a while.

The authorities had imposed a 1:00 a.m. curfew on military personnel. The Seals, therefore, rented girls and rooms upstairs for the night and would party in the bar until the wee hours. Then they'd take their woman upstairs until the sun came up. McConnell had taken his girl upstairs about two o'clock and screwed her for about an hour. The two of them now lay on the bed, the girl asleep, snoring gently. He was lying there awake thinking about Jack and how he had felt about the girl, MyLing. It was bullshit, he thought, but at least there was some feeling, some meaning, however bogus, to Jack's flings with the girl. Her death wasn't just another body bag. Another gook. McConnell glanced over at the girl lying next to him and tried to recognize some feeling. Something good. Anything. He could not. His sexual tension was satisfied, and she was now like a scar that he had to look at until morning. She was attractive and a nice person. The sex was enjoyable. Christ, getting your rocks off was enjoyable. Hard to mess that up. But it was over, and the memory wasn't as pleasant as the act.

It was just before midnight. Harsh lights gave the launch area a surreal feeling. Wind and dust from the rotor wash peppered and tugged at everything. The patrol was loading aboard the insertion helicopters. Intelligence indicated heavy enemy troop movements in the delta and the Seals were tasked to verify and locate that activity. Their job was to find them and then call in the big boys—air cav., marines, B-52s, whatever. The patrol would be a minimum of three days. The helicopters would drop the team off at the edge of the U Minh Forest (nicknamed the "forest of death" by somebody who recognized it as heavy-duty VC territory). For two days, helicopters had been overflying the area, making false drops to throw off enemy observers. Hopefully the patrol could insert without detection, locate enemy concentrations, and call for extraction before the shit hit the fan. It always sounded reasonable on paper. Well, almost always.

Retino, Friendly, McConnell, Constanza, Blackly, Thompson, and Weatherby made up the patrol team. The choppers lifted into the night and disappeared in the darkness. At 0045, after two false insertions, the patrol was dropped into the bush and left behind in a crushing silence. After moving about a hundred meters away from the drop point, they sat in a defensive circle to ascertain whether or not anyone had observed their arrival. The audacity of their tactics, dropping into enemy-held jungle in the middle of the night, was their greatest asset. Who would be crazy enough to do it? How much energy would the enemy put out to look for such a crazy possibility?

Retino passed the word. "We go in five minutes." It was dark, and movement would be slow. But eyes adjusted to the darkness, and experience allowed them to make pretty good time. They were headed to a low-lying ridge overlooking what appeared to be a junction of several large trails. The patrol would split up, separating about one hundred meters, so each unit could watch effectively in a different direction. Their separate vantage points allowed them to watch a large expanse of heavily vegetated savannah, elephant grass spotted with thick pockets of woods and vegetation on either side of the ridge. The VC were masters of camouflage, utilizing bunkers covered with earth and natural vegetation or underground caves and tunnels, which made observation from the air extremely difficult and usually futile. Retino expected only individual or small-group movement during the day. More likely, contact would be at night. This being the case, he set up a watch schedule that would allow the men to get some rest during the day and be more alert at night. Each man had a starlight scope that helped see into the night. They all wore some form of ghillie suit, a sort of tattered rag blanket, which, when worn over the body, made detection very difficult even at close quarters.

By 0500, the patrol was in position. The sun began its rise, throwing heat into the air. It would be an uncomfortable day. Time passed slowly. The fear of discovery made them emotionally uncomfortable. The heat and dirt made it difficult to stay still.

Late in the afternoon, the ground hot to the touch, Friendly, McConnell, and Constanza lay in the brush, watching. To Friendly's left, about thirty feet away, the ground moved, just a few inches. Friendly thought he saw it move but, in the absence of any additional movement, he couldn't be sure. He nudged McConnell, next to him. His lips moved without him actually talking. "Watch over there." McConnell nodded.

Several minutes later, the ground moved again. It was a concealed trapdoor, now opening wide. A short man armed with an AK-47 rifle emerged from the hole, closed the door, and brushed dirt and dried grass back over the door. The man, wearing a loose black shirt and pants, stood

59

up and looked around. He started walking in a direction that would take him within ten feet of the Seals. As the man scanned over the area his eyes, by chance, locked with Friendly's eyes. A shocked surprise spread over his face. He stood there for a moment, digesting the information his eyes brought to him, then began to swing the rifle toward the enemy intruder. Friendly pointed a silenced nine mm pistol at the man's face and fired twice. Both rounds hit the man in the head. He jerked straight up, dropped the rifle, and fell to the ground. The three Seals lay frozen in place. Their eyes moved between the fallen man and the trapdoor. Nothing else moved.

Several minutes later, Friendly slowly brought up his low-frequency radio and called for Retino.

"Lou. I just shot a gook with the hush puppy. Quiet. He came out of a trapdoor almost right underneath us. We could be sitting on top of a huge bunker. Don't know if anybody heard. Nothing's happenin'."

There was no response from the other end. Friendly knew the news he'd sent would hit Retino like a brick. If the VC discovered the patrol here, getting out would be difficult, to say the least. "Hold." Retino's response was terse.

Retino reconfirmed his location coordinates with each of his support units; helicopter gunships, F4s, artillery, offshore ships, and his extraction Sea Knight helicopters. There was no hard news to report, but the trapdoor—and the dead VC—was reason to get prepared for quick response. If there was a bunker complex here on the delta, it was significant intell and a lot more VC than anticipated.

"Bob, get down low," Retino instructed. What he meant was to make yourselves invisible, really cover up. "Avoid contact if at all possible. Keep me posted on activity. Be ready to move out quickly if we have to."

"Roger that." Friendly put the radio away. "Let's dig in deep. Keep a sharp eye. No contact. Have your shit ready to go quick." McConnell and Constanza both nodded and did as instructed. Friendly moved out, covered the body, and returned to their hole. They made their individual holes a little deeper, roughed up the ground around them and fluffed up the ghillie suits. They all understood the situation.

The sun had dropped, and there was only a crescent-shaped hunter's moon. The darkness was pierced by the starlight scopes, and the men watched an eerie gray-green landscape. They had seen several people moving about in the distance. On two occasions, armed VC had walked along the ridgeline passing between the two groups of interlopers. These were thought to be guards on rounds. Guarding what, was the question.

Somewhere around 0200 hours, movement and sounds could be heard on both sides of the ridgeline. The scopes picked up several large groups moving toward the ridge. In several places large, well-camouflaged trapdoors opened wide, revealing mine-like tunnel entrances. Columns of NVA troops pulled carts loaded with what appeared to be supplies and ammunition. Several smaller artillery field pieces were also in tow. The carts and field pieces were pulled into the invisibility provided behind and beneath the expertly concealed the trapdoors. The majority of the troops spread out, and several small cook fires flared up beneath the canopies of trees. They were setting up bivouacs. Guard patrols began to move out. Retino's estimate placed the number of enemy troops at about 250. That did not include any inside the bunkers. God only knew if there were any other groups further inland or how far the bunker system went.

Retino made the decision to begin a slow reconnoitering withdrawal in the direction of the ocean. That way they could put some distance between the patrol and the enemy before dawn, and at the same time, determine how far the bunker system went in that direction. Sitting here longer would garner little more useful information and put the patrol at risk. He passed the word to Friendly. The two groups began to withdraw, scanning their route with the night-vision scopes and then proceeding a short distance before scanning again. Another bivouac area appeared along their exit route. Fortunately, there were few trees along the ridgeline. The lack of cover for cook fires or quick concealment from the prying eye of US aircraft created a path between the bivouacked troops that allowed the patrol to move, albeit low and cautiously, through the enemy camps. Retino had reported in, and both artillery and air strikes were preparing to attack. Air cav. was also scrambling to get a piece of the action. Extraction helicopters were standing by to rush in to pick up the patrol as soon as they cleared enemy proximity.

Paul Weatherby crawled through the grass and low shrub. He failed to notice a trapdoor open about six inches. The Viet Cong guard manning the spider hole was caught completely by surprise when he looked up and saw a body slithering past his hole. Had the movement not been only two feet away he might not have noticed it at all. But he saw it and opened up with his AK 47. The blast almost cut Weatherby in half. Jack Thompson, immediately behind Weatherby, was stunned by the noise but saw the muzzle flashes and recovered quickly enough to slip a grenade into the hole.

"Fire in the hole!" he yelled as he buried his head in the dirt. The explosion blew the trapdoor off the spider hole but neutralized the immediate threat. Retino radioed for immediate extraction and fire support.

"Let's move out," Retino calmly instructed the men. "Thompson, you take Weatherby."

The men stood and began to move in a crouched walk, moving as quickly as Thompson would let them. Retino and Friendly prepared but did not activate strobe lights, which would mark their position for the gunships and extraction helicopters. Enemy movement was seen and heard all around them. The dim hunter's moon helped their situation. The enemy only heard a quick burst of unexpected small-arms activity. They didn't know what was happening but would investigate. There were several scattered beams of light in front of the patrol now. Flashlights probing the area to discover now passive intruders.

Several rifles opened up on the patrol from a distance, and bullets whizzed around the Seals. They kept moving. Blackly took Weatherby's limp body from Thompson. Each Seal would take a turn carrying the body allowing the group to move faster.

"No one return fire. They haven't really pinned us yet. Don't give them a target," Retino cautioned. His radio squawked, and he listened for a moment. "Birds six minutes out."

The patrol made about a hundred meters without further gunfire. Suddenly from about fifty feet away, an AK-47 opened up. Friendly grunted and went down.

"Shit!" Jack Thompson hissed through his teeth.

"Who's hit?" Retino yelled. Blackly and McConnell returned fire and cut down the AK-47.

"I'm hit in the arm," responded Thompson. "I'm OK. I'm good to go."

"My leg," said Friendly. "It's broken good. God damn it. You guys keep goin'. I'll do a little rear guard action."

The sound of the helicopters in the distance gave Retino an additional option, better than anything else he had. "Bob, get your strobe ready but don't use it yet. John, stay with him. We'll move toward the birds, get picked up, and move forward to you. When the gunships are close, pop your strobe. We'll all know where you are then, so wait till the last second. Let's move out," he commanded the others.

The extraction helicopter saw Retino's strobe and came in low and fast. Retino's group was about forty meters from McConnell and Friendly.

A grenade landed some twenty-five feet from the two men. McConnell felt the shrapnel fly above them as he pressed hard against the ground. Gunfire opened up from two sides. Now three sides. They held fire. The sounds of gunships prompted Friendly to pop his strobe. Immediately they received more fire now, coming in closer than before. McConnell felt a slug smack the back of his left arm. There was no pain. Only an awareness that he had been hit. The fire increased and was getting closer all the time. Friendly's Stoner opened up, and there were screams only yards away. John's shotgun barked. From heaven, the gunships finally opened up. The ground all around the strobe jumped and shook. Screams in the night spoke clearly of the number of enemy troops in the vicinity. From out of the night, a man screamed and rushed in on the two Seals. John's shotgun swung up and caught the man on the neck, knocking him to the side. A second man, following the first, now rushed directly into the muzzle of the shotgun. John fired, and the man blew backward into the darkness. The shotgun swung back down on the other man and roared again. The action was purely reflexive. There was no time for the contemplation of right and wrong.

Suddenly the air was whipping around them, and noise from the heavy rotors was deafening. The extraction helicopter was almost directly above them and came down several feet away. As Friendly was being loaded aboard, Retino yelled, "Where is Thompson?"

"He's not with you?" screamed McConnell.

"No!"

McConnell moved back along the route they had taken. Fire was being directed at the helo, but it was answering with .30-caliber miniguns and sister gunships. Artillery rounds began to fall on the ridge a quarter-mile up, where the first concentration of enemy troops had been reported. Now everyone was in the shitter. Good guys and bad. McConnell saw the body lying on the trail and raced to it. He didn't wait to examine Thompson's condition but immediately picked up his comrade and friend. A VC trooper running toward the helicopter literally ran into them, sending them all sprawling. McConnell yanked out his combat knife and jumped at the other man as he started to bring up his rifle. The knife arched in from the side and plunged into the man's neck. Blood spurted everywhere. The dead man's reflex action pulled the trigger and the AK-47 fired into McConnell's side. His eyes went wide with surprise and pain. Adrenaline pumping hard, he stood up and reached down for Thompson again. Falling to his knees, he managed to get Thompson over his shoulders and, with all of his strength, stood up. He turned toward the helicopter and stumbled toward it. He felt hands taking his load, took a deep breath, and relaxed. He could do no more.

CHAPTER FOUR

San Francisco, California

August 1968

Rebecca awoke tentatively. The strange surroundings had her slightly disoriented. Her memory of last night slowly came into focus, and with it, the events that had taken place. She took a deep breath, glanced cautiously over, and confirmed that Scott Markham was still asleep in bed next to her. They had gone to a Santana concert at the Berkeley Community Theater on the Cal campus, had a late dinner of french onion soup, Caesar salad, and white wine at the Bistro and, albeit with reservations, went to Scott's apartment and made love. "Well, had sex, anyway," thought Rebecca.

Subconsciously she had been feeling a little left behind in the throes of the sixties sexual revolution and was ripe for a relationship. An analysis of her male friends put Scott on the top of the list of potential partners. He really did like her. She knew that. He was on what appeared to be a successful career track for the Foreign Service and was admittedly good-looking. Their sex had been OK but not what Rebecca thought it was going to be. Perhaps she was looking for too much. Had "great expectations." She smiled at the literary reference. It was as if she had run an important and competitive race and had come in second. Not bad, but not like winning.

Scott would wake up soon, and she did not want to be in bed when he did. "Last night was enough," she thought. "I need to get out of here graciously and quickly." She very gently drew the light cover aside and swung her legs to the floor. With exaggerated slow movements she got out of bed and walked to her clothes on a chair by the dresser. "I'll have to shower at home. God, I feel like an old onion. Oh well." She didn't feel bad about the evening, but the warm and fuzzy feeling she had anticipated was nowhere in her senses. It was an intellectual analysis that told the tale and projected a Rebeccaless future for Scott. They might remain friends, but even that was probably a long shot under the circumstances. As she walked to the bedroom door, shoes in hand, Scott rolled over and snorted in his sleep. She stopped, standing still, until he resumed his regular breathing. In the kitchen Rebecca left a note, as upbeat as she could, explaining she needed to get to her parents' house in St. Helena and didn't want to wake him. There was no "love" or "see you." Just "Rebecca."

The hot water splashed over her as she washed down with Dove and a real sea sponge. The sponge was a little rough but felt good on her skin. She dried herself with an oversize mauve towel, and finished with a moisturizing lotion. A glance in the mirror reassured her that she was athletic and attractive. "So where's my knight in shining armor?" she asked her image in the mirror.

"Who were you talking to in there, Rebecca?" Her roommate Charlene Bascomb didn't miss much, and she initiated her inquiries about Scott almost as soon as Rebecca walked through the door. "How's old Scott doing this morning?"

"How would I know?" Rebecca responded defensively, hoping to avoid the inevitable.

"Oh, I'm sorry. What, did you sleep under the bar at the Camelot? Scott dropped you off at two o'clock and then went home?" Charlene was laughing, and Cathy wore a broad grin. They were all friends, and there were no virgins living in or around the apartment. Rebecca was a little more conservative, and it was something of an event when she expressed serious interest in a man. Everyone, it seemed, wanted Rebecca to fall in love and be happy.

"It's not a big deal," Rebecca conceded to the evening's assignation. "I mean he's nice … and it was nice. But we're just friends."

"I'm sure he thinks you're just friends. He gets a big erection with all the girls." All three girls broke out in laughter.

"He is nice. He's just a little too…diplomatic for my taste." Cathy put in her two cents.

"Plus, he's got a flat ass." Charlene put the final kibosh on poor Scott. More laughter. Nonetheless, all three were disappointed that Rebecca had missed the brass ring and was back in the pool of women looking for true love or any facsimile thereof.

"Are you heading out to see your folks?" Cathy asked.

"Uh-huh. I'll be back around ten. There's a wine tasting. You want to come with me? It'll be nice." Rebecca would welcome the company on the drive.

"Thanks, but George and I are going to Golden Gate Park. We may do a little wine tasting there," Charlene responded.

"I've got an early day tomorrow. I'll be asleep by ten," said Cathy. "We've got a spring line presentation for the Emporium on Wednesday, so everybody's pushing, or else I'd go with you. Say hello to your folks, though."

"Yeah. They're a kick," said Charlene.

"Will do. I'm gone. If any of the girls call, tell them practice at five tomorrow. And to bring their playbooks."

St. Helena was an agricultural community in the center of the Napa Valley that predominantly grew grapes for local wineries. To the surprise of many, the first winery in St. Helena, Charles Krug, had begun operations in 1800, making the vineyards part of a long and interesting tradition. The wine-making operation ceased briefly during Prohibition and again during World War II. They probably didn't actually stop in the twenties but went underground admitting only to making sacramental wine. In the late sixties, California wines and champagnes were just starting to come into their own in the national and international markets, and demand was making life for the growers very comfortable. A bad year, however, could put you in a hole very quickly. Rebecca's maternal grandparents had acquired the vineyard years before and expanded it to its current size. Her parents took over when her grandfather passed away eight years ago. They had remodeled and expanded the house and upgraded the stable and barn. Her father, Ed Saunders, came from a farming family back in the Midwest. An army paratrooper, he had been discharged from the 101st Airborne Division after the war, met Rebecca's mother, Emily, in Georgia, and followed her back to San Francisco. After they married, Ed went to work for Emily's father and in time ran the entire operation. The Saunders were hardworking people. Although there had been several years of hardship with crops gone bad or prices down, overall they were financially comfortable. They owned 320 acres of land, two hundred of which were in grapes. The majority of their vineyard was in a White Riesling varietal grape and sold primarily to Korbel, a well-known champagne maker located up the road on the way to Guerneville. Several years prior, Ed had decided to diversify and now maintained, in smaller vineyards, at least two other grape varieties, Chardonnay and Cabernet Sauvignon. Although it meant more work and closer scrutiny at harvest, he felt more comfortable dealing with the wineries in three areas of their production.

The countryside—with its perfectly laid out rows of grapevines, rolling hills, and intermittent oak groves—was breathtaking, and neighbors were friends. The population was spread out, and deer and raccoons were as commonplace as horses and cows. In this area, 4-H was still a big part of the community. Rebecca had grown up with the vineyards, raised rabbits to show at state fairs, and was given her own horse when she was twelve. Fields of hay were not uncommon, and Rebecca always thought of the inside band of a music box when she saw the baled hay spread out in the fields. She was also something of a wine connoisseur, given her proximity to the business; and the fact that her parents had often let her taste new wines, even at a relatively young age. Rebecca loved coming home to St. Helena and family. The place held nothing but pleasant memories for her. During summer breaks from school, she had worked for several wineries as a tour guide and in the retail shops, and the owners loved her. She was pretty and outgoing, and she knew a lot about the product. Several wineries had extended open job offers upon her graduation from Cal. Her choice to pursue a master's in education was based partly on her love of children, but it helped that the volleyball-coaching job included tuition and a stipend large enough to afford her some financial independence.

This afternoon was a major wine-tasting event. Several wineries, including Beringer, Charles Krug, St. Clement, and Mondavi, were presenting new releases at the Christian Brothers facility. Driving into the Christian Brothers Winery was always an impressive experience. The main building was a massive, three-story, stone-walled structure; ivy growing halfway up the walls giving life to the red-gray stone. Bronze stars, unique to this building, adorned the walls high up. The stars were actually the ends of long metal bars infused into the stone for added structural support against the ever-present possibility of earthquake. Some monk years ago decided stars would be appropriate, consistent with the Christian philosophy. Olive trees and long rosemary hedges adorned the grounds. Huge barrels of wine and brandy lined the interior halls in what seemed like an unending supply of spirits. There was a semiselect invitation list, and as growers, the Saunders family was always on the guest list. Rebecca was pleasantly surprised to find her grandmother there. Her grandmother had elected three years before to move to the city of Napa a few miles up the Valley to live with two other widowed ladies, longtime friends who were, one way or another, associated with the wine industry. She was, at seventy-one, in no way slowed down or intimidated by gray hair or touches of arthritis. She wore a bright smile and a twinkle in her eye.

"Grandma Nell!"

"Rebecca. You look more beautiful every time I see you." The two embraced with genuine affection. "How are you? How is your ladies' team doing?" inquired the older woman.

"Just fine. And you? How are you doing? You look great. I love your outfit. Where did you get it?"

"At the boutique right here in Napa," laughed Grandma Nell Covington. "Hi Emily. Ed." She greeted her daughter and son-in-law with hugs and a pat on Ed's shoulder. "Have you started yet? I hear there are some really high hopes this year. Bob Mondavi thinks this is a breakout year for the Napa Valley. We had lunch with them last Wednesday."

"Our wines are as good most French wines," said Ed. "But it's going to take some good marketing to get them on the tables. Then they'll speak for themselves. I know they're trying to lock up production four, five years down the road."

"Well, let's see what they have for us," said Emily Saunders as she took her mother's arm. Ed put his arm over his daughter's shoulders, and the four of them moved to the tasting tables set up in one of the cavernous halls. The ambiance provided by huge, ten-foot-high barrels of wine adorning the halls gave the new releases a definite edge, joining decades of aging spirits and successful wine production, creating a positive mental attitude for today's tasters. Guests would get their wine—with a short explanation of who, what, when, and where the wine was born—then move about the facility or out onto the open air verandas. The day was warm and sunny; people were, for the most part, dressed up in summer finery. Small lines were forming in front of various tables, and greetings of recognition rang back and forth among the small crowd. Ed always went to look at Brother Timothy's corkscrew collection, eighteen hundred corkscrews displayed near the entry. They enjoyed the afternoon tasting and chatting with friends. Rebecca flirted innocently with some of her old high-school friends and made vague plans to get together soon. Ed took the women out to an early dinner at a genuine Mexican restaurant in Calistoga. By eight o'clock, Grandma Nell was on her way home, and Rebecca was on Highway 101 headed back to the city. News of the war in Vietnam was on the radio as she approached the Golden Gate Bridge but since her brother, Dennis, a former marine, was back from his tour over there and discharged, she really didn't follow it much anymore. "Why don't they just resolve the damn thing, one way or another, and be done with it?" she mused and punched the button for some music.

Rebecca put first aid cream on the knee of one of the girls who had dived for a dink shot and slid painfully across the hardwood floor. She spread the cream around and placed an adhesive pad over the raw friction burn. "Good hustle, Carolyn. That's the way we're going to win games." Rebecca patted the leg and called the other girls over. "Gather round. We have our first league game at Stanford on the sixteenth of September. That's a Thursday. We'll leave at three o'clock and go down in the bus. Probably be back by nine o'clock. Take care of homework. Don't give the faculty an opportunity to give us grief. Start thinking about the game now. Think about Putnam, Schmidt, and Olsen," she said, referring to three of Stanford's standout players. Rebecca had handed out profiles on the other team's players and wanted her girls to "know" them before game time. "They're good, but we can beat them if we stay cool and work our plays. We're a team, right?"

"Right!" the girls yelled back.

"What are we?"

"A team!"

"The team!" Came a voice from the group.

"That's right! The team!" shouted Rebecca with a laugh. She extended her arm, and all the girls reached in and grabbed hands.

"One. Two. Three. SF rules!" the team yelled enthusiastically.

"OK. See you tomorrow. Study the plays. The more you know when you get here, the more we can actually practice them."

"Good night, Coach."

One of the girls hung back and asked Rebecca if she could ride home with her parents after the Stanford game instead of coming back on the bus. "Not a problem, Kit. But I want to see your parents there and make sure that's who you're going home with. If anything happened, the school and I would be responsible. So if that's the case, fine. If not, no way."

"No that's fine, Coach. They'll be there. We live in Palo Alto, so it's close. They wouldn't miss the game anyway. Thanks. Good night." The girl smiled and started for the dressing room.

"Good night, Kit." As Rebecca looked up, she saw Scott Markham sitting in the bleachers by the entry. He waved and started toward her now that the girls were gone.

"Hi, early bird." He smiled showing white, even teeth. "How was the wine tasting?"

"Good," she said. "We'll give those Europeans a run for their money this year. You would have enjoyed it."

"I was hoping to."

"Well, it was a little stuffy. My parents and grandmother. Lots of business talk and a little wine tasting." Rebecca felt really awkward. She didn't mean to lie. She didn't really know what she would do or say. It just sort of came out. Clearly she didn't want to nurture this relationship. But how to get out of it without hurt feelings?

"Maybe next time."

Rebecca nodded. "Maybe next time."

Scott was not stupid. Rebecca was obviously not on the same cloud he had been on since Saturday night. It was a little bit of a shock that she didn't share his feelings, but he was, after all, a diplomat. He avoided scenes whenever possible, took light early losses when victory seemed distant ,and kept his ego intact for the next encounter.

"You don't seem too enthusiastic about that, Rebecca. I thought we had something going."

"Oh, Scott. It's not you, it's me. I'm so wrapped up in school and volleyball I...I don't know. I guess I'm not ready for a relationship. Other than as a friend. You know what I mean?"

Yes. He did know what she meant. "Salvage what you can," he thought. Then he said, "Sure, I know. It's always nice to dream and jump into the deep water once in a while. Our Saturday night in bed will always be a wonderful memory. San Francisco. College days. A beautiful woman. But I do value our friendship. Don't want to lose that. Who knows what will happen down the road?"

Rebecca listened to his calm, well-thought-out reply. "You slippery bastard," she thought. "It may be a pleasant memory for you. Deep water. What bullshit."

She smiled and said, "Thanks, Scott. Hey could you help me gather up these volleyballs. If I don't tell them, they don't do anything."

Rebecca turned out the light and fluffed her pillow. It hadn't gone badly with Scott. He was an arrogant, self-centered ... "What was I thinking? Was he really the pick of the litter? Well at least there had been no yelling or accusations. I can keep him at arm's length in the group. Damn," she thought. "Now what?"

CHAPTER FIVE

USS *Repose* (AH-16)

South China Sea

July 1968

Awareness drifted slowly back. McConnell's eyes remained closed, and there was no indication he was awake. As disoriented as he was, he nonetheless listened carefully, trying to ascertain where he was and his situation. Muscles throughout his body ached when he tried to tighten them, and he was sorely reminded of the hits he had taken. His memory recalled the retreat, Friendly and Weatherby, the helicopters, the noise, and the killing. A clearly defined pain in his left side and belly spoke of the AK-47 round. The area surrounding him was quiet. His eyes opened, and he squinted for a few moments as they adjusted. Nausea and a mild headache accompanied the survey of his surroundings. A small, dimly lit, pea-green painted room with a heavy metal beam running across the low ceiling held what appeared to be his hospital bed. There was a second bed in the room, but it was unoccupied. An IV bag with plastic tubes plugged into his forearm hung from a stainless steel rod next to the bed. There was movement. He could feel it, but he couldn't identify it. "Maybe medication," he thought. "Let's find out what works." Tentatively he started moving his fingers, then his hand, and finally his arm. Glancing down at his arm, he saw it was bandaged and strapped to the length of his body. His upper arm was sore as hell, and he lightly tensed and relaxed his bicep to determine how bad it was. It was still there, and for now that was good enough. He noticed the IV bag swaying slightly and recognized the movement as being from a ship at sea. "I must be in a sick bay aboard ship. Maybe a carrier."

He had been awake about thirty minutes when the door opened. A white-clad woman entered, carrying a tray. She closed the door then glanced over at him. Her face brightened when she saw he was awake. "Well good morning, Mr. McConnell. Welcome back," she said with a smile as she moved to the stand beside the bed and fussed with items on the tray. "How are we feeling?"

"Great. Where am I?"

"Aboard the *Repose*. The hospital ship," she explained. "We were the closest medical facility, so they dropped you and your buddies here. You guys really lit up the sky the other night." The USS *Repose* (AH-16) was a hospital ship that provided top-of-the-line medical care on station in the Gulf of Tonkin. It carried state-of-the-art medical equipment and a full complement of highly skilled doctors, dentists, and surgeons. The ship, deactivated after the Korean War in the midfifties and mothballed on Suisun Bay in California, was refitted and recommissioned in 1965 and had been online in Vietnam since 1966. Many lives and limbs were saved because of the proximity of the *Repose* and her sister ship, the *Sanctuary*.

"How long have I been here? Where are the others? How many others?" McConnell's concern for his teammates flooded over him. The little bit of effort he exerted just asking the questions left him exhausted and weak. "How bad were they hit? Can I see them?" he persisted through the lethargy that enveloped him.

"Take it easy," the nurse said, seeing his eyes flutter. "You've been out for thirty-six hours. It's Thursday afternoon. There were two others. Chief Petty Officer Friendly and, um …Thompson. They'll be OK, but they're not mobile yet," she informed him. "You a little woozy?"

He nodded in the affirmative. "And Weatherby?"

The nurse looked at him but didn't say anything.

"I know he's dead," McConnell said softly.

"There was one DOA," she said gently. "I'm sorry." She stood there for a few moments then busied herself with his IV bag and checked his dressings. Pursing her lips, she took a deep breath and told him the doctor would be in to examine his side soon. She moved to the door, hesitated, and looked back at him. "I'm sorry, John. About your friend…there was nothing we could do." The door closed quietly behind her, and he was alone in the small room again. Like many medical professionals in Vietnam, the woman took every loss personally. Every life. Every limb. Every boy whose youth was ripped away and replaced with cynicism and bad dreams.

"I know," he thought. "He never knew what hit him."

It was another full day before Jack Thompson arrived in a self-propelled wheelchair to visit. "Hey, dirtbag! You gonna lay around around all day?" Thompson chided him.

"Hey, Jack! How the hell are ya? What happened?" McConnell nodded at the bandages on his friend's head.

"Aw, I got nicked on the arm. No biggie. Then something went off right next to me. Didn't hit me, but the shock wave gave me a concussion. Knocked me for a loop. Busted an eardrum. Understand I owe you a beer for dragging my young ass out of there."

"Just understand I want a Heineken—not some fucking watered-down snake piss." The two men laughed, as much from the joy of seeing each other as from the joke. "Glad to see you're OK. Last time I saw you, you were just a lump. Why the wheelchair?"

"The head's still ringing a little. Got some dizziness. They make every-one use a wheelchair anyway. Between my friggin' head and the rolling of the ship, I was banging off the walls and grabbing on to the nurses so I didn't fall down. The good-looking ones love it. The others run for the wheelchair. How's the side?"

"Don't really know yet. The round went right through. The doc told me it nicked part of my stomach and kidney. They operated on it. Stitched it up or something…I'm not quite sure. Now it's wait and see if it heals right. Christ, I just woke up yesterday afternoon. I feel like shit. But I'm OK."

"Your arm, too?" Jack looked at the bandaged bicep strapped against McConnell's trunk.

McConnell took a slow, shallow breath. "Yeah. Arm, too. But the bullet didn't hit the bone. Put a nice hole in the muscle, though. Call me doughnut arm." He laughed then quickly winced. There was both pain and laughter in his eyes.

"Hell, you're fine, John. We need to get you back on patrol ASAP. This lying-around shit will make you fat and lazy. Hey, Bob Friendly said to say hello. His leg is fucked up good. Got a huge cast and traction. They've got him pretty well tied down to that bed."

"Everybody else make it out OK?" McConnell asked.

"Yeah. The usual bruises and scratches. But yeah, they're OK. You know about Weatherby."

McConnell nodded.

The two men talked for a while. Thompson left when the doctor came to check on the status of McConnell's insides. He was looking for infection and the proper functioning of his organs. "We'll have to wait for you to be a little more mobile before we can really tell what's going on, John." He took the thermometer out of McConnell's mouth and checked the mercury level. "But no fever. Only a little redness around the entry. So far, so good. We stitched the muscles in your arm together. That will heal in time."

"How long will I stay on the *Repose*, Doc?" McConnell asked.

"You, Friendly, and Thompson will be transferred back to San Diego pretty soon. Balboa Naval Hospital is right close to home. You and Friendly aren't mobile, so we're waiting for stretcher transport to Subic Bay and then back to the world. Won't be long."

"How long before I'm mobile?"

"Depends. John, you took a bullet through the left side of your stomach. It did some damage but it's difficult to ascertain if—or how quickly—your own system will essentially heal itself. We went in and patched up the few things we could. You're sore. You could get hit with a major infection. Or not. You're on antibiotics. We'll keep you on them for a while. For now, rest. Not a lot of exercise initially. And be patient. That help?"

"Is there anything I can do to speed up the process?"

"Not now. After we know the organs are OK, and you've had time to heal internally, then you'll have lots of opportunity to get the arm and the abs back into shape. That, my friend, will be a real ballbuster. So save your energy for that and rest now." The doctor wrote on John's chart, smiled, and left the room.

Six days later, the three Seals were admitted into Balboa Naval Hospital in San Diego. Thompson was discharged the next day as an outpatient. He would remain on medical leave until the condition of his ear was stabilized. Then he would be returned to light duty until he was determined fit for duty. For a diver, a ruptured eardrum was a delicate matter—one that could determine his future in the Seal Teams. Friendly and McConnell would be in the hospital for a while as their wounds healed. They both faced some tough recovery and rehabilitation time.

John McConnell was young and strong. With the attention of the hospital staff and his own healing power, fueled by an intense desire to get out of the goddamned hospital bed, he was released to outpatient status seventeen days later. He was provided with crutches and a wheelchair, instructed to go slow, and given a medication and examination schedule. "If you try to rush things, John, we'll have you back here for another few weeks," his nurse told him. She was a thirty-five-year-old single mom who thought he was cute. She enjoyed the boisterous Seals who came in and out of the hospital visiting her two warrior charges. She would've loved to see him back and thought seriously about asking to make house calls to check on her outpatient's progress. For the last two weeks, there had been a mock chase for her affections. Unfortunately, he wasn't really interested in catching her, and she was really hoping he would catch her. She was, however, mature enough to recognize the patient/nurse love scenario for what it was and waved cheerily as three Seals in BDUs assisted him in his wheelchair back to his world.

McConnell was on medical leave. Permission was granted for him to stay at a civilian residence, rented by eight bachelor Seals, right on Mission Beach in San Diego. The single-story, four-bedroom house became a home away from home, a place to get away from the military for a little while. It was a great house for parties, time away from the base at Coronado, bringing lovely ladies for assignations, and a fun place to spend free time. The sandy beach right off the back patio was perfect for surfers, volleyball players, and girl-watchers. It was understood by the renters that if things got too out of hand, the navy would be informed, and the lease would be terminated. Trouble happened occasionally but was quickly and carefully taken care of internally with everyone pitching in to placate injured parties. Being right on the beach, the setting couldn't have been better for John, who immediately set up camp in a lounge chair on the patio overlooking the ocean. He gloried in watching the waves; the parade of people moving back and forth; the almost naked, round-eyed girls in their two-piece bathing suits; the sunrises and sunsets. He read a lot during the day, refereed beach volleyball games on weekends and late afternoons, and turned brown as a berry beneath the Southern California sunshine.

Almost immediately he began exercising. He squeezed a tennis ball, gently at first, then more and more vigorously. A sixteen-ounce can of corn kernels became a weight for doing curls as he tried to get his left arm back up to speed. Within a week he was taking short, slow walks along the beach, each day going a little faster and a little farther. In three weeks he was able to jog for a hundred yards or so before tiring or feeling it in his side. He was careful not to overdo the exercise, maintaining a discipline that was very difficult for a Seal accustomed to ignoring pain and pushing to the limits. Around this time, at a weekend house party, he had his first sexual encounter since Vietnam. The girl was understanding of his condition, but it was explosive, repetitive, and almost 100 percent physical. He was back in the world. She stayed with him Saturday and Sunday, both of them enjoying the sun, suds, and sex. But when she left on Monday morning, he felt little different than he had in Vietnam. The girl kissed him good-bye, and he was happy to get back to the beach and his regular exercise. He thought he should have felt more.

By the beginning of October, McConnell was jogging or swimming five miles almost every day. He did push-ups and sit-ups and lifted weights in the gym, and he had been returned to light duty at the base. When he received his medical clearance to return to full-duty status, he immediately went to the Seal personnel office to get orders to return him to Bravo Platoon, still operating out of Rach Soi. Personnel pointed out that the platoon would be back to Coronado in less than three weeks and they were reluctant to send him over only to be brought home in a few weeks. McConnell got angry and made a scene. He went to the team's master chief seeking support for his request and was told to relax. The platoon would be back soon, and he was only just returned off medical leave. "Stand down, McConnell." he was told. Dismissed."

Two days later, as McConnell was inventorying ammunition and gear in the supply building, the phone rang. "McConnell?" the voice on the other end asked.

"Yeah. What's up?"

"It's Chip. Report to the admin office ASAP."

"What's up?" McConnell repeated. Chip Mihok was the duty yeoman. A call from him meant the master chief or an officer had something for him. ASAP meant just that. Right now.

"A medical officer is here. Other than that I have no clue, sorry. But Andy wants your butt up here. OK?"

"On my way, Chip."

About four minutes later, McConnell was standing in front of his E-9 Master Chief Andrew Ryan. The man was like a king. He ruled the operations and readiness of Seal Team One. His way was the way it happened. There were no tantrums or arguments with the master chief. He told you to do it. You did it.

"Reporting as ordered, Chief. What's up?" Out in the field it was first-name basis. In the office or in the presence of officers, it was the more formal "Chief" or "Master Chief."

"A doctor here to see you, John. He's waiting in the briefing room. Go talk to him." Andy Ryan was tough as nails. He didn't say a lot but was very clear when he did speak. Today was not a day for chitchat.

"Aye, aye, Chief. You know what he wants?" McConnell pressed.

Ryan looked him directly in the eyes and said, "He wants to know why you want to go back to Vietnam. Tell him." The master chief pointed at the door to the small briefing room, indicating that their conversation was over. With a perplexed look on his face, McConnell entered the briefing room and looked at a lieutenant commander with medical insignia on his shoulder bars sitting at the briefing table. The officer stood up and extended his hand. "Hello, John. I'm Doctor Barnard."

McConnell shook the man's hand. "Sir." The doctor was about thirty-five, tan, and relaxed. He had an unopened briefcase on the table. John had a sinking feeling that something in his stomach was amiss. Some relapse of his wound. But he felt fine. "What the hell is going on?" he thought.

"Please sit down." Dr. Barnard motioned John to a chair and sat back down across the table. "You look healthy, John. Pretty much recovered from those wounds?"

"Feel great, sir. Should I?" he inquired, anxious to find out what this was about.

Dr. Barnard shook his head and smiled. "I'm not a medical doctor, John. I'm a psychologist. I'm sure your recovery is fine. That's not why I'm here. We're getting more and more cases of what the military is calling post-Vietnam stress disorder. Psychological wounds. We don't really know what it is, but that's the label we're putting on it for now. You heard of it?"

"No, sir. You think I have this stress disorder?"

"I have no idea. We're studying the disorder itself as much as we're examining any individual. There is no standard list of symptoms that we can put our finger on yet. But men come back from Vietnam, and many are a little confused. Have difficulty adjusting back into society. Sometimes they drop out. Sometimes get violent. Difficulty with marriages … jobs."

"Why are you talking to me?"

"Well, it has come to our attention that you want to go back to Vietnam, back to combat patrols. Among you Seals, this is not altogether unusual. You guys are pretty gung ho. But you have served three tours in two and a half years. You got the shit knocked out of you on the last tour, and now you're pushing pretty hard to go back. Do you like Vietnam, or are you not liking it here at home anymore?" The question came across hard. It wasn't accusatory. Nor was it threatening. It was direct. But what was the answer?

It was silent for more than a minute. "I have buddies over there. Maybe I can help them. Or save a life," McConnell finally replied. "What other reason could there be?" he thought to himself. Aloud he said, with an edge on his voice, "A Seal is a warrior, sir, and warriors go where the action is."

"I understand, John. Realize I am not here to make trouble for you or accuse you of anything. I'm here to maybe learn something about post-Vietnam stress disorder. Consider this research. And you're in a position to help us figure this out." He paused and then said, "You really want to go back there, don't you? Even though your buddies will be home in two weeks." The statement made John wonder. It sounded wrong the way the shrink said it.

Lieutenant Commander Barnard was being completely honest with the man sitting across from him. But as they spoke, he sensed there was something there that the young Seal was hiding. Probably not consciously. He really did want to go back. But it wasn't to save his buddies. Oh, he was sincere about that, but that wasn't the main reason. Why would a man want to go back to war? Especially this war.

The two men talked for about an hour. It seemed casual to McConnell, and he answered questions as truthfully as he could. The officer seemed to be a pretty good guy. There didn't seem to be any continuous line of inquiry. They just seemed to be talking about Vietnam in general and the tough time a lot of guys had coming home.

"John, I'd like to review my notes; see how or if any of what you have told me might fit in with our research. And I'd like to meet with you again, if that's all right with you. Maybe we could talk over lunch. You know, as public protests over our involvement in this war get more vocal and visible, it's going to be even more difficult for the guys returning. I'm convinced that's a big part of this stress disorder. Coming home used to be parades and free beers. Now guys don't even want to wear their uniform. They want to hide. Maybe you can help me to help some of those guys."

McConnell nodded. "Sure, Doc. I understand what you're saying. Sure. Lunch whenever you say. Just clear it for me with the master chief."

"Thanks, John." The doctor rose and extended his hand again. "I appreciate your help. I'll give you a call to set it up."

That afternoon the doctor sat at the desk in his office reviewing his notes on McConnell, pondering the man's replies and position on Vietnam. Some men gloried in war. Patton. But this man was a foot soldier, in the trenches. As the doctor read through McConnell's file, he noticed that it was almost exclusively night patrols. Ambush. Pointman. Shotgun. Hand-to-hand combat expert. Did this man love his work that much? He was certainly good at it. Barnard noticed that Seal Platoon Bravo had an extraordinary enemy KIA record. This man has seen a lot of killing. Has done a lot of killing. "My God! Is that why he wants to go back there? The taste of killing. Oh shit! He's not aware of that." Barnard sat back in his chair and thought about the personable young man with the fire in his eyes. "How do I help this man come back without crushing his self-esteem? Here's another syndrome to add to the pile."

Lieutenant Lou Retino and Bravo Platoon had returned a week ago. There was a great reunion of the platoon with Thompson, Friendly, and McConnell backslapping, catching up on patrol stories, and helping the platoon unpack the gear returned in the shipping containers, including stereos and dishes. McConnell was glad for the distraction. He had met again with Commander Barnard. The subject of his desire to return to Vietnam had again been the main topic of their conversation. But John had been thinking about that on his own since their first meeting. Even after the platoon had returned, he thought about going back and was trying to figure out, in his own mind, what was motivating him. Barnard never came right out and said it but implied that it wasn't the people or the camaraderie but rather the work that needed to be examined. "Some soldiers," he had said, "get caught up in the excitement of the hunt; the thrill of individual victories. 'I win: the enemy loses.' Very clear. Very powerful."

Barnard never used the word "kill." John figured that out for himself.

"Sometimes it takes a while to get that mindset to go away. Like not taking a shotgun to some asshole because he cut you off on the freeway." Barnard's reference to the shotgun was not lost on McConnell. He and Jack Thompson also talked about it in nonspecific terms. John was surprised to learn that Thompson would go back to Vietnam but wasn't eager to get back.

"Why the hell would I want to go back there? To get killed? To find another MyLing? To lay in the fucking jungle all night shivering? I'll go if that's where they send me, but my first choice would be Makapu Beach in Hawaii." Thompson laughed. "John, Coronado ain't that bad either. The beach house…" He raised and lowered his eyebrows like Groucho Marx.

"Speakin' of going back, how's the eardrum?" McConnell asked, changing the subject. "Gonna be all right?"

"It's not good, John. It might be all she wrote for me here. The chief is stringing it out for me, but I can't do my dive quals. And a Seal who can't dive ain't worth shit."

"Jesus, Jack. There's lot's of billets you could fill on the team. Yeoman, topside support, weapons."

"Would you be happy doin' that, John?"

McConnell paused. He looked at Jack and thought about his own dilemma. "No, Jack. I don't think I would. So what would you do?"

"I think get out of the navy. Maybe go back to school. Find a round-eyed MyLing and start a family. I'm not really sure." The two men sat quietly for a while. "Hey! Did I ever buy you that Heineken I owe you?"

"I sure can't remember. But if you buy me one, then I'll buy you one. How's that? How's about a little liar's poker?" A poker-like game using the serial numbers on dollar bills was a popular way to gamble for rounds of drinks. Some guys were good, but more often than not, at the end of a month everyone had bought the same number of beers.

"You're on, pal!"

The two men dug into their wallets, pulled out dollar bills, folded them into their cupped hands, and looked back and forth suspiciously between the bill in their hand and the other man. "Two sixes." McConnell started the game cautiously.

Thompson's eyes rolled skyward. "Oooooh. A ballsy start. Two sixes. Where do I go from there?" he said in mock dismay. Then he leered up at McConnell and said, "Three tens, smart-ass."

McConnell had confided in his commanding officer and comrade, Lieutenant Lou Retino, about his now nagging problem. The two men sat at the bar in the Seal's quasi-private EM Club.

Retino was speaking. "I guess it boils down to what you feel and how strongly you feel about it, John," the officer said. "It's a tough call. For some men, that feeling, or something akin to it, rules their life. They're career men because they like the work. Some are psychotic. I've seen them. Worked with them. They're great to work with but usually fucked up when they're not in a combat zone. For others, they like the work, but they don't take it home with them. Sometimes it takes a little while to let go, but they do eventually. For some it's a job. They don't like it but do it because their country says it's necessary."

"Which are you, Lou?"

"Me? Maybe a little of all of them. But I'm comfortable with where I am and what I am. If you're not, then move on to something else. It's a personal call, John. You are a hell of a Seal. You know that. But is that going to be your life? If it is, why?"

"It's your life, Lou."

"The navy is my life, John. I was in it before there were Seals. I'm an officer, and I have a family. Thank God Susan is the kind of woman she is, or I wouldn't have a family. Unless this Vietnam thing goes on a whole lot longer than I think it will, this could be my last combat tour. Oh, there'll always be some shit going down somewhere, and Seals will always have work to do. But hell, I've got a daughter about to go into high school."

"I didn't even remember you had a daughter. You should bring her around."

"Right! Maybe she and Constanza could go out to the drive-in." He laughed. "Right. Over my dead body." His eyes hardened involuntarily. "Or his!" The two of them laughed again.

"Here's my advice, John. I have an old UDT buddy up in San Francisco. He runs a marine engineering and salvage operation. Pretty big company. I'll call him and see if he has any work you might be interested in. You still have your welding and hull inspection certification, don't you?"

"Yeah. All current."

"OK. I'll set up a meet for you. Take some leave and talk to the guy. See what he has to say. Screw a hippie or two, walk through Golden Gate Park. Go to a 49ers game. See what's going on in the world."

"OK. Thanks, Lou. I appreciate your time."

The next morning the platoon was working in the gear locker inventorying the returning weapons and equipment. The mood was light. The men were talking and were, for the most part, relaxed. Lt. Retino entered and walked across the locker to the wire cage where weapons and ammunition were locked. He went over some paperwork, finished up a few minutes later, and started for the door. Constanza was sorting Stoner ammunition links, engrossed in his task. As Retino passed him, he slowed and said in a reasonably loud voice "Constanza! You stay the hell away from my daughter!" Constanza's head jerked up, his eyes filled with concerned surprise.

"What? What'd you say… sir?" He looked around the locker. Every eye was on him. "What?"

"You heard me, you son of a bitch! Just stay away!" Retino scowled at Constanza. As he turned back to the door, his eye caught McConnell's, and he winked as he stormed out, slamming the door behind him.

"What the hell was that about?" There was real concern on Constanza's face. Nothing but hard looks came from the men around him. Retino's daughter was only maybe fifteen. He was their leader and mentor.

McConnell, having caught the wink, only just realized how perfectly Retino had set Constanza up. He contained his laughter as long as he could. After only a few moments he burst into full-bellied laughter, tears streaming down his face. The others looked at him questioningly and in dismay. When McConnell looked at them and then at Constanza, his laughter took on monumental proportions. Some of the others sensed a practical joke, slowly realizing that Constanza had been had. The laughter spread and soon Constanza alone sat with his mouth open, still waiting for Retino to storm back into the room, this time with an ax ... or worse.

It was Friday night, and a party had been brewing all week. A keg of beer was tapped and on ice. LP records on the stereo were setting the music mood, and the boys were ready. A number of women were there, some regulars and some new faces. Chip Mihok, a Seal from Alpha Platoon, was sitting outside on the brick patio that bordered the beach. He was talking with a woman who was attractive and animated. Chip had a beer in his hand, and the girl a glass of white wine. They appeared comfortable with each other, and John had the impression that Chip was either not on the make or had already partaken of the lady's favors. John had been running on the beach and wore shorts and a gray sweatshirt with the sleeves cut off at the shoulder.

"Hey, Chip," he said as he walked up from the sand and onto the patio. He nodded at the girl.

"Hey, John. You look like you could use a beer."

"Maybe a shower first."

"John, this is Charlene Bascomb. I met her in San Francisco last year. A good lady. She's down visiting relatives. I talked her into coming over tonight."

"Hello, Charlene. Nice to meet you. I'm John McConnell. " he introduced himself. "Glad you could make it. You live in San Francisco?"

"Hello, John. Nice to meet you. Yes, I live there. Wish we had your sunshine up there." She extended her hand and gave McConnell a firm handshake.

"Well you have the cable cars. You can't have everything."

"True." She laughed.

"Hell, why don't you have a beer and then a shower," Chip suggested.

"Hell, why not? Can I get you guys anything while I'm in there?"

The three of them sat on the patio, talking and watching the sunset. Several others joined them, and the conversation was enjoyable and fun.

"Well, I've got to pack. I'm headed up to San Francisco tomorrow morning. Want to get an early start. If I don't pack now, I know I'll forget my toothbrush," McConnell said as he stood up and excused himself.

"Where are you staying?" Charlene asked. "You can stay at my place. I'm sure my roommates won't mind. I could call and tell them you're coming."

"No. I'm sure that would be a bother. But I appreciate the offer."

"No bother. Heck, they might not even be home."

"You know what a hotel room costs in the big city, John?" Chip Mihok offered as further inducement.

John shrugged his shoulders. "If you're sure they won't mind."

Charlene dug into her purse for a ballpoint and wrote her address down on a paper coaster. She then tossed John a key. "Leave the key on the kitchen table. My room is the one with the white door. I hope I remembered to clean up." She smiled.

"Well, thank you. When will you be home?" John asked.

"Not for two weeks."

"Maybe she can use your room here." Chip laughed. Charlene didn't think that was funny, and she glared at Chip. "Sorry, babe. You know I was kidding."

McConnell didn't get to bed until two and didn't get on the road until ten thirty the next morning.

There was really no rush. McConnell took the longer but more pleasant route up coast the Pacific Coast Highway. He drove a dark-gray 1964 Chevy pickup. It had a camper top but, to save on gas, he left it at the house. The truck was well tuned, in good shape. He looked forward to the drive and the time in San Francisco. An opportunity for adventure. Maybe a little mild after Vietnam, but something different. A couple of hitchhikers helped him pass the time for a while. A laugh came to his lips when he thought about warnings against picking up hitchhikers. His KA-BAR combat knife and a loaded .45 were tucked under his seat. Being armed was a hard habit to break. From what he heard, San Francisco had no shortage of drug addicts and, flower children or no, better to have a big stick than not. The ocean off to his left reflected the sun in a million directions and the offshore breeze carried that wonderful salt-and-seaweed smell up to the road. He observed whales blowing as they moved down the coast to Baja, and he crawled through tourists stopped by the side of the road to watch the whales and sea lions sunbathing on the rocks or surfing the near shore break. The radio gave him a indication of what was ahead as Scott McKenzie sang, "If you're going to San Francisco, be sure to wear some flowers in your hair, If you're going to San Francisco, you will meet some loving people there." "A far cry from Vietnam," thought McConnell as he envisioned the contrast. The drive afforded him some privacy, something you didn't get a lot of in the military. He enjoyed the time.

At Half Moon Bay he stopped for a late lunch. eating codfish and chips on a pier that hung out over the waves. Several older men were fishing off the end of the pier, talking among themselves in the afternoon sun. He didn't see them catch anything. He didn't think they minded much. John thought about the job interview and the possibility of leaving the team. It was difficult to imagine his life other than as a Seal. It was equally difficult to imagine himself as a killer with an insatiable bloodlust. Gung ho…yes. He was looking forward to San Francisco but not to making that decision.

As he sat eating lunch, he looked over a city map to locate Steiner Street. The address on the back of the Black Label beer coaster read 311 Steiner. He was a little apprehensive about dropping in without calling first, but he hadn't thought to get a phone number. Calling was not an option. He hoped the girl, Charlene, remembered to let her roommates know he was coming. "God! What if her roommate is a guy?"

The truck struggled through the strange environment of the city. He finally found Lombard Street following it west until the Steiner Street sign appeared. He made a right, saw the numbers getting smaller, and went around the block to cross Lombard and go the other way up the steep hill. Not too far off Lombard, the numbers 311 hung on the door of a two-story white house on his left. All the houses were scrunched right up against one another. There were no yards or driveways. The neighborhood, though, was clean and well kept, the occasional potted plant or window box with flowers providing bright pockets of color. There was no parking spot in sight, and he cruised slowly, looking. Three or four minutes later, a spot opened up about a block away. "Where do they park?" he wondered. "Do they drive around like this every night?" John decided to leave his travel bag in the truck and see what was happening at the apartment. There were no lights on that he could see as he walked up the steps. He heard the buzz inside when he pressed the doorbell and fidgeted while he waited. There was no response and he fingered the key in his pocket. It was only six thirty. "Shit," he thought. "I don't know if they're expecting me. I'm not going to just walk in and take a shower. I'll come back later" he decided "Maybe there'll be somebody home then."

On the advice of Mako McDaniels, he sought out Union Street as a hot spot for San Francisco nightlife. There were lots of shops and not a few pubs and restaurants. Union Street was lively, colorful, and brightly lit, with a good number of shoppers and animated people casually strolling the side-walks. "Looks like a good place to get a beer," McConnell thought as he pushed through the swinging doors that led into the Camelot. It was still early. A couple sat at the bar. Most tables were filled with people having dinner. It smelled like a good place to eat. He would come back, maybe tomorrow night. Music rolled out of a jukebox turned down for the dinner crowd. It was noisy but not boisterous.

A bartender in a white shirt, sleeves rolled up inside, appeared in front of him, looking at him, waiting for him to order.

"A draft. Bud if you have it."

"Have Oly and Michelob on tap. I can get you a bottle of Budweiser," the man said pleasantly.

"A bottle a' Bud will do it."

He enjoyed watching the people. More couples arrived and a lot of single guys. Girls in twos and threes arrived with less regularity. A large girl wearing black leather offered to buy him a beer. He was tempted but politely declined, explaining he was waiting for someone. It was starting to fill with singles, some good-looking women. Although the dance floor was filling with waving arms and legs, by nine o'clock his ass hurt from sitting on the barstool, and he decided to go back to the apartment.

There were still no lights on as he waited for someone to answer the buzzer. "Maybe there'll be no one there." He remembered the girl offering that possibility. "Oh shit," he thought as he turned the key and entered the foyer. "Give me a night patrol anytime." He chuckled to himself. The rooms were smaller than he thought they would be. He switched on the light in the kitchenette and noted that the house was clean with a smattering of eclectic furniture, lots of pillows and family photos, and some trophies on top of a bookcase. Neither a bedroom nor a white door was part of the downstairs and he surmised it would be up the narrow flight of stairs against the wall. An awkward feeling hung over him. He felt like he was sneaking around someone else's house. "Well shit!" he thought again uncomfortably. "That's exactly what I'm doing." The fourth stair creaked slightly as he went up. The white door was at the top of the stairs. He opened the door and stood in the doorway. There were women's clothes, stockings, curlers scattered throughout the room and over the bed.

"Fuck this!" he said aloud. "I can't stay here." The discomfort he felt from the beginning of his acceptance of this idea flooded over him. He couldn't wait to get out. As he turned to go back down the stairs and leave, he heard the door open. His chest tightened. He felt like a thief in the night. It was ten o'clock.

He started down the stairs. A woman came through the foyer and immediately saw the movement on the stairs. Her head jerked up and her eyes, wide with fear, stared directly at him.

"Hello. I'm John McConnell," he said quickly before she screamed. Charlene's name was nowhere in his available memory. He stood on the stairs, trying desperately to remember her name. The woman's eyes never left him. He couldn't think of her name. "Don't be afraid." It was all he could think of to say. "Your roommate said I could spend the night. That she would call and tell you I was coming." With mounting despair he thought, "What the hell was her name?" Anger was pushing through the woman's eyes. The shoulders beneath her gray-and-black sweater were heaving slightly, as if she was short of breath.

"What are you doing upstairs?" she blurted out.

"She said to use the room with the white door. I was just checking it out."

"Who said?"

"Charlene!" The name mercifully popped back into his head. "I met her in San Diego. She said she would call. Jesus, I'm sorry about this. She didn't call?"

"How did you get in?"

John fumbled in his pocket and produced the key. He held it up, thanking God he had it. The woman was beautiful. "Charlene gave me her key."

"Well, no one called me. I'm sorry, but you can't stay here. I have half a dozen of my volleyball players coming over," she lied, still frightened by the man with the fierce eyes and the direct stare. Both of them continued to stare at each other, until Rebecca moved to the kitchen table, put down her purse, and turned back to the intruder. Her eyes were still wide with both fear and anger. She was trying to decide what to do. He felt like an ass.

"I can find a hotel. No problem. I would have called first, but I didn't have a number." McConnell moved to the bottom of the stairs. "I'm really sorry I frightened you."

"Charlene is a little bit of a scatterbrain. If I had known you were coming…" Her voice trailed off. She was less uncomfortable but still intimidated by the man who had violated her space and still stared at her with those eyes. "But it's impossible. The girls are coming… it just wouldn't work."

"No. That's fine. I'll be fine. I apologize for scaring you. Really."

"It's OK." She stood there looking at him. Waiting for him to do something. Hopefully leave.

"I'm going to be up here, in San Francisco, for three or four days. Maybe I could take you out to dinner. Sort of apologize." John thought the woman was incredibly attractive. Her face was tan and strong. A blush of red lingered on her cheeks, he was sure from being so scared. She looked athletic. And a good build considering the swellings pushing her sweater out. He felt his chest tighten again as he waited for her to reply.

"Is he asking me out?" she thought incredulously. "What a pair of balls."

"I don't think so," she said. Um…. "I have a really busy schedule… volleyball games, work. But thank you. Maybe when Charlene gets back." She couldn't resist the dig. His eyes closed and opened slowly as he nodded his understanding. A look both icy cold and yet… hurt… lurked in the blue-gray.

"God. I think I hurt his feelings," she thought.

"Charlene is pretty involved with a friend of mine. And I'll be long gone by the time she gets back. Well…" He moved to the door, dropping the key on the table as he passed. Then he turned and looked back. "Good luck with your volleyball games. I'll be on my way before the gang gets here. Sorry again." He went through the door and closed it gently behind him. As he walked to the truck he thought about the first girl he met in San Francisco. "Well I sure made her feel comfortable. Maybe that's the way it's going to be. Maybe I should have shown her my KA-BAR. Or the 12 gauge. That really would have scared the crap out of her."

Rebecca moved to the door and locked it. Her fear was subsiding, but her chest still heaved. "What a strange man. What eyes. Imagine him sleeping upstairs." The thought was both terrifying and ... what?

CHAPTER SIX

San Francisco, California

November 1968

It was that time of the year in San Francisco for wonderful, cool autumn days, when the pure-blue sky was clear, and the golden sun shone bright and clean on everything. Everyone was outside, mellow and enjoying life. Joggers, Frisbee players, people walking dogs, and bicycles were everywhere. Touch football games filled every grassy corner Golden Gate Park had to offer. Lawn bowlers and hippies; gays and straights; young and old; everyone wore love beads. Sailboats of every size and description cut through the soft, white-mustached waves of the Bay. Colorful spinnakers billowed out majestically, lording over the Lasers and Cal 20s darting back and forth like frantic flying fish. Cars, boats, and bicycles ventured across the water to the delightfully quaint towns of Sausalito and Tiburon. Passenger ferries plowed back and forth to Angel Island and Alcatraz, that enigma in the middle of the city of love.

John McConnell felt comfortable at Berg Marine Engineering from the moment he drove through the gates on Monday morning. The saltwater, the docks, the boats, coils of thick rope, buoys, propellers; it was not unlike a navy base. There was a man welding something. He could see the sparks flying. A small group of men worked on and around what looked like an old navy Mike Boat converted to a floating work platform. Another burst of sparks splashed across its deck. A large ocean-going cargo ship was passing by, headed for the potato patches under the orange span of the Golden Gate Bridge and the blue water of the Pacific. Seagulls wheeled and squawked, their white droppings a visible part of the environment. A sign indicating the office caught his attention, and he pulled the truck into a parking spot labeled VISITORS ONLY. He sat in the truck for a minute, getting his bearings, gathering himself for his meeting with Lowell Berg, owner and operator of the business. Berg had been a Navy Underwater Demolitions Team diver during World War II. He had been recalled for the Korean conflict and had worked with a very young seaman, Lou Retino, at Pusan. McConnell had talked with Berg on the telephone. The man had been nice enough, very direct. Said he could always use experienced divers and was willing to talk with McConnell. Always nice to walk in and talk to the man in charge.

He walked through the office door at 9:57 a.m., early for his ten o'clock appointment. The reception area was not that big, but two large picture windows gave it a bright and roomy feeling. Maritime photos and artifacts caught your attention right away. A six-by-four-foot, large-scale map of the Pacific Rim hung on the wall, colored pins marking the locations of something, presumably jobs or projects. The number of pins was impressive. John thought how easy it would be to add a few pins; puff a little. A brass binnacle stood almost in the center of the room. A secretary looked up when he entered. She smiled as he approached her, looked down at a book on her desk, and then, looking up, said, "You must be Mr. McConnell."

"Yes, ma'am."

She smiled. "I'll tell him you're here." The woman was in her midforties. A dozen photographs adorned her desk and the wall to her right. The pictures proudly displayed four kids, a husband in a police uniform, a beagle. It was a nice-looking family. She still had an attractive smile. The intercom crackled when she pushed a button and spoke into it. "Mr. McConnell here to see you, Mr. Berg." His response presumably came back through the headset the woman wore because she looked back up at John and said, "He'll just be a few minutes. You can have a seat there. Can I get you a cup of coffee?"

"No, thank you. I'd like to look through that brochure, though." He indicated with a nod of his head toward a corporate brochure lying on her desk. The brochure was color, glossy. Even without reading it, it told you John a lot about the company—that it did things right.

"Oh, by all means. I have another one, more detailed, if you'd like."

"Great. Thank you." John noted six or seven offices along a hallway off the reception room, several of which he could see had drafting tables. He could hear muffled conversations and knew that people were working. Blueprints rolled up, tacked up, and boxed seemed to be everywhere, along with the faint smell of ink or alcohol, or whatever that chemical was they used to print them. There was a door marked CONFERENCE ROOM.

He browsed through the information in the brochure, surprised at how large and diversified the company was. Ship overhaul and repair, hull inspections, oceanfront architecture and engineering, from docks to marinas, demolition, salvage. And it looked as though they worked all over the world—the Pacific Rim, anyway. Christ, the place didn't look that big. Or that impressive. Of course, neither did eight men in dirty clothes and green face paint. But they were. Looks could be deceiving. While he was reading about a waterfront renovation project in Oakland, a door opened and a large man with close-cropped whitehair burst into the room. His energy was palpable. He looked toward John.

"Mr. McConnell! Welcome to San Francisco." The two shook hands. John's hand felt small in the other man's grip. "Come in. How's old Lou?"

"Mr. Retino's just fine, sir. Sends his regards."

"He's come a long way. Lieutenant. Seal. He's a good man. Knew him when he was a snot-nosed kid. Tough, though. Dependable."

"Yes, sir. He is that."

Berg waved John to a couch beneath a large photograph of a navy submarine with a dozen men in bathing suits and swim fins standing along its railing. There were signatures scribbled on the old photo, and John couldn't resist extending his glance.

"My old UDT unit used to launch from the Tigerfish. In Korea. Reminds me of the old days. My only regret is that we never did finish that job. The Korean War. So you're thinking about getting out of the navy?"

"I'm thinking about it. To be honest, I haven't made up my mind yet."

Berg looked at the young man. "Something about Vietnam. Not wanting to go back. Or wanting to. I can't remember." He was watching John intently.

McConnell didn't make any outward sign that the man had struck a nerve. Nonetheless, he felt a need to defend himself. "Sir, I've done three tours. Done a good job. I'm just thinking maybe that's enough. If I were ordered back tomorrow, I would go without batting an eye. And do a good job."

"An outstanding job, according to Lou."

McConnell nodded. The two men looked at one another for a few moments.

"You've got all the necessary underwater qualifications. All current. Demolition." Berg noted as he read from the resume McConnell had sent up a week before. "You would have to take some civilian certification courses, but that's nothing. Your navy occupational rate is shipboard electrician. How good are you?"

"Went through 'A' school. Had to take the tests to advance. But I'm a little rusty. In Vietnam, we didn't spend a lot of time on shipboard repair."

"I understand. You must know your way around shipboard electrical systems, though. I understand you have some college."

"Yes, sir," John replied, surprised at the question. "Three semesters at Rutgers."

"Any thoughts about continuing on? Getting a degree?"

"Well I haven't thought about it for a while. Always thought I would finish up. If the opportunity presented itself, I would grab it." John's mind was racing. This might be a great deal. "Do you have a program here? I mean for college?"

"No. Not a formal program. If someone comes along with talent and drive, I would bend over backwardsward to help him. You know, you can get college credit for some of the navy schools you've attended. Depending on the major, of course."

"I didn't know that. I'll look into it." It was quiet for a moment. The intercom buzzed and the secretary informed Berg he had a call.

"Excuse me a minute, John. This'll only take a few minutes."

"Would you like me to wait outside?" John asked.

"No. You're fine."

John sat, not listening but hearing Berg's conversation. He was talking about some project. His questions were direct and clear; his answers were the same. No bullshit. Clear and to the point. John liked the man's style. And his inference that support for college might be available was an interesting and attractive idea. He wondered how he would fit in with a college crowd after his experiences as a Seal…a combat Seal in Vietnam. What if he took this job, assuming one was offered. The girl at 311 Steiner passed through his mind. He could hear the seagulls squawking through the partially open window. The sound of the Mike Boat's engine rumbled through the salt air.

"Sorry about the interruption, John." The men talked for another thirty minutes, Berg explaining what sort of things John could be doing, if he decided to pursue this. He would work primarily out of this office, with some time off-site as needs demanded. "This office is our headquarters, where things get planned, set up, marketed, and sold. Although we do some hands-on work here, most of the work is off-site, maybe here in town or in Oakland, or maybe Hawaii. Almost anywhere. Consultant teams are put together based on need, experience, timing, and availability. Location teams work on-site, wherever that might be, coordinating with the home office as necessary. There could be significant travel, if you wanted to go that route. Or if you got involved with, say, college, that would be given priority consideration. I like to get good people, John, people who do a good job, who can work well on their own or on a team, and whom I can trust. To keep them, I pay a good wage and treat them well. You have any questions?"

"You make it sound pretty good, Mr. Berg. I'd like to look into getting college credits for navy classes. And what kind of majors would be involved?

What kind of majors would you be looking for? Actually, my enlistment is up in January, so I wouldn't even be available until then. How much of my work would be in the field and how much would be at a desk?" John knew that was a dangerous question, but he really didn't want to be a desk jockey.

"Well there is a lot of paperwork involved in the business, John. But I think there's a pretty good ratio of field time to paperwork. The paperwork drives the business, though, so it can't be avoided altogether. Once you got a feel for how we operate and vice versa, I think you'd see enough field time. As to what majors I look for, that really varies over time. We can look into that when the time comes. So you're at least still curious? Still interested?"

John knew the interview was over. Berg looked straight at him. John liked the man. "Yes, sir. What's the next step?"

"How long you going to be up here?"

"Three or four days. Another day or two if necessary." He thought of the sunshine, the Golden Gate…the girl.

"Well tomorrow I'm going over to Oakland to look at our Marina project there. You're welcome to come along and see what it's about. On Wednesday I have a crew finishing up a hull inspection on a barge over in Sausalito. You can tag along and meet some of the guys. Before you go back, we'll talk again and see where you are. How's that?" Berg had a sort of twinkle in his eye. Clearly he liked John and was presenting him with an opportunity. John wondered what Retino had told him. Must have been good.

The next two days were way more interesting than John thought they would be. There were all kinds of things going on at the Oakland project, multiple disciplines interacting, any one of which required skills which John either already had or would like to have. He was with Berg in Oakland almost all day Tuesday. Berg simply introduced him; didn't say who or what he was. John was included in discussions and presentations, asked his opinion, and made to feel like part of the team. He recognized and appreciated what Berg was doing. This was part of society's creative process, building things up, the other end of the destructive process he was so familiar with. It was interesting.

Wednesday he spent with a hull-inspection team in Sausalito. They wouldn't let him dive—insurance restrictions—but they made him feel welcome. The guys were competent professionals, not Seals, but very good at what they did. After work he was invited along for a few beers and a taste of Northern California. Several pubs along Bridgeway Avenue stood out as potentially interesting places to have a cold one. The Cat and the Fiddle, the Two Turtles and one that had nothing on the sign that hung outside—of course, the No Name Bar. Sausalito was quite a place. Damn near the whole town was waterfront and every house on the hills above Bridgeway had a spectacular view. And it was only five minutes to the Golden Gate Bridge and the big city. Between the bridge and Sausalito, two large US Army-owned tracts of land, Fort Cronkite and Fort Baker, protected the town from outrageous development and provided a somewhat pristine recreational area for locals. Looking across the bay at the Oakland hills, the reflection of the setting sun on hundreds of glass windows glowed gold like a field of campfires, like an invading army gathering for an attack. "Too much Vietnam," thought John. "Maybe it's Boy Scouts on a camporee."

On the way back to his motel that evening, he passed Steiner Street as he drove up Lombard, and the girl popped into his mind again. Without thinking about it, he turned and drove past 311. Again he felt awkward and nervous. This was definitely not his MO with women. He felt maybe he should apologize one more time. Maybe ask her out for a drink or dinner. A parking spot appeared, as if a signal to do it, and he pulled in. As he walked slowly to the 311 stoop, he looked for signs of activity in the house but saw none. Once more he rang the buzzer and waited impatiently. His chest was tighter than if he had been on a night ambush. Jesus. He rang again. No answer. Two or three minutes passed before he accepted the fact that no one was home. He thought about leaving a note but decided that that would make him look like a bigger jerk than he already felt.

Thursday afternoon, Berg invited him to lunch. "To wrap up our visit. See what you want to do," he said. They had lunch at one of the smaller restaurants along Fisherman's Wharf that seemed to cater to working locals.

Men in boots and sweaters were having coffee or eating. For those associated with the crab or fishing industry it was near the end of their workday. Almost everyone knew Berg, greeting him as he and John entered. Berg didn't even pick the menu up. He recommended crab Neptune, a version of eggs Benedict that used Dungeness crab instead of ham or Canadian bacon. It was delicious, and John filed the recipe away for future use in his seduction cookbook. John McConnell, Seal extraordinaire, mildly surprised himself by telling Berg he was very interested in pursuing this opportunity and working for Berg Marine Engineering. That he would be available in January, just two months away.

"Are you curious about what salary I'm ready to offer?" Berg asked with a smile.

"Actually I'd like to do a little research on that subject first, no offense," John countered. "This whole thing is new to me. I'm sure yours will be a fair offer. I'm not concerned about that. And I want to get a little more information on colleges. The bottom line, Mr. Berg, is that I would like in. It looks like an opportunity too good for me to pass up." General George S. Patton's quote "Audacity, audacity, always audacity" crossed his mind, and he felt a little less guilty about abandoning the Seals and better about the decision.

Berg gave John a telephone number and told him to stay in touch. "We can work out details on the phone. John, it's a pleasure to have you coming on board. Give my warmest regards to Lou and Susan. Tell them it's time for a visit. I haven't seen my goddaughter for almost two years." The horrified look on Constanza's face popped into McConnell's mind, and he had to work to keep from laughing at the image of Retino and Berg, both armed with two-by-fours, chasing poor Constanza around the compound. They shook hands and left the restaurant, each back to his own world.

That afternoon, McConnell went over to the University of California, Berkeley, and to the University of San Francisco to gather up material on class offerings, tuition, GI Bill, and student assistance programs. The Berkeley campus was loaded with bizarre people, thousands of young girls in tie-dyed tank tops and guys with shoulder-length hair and beards. His own crew cut, high and tight, stood out like a third eye. "This would be tough," he thought. "No KA-BARs or shoulder holsters here." He smiled as he walked over to the engineering department. The aroma of marijuana wafted over him. He wondered if it really was and then where it came from. The college campuses were like other worlds to McConnell, different even from the city and Berg Marine. "Back to the world," he thought. "Which one?"

It would certainly take more balls to be on the Berkeley campus than out on night patrol. However, although he may not have realized it just yet, San Francisco had captured his heart and imagination. That evening after dinner, he drove past Steiner Street again. There were no lights on at 311, and he decided not to ring the damn buzzer again. Tomorrow he would head back to Coronado; demolition training, hand-to-hand combat exercises, and running the forty-five-minute ballbuster obstacle course … back to a normal life. Grace Slick, the lead singer for the new rock group Jefferson Airplane, wailed out "If you want somebody to love, if you need somebody to love, you better find somebody to looooOOOoove." After New Jersey and Vietnam, this was truly like another planet. One worth exploring.

On Wednesday night, Rebecca Saunders turned onto Steiner Street at about a quarter to nine. She immediately began looking for a parking spot, an almost-daily act of drudgery shared by most of the neighbors. "My lucky day," she said aloud as a dark-gray truck pulled out fifty feet ahead. The Mustang drew ahead of the choice real estate and, with a single reverse twist, settled into the spot. The volleyball team, carpooling in their own vehicles, had driven to the University of Oregon in Eugene for a six-team tournament and had only returned earlier that evening. USF had come in second, serving notice that they were hungry for league respect and would be fierce competitors for this year's honors. Cal had lost to Stanford but won the overall tournament and taken home the trophy. Rebecca was tired but happy about things. She had put more time and energy into the team than usual, primarily to avoid Scott Markham. This had gone well, and she felt he had definitely gotten the message. "The frost is off the pumpkin!" It was still a little awkward when they both showed up for a group event, but she held the edge there, and it was getting better.

The rest of this week would be spent catching up on papers coming due for her master's work and working up the lesson plans she would need for her week of student teaching the second week of November. It would be fifth grade. She was looking forward to it. She had not yet made her decision about what grade level she wanted to teach. The younger children were cute and nice and open to learning. The older, high-school kids were more into their peers and adolescence, but afforded an opportunity to coach, which was also enjoyable. Something would tip the scale one way or another. Probably an actual job offer. As she unlocked the door and entered the house, she looked toward the stairs and thought again of the man who had so frightened her on Saturday night. When she thought about it, she realized that he was probably as embarrassed as she was frightened and had made every effort to apologize. She had not been gracious but, under the circumstances, he was lucky she had not screamed or called the police. Rebecca was looking forward to talking with Charlene. How could she just give her key to someone—some stranger? How stupid.

The telephone rang. Cathy Ventura was at the Camelot with several guys from her work, and she was rounding up good-looking women to join them for cocktails and dinner. "They're a nice bunch of guys, Rebecca. Not a letch in the group, if you don't count Norman Kuyper." Rebecca knew him and thought he was an ass. "They're going to Scoma's on the Wharf. Good dinner. Their treat." Cathy tossed in a bribe.

Rebecca smiled. It was tempting, but she really was tired and had work to do for school. Charlene was always good for a last-minute party, and normally, so was Rebecca. But not tonight. Tonight was a hot bath, a salad, homework, and a glass of wine before bed. After the long drive back from Oregon, that didn't sound too bad. While she made her salad, the television news showed Secretary of Defense Robert McNamara telling the American people about all the things we were accomplishing in Vietnam. Newsreels of helicopters shooting rockets, marines firing weapons at a distant tree line, and tanks on a search-and-destroy mission rolling down some dirt road alongside women stooped over picking or planting rice in square fields of water. She thought of her brother, Dennis, and the year the family, especially her mom, worried that they would see him on a stretcher on the six o'clock news. It was scary. Although he was a pretty macho guy, she wondered how he could live like that for a whole year. Well, he had come home in one piece, and the family had let out a collective sigh of relief. There was a mounting protest here at home against the war and some were targeting returning veterans instead of polititions. What a lousy situation she thought.

The math and English lesson plans were finally finished. Rebecca was trying to work in something fun for each day she taught her fifth-grade guinea pigs. She believed that school should be fun, and learning would follow. As she worked on the plans, she thought about children in general, trying to imagine what her own babies would someday look like. A warm feeling flowed up within her as she thought about these mysterious children of the future, perfect yet still needing their mother to protect and teach them. And their father. Her own father was wonderful a role model, a super guy, one in a million. Where was the father of her children right now? What was he doing? Would he love their children as much as she would? "Of course he would," she thought. 'I wouldn't marry a man who couldn't love his own children. He'll be a wonderful dad. He'll teach them to ride a bike, throw a ball. Take them, us, to the beach. Take the boys fishing. Heck, take the girls fishing, too!"

Rebecca worked and fantasized until eleven. Then she poured a glass of wine and packed up her papers for tomorrow. As she sipped her wine, she thumbed through one of Cathy's fashion magazines, wondering who, if anyone, actually wore the dresses and gowns pictured there. It was fun, though. She looked for something she could or would actually wear, keeping her thumb over the price to keep her objectivity. At eleven thirty she turned the lights off and snuggled against her pillow, visions of little children tugging on her skirt fading as sleep crept upon her.

John McConnell's decision to leave the navy and the Seals came as a surprise to most of the people who knew him. The embarrassment he felt about leaving was mollified by the fact that Jack Thompson's eardrum was ruptured and his dive career over. He, too, elected to get out. His reenlistment-or-departure date was in June, so he would be acting as radio and weapons instructor for new members of the team. It always helped to have someone who had actually been in Vietnam teaching you the ropes. Jack would hang in there until June then boogie back into the civilian world. He already had resumes out to several weapons and communications manufacturers to work as a liaison to the military buyers. The fact that he was a Seal was both a bane and a blessing. On the one hand, most people didn't know that Seals even existed, their work usually being classified secret. On the other hand, Seal units, given their smaller size and wide range of expertise, were often given the job of field-testing new technology, new weapons. Once manufacturers knew that, a man with Seal contacts could be very much in demand. The two soon-to-be ex-Seals often sat over a beer and talked about the future. How different things would be. Jack, being a little on the romantic side, would talk about finding a woman and getting married. He was ready to settle down.

John confided to his friend the possibility of post-Vietnam stress disorder that Dr. Barnard had described. His desire to go back to the killing was not a positive aspect of his personality that some nice American girl would find attractive. And if she was a nice girl, how could he tell her that about himself? And how could he not tell her? This catch-22 bothered him. Raised concerns about his ability to meld back into society. Thompson gently chided his friend, saying it was just a matter of time. That John was a good guy, and he would find a good woman. That Vietnam was a shithole that warped your mind, but it was not permanent. Not permanent unless you let it be. So stop dwelling on it and go find a San Francisco flower child. For John McConnell there was nostalgia in his heart in anticipation of his departure. He carried more than his load, helped the new guys as much as he could, and partied hard at the beach house. He knew he would miss the camaraderie, the action, the elite status of the Seal community. He still could not differentiate, could not be sure, how much of that nostalgia was misplaced for the cordite smell of the shotgun and the heat of battle. Time would tell.

Lowell Berg was true to his word and had McConnell set up and ready to start anytime in January that he wanted. Not only was the salary (and hourly dive rate) much greater than McConnell anticipated, but Berg had a partially furnished corporate apartment not far from work, available with a year's lease if he wanted it. John could have it at the company's cost plus utilities. Lou Retino was glad McConnell would be working with Berg. He knew Berg would watch out for him while he was adjusting and that it was a good career path for the young man. Retino had an open door to Berg Marine Engineering whenever he was ready to retire from the navy. He and McConnell could be working together again someday.

John decided to take four or five days of leave prior to his discharge to go home and visit his father, stepmother, and fourteen-year-old sister, Jennifer. John's mother had died of cancer when he was eight years old. His father had remarried two years later. Elaine was a nice woman, whom John liked but did not think of as Mom. More like Aunt Elaine or a close family friend. Two years later Jennifer was born, and John had a baby sister. Jennifer truly had a big brother to look up to, and John got a kick out of spoiling her. John was comfortable enough with himself, even in high school, that he didn't mind taking her along occasionally to the beach, a ball game, or the Fourth of July parade, which meant that she usually had four or five "big brothers" looking out for her. Jennifer loved it and adored her big brother. The family had moved from New Jersey to Tampa, Florida, shortly after John enlisted in the navy. So going home was really going to a strange place and, although he had not been home for almost two years, after two or three days everything had been said and done, and John was ready to return to Coronado. Jennifer wanted to come out to California on summer vacation. She was a cutie, and John was sure, in that event, he would need the shotgun to keep the California boys at bay. He and his dad had talked long into the night, catching up on old memories and discussing John's work and college plans. His father was glad his son was finished with the dangerous profession of being a Seal and getting on with his life in what seemed a promising situation. He was, however, very proud of his son, of his courage and self-reliance. John did not mention to his father the stress disorder he might or might not have. He would deal with that on his own. Amidst promises to write, telephone, and come visit again soon, McConnell was off to the airport. Just before he left, he gave Jennifer his gold ten-jump parachutist wings, maybe to help ward off the group of teenage boys who had been hovering around Jennifer the whole time he had been there. Nice kids, but the hormones were beginning to rage. Better than Haight Ashbury, though.

As he was packing up his personal things, McConnell was surprised at how little he owned. There were a couple sets of camouflage BDUs, dive gear, a parachute, guns and knives, photos, casual clothes, jeans and sweatshirts, and one sports coat. The stereo system, dishes, camera, knickknacks, and other goods acquired during his overseas tours didn't even fill up the back of his pickup. During his last weeks, he scavenged all kinds of field gear that would have turned up missing or lost anyway. He also made a run through the PX, stocking up on bourbon, underwear, toiletries, and other miscellaneous things he would need in civilian life. His last chance to buy at PX prices. There were several major parties in his honor, at the beach house and at the EM club, lasting until the wee hours. The team formally presented John with a short, wooden paddle, like the ones used during BUDS training to paddle an IBS (inflatable boat, small). The paddle had a bronze plate with John's name and unit inscribed on it. The inscription "Keep your powder dry, your knife sharp and aim to kill" had been painted on the flat part of the paddle. Several guys from Bravo Platoon chipped in and presented him with a twelve-by-sixteen-inch photo of a heavily armed Bravo Platoon posed on Chief Jackson's PBR in Rach Soi, autographed, and framed in koa wood. A cloth Seal patch was under the glass. There were no tears. Seals don't cry.

On January 27, John McConnell drove through the gate at the Coronado Navy Base and aimed his truck north. It was like leaving home, leaving family and friends, to start out alone in a strange new world. While there was sadness and regret, there was also a sense of adventure, an excitement fueled by the new job, the magnificence of the city of San Francisco, and the promise of something new, something different. Again he drove leisurely up the coast highway, an errant knight, flirting with the sun, the highway, and any traveler in distress or willing to flirt back. He picked up hitchhikers and even bought one scruffy but mellow hippie couple lunch at a drive-in burger place. Lowell Berg had sent down the address and key to the apartment so he could unpack and get settled as soon as he arrived. He would report for work on Monday morning. Thursday he spent the night in the truck at a highway rest stop, reluctant to leave all his worldly goods unattended while he slept in a motel.

He came through the back of the city, got lost, and finally pulled into the parking area for his new residence. It was a pretty nice place, a lot nicer than he anticipated. There appeared to be ample parking, even a spot reserved for his apartment number. Apartment number 303 was, of course, on the third floor, the top floor, and there was no elevator. He hiked up the stairwell and entered a bright, roomy, one bedroom apartment with a small kitchen. A dining area lay immediately off the kitchen toward the rear of the apartment, opening onto a large living room. Double picture windows offered a view of the bay and the waterfront. Wow! After six years in the military, these quarters were almost palatial. The place was partially furnished. It had a simple round glass table with four oak chairs in the dining room and a sleeper couch, coffee table, and one lounge chair in the living room. A queen-size bed, a pair of night tables, and a single chest of drawers made the bedroom ready to go. There were a few pots and pans, plates and silverware for almost three, a coffeepot, and some Tupperware. There was a small, opened jar of instant coffee and several tea bags in one of the cabinets. All in all, not a bad start. He did have some shopping to do, though. He walked over to the bay window and, looking out over the water, thought about what lay ahead.

There was really nothing in the back of the truck he could not carry up the stairs himself although it would take many trips. Late in the afternoon a woman in a nurse's uniform, maybe thirty-five, parked in the adjacent stall, went up the stairs to the third floor and entered the apartment next to his. A few minutes later she emerged in jeans and a T-shirt. She walked up to John and extended her hand. "I'm Molly Haffner. You must be my new neighbor."

"Hello, Molly. I'm John McConnell. Nice to meet you. You're a nurse?" he said as they shook hands.

"Children's Hospital. Emergency room." She nodded. "You look like you could use a hand."

"Oh, there's nothing heavy. Just a pain walking up and down a hundred times. I can manage. But thank you for offering."

"I don't mind, and we can get acquainted while we walk up and down together. Then when I ask you for help, I won't feel so bad." She smiled and walked to the back of the truck.

John pulled at one of his footlockers, sliding it to the tailgate. Molly grabbed the other end and lifted. "Holy cow! Nothing heavy? What do you have in there? Rocks?" As luck would have it, this was John's box of dive gear, including his bottled-air tanks, weight belt, automotive tools, an ammo container of .45-caliber ammunition, and various technical manuals.

"This one is a little heavy," John conceded.

"You know we each have a storage locker down here on the bottom floor. I leave things I don't need a lot or heavy stuff in there. The manager can get a key for you."

Two hours later they were done. "I would offer you a beer or something to drink, but I don't have a thing in the reefer. I can run down and get something," John offered, genuinely appreciative of the neighborly assistance.

"I've got beer." A few moments later she was back. "Welcome to the neighborhood," she said handing him a cold, dark San Francisco Anchor Steam beer.

"Thanks." John took a long draft, almost finishing the twelve-ounce bottle. "I think I'll do my shopping tomorrow. I owe you, Molly. You ever need help, you call me."

McConnell was relatively comfortable financially. A bond-a-month plan over six years and a fifty-dollar monthly savings deduction, coupled with separation pay and numerous whole paychecks put into savings during his tours in Vietnam, had built into a sizable savings account. He could afford to stock his civilian world without worrying about every dime. And by starting at Berg's on Monday, he wouldn't even miss a paycheck. The stereo, dishes, and other overseas purchases, some of which had seemed frivolous at the time, were wonderful additions to the spartan furnishings. The rest of the weekend was spent shopping, unpacking, and organizing his new living quarters. The elaborate stereo system made the house a home.

The first month of McConnell's new existence went by quickly. The job and the apartment took up most of his time, and he enjoyed being busy. He spent free time with newfound friends at work, in particular, Hank Cooper and his wife, Judy. Hank was a fellow diver, and they had developed an almost immediate friendship. Hank was an avid sports diver. Surprisingly, that was not common among professional divers. When time and weather allowed, the two of them dove for crabs or fish, bringing their catch home to Judy, who had a hundred seafood recipes. Molly and her semi-live-in boyfriend also had John over for dinner or drinks on a regular basis. John reciprocated by keeping them supplied with fresh seafood. The apartment was taking shape, molded by John's simple decorative tastes and a lot of his military memorabilia. Bravo Platoon hung in the bedroom above a pair of crossed Vietnamese rice cutters.

In early March, John was driving back from a day with consultants at the Oakland project. After work on Tuesday a group of them invited John along to dinner and cocktails. Some business would be discussed for expense-account purposes, but it was basically an evening to relax. The weather had turned stormy, and by ten o'clock the sky was dark, and wind blew sheets of rain across the road as John came through the tollgate onto the Oakland Bay

113

Bridge. Traffic was light. What there was, was moving slowly. John pulled in behind a blue Mustang, leaving a good fifty or sixty feet between it and his truck. About halfway across the span the Mustang's brake lights went on, the car jerked to the right and slowed quickly to a stop.

"The poor bastard has a flat tire. What a night for that," John thought. "Dangerous, too." He slowed and came to a stop fifteen feet behind the now stationary car. Flicking on his high beams to provide light for a fast change and his own flashers to warn off other cars, he set the brake and got out to lend a hand.

A woman got out, walked around to the right front of her car, and stared at the flat tire. Her shoulders slumped.

"Got a spare? I'll give you a hand," he said as he approached and looked with her down at the faulty tire.

"Yes. Thank you for stopping." She continued to look at the tire as the rain pelted down on the hood of her rain hat.

"Ma'am, I'd suggest we move fast. The bridge has a tow truck on call. It'll be here in five minutes, and they charge sixty-five dollars."

The woman moved to the trunk and popped it open. John moved in alongside, unscrewed the spare, and removed the tire and lug wrench. "Grab the jack. Bring it up here," he said as he moved to the front of the car.

The woman wore a raincoat and had a rain hat pulled hard down on her head. A gust of wind drove the rain through the light jacket and jeans John wore. "Just like the good old days," he thought. "Night patrol." He smiled to himself.

Without rushing, he worked fast and quickly had the tire changed. Lowering the car onto the new tire, he grabbed the jack, the flat tire, and the lug wrench, carried them to the back of the car, and dropped them with a thud into the trunk. Flashing lights from the tow truck were coming through the tollgate a half-mile behind them. John closed the trunk cover, turned and looked into the eyes of the woman. When their eyes met, a flash of recognition caused him to blink. His chest tightened and he swallowed. It was the girl from 311 Steiner Street. They looked at each other for a few moments. John was dumbstruck. The flashing lights approached. Recovering, he advised her, "You better get going. They'll charge you if they get in front of you." She stood there looking at him. He didn't know what else to say. "Get going and don't stop."

The girl nodded. Both of them moved to their cars. As John opened his door he heard her call. "Mister." He turned to look at her again. She was staring at him. "Thank you." He waved acknowledgment. The flashing lights were almost upon them. She got in and drove off. John sat there and the tow truck pulled in front of him.

"It was a woman. Her baby fell out of the car seat. She had to strap it back in. Didn't want her to get rear-ended, so I waited with my flashers on," John explained. The tow truck driver wasn't too sure about the story, but there wasn't much he could do. A woman with a baby. What bullshit.

The Mustang was long gone by the time he got going. He wondered if she had recognized him. If she did, he wondered what she thought about him. He thought about going to Steiner street, to sort of check to see she made it home all right. Hell, she didn't recognize me. Maybe I should put some face paint on and really scare the crap out of her next time. Maybe then she'll remember. He turned on the truck's heater and drove home. No sense beating a dead horse. This was just not meant to be.

CHAPTER SEVEN

San Francisco, California

March 1969

The volleyball season was in full swing. The team was seven and two, winning their last five in a row. Practice had become more intense, the girls more into it, realizing they actually had an opportunity to win their conference. Rebecca spent afternoons in the gym and evenings working on her master's thesis and preparing for her student teaching. It was a bit of a grind, but she still managed to get out with the gang once in a while and home for dinner in St. Helena once every three weeks or so. The previous weekend, her parents had come to the city for one of their periodic weekend shopping sprees. Usually Rebecca went out to dinner with them and occasionally to a show. This time was no different. They went to Dimaggio's down at the wharf. Her father knew the manager and brought him a couple of bottles of recently released reserve wine. They, in turn, got VIP treatment and had a great dining experience. They always told Rebecca that if she had a friend she wanted to bring along, it was OK with them. Sometimes she brought Cathy or Charlene. Her parents' intention was to see whom, if anyone, she was dating. To their knowledge, Rebecca had lots of suitors and dates, but never a serious relationship. They were not nosy or interfering. Just interested in their daughter.

On Tuesday night, Rebecca went to a sports-medicine lecture over at the Berkeley campus from seven o'clock to nine thirty. It was a good lecture;

good stuff for a coach to know in case one of her players got hurt. She knew several others attending, and they talked shop for a while after the lecture. Outside the weather had turned; rain and wind mixing it up for a good old-fashioned downpour. Storm clouds made the night seem even darker than it actually was.

"The raincoat was a good decision," came to her as she ran through the parking lot, pulling on her rainhat and holding the front of the coat close around her. In a few minutes, she was driving off campus headed to the Oakland Bay Bridge and San Francisco. She tossed the exact change into the toll collection machine and cruised through, staying in the far right lane. There was always some crazy driver who had to go seventy miles an hour even in a downpour like this. She thought, "I'll just take it easy." When the wind gusted, the wipers could barely keep up, and her knuckles tightened on the wheel. The radio was on, but she was tuned into the road and handling the Mustang. The bridge was safe, but she was still only a couple hundred feet above the dark, roiling waters of the bay.

Suddenly Rebecca felt a thumping in the steering wheel. Her foot automatically went to the brake. The car tugged to the right and the thumping became more pronounced. "Damn! A flat. Damn!" She pulled as far right as she could and stopped the car, partially blocking the far right lane. Headlights were coming up behind her, and she momentarily panicked, thinking someone not paying attention would crash into her. Instead they slowed and stopped behind her. High beams clicked on. She snapped her raincoat closed to the neck and put her rain hat back on. Taking a deep breath, she opened her door and stepped out into the inhospitable weather. Leaning into the wind she walked around the front of the car and saw that the right front tire had somehow blown out. That old sinking feeling settled over her as she stood in the rain, letting her misfortune soak in.

A man was suddenly beside her. He was looking at her tire, his hair already soaked, then asked, "Got a spare? I'll give you a hand."

"Yes. Thank you for stopping," she said and continued to look down at the tire.

"Ma'am, I'd suggest we move fast. The bridge has a tow truck on call. It'll be here in five minutes, and they charge sixty-five dollars."

Rebecca was instantly motivated to action. Moving to the rear of the car, she opened the trunk. The man was reaching in before it was fully open. He loosened the spare, yanked it out, and grabbed the lug wrench. He told her to bring the jack, which she did, getting it set up as he loosened the lugs on the wheel. She watched him work calmly and proficiently, getting absolutely drenched in the process. She wondered if she should offer to pay him. "Jesus, how much would be enough?" she wondered. In minutes the car settled back down onto the thankfully fully inflated spare. He cranked on the lugs one more time, grabbed the tire and the jack, tossed them into the trunk, and closed it. Drops of water flew off his head as he stood up and turned to look at her, his eyes catching hers directly. He didn't say anything. He blinked once. His eyes were locked on hers. Those eyes. She knew those eyes. Rebecca wanted to thank him, but her mind was focused on the eyes, trying to remember what it was about them. She knew this man. But where?

"You better get going," he finally said. "They'll charge you if they get in front of you." Water ran down his face. She wanted to reach over and wipe the rain off. "Get going and don't stop."

All she could do was nod and walk to her car. "The eyes! The man in the house that night! The one I threw out! It's him!" She remembered with instant clarity. "What was his name?" Her mind was a blank. Nothing. She turned and saw him almost to his car, the flashing lights of the tow truck approaching. What was his name?

"Mister!" she called. It sounded so stupid, but he turned and looked back. The glare of his headlights made it difficult to see, but she saw him standing silhouetted in the glare looking at her. She couldn't see his eyes, but she remembered them and felt them on her. "Thank you." she called. Still no name came to her, and the words hung there lamely. He waved his hand then got into his car. She drove into the night as the tow truck pulled in front of his car. "They wouldn't make him pay! That wouldn't be fair." She hesitated and then remembered what he had said: don't stop. Her foot went back down on the accelerator, and she continued on across the bridge. Although it was not hers, she took the first exit, pulling over at the first opportunity to wait, in hopes he might do the same. It only now occurred to her that she had no idea what kind of car he was driving. All she saw were headlights. He would have to see her Mustang. The rain pattered down on the car for twenty minutes, her hopes that he would come by washing away with the raindrops. Finally, reluctantly, she pulled out and drove home, a feeling of unfinished business hanging heavy upon her.

Rebecca removed and shook out her raincoat before entering the apartment at about eleven o'clock. She went immediately to Charlene's room, knocked, and then entered. Charlene was asleep. Rebecca shook Charlene's foot and half whispered, "Charlene. Wake up. Charlene."

"What. What's wrong?" The startled, Charlene came roughly out of her sleep. "Rebecca! What's the matter?"

"I'm sorry to wake you. Do you remember the man you gave your key to? The man who was going to stay here while you were in San Diego? Remember him?"

"Christ! Do we have to go through that again? I forgot to call. I'm sorry. End of story. Good night." Charlene had taken justified verbal chastisement for that fiasco and thought it was over. She pulled the covers back over her head, hoping to escape.

"No. No. I just saw him again. Tonight. He helped me fix a flat. I didn't recognize him right away. Do you remember his name?"

Charlene sat up, relieved it was not more abuse. His name? "God, Rebecca. That was four or five months ago.' She searched her memory. "I met him when I was sitting with Chip…on the patio. He came up from the beach. He was running or something. John! His name was John." She looked at Rebecca with victory in her eyes.

"John what?"

"God, Rebecca." Charlene sat thoughtfully for a few moments. Finally she looked up at Rebecca and shrugged. "He was up here interviewing for a job, I think. I don't remember his name. Nada." Fifteen minutes later, they both gave up on a lost cause. Charlene promised to call Chip Mihok the next day and find out. "I still can't believe you threw him out. He was really a nice guy. And a hunk."

"Well the circumstances were not ideal, Charlene. If you had called, it might have been different."

"Good night, Rebecca. Please close the door behind you."

Rebecca puttered around for an hour before getting into bed. She couldn't stop thinking about the bridge and the man. "Thank God I didn't offer him five dollars. He must think I'm a real putz." It was a term her father occasionally used. "He was absolutely soaked. The poor guy. At least I said thank you. Big deal." She tossed and turned most of the night and reminded Charlene in the morning to call her friend in San Diego. "I'll even pay for the call."

Chip Mihok was on assignment and not available. She could leave a message, and he would get it at some undetermined future date. "Sorry, ma'am. Best I can do for you. No we do not give out rosters of our personnel. National security reasons, ma'am." At a dead end, Rebecca refocused her attention on volleyball and school. It was a loose end that bothered her. The image of the rain rolling down his face occasionally popped into her thoughts. His eyes, intense and unreadable.

The following Sunday the gang—five gals and four guys, including Scott Markham—headed north to whale watch and spend the day at Sir Francis Drake's Beach near Point Reyes. It was still cool, but the sun was shining. The ocean was touched only occasionally by an errant whitecap. They had set up a volleyball net and played what Rebecca thought was really lame volleyball. It was not the competitive game she was used to but OK for just fooling around. They actually saw several whale spouts in the distance, and watched as the behemoths moved north to the rich feeding grounds in the Bering Sea. Jim Howe set up a powerful telescope with a camera attachment and shot off a roll of film on the spouts and possibly a tail slap. The gang posed for some silly "candid" scenes. Two of the guys raced in and out of the chilly surf in their underwear, one dragging "Moby" out of the water under protest. All in all, it was a fun afternoon. On the drive back they decided to stop for dinner at a bar and grill in Larkspur renowned for its hamburgers and sloppy joes.

At six thirty, the nine of them made a boisterous entrance into the Blue Fox Inn, taking two booths against the wall opposite the bar. Half a dozen tables were set between the booths and the twenty-foot-long bar. The place was more than half full. Music was playing on the jukebox, and people, most of them there for the popular burgers, were talking. It was a typical cheery bar/restaurant; good food, cold beer, and friendly banter. The only thing out of place were two bikers in black leather vests, dirty blue jeans, and heavy leather boots. They sat at a table between the bar and the two booths occupied by Rebecca and her friends. There were several empty beer bottles on their table. They drank their beer out of the bottle, feet stretched out and backs leaning hard against their captain's chairs.

A waitress came to take orders from the four and a half mildly boister-ous couples in the booths. Five minutes later she brought a tray of drinks: three beers and four glasses of wine. Rebecca and Cathy had decided not to have drinks and sipped at their water. The food was slow in coming, but no one was in a rush, and another round of beers and wine was ordered. Still waiting for their food, Rebecca decided to have a glass of Chablis after all. Rather than attempt to catch the harried waitress's attention, she got up and walked across to the bar. On her way past the bikers' table, she felt a hand pat her behind. She turned sharply and looked into the leering smile of an unshaven man, long, unkempt hair hanging over his shoulders.

"Watch your hands!" Both anger and fear welled up in her chest. She moved to the bar quickly and ordered her wine. Her breath was coming more rapidly. "That son of a bitch," she thought, her adrenaline rising. She thought about walking back the long way, around the tables altogether, but felt that would be giving in to intimidation. She came back through on the opposite side of the table trying to act calmer than she felt. As she glared at the biker with the loose hands sitting across the table, the other biker moved quickly, grabbing Rebecca with two hands by the cheeks of her backside. "Get your hands off me!" she yelled. He started to pull her body toward his face. Rebecca threw her wine into her assailant's face. Then she slapped him hard across the face. He let go but immediately grabbed both of her wrists and pulled her to him. He was laughing. She could smell the beer on his breath; his sweat. Rebecca yanked with all her strength to free her hands but could not move them. The man easily pulled her toward him and buried his face in her breasts. She had no leverage now and couldn't kick him in the crotch, because he was sitting in the chair.

"Let the lady go." The words were calm but very clear. Rebecca felt more than saw someone standing slightly behind her. She continued to pull, now with renewed vigor, against the hands restraining her. Suddenly the biker let go of her right hand. It flew backward, the momentum moving her whole body back. The left hand was still in his grip. "Let her go," the voice behind her said. There was more tension in the voice now. It was more command-ing. The biker let go of her other hand and stood up to face the challenge behind her. Rebecca's anger raged and she slapped at the biker's face. She slapped again. Then she felt hands gripping her by the waist, lifting her off the floor moving her away from the menacing leathered threat standing in front of her.

"Would you please get out of the way?" the voice said, and she was deposited away from the threat. Her eyes were wide open. She wanted to continue slapping the bastard, to wipe the smile off his face, but stepped back, barely in control of her rage at this violation.

"You're spoiling my fun, asshole," the man in leather said, losing his smile as he leaned forward to take on the interruption. After depositing Rebecca, her rescuer had turned back to the man in black leather. He stepped forward. His hand moved so quickly it was a blurred part of his step forward. His fist hit the other man square in the chest, right on the solar plexus. The biker's eyes opened wide. He gasped, struggled to catch his breath but couldn't, and dropped to his knees. His face turned bright red, and finally, he sank to the floor, helpless. A moment later a loud crash electrified the room. Glass flew; its tinkling against the floor reverberating like thunder in the stunned silence of the crowd. The second biker had broken a beer bottle against the table and now held the jagged glass by the handle. He waved it slowly at the man who had so easily disposed of his companion.

"You're a real pain in the ass. I'm gonna have to teach you a lesson. I'm gonna cut you a little. Then I'm gonna have a taste of your lady friend." He was tall and thickset. Tattoos rippled on his shoulders and forearms. Trouble. Rebecca's defender picked up a chair and held it out in front of him like a lion tamer to keep the jagged glass at bay. He looked around quickly and counseled everyone to stay back. The owner of the bar yelled from behind the bar, "I've called the cops. They'll be here any minute!"

Undeterred by the owner's warning, the biker thrust the bottle forward. The other man parried the thrust with the chair. The biker feigned another thrust with the bottle then kicked out, trying to catch the other man's groin. The latter twisted sideways avoiding the kick and countered by thrusting the chair forward, catching the biker hard on the shoulder with a leg. The two stalked in a circle waiting for an opening. Suddenly the biker lunged into the chair grabbing it with his left hand, jerking it hard to the side. Just as quickly, the other man let loose of the chair and had the arm with the glass weapon held straight up in an arm lock. He applied pressure, and the biker groaned.

"Drop it, or I'll put your shoulder out of its socket." He applied a little more pressure on the arm. The man in black leather gritted his teeth and looked into his opponent's eyes. His grip on the bottle loosened, but he did not drop it. Instead he spit into the other man's face. A split second later there was a loud 'pop' as the shoulder snapped out of its socket. The piece of glass fell to the floor. With a gentle push on the chest, the groaning man stumbled backward and flopped into a chair. The beaten man looked up, his eyes black with rage and pain. "You cocksucker."

This accusation apparently did not sit well with the tall man standing in front of him. He stepped over to the sneering man still unwilling to accept defeat. The tall man's fist shot out so quickly you would have missed it if you blinked. "There are ladies present," he said. "Watch your mouth." Blood began to trickle from the seated man's nose. His defiance slowly slipped away before the unforgiving strength of the stranger looking down at him like a hawk about to feed. He was not used to himself being intimidated.

Rebecca, like everyone else in the bar, had watched the entire encounter in a kind of trance. The whole thing had taken only minutes. Watching the violence was like watching a cobra. It held you spellbound. Your muscles went limp. Fear overwhelmed your sense of survival. You were out of breath just standing there watching. No one knew what to do. It was dead quiet, except for the gasps of the man lying on the floor.

The owner finally came over, a small baseball bat in his hand. He looked at the two fallen bikers then at the man. "You OK? Jesus, I think you saved the day. The cops are on the way. You want a drink?" From experience the owner knew that this would make everyone leave, queasy with fear, or make them stay, have a few drinks, and relive the incident from a more comfortable place. "Sit down, folks. It's all over. If anything spilled we'll replace it, on the house. Please. Sit down."

Rebecca moved over to the man who had interceded on her behalf. She touched his shoulder, and he turned to look at her. The left side of his face was covered with blood; it had dripped down onto his shirt. She looked at him and lost her breath. Her emotions flooded up inside her, and she almost burst into tears. It was the man! The man with the rain on his face. The man with those wonderful, scary eyes. He smiled sheepishly at her. Like a little boy, he said, "Hello."

CHAPTER EIGHT

Larkspur, California

March 1969

McConnell didn't sleep well that Tuesday night. After changing out of his wet clothes and showering, he popped a beer and put on the TV. Nothing of interest was on. His mind relived the changing of the flat tire and the girl from 311 Steiner. Just when he had stopped thinking about her, there she was, right there in front of him. And he says nothing. Like friggin' Elmer Fudd. Mister Dip. "You asshole," he thought. "You could have at least said hello. Well, she didn't recognize you, anyway." He was unaccustomed to this lack of confidence in himself. While he considered himself to be a quiet person, it was more because he elected not to say something; not because he didn't know what to say or couldn't speak. "What a pussy." He chastised himself relentlessly. The thought of driving over to Steiner Street crossed his mind and was again rejected. What would he say?

The remainder of the week passed quickly as McConnell threw himself into his work, spending long hours on jobsites or in the office. Although he wrestled for days with the idea of driving over to Steiner Street, never fully satisfied with the negative answer that kept coming up, he did not. The thought of post-Vietnam stress disorder lurked in the back of his mind; "an inability to readjust to society," as he recalled Lieutenant Commander Barnard saying. "And saying hello to a pretty girl." He added a symptom of his own.

Hank and Judy Cooper had him over for dinner on Saturday night. They told him to bring a date if he wanted to. He brought an apple pie for dessert and two six packs instead. They talked, watched a little TV, and went over rough drawings of a house Judy swore they would one day build. McConnell enjoyed watching the couple, the two of them happy and comfortable with each other, planning for the future. Judy was also trying a little matchmaking and gave John several choices as future potential dinner partners. "Blonde, brunette, or redhead. My office is like a dating service. They're nice girls, too." Hank and Judy liked John, and they both realized he was going through a period of readjustment. Their intentions were good.

John smiled. He'd had a few dates since arriving in San Francisco, but no one had caught his fancy. One night at the Buena Vista Pub at the foot of Hyde Street, he had been picked up and seduced (he almost didn't go along) by an attractive woman. After their sexual encounter had climaxed, the woman lit up a joint and, sitting naked in bed, holding her breath most of the time, told John about her last boyfriend. John tossed her business card in the trash shortly after leaving her apartment.

There was a gun show up at the Sonoma County Fairgrounds on Sunday, and John decided to drive up and browse around. The smell of gun oil and the clack of bolts snapping closed rekindled familiar memories. He didn't buy anything. Christ, he had more weapons than he would ever need. There was a lot of surplus military equipment, mostly from World War II, but some from Vietnam. Veterans were in evidence, old army jackets and camouflage pants flagging their presence. He talked with some. Not about the war.

On the drive back to the city, he remembered a tavern with great burgers where he and some of the guys from work had eaten. He was hungry and had no dinner plans, so he decided to grab a burger and a beer at the Blue Fox. He remembered roughly where it was and, after a few wrong turns, spotted its blue neon sign on a two-story building on the corner. "What a cool name for a town," he thought. "Larkspur." A parking spot beckoned not too far from the corner entrance and he slid the truck into it.

Compared to the light outside, the bar was dark, and it took a moment for his eyes to adjust. He walked to the service section and scanned the blackboard menu hanging over the brass draft handles. The list of about thirty different kinds of hamburger occupied him for several minutes. A middle-aged bartender, probably the proprietor, came over. "What can I do for ya? Got a special on Polish Sausage. Spicy or regular."

"Bacon cheeseburger, deluxe, and a draft."

While John waited for his change, he looked at a row of booths along the far wall. A booth toward the back had a newspaper lying on the table. When the barman brought his change, he told him he would be in the booth. On his way over he observed a pair of rough-looking motorcycle riders wearing leather vests, lounging at a table. They seemed out of place but were quiet, not even talking to each other much. They looked bored.

Twenty-five minutes later, John, still reading the newspaper, had almost finished his meal and was nursing his second beer. Noise from a group of people entering the tavern caused him to look up. They stood by the entrance, eyes adjusting to the dimmer light inside, deciding where to go when John saw her. She wore blue jeans and a gray sweatshirt. Her face was a golden red. She had been out in the sun. She was much prettier than he remembered, a casual athletic grace accentuating her attractiveness. There were four males in the group, and he assumed one of them was with her. Even though she hadn't recognized him on the bridge, he moved back into the shadow to avoid detection. The man behind the bar came out and waved them to booths against the wall. Since the booths only held six comfortably, there was a discussion about who would sit where. It ended up with two couples at one booth and two couples and one girl at the other. One of those two guys must be her date. John felt uncomfortable. He was ready to leave, but he didn't want to risk confronting the girl, as much as he might have liked to under different circumstances. He decided to wait it out.

They were not visible from where he was sitting, but bits and pieces of their conversation could be heard if he focused in. The waitress took their order and five minutes later brought a tray of drinks. The waiting reminded

John of the patience required to sit still on night patrol, waiting for something to happen. Suddenly the girl was walking over to the bar. She turned and said something to the motorcycle guy at the table, who leered suggestively as she continued on to the bar. A minute or two later, she turned with a glass of wine in her hand. She moved past them, now on the other side of the their table, past them, giving them a hard look as she did. The other man at the table suddenly reached out and grabbed the girl. "Get your hands off me!" John heard the girl yell. The man had his hands on her ass and was drawing her toward him. She threw her drink in his face and slapped him hard. The slap was like a gunshot in John's ears. Without consciously thinking about it, he was on his feet and moving to her aid. The biker now held her by the wrists and had pulled her chest against his face. John was incensed at this violation of 'his' girl. He came up behind and slightly to the right of the struggling girl and the laughing biker. "Let the lady go."

The man looked up from Rebecca's breasts at the words. The girl struggled harder. The man let go of the girl with his left hand, freeing it to confront this intrusion. As soon as he let go, the girl's right hand flew back and, with force, caught John's left cheek high on the bone. The blow caught John by surprise. His head turned slightly at the impact, but his eyes remained on the other man still holding the girl by one wrist. "Let her go," he said again, some of his emotion, mostly anger, now in his voice. The biker let go and started to rise, but the girl now moved forward, slapping him. "God damn it, get out of the way. She's gonna get hit by this son of a bitch," John thought. He grabbed her by the waist, lifted her up, and deposited her behind him. "Would you please get out of the way," he said to her quietly. She glared at her assailant but stepped back out of the way.

"You're spoiling my fun, asshole," the man said as he started to move toward John. John countered by stepping forward, simultaneously bringing his fist up hard with a crunching blow to the man's solar plexus. The man gasped, wide-eyed, and John knew he had hit the sweet spot. This guy was finished. Gasping for breath, the man fell to his knees and finally rolled over onto the floor, still gasping.

A crash alerted McConnell to the other man at the table. He had broken a beer bottle on the table and stood up. His eyes were mean. He was in his element. "You're a real pain in the ass. I'm gonna have to teach you a lesson. Gonna cut you a little." He looked at McConnell. "Then I'm gonna have a taste of your lady." If he was trying to piss McConnell off, he was succeeding.

McConnell picked a chair up by the back. It was the most readily available defense against the dangerous shard of glass. The bartender yelled something about the cops. It meant nothing to the other man. He thrust the jagged edge of the bottle toward John but was deflected by the chair. Another thrust! Now a kick! John struck back with the chair and simultaneously twisted like a matador to avoid the kick to his groin. The two gladiators stood crouched, circling, looking for an opening. A man's eyes often signal his intentions. If you're fast enough, however, your move can be accomplished before your opponent can react to that signal. Suddenly the biker lunged in, catching the chair with his left hand, yanking it off to the side.

John realized his defense had been breached. Letting go of the chair, he went on the offense, going for the arm holding the glass, taking advantage of the other's attention on the chair. In a moment, McConnell had applied an arm lock with which he knew the man could be disarmed. Applying a little more pressure to get the man's attention, he said, "Drop it or I'll put your shoulder out of its socket." The biker was strong. John applied pressure until the man winced, his grip on the bottle loosening. Through gritted teeth, the man looked at McConnell and, instead of dropping the bottle, he spit into McConnell's face. McConnell's reaction was immediate and severe. The man's arm jerked backward, a distinctive pop signaling the end of the fight. John stepped back, watching the man clutch his arm. With a soft push, McConnell dropped the man backward into a chair. He groaned as he plopped down. His eyes looked up at McConnell with malice and pain. "You cocksucker." The words dripped with hate.

McConnell stepped over and, with a short, solid punch, hit him square in the middle of his face. "There are ladies present. Watch your mouth."

As blood began to trickle from his nose, the tattooed man in black leather finally began to realize his ass had just been kicked. More defiance would result in more pain, more humiliation. The man standing over him watched with emotionless eyes riveted on him, as though he hoped for another opportunity to punish him. As quickly as it had started, it was over. The room was completely silent. No one moved. Finally the owner, thankful it was over and anxious to settle things down, came out from behind the bar holding a baseball bat in his hand. "You want a drink?" John heard him ask.

Something touched John's shoulder. Knowing...hoping it would be her, he turned and looked into her eyes, her face flushed with excitement. Her eyes opened wide and filled with tears as she looked at him. She swallowed but did not speak. Again he felt awkward. Not knowing what else to say, he said, simply, "Hello."

"My God!" she finally blurted out. "Your face is bleeding. Did he cut you? Are you all right?" His hand reached up and felt his cheek. There was blood on his fingers and, he noticed, on his shirt. Without waiting for a response, Rebecca ran to the bar, demanding a clean, wet towel. Returning to him with eyes now full of concern and determination, she stood close to him and dabbed at his cheek with the moist cloth. He felt wonderful, relaxed, basking in this attention. "You'll need stitches for this," she informed him while tending to his wound. "How did he cut you? I didn't see it." John took her by the hand, gently holding it up for her to see. Her ring, braided grapevines of sterling silver with leaves on either side of a single bunch of grapes colored deep red with garnet chips, held bits of flesh. The back of her hand displayed a smattering of blood. She looked at the ring, her hand, and then back up at him. "I don't understand. What happened?"

"It's nothing. One of those things that happen when arms and legs are flying. It's really nothing." A look of horror spread over her face as it registered on her that she had struck him in the face. She had cut him. After another look at her hand, as if to confirm its guilt, her eyes looked back into his; a tear pushed its way out, rolling down her cheek. "I'm so sorry.

Please…forgive me." She spoke slowly, trying not to lose her composure completely. His hand, so brutal just moments before, reached over and gently brushed the tear away. As blood continued to seep out of the cut on his cheek, she resumed cleaning the wound, almost like therapy. When he flinched in a moment of pain, she held his other cheek and continued dabbing softly at the cut.

The police entered the Blue Fox a few minutes later. Everything got very formal; witnesses came forward to give accounts of what had happened. In the end, the bikers were hauled away, but not because of the assault on Rebecca or the fight. One of them had a small box of hand-rolled joints, which led to a search of their motorcycles and the discovery of a gun and a significant amount of acid. No charges were brought on McConnell, although one police officer did ask if he was ex-military. John simply said, "Navy."

As the investigation wrapped up, Rebecca informed the police and John that she would be taking John to the emergency room for stitches, and it was time for them to leave. She had words with her friends, apparently not pleasant ones with the guys. Taking John by the hand, she led him to the door. Outside, she stopped, perplexed. Turning to him, eyebrows raised, she asked, "Do you have a car?"

"Yes."

"Give me the keys."

"I can drive. You know, we don't have to get stitches. It's fine."

Rebecca looked at him sternly. "I can see your cheekbone. You've lost blood. Please stop the macho bullshit and give me the keys."

Inside he smiled at her tenacity, meekly handed over the keys, and led her to the truck. As they crossed over the Golden Gate, Rebecca informed him that she was going home to get her checkbook. She felt obligated to pay for the stitches. "No way. I have insurance. It won't cost me anything," he replied.

"I feel responsible. You helped me out today, and I would like to do this for you."

"It's silly for you to pay when you don't have to. Just taking me over there is really nice. I appreciate that. If you insist on paying, I won't go in."

Rebecca watched the road, considering her course of action. "OK. But I get any out-of-pocket costs." She looked over at him. "Promise?"

"Promise," he agreed, holding up his right hand as if taking an oath.

They drove on in silence for a while. Rebecca finally said, "You're the man who helped me on the bridge on Tuesday, aren't you?"

"Yes."

"And the man I threw out of my apartment."

"Yes," he responded, not quite certain what would come next.

"It's lucky for me you came to San Francisco, John. I'm Rebecca Saunders. Thank you again for your help."

"You're welcome, Miss Saunders." He wanted to add 'pretty lady' but didn't dare jeopardize his foothold with the girl he had thought about so much. "I'm John McConnell."

"After you fixed the flat, I felt really bad about not letting you stay that time. You know, I didn't recognize you right away on the bridge. Then I couldn't remember your name. I called you 'Mister.' Remember?" John nodded affirmatively. "I feel even worse about it now."

"Nah. It was mostly my fault. I frightened you when you walked in. You did the right thing."

"John McConnell, did you ever go to knight-in-shining-armor school?" she asked with a grin. "Graduate magna cum laude?" They both laughed.

"Nope. US Navy."

Rebecca parked the truck close to the entrance of the emergency room at San Francisco General. After a half hour of paperwork they sat down, waiting to be called. There were half a dozen others sitting in the room. Periodically Rebecca would check his wound, which was held closed by a too-small Band-Aid. During the course of their small talk, Rebecca asked, "Did you get the job? The one you came up to interview for." He looked at her with a question in his eye. "Charlene thought that's what you came up for. I guess you got it, eh?"

"Yes. I did," he answered, thinking, "She must have talked about me at least a little." A doctor came into the room calling for a Tom Jackson. An older man got up and limped to the doctor, his wife supporting him as he hobbled across the room.

"What kind of work do you do?"

"It's with Berg Marine Engineering. Their home base is here in San Francisco, but they have projects all over."

"What do you do?" Rebecca asked again, curious about the man.

"Well I'm primarily a diver. Underwater work. But I'm also a sort of jack-of-all-trades. They've got me involved in all kinds of things. There are five or six projects from hull inspection to salvage to project management for waterfront development. It's pretty interesting."

"Sounds really neat. Do you travel much?"

"Some. Right now I'm still getting familiar with all the projects. I'm thinking about going back to school, getting a degree. I've not quite focused in on what my major should be. I'm thinking engineering, but maybe architecture."

Rebecca looked at him, remembering how frightened she was the first time she saw him. "And now," she thought, "I could never be afraid of him again." She barely knew him but felt that she trusted him almost implicitly. "You got your diving in the navy?" He nodded. "So you're a professional diver. Do you dive for fun, or is it all business now?"

"It's funny you should ask that. A lot of divers I know really don't like to dive. It's their job, and they avoid the water if they're not working. I love to dive. I spearfish, go for abs and scallops, collect shells. I love the quiet and all the activity of that whole underwater domain. Haven't had the opportunities to dive much up north here, but I will."

"Abs? You mean abalone?" Her eyes were lit up, excited.

"Yeah. You like abalone?"

"I love it. But my dad really loves it. Whenever we get some, it's a ritual with him. Has to be pounded just right, seasonings just so. He's fun to watch. It's so expensive, though. And not that easy to find. Usually he gets it in a restaurant."

"When I go, I'll bring some back for your dad." John's thoughts were now focusing on a future meeting with this special woman. "What is it about her that's so different?" he thought. "Something."

"John McConnell." A doctor holding a clipboard stood looking at the people seated in the waiting room, focusing on John and Rebecca when they stood and started toward him. He saw the blood on John's shirt and looked to the cheek. "Need a few stitches in that?" he asked.

"Yes," answered Rebecca. "We don't want a scar if it can be avoided. We'd like to have very fine sutures. Can you do that?"

The doctor looked at Rebecca, then at John. "No scar," he said, neither a statement nor a question. John shrugged and nodded toward Rebecca, deferring to her judgment and direction. "OK. Follow me." He turned and led the way to a bed, indicating John should sit on it while he drew the curtain around them. "Mrs. McConnell, if you would come around here, you can sit on the other end. You won't faint on me now, will you?"

Rebecca blushed bright red, looking at John, embarrassed and not knowing quite what to do or say. John smiled a broad smile, almost a chuckle. "Sit down, sweetheart. Let's get this done so we can get home." Rebecca wanted to stay in the room, so she didn't correct the doctor's mistake. Still blushing, she feigned an angry look at John, walked to the other edge of the table, and sat down. The doctor didn't know what the hell was going on. After closely examining the cut, he announced, "This will leave some scarring. The wound was made with something fairly blunt. It's more of a tear than a cut. What happened?" They explained as briefly as possible, Rebecca showing the doctor the ring. "That hit with quite a bit of force to gouge that deeply. I'll give you a prescription for antibiotics…for infection." Said the doctor eyeing Rebecca suspiciously.

Under Rebecca's watchful eye, the cheek was sutured, a butterfly bandage applied, and directions given for washing and suture removal. It was almost eleven o'clock when they left. John drove to 311 Steiner, pulling up in front of the building and setting the parking brake. He left the engine running.

"Thanks again for taking me for the stitches, Becky. I appreciate it. That is the nickname for Rebecca, right? Is that what they call you? Your friends."

It sounded good the way he said it. It was a name she hadn't heard for a while. Hadn't permitted for a while. Now it was his name for her. "Some people do. You can call me Becky if you like," she replied, releasing Rebecca to obscurity. "And don't be silly. I owe you a lot more thanks than you owe me. I don't know what would have happened in the Blue Fox if you hadn't been there. It's scary to even imagine."

They sat in awkward silence for a minute, having just talked for several hours, knowing it was now time to say good night. "Well, good night, John. Thank you one more time."

"Hey, when I get that abalone for your dad, if you give me your number, I'll call you."

"Oh right. He'll love it," she said as she dug through her purse for pencil and paper. "How could I forget that?" she chastised herself. Scribbling down the number, she handed it over to him with a bright smile, happy she would be hearing from him again.

He took the scrap of paper, looked down at it to verify its legibility, and placed it carefully in his shirt pocket. "OK then. I'll call you when the abs are in."

Rebecca nodded. She looked at him, her face now serious. Her hand came up, softly touching the stitches in his cheek. Their eyes connected for just a moment, and then she got out of the truck and walked quickly into the house, not looking back. John felt alone. He touched the pocket with the telephone number and felt better.

First thing in the morning McConnell tracked down Hank Cooper to find out about abalone season. When? Where were the best spots? Let's get set up to go.

"Two weeks! Opens the fifth of May." Hank laughed at his friend's excitement. "What the hell happened to your face?"

"Cut myself shaving. Let's get set up to go ab diving. You've been before, up here?"

"Last year they let us take the boat out. Means we have to go on a Sunday, but that's fine. We went under the Golden Gate and north a little. Off Fort Cronkite. Rocky cliffs and rocks offshore. Twenty to forty feet. Pretty good abalone. Hard to get to. Not a lot of guys dive there. There's good diving up north of Jenner, too, up by Salt Point State Park. It can get a little crowded, but if you look around there's miles of coast, most of it rocky kelp beds. The tougher it is to get to the water, the better the abalone. Course, the deeper you go, the less the competition."

"May tenth is a Sunday. Let's arrange for the boat." John was hot to get it set up.

"Mother's Day? I don't think so. Judy would slap me silly. Maybe the week after. What's the big deal? You hungry?"

"It's important, Hank. Plus, I would really like to go. Let's do it the third Sunday."

They met several times after work to plan and get equipment ready. John was surprised to learn that no SCUBA tanks were allowed for the pursuit of abalone in Northern California. Free dive only. "That's what Hank meant about going deep. No SCUBA tanks. A good thing," thought John, "Makes it tougher. Weeds out the old and the sick."

Hank explained how he used an inflated inner tube wrapped in two-inch netting. The netting was held on with surgical tubing strung through the net, creating a tight, five- or six-inch circular opening in the top. "You put your catch—abalone or fish—in through the tubing to hold it while you dive. Then, even if the tube is tipped over by a wave, you wouldn't lose everything. It also provides a place to rest between dives to the bottom. You can lie on your tube and take a nap."

An abalone iron—a flat pry bar to pop the single-shelled mollusk off the rock—was the only other thing needed. And of course a full wet suit, hood, booties, and gloves to protect against the colder water. And dive weights, fifteen to twenty pounds, to compensate for the buoyancy of the quarter-inch-thick neoprene wet suit.

"Carrying all that shit to the water's edge can be a ballbuster if you have to hike a ways. On top of that, you have to hump the fifteen to twenty pounds of abalone out," John added.

"Hooyah. Just like Seals off for a crawl through the mud," mused John, excited at the challenge and the thought of seeing the girl again.

When access to the boat was finalized, an idea struck John. Maybe she would like to go along. Maybe she would like being out on the boat. Hank had no problem with her coming along, understanding better now his friend's excitement.

The Friday before Mother's Day, John dialed the number from the scrap of paper. His chest was tight as the phone rang. "Hello," a voice answered.

"Becky Saunders, please."

"Who?"

"Becky Saunders. Is this 376—?"

"Hold on," the voiced interrupted. The line was quiet. Then, in the background, "It's for a Becky Saunders. Anyone here by that name?"

"Hello."

"Becky?"

"Yes. Is that you, John?"

"Yeah. How're you doing?" he asked awkwardly.

"Fine. I'd almost given up on that abalone. How's your cheek? Did they remove the stitches? Is there much of a scar?"

"It's fine. Hey, abalone season opens this Sunday and, well, since that's Mother's Day, we're waiting till next Sunday to go. But I thought you might like to come along. We could get you a fishing license and be able to get another limit of five abs. We'd be going out in a boat under the Golden Gate along the coast. Maybe catch a fish or two. You could send a seafood platter to your dad." He stopped talking. His heart was in his throat. "It's just a thought. I'd bring you some abalone in any case."

"I don't know how to dive. Would I be in the way?"

"Heck, I'll dive for you. There's plenty of room. It's a twenty-four-foot boat. We'd be back by midafternoon." Again he waited nervously.

"If you're sure I won't be in the way, it sounds like fun. We'll knock Daddy right off his feet." Rebecca was thrilled to hear his voice and excited at the prospect of entering his world. "Actually, I'm glad you're going next week. I'm headed out to my parents' house first thing tomorrow morning. You know, Mother's Day family dinner and all. But I look forward to going with you, John. You'll call me to tell me what time and what I can bring?"

"You bet. I'll call you on Wednesday." They spoke for a few more minutes before hanging up. Both were elated, each of them wondering how they could make nine days go by faster. John was thankful for Hank's recognition of Mother's Day as a no-no for the dive. He popped a cold beer and sat on the couch, looking out of the picture window at the bay. Things were looking up. On Saturday morning, he called Hank to tell him his date was on. Twenty minutes later the phone rang. It was Judy. "Three's a crowd, John. So I'm going along, too. Who's the mystery girl? You've been holding out on me, John." She laughed. "Good," thought John. "Becky won't have to sit alone in the boat while we dive. Definitely good. She'll like Judy. Yes, things are looking up!"

When he heard Becky's voice on Wednesday, it was like the sun coming up on the horizon, like cool water on a hot day, like everyone coming back from patrol—but better. She had brought some newly released reserve wine back from St. Helena and offered to bring it along with cheese and french bread. "Hey, that sounds great. You can teach me a little about wines. Be fun to learn."

"I'm no expert, but it's really kind of involved and interesting. My dad's the one who can tell you about it. I'll give it a try, though, if you're really interested."

"Right now I know red and white. If you have samples, I promise to be a good student." They both laughed. He would pick her up at eight o'clock. "If you have a cooler, bring it. For the abalone."

The weekend dragged by for John. Sunday morning he was up at five thirty loading the truck. They would meet Hank and Judy between eight thirty and nine o'clock at the boat. Hank would bring herring and worms for bottom-fishing bait. John would bring coffee and donuts for breakfast. On Saturday afternoon, the boat had been gassed up, fishing poles brought aboard, and a general cleanup performed. The engine hummed obediently. The toolbox was stowed below, just in case.

At 7:57 a.m., John pulled up in front of 311. Becky was sitting on the stoop with a basket, a cooler, and a small tote bag. She had on what looked like the same blue jeans and sweatshirt as the last time he had seen her. The collar of a yellow blouse hung out over the top of the sweatshirt joining with her light brown hair to frame her tanned, smiling face. "Good morning. You're early."

"Good morning. The early bird gets the worm. You all set?"

"Ready to go." As they began loading her things into the back of the truck, Becky stopped him, turning his head sideways to inspect his cheek, brushing it with her finger. It was still slightly swollen and red. "I tell people I got hit with a bunch of grapes," he said. "Nobody believes me. They think it's a dueling scar."

"You'll have a scar, all right. The doctor was right."

"But it looks good. Don't you think?"

"Yes," she said, vividly remembering the incident in the Blue Fox, "it does look good. And you've earned it."

"Did you remember to wish your mom a Happy Mother's Day?" Becky asked brightly.

"My mother passed away when I was eight. Cancer," he softly informed her. He had thought about his mother on Sunday. It was a long time ago.

"Oh. I'm sorry. That must have been very difficult for you."

He shrugged and nodded.

Stopping at a bait shop, Becky got a fishing license, refusing John's offer to pay for it. The thermos was filled with coffee. John got a dozen donuts, ice, and several hooks and weights. Standing close together at the counter, Becky looked up and asked, "What are you wearing?"

"What?" John answered, not comprehending what she meant.

"Your cologne? It smells really good. What is it?"

Embarrassed, John smiled. "Old Spice. Yo, ho, ho. It kills the fish smell."

"Between your dueling scar and your Old Spice, you're going to be a handful," she kidded him.

"You have no idea, Miss Saunders. You have no idea," he thought happily.

Judy and Hank were already loading their things on the boat when Becky and John arrived at the pier. John introduced them and was thankful Judy didn't describe in detail his pitiful love life. Hank started the engine, while John finished loading their things aboard. Fifteen minutes later, the boat swung away from the dock out onto the bay. The sun was still low on the horizon, but it promised to be a beautiful day. The water was mildly choppy, a three on the Beaufort scale, nothing to worry about. They hit the potato patches a few minutes after passing under the bridge. The patches were where wind and wave met tide and current from the water coming down the Sacramento River. It created a turbulence that shook the boat for a few hundred feet. Hank explained that in the old days, Russian farmers in Mendocino would boat their potato crops down from the north, sometimes losing poorly tied sacks of potatoes stored on the deck overboard to the choppy water; hence, the nickname "potato patches."

Once clear, however, the ride was smoother, the warmth of the sun beginning to make the salt spray less chilling. Hank steered for the cliffs below Fort Cronkite, cruising about fifty feet offshore. The women were given a lesson on how to start and drive the boat, just in case it became necessary for them to move it while the men were in the water. The two men looked for rocks, both to avoid and to signal the presence of abalone. Patches of kelp helped to suppress the small waves. In some places they could see the bottom, algae and sponges reflecting reds, greens, and yellows up through the water column. About an hour out, they decided to drop the anchor and give it a try. To Becky's surprise, John began taking his pants off right there on deck. She watched with raised eyebrows, bemused, until she realized he had bathing trunks on beneath his jeans. The process of getting into a full wet suit, complete with weight belt, was fascinating to watch. They yanked and stretched, pulled and pushed. It seemed so heavy and cumbersome, the rocking of the boat throwing them off balance occasionally. Finally they sat, black forms on the gunwale, fins on, masks atop their heads, abalone irons looped around their wrists. Judy tottered over to Hank and gave him a big kiss on the lips. "Go get 'em, cowboy." She patted John on the knee. Becky looked at John. She would have liked to kiss him, too, but gave him a thumbs-up instead.

"Tallyho!" John said, pulling his mask over his eyes and nose. With that the two of them pushed over and splashed backward into the sea. The wet suits were not waterproof. Cold seawater seeped under the quarter-inch-thick neoprene, making the first few moments in the water chilling ones. Once inside the suit, however, the water was trapped and warmed by body temperature, creating a kind of warm bath. John waved to Becky to throw in his tube. The search was on. They swam off together but fifteen to twenty feet apart, fins kicking gently, heads face down in the water. Occasionally a spray of water would blow out of the snorkel, much like a whale spouting. Suddenly John's body arched, his fins swinging up over his head and then kicking down into the water. In an instant, he was gone. Hank promptly followed him out of sight.

"Kind of scary to watch them disappear like that, isn't it?" Judy said softly. "I can't imagine going under out here. There are sharks and big sea lions and God knows what else. But that's what they do." She looked at Becky. Then she smiled and asked, "Do you want some suntan lotion? You look pretty tan, but this will keep your nose from peeling." Becky hadn't even considered sharks.

"Thanks. How long have you and Hank been married? You seem like newlyweds," Becky asked as she spread the lotion on her nose. "You seem very happy together."

143

"I love him very much. Can't imagine being without him. His work scares me sometimes. That something could happen. But that's part of him. We've been married coming up on two years."

Becky was a little taken aback by Judy's directness. To say in all seriousness that you loved someone was an incredible admission. It made you vulnerable. Set you apart from the rest of the world. Becky knew her parents were in love. They said it sometimes to each other and, of course, all the time to her. But this was different. Judy wasn't much older than she was. But you could see a maturity in her face. She had reached a plateau in her life far above Becky's, even with all the schooling and volleyball. Judy was in love.

"And John McConnell is another piece of work. If I didn't have Hank, you'd have a run for your money."

Becky laughed. "I hardly know John. It's a very weird story about how we met. It's funny, though, I feel like I've known him for a long time. Has he told you about me at all?"

"Nary a word. But he has been excited about this dive. And I don't think it's the abalone he's excited about. You know, he's only been back from Vietnam a few months." Becky thought about her brother. Oddly she felt the same relief that John was back as she had when her brother returned safe.

With some concern, Becky asked, "How long do they stay under? Haven't they been down a long time?" As she spoke, a black body burst through the surface, its momentum carrying head and shoulders out of the water before settling back below water. The diver kicked toward his tube and placed something into it. A second body burst up with a splash. Twenty minutes later, John and Hank approached the boat. Pushing the mask off his face, John instructed Becky to take the tube aboard. She reached for it, tugging lightly to bring it aboard. It weighed a ton. She couldn't budge it. John pushed from below, and she finally managed to muscle it into the boat, its cargo clunking to deck, saltwater splashing all over her white sneakers. The two divers climbed aboard, scattering the girls' reflections amidst the wash of seawater, tubes filled with ocean-scented abalone, and two dripping men.

The legal limit for the red abalone was five per day, minimum size seven inches across the length of the shell. John reached into his tube, removed a nine-inch abalone, and held it up for Becky to see. It didn't look like much in the way of gourmet dining, but they all knew better. "Put them in a cooler. Then we'll fill it with sea water to keep them alive," John explained. "If we change the water every so often, they'll stay fresh right into the freezer."

"We'll have a cup of coffee and move the boat. We don't want to take all the abs from the same spot," Hank explained to the girls. "There's some nice fish down there, girls. Lingcod and cabazon. Good size. We'll rig up some poles so you can fish while we're down."

The four young people drank coffee and munched a second round of donuts. Fishing poles were rigged and baited, and the lines were dropped over the side. Becky was curious about what it was like to be underwater, what they saw, and how they could hold their breath so long. "You teach me about wine and I'll teach you how to dive," John offered. They talked and laughed, enjoying one another's company, the sun, and the ocean. The men went back into the water a few hundred yards farther up and within thirty minutes got the third and fourth limits, bringing the total number of abalone to twenty. The fact that none were smaller than eight and a half inches across was a tribute to their dive skills. Becky was amazed at the size and number of abalone. Two more fishing lines were dropped over the side.

Hank and John struggled out of their wet suits. When they got down to their swim trunks, John asked the women to please look away while he changed into dry clothes. "What, you got somethin' to hide, big boy?" Judy retorted. She and Becky looked out off the stern, giggling together at John's shyness.

Without warning, Becky's fishing pole jerked hard. Then again. "Fish on!" yelled Hank. Becky jumped to her pole, setting the hook and reeling, careful to keep tension on the line. John struggled with his pants, catching his foot in the leg hole of his jeans locking his feet together. He fell forward into the back of Becky's legs. Her legs knocked out from under her, Becky sat down on top of John but maintained as much control of the pole as she

145

could. The two of them, Becky with two hands on the pole and John with both feet caught in his jeans, were hilarious in their efforts to regain control. John—with abalone slime on his underwear and Becky's behind wiggling back and forth against him in her efforts to stand up—had a look of mortification and helplessness totally out of character for him. Judy and Hank had tears of laughter rolling down their faces, unable or unwilling to help. When things finally settled down, Becky, with a triumphant smile, brought up her fish, a fifteen-pound lingcod, which Judy captured on her Instamatic camera.

They caught several more fish, none as nice as Becky's lingcod. At about one o'clock, Becky's reserve Pinot Noir was broken out to complement the cheese and french bread. She had wrapped four glass wineglasses in cloth napkins, which lent an air of sophistication to lunch. They swirled the wine, sniffed it, and mouthed each sip, garnering all its aroma and flavor. It was a very good wine.

On the trip back, Judy asked the question, "What's the best way to have abalone?"

"Dipped in bread crumbs and sautéed in butter."

"Seasoned bread crumbs."

"Olive oil." Came the responses, all sounding pretty accurate.

"Nope," Judy corrected. "Fresh! How about we go over to our house and cook up an abalone dinner tonight? By the time we get in, clean the boat and the abalone, and do some shopping, it'll be time for dinner. What do you say?"

John looked over at Becky then back at Judy. "I told Becky we'd be back by four. I don't know if she has other plans," he explained, giving Becky some latitude if she didn't want to come.

"It sounds great to me," Becky said without any hesitation. "I can make a Caesar salad if you like. And we still have another bottle of that reserve."

"Good idea, babe. And I love Caesar salad. We're good to go." Hank cast the idea in stone. "John, you'll have to eat out on the deck unless you get that slime off your underwear." Everyone but John laughed. He just smiled.

The group flew into action as soon as the boat docked. "Hank and I will clean up here and bring the gear, while you guys go the store. We'll meet at your house." John choreographed the operation. As he handed Becky the keys to his truck, he slipped her a twenty-dollar bill. "Don't let Judy pay for everything. She'll do that if you let her."

"I have money," Becky said trying to return the bill. But he was already moving back to the boat.

"Hank. Bring the fish home filleted. Leave the guts for the crabs," Judy called as John's truck rolled by on the way out. The guys downed a couple cold ones as they cleaned up the boat, rinsed their dive gear with fresh water, and loaded up Hank's van.

Becky had never cleaned an abalone, so she watched intently as John prepared the esoteric mollusk for the frying pan. He had taken a wooden coat hanger, the kind with a flat arc of wood about a quarter inch thick, and removed the metal hook. The roughly sixteen-inch arc of wood was then cut in half and tacked to a thicker, wood cutting board maybe fifteen by twenty inches. The coat hanger pieces , creating a kind of horseshoe, each piece about six inches apart curving inward. The quarter-inch-deep cavity in the horseshoe allowed the meat of the abalone to be placed within it. John ran a sharp filet knife along the top of the curved wood, leaving a perfect, quarter-inch-thick abalone steak inside the cavity. A few swipes of the knife trimmed the steak of its black edges, and the steak was ready for pounding. "What a neat…abalone steak cutter," Becky said, fascinated by the obviously home-made gadget. "How did you come up with that idea?"

"You know, I don't remember. One day I built it. It took about three minutes to build, but it works like a charm. I'm glad I remembered to throw it in my dive bag. Anyway, you have two choices for your dad, Becky," John explained. "We can clean them now and wrap them in freezer paper or keep them in the shell, freezing them in salt water. That really keeps in the fla-vor, but he then would have to clean them each time. And it takes up more freezer space. What would you like to do?"

"Let's clean them now. Actually, I'd like to learn. Is that OK?"

147

"You got it." They cleaned seven of their catch, two for dinner and the rest for Becky's dad. Becky took a break from the cleaning to fix the Caesar salad, toasting her own croutons in a pan of olive oil, as she had seen her mother do many times before. At seven thirty they sat down to a scrumptious dinner, a challenge to any the finest San Francisco restaurants could produce. Their conversation relived the day and spoke of future trips to the realm of Neptune. Becky insisted Hank and Judy keep her lingcod fillets for another time. Judy brought out their architectural drawings, John's interest rekindled by Becky's excitement and enthusiasm at the thought of designing a dream house.

Becky felt a strong sense of friendship with Judy and Hank, giving them both a big hug when they left at around ten o'clock. "I really like them," she told John as they drove to Steiner Street. "You have nice friends. I'm glad you invited me along."

John carried the cooler of now cleaned and wrapped abalone into the apartment. Both Charlene and Cathy were there and curious about their roommate's budding relationship. John begged off a glass of wine explaining he had to dive in the morning. No more alcohol. A few minutes later, Becky walked with him to the top of the steps outside. He turned to her and said shyly, "I'd like to call you sometime. Maybe have dinner."

"That would be great. I look forward to it." She smiled at him, recognizing that the awkward question—to kiss her or not to kiss her—was probably running through his mind. She thought her look was pretty encouraging, but he started to back away. She caught his shirt with her hand and tiptoed up to brush her lips against the red line on his cheek. "Good night, John," she whispered. Then the door clicked closed behind her, and she was gone.

CHAPTER NINE

Northern California Coast

June 1969

His Seal training and self-discipline was crumbling. His impatience to confirm a weekend date with Becky made him feel like a raw recruit, a cherry, and a high-school sophomore all rolled into one. By Tuesday, John couldn't wait any longer, and he dialed her number. Becky answered the phone on the third ring. "Hi, Becky. This is John. How ya doin'?"

"Just fine, John. And how are you? Ready for your wine class?"

"Ready anytime. Even have an apple for the teacher. Or should I bring a grape?"

"The final exam is when you take me out to dinner at the Top of the Mark and order wine so the sommelier—that's the wine steward—says, 'Very good choice, Sir,'" Becky teased. "Of course, we may have to take out a mortgage on the dinner when the check comes."

The pronoun "we" was not lost on John. It sounded good. "We'll make it happen," he said. "Even if we have to eat beans and abalone steaks all month." They laughed together at the incongruity.

"It would be worth it," Becky agreed. "I'll grow lettuce in a window box so we can have salad."

"Speaking of dinner, how about Friday night? We'll start off small and work up to the Mark. Maybe have a little Red Mountain dinner wine. Seriously, if you're free, it would be my pleasure." The die was cast.

"John, Friday is a bad night." His heart sank. He was ready to say something like, "It was a stupid idea anyway." But she explained, "I've already committed to a kind of faculty cocktail party. The head of the English department is throwing a party at his house and … well, one of the professors asked me two weeks ago if I wanted to go. I told him I would. But I'm free on Saturday, if that works for you."

A momentary pause almost prompted her to say, "The hell with the party. Let's go out on Friday." John came to her rescue again and said, "Hey, Saturday'll be fine. I'll pick you up at … seven?"

"Seven sounds fine."

"Do you have any favorite place?"

"No. You pick somewhere. Someplace without a wine steward. Someplace cozy."

"OK. I'll see you at seven on Saturday."

"OK. Thanks for calling. By the way, Sunday was really a fun day. Thanks again for that."

"You're welcome. See you Saturday."

"Okay. Bye."

Work was going well for McConnell. Lowell Berg had him spread out all over the place, involved with consultants, disciplines, and procedures that covered a wide spectrum of the business. Berg as much as told him to find out what he liked the most and focus on it. As much as John enjoyed the hands-on action of doing things for himself, he found it interesting to be involved in creating a project, planning it, and helping to bring it all together. Architects and engineers, marketing guys and money men, general contractors and subs, government research and science projects, trying new technology, watching out for the environment—there was so much to choose from, picking one area was almost impossible. But involved he was, staying late and bringing reading home with him. To fight off the bulge in the waistline, he joined the YMCA, swimming and working out as often as he could. His goal was to swim or run five times a week, and occasionally he was on the run or in the pool at five thirty in the morning. He missed the competitive press of working out with Seals, always pushing one another closer to the edge, closer to your full potential, but continued going through his hand-to-hand combat routines and holds, often working out with Hank or Pete Rowley, an ex-marine who also worked at Berg Marine.

On Thursday night, about seven, the doorbell rang. John opened the door to find a man, about forty-five, with a gray-flecked beard and brown tweed jacket, standing there. The man began nervously. "Hello. I'm Joe Powell. I live almost directly below you … downstairs. I'm at the University of San Francisco, and I'm having a few colleagues over for a get-together tomorrow night. Not too many people, but I wanted to let my neighbors know and invite you down for a drink, if you'd like. About eight. "

"Hello. I'm John McConnell. The University of San Francisco?" John wanted to confirm. "Well, Joe, I might just stop down and say hello. Thanks for being such a good neighbor."

"I'm sure they won't make a lot of noise, but, you know, better to avoid trouble." He smiled. "Well, then, we'll maybe see you tomorrow."

As John closed the door he couldn't believe what he had just heard. This had to be the same cocktail party Becky would be at. It had to be. "You bet your ass I'll be down for a drink, Joe, old pal, old buddy."

Rebecca wasn't comfortable as she got dressed for the cocktail party at the head of the English Department's home. She knew some of the people who would be there, but not well. This was a potential opportunity for her to make some contacts among the faculty at the university, to enhance things for her volleyball team and, possibly, her own career as a graduate student and Education major. She had minored in English. This could mean additional references on her resume. All she knew was that it was a cocktail party. What should she wear? How casual? How dressy? James Feit, the professor who had invited her was about thirty-five, a sort of bland man—not great, not bad. But every time she thought about John McConnell, James Feit became less and less attractive, until she seriously considered canceling the whole evening. The die, however, was cast. She selected a simple black dress, a silver chain with a cross, her silver grape-cluster ring, and black shoes with medium-high heels. Better to be overdressed than underdressed.

Feit picked her up exactly on time, assisted her awkwardly into his blue Porsche, and kept up a banter of small talk all the way to the party. He wore a blue blazer over a turtleneck, removing any concerns Rebecca had about her dress selection. He pulled the Porsche into an attractive, three-story apartment complex, failed to find a parking spot, and had to look out on the street. Walking into the complex, Feit was looking for the apartment number in his wallet. The door to the apartment was open however, and music, incense, and muffled voices wafted out to identify the location of the party. Feit quickly got Rebecca a drink, a mediocre Chablis, and began introducing her around. He would slip his arm around her waist as they moved through the apartment, leaving it there during introductions, trying to give the impression that he and Rebecca were a lot closer than they really were. There were about twenty people there, more drifting in as the night progressed. One couple started dancing. Several others immediately followed suit, squeezing everyone else to the periphery of the living room and into the dining area. Rebecca found herself on the dance floor with Feit, who swung his arms and legs in exaggerated motions. He seemed to be trying to watch himself, looking down at his legs and out at his arms, only occasionally glancing at Rebecca, smiling as if to confirm the terrific time they were both having.

Just as Rebecca was thinking this was going to be a long and tedious night, she caught sight of—John McConnell?—standing across the room talking to the head of the English department. Their eyes met, and John winked, the mirth on his face undermining his effort to remain implacable. As soon as the music stopped, Rebecca excused herself from Mr. Feit and weaved through the crowd to John. "What are you doing here?"

"Too early for my wine lesson?" he asked with eyes opened wide with innocence. "I stopped by to have a drink with my old pal, Joe Powell."

"Like heck!" Rebecca challenged under her breath. She was happy to see him but at a total loss as to how he managed it. "Really?"

"I live upstairs," he confessed. "In 303. It turns out ol' Joe and I are neighbors. I thought you might be surprised."

"You never cease to amaze me, John. We could have invited Joe Powell over for abalone, and I could have skipped this party altogether."

The music had started up again. As James Feit approached Rebecca for another dance, she initiated introductions. "James, this is an old friend of mine, John McConnell. John, James Feit." McConnell started to raise his hand to shake hands with the man, but Feit threw him a cursory glance, mumbling, "Nice to meet you." He half led, half dragged Rebecca out onto the dance floor. Rebecca shrugged, mouthed "sorry," and melted into the crowd. John did not like James Feit dancing with Becky, but he realized that he was the intruder. He was not being fair to Becky by being here. Leaving the glass of wine on the kitchen counter, he slipped out of the party and went back upstairs, where he poured a cold beer. He put Los Indios Tabajaras's *Maria Elena* album on his tape deck and began thumbing through a *National Geographic* he had brought home from work. As he listened to the clear, mellow guitars of the Indian musicians, his mind kept drifting back to Becky in the black dress and silver jewelry.

Twenty minutes later, there was a soft knock on his door. He opened it to find Becky standing framed in the doorway, a glass of wine in her hand and a look of apology in her eyes. They stood looking at each other for almost a minute, the gentle music perhaps speaking for them. Becky finally broke the silence. "I'm sorry about him. That was rude." Another pause. "May I come in?"

"Of course," John said recovering from his surprise. "Come in. No apology necessary. If I was with the prettiest girl at the party, I'd want to dance with her, too." Becky smiled at the compliment, walked over to the couch, and sat down. "You look good in black," he remarked.

"I just didn't want you to think I condoned his behavior. He acted like a jerk. I wanted to tell you that." They talked and listened to the music for about ten minutes. Small talk, about their date the next day, Los Indios Tabajaras, and the Coopers. Becky had called Judy, and they were going to have lunch the following week. Becky seemed to be getting sleepy. Her eyelids started drooping. She would open them wide for a moment, only to have them close even further.

"Are you OK, Becky?" John asked with some concern. "You feel all right?"

"I'm not sure. I feel funny. Dizzy, kind of." Her head lolled back and forth. The wineglass dropped from her hand onto the floor. Finally her eyes rolled back, and she slouched forward, about to fall to the floor. John leaped over and caught her, gathering her to him. He picked her up and then laid her back onto the couch, kneeling beside it in order to release her gently onto its cushions. "What the hell happened?" he thought, his heart pounding with concern.

Quickly picking up the phone, he dialed for Molly next door. She was the closest medical person he could think of. "Molly. This is John McConnell. A friend of mine just passed out here in my apartment. Can you take a look at her? Please."

"Be right over."

In moments Molly was kneeling next to Becky, taking a pulse, looking into her pupils, and feeling the lymph nodes under her jawbone by her neck. "Has she taken any drugs, John? Be honest."

"She's been at the faculty party downstairs. She isn't into drugs. I'd have to say no."

"Her vital signs are slow but OK. She's not in any danger that I can see. But I don't know why she fainted. She probably should get medical attention." As Molly spoke, the faint wail of a siren could be heard getting closer. Two minutes later an ambulance pulled into the parking lot downstairs. The attendants were brought to Powell's apartment downstairs. Something was amiss at the party. "Let me go down and see what's happening, John. You keep an eye on her." McConnell took Molly's place on the floor beside the couch. He took Becky's hand in his, feeling its softness, trying to will his strength into her, watching her eyes for signs of her awakening.

Twenty minutes later, Molly returned with interesting news. "It appears someone at the party was slipping Mickeys into the girls' drinks. Three others are out cold. They're OK, but the ambulance is taking them to St. Francis Hospital for a checkup. They can't just leave them here at the party. I didn't say anything about your girlfriend. That's your call, John."

"Let me go down and talk to them. Give me five minutes, Molly." He went quickly downstairs to the ambulance driver, who was standing at the back of his rig watching one of the girls lying inside. "Are they OK?" John asked the driver.

"Yeah. We've been getting calls on these Mickey Finns lately. It just knocks them out for a few hours. They wake up with a headache. And maybe pregnant." he added.

"What about these girls? What's the procedure for them?"

"We have to take them in. Can't leave them unconscious at the scene of the crime, or we'd be liable. When they wake up, we'll release them into the custody of their next of kin … mother, father, husband."

"Thanks," John told the man, his decision to keep Becky away from the hospital made by the attendant's last statement. Back at the apartment, he asked Molly to give her one more check, make sure she was not in any danger. He explained that he would keep her in lieu of the hospital calling her parents. Molly understood. "Call me if you need me. I go to work at noon tomorrow." John picked Becky up and carried her to his bedroom.

"Molly, if you could just sort of tuck her in, I would appreciate it." Ten minutes later Molly closed the bedroom door, leaving it slightly ajar as a precaution. "Thanks, Molly."

"Good night, John. I'll talk to you in the morning.

John got a blanket out of his linen closet and prepared the couch for himself. He peeked in at Becky before lying down. She was breathing deeply, sound asleep. She looked small tucked in beneath the blankets, curled up like a kitten.

Becky's eyes blinked open. Her head ached. The room was dark, but she knew it was a strange place. Nothing was familiar. She was in a bed, wearing a T-shirt and her panties. Somebody had undressed her. The throbbing in her head and a slight nauseated feeling told her something was amiss. Rape entered her mind, and she tried to focus on her body, her vagina, for an indication of violation or damage. She felt nothing amiss except for her headache. Swinging her legs over the side of the bed, she sat up to a wave of dizziness. Several deep breaths gave her the will to stand and walk over to the door, which was slightly ajar. She tried to peek out, to see if anyone was in the other room. She was a little frightened. Pushing the door open slowly, she saw a darkened living room; no one was readily observable. Walking into the room, her eyes scanned for some indication of what had happened. "I was talking to John. Suddenly everything went dark. What happened?" Her fear was mounting, fueled by the unknown cause of her disturbing circumstances. A movement on the couch prompted her to cry out involuntarily. A dark form shot up off the couch, crouching in a kind of defensive attack position. Becky's mouth opened but nothing came out, her breath gone in surprised shock.

"Becky? Are you OK?" Becky took two or three steps backward, stopping only when her back came against the wall. "It's me, John. Everything's all right." He reached over and turned on the lamp at the end of the couch. In the light he stood up straight, extending his hands out palms up. "It's OK," he said again softly.

Becky's head throbbed; she was on the verge of vomiting. Her breath was short, making it difficult to breathe or speak. "What did you do?" she finally said, both asking and accusing. "What happened? Why did you take my clothes off?" Her questions built a case against the only person available, and her anger mounted. Suddenly bile was in her throat. She put her hand to her mouth knowing she was going to throw up.

John saw what was about to happen. He ran to the bathroom, opened the door, and turned on the lights. "In here!" Becky stumbled to the bathroom, went in, and threw up mightily. John watched only to make sure she didn't fall or otherwise need his help. "She thinks I did this. Maybe I would be better off in the jungle. Leave innocent girls alone," he thought. When she was down to dry heaves, he went to the telephone and called Molly.

When it was over, Becky washed her face and rinsed her mouth. She helped herself to several capfuls of Scope. The purging made her feel much better, but she looked like something the cat dragged in. There were several drops of vomit on her T-shirt. She walked to the door, saw John standing there helplessly, and asked calmly, "May I please have a clean shirt?" As she spoke, the doorbell rang, and John let in a dark- haired woman wearing sweatpants and a T-shirt. She looked like she had just gotten out of bed. Becky went back into the bathroom and changed into a fresh shirt, which had NAVY emblazoned across its front, first cleaning her chest of any remnants that might have soaked through the old shirt. Only just now realizing she wore only panties underneath her T-shirt, Becky wrapped a towel around her waist and walked with whatever pride she could muster into the living room.

John immediately introduced Becky to Molly, explaining who and what she was. "I'll let Molly explain what happened." Molly went on to tell Becky the details of what had transpired, the Mickey Finns, her conversation with the ambulance driver, and her examination of Becky's vital signs. "It was John's decision to keep you here rather than let them take you to the hospital. He can tell you about that. He carried you into bed and asked me to tuck you in. I didn't think you would want to sleep in that nice dress, so I put the T-shirt on you. Your necklace is on the dresser. You look fine, but I'll be happy to check your signs again if you like." Molly finished.

"Yes, thank you."

After a quick check, Molly pronounced Becky to be fine. "The nausea was from the Mickey. It actually helped to clear out your system. Well, folks, unless there's something else, I'm going back to bed."

"Thanks, Molly. I owe you," John said sincerely.

Becky stood up and walked over to Molly. Extending her hand, she said, "I really appreciate your helping me. If there's any way I can repay you, please let me know." The two women shook hands, Molly taking Becky's in both of hers. "Any friend of John's is a friend of mine. You'll be fine. Maybe next time, under better circumstances, we can all have a glass of wine. Good night." With that, Molly was out the door, leaving John and Becky standing in the silence of the early morning.

After several long moments, Becky went over and sat down on one of the chairs. John remained standing, bracing for whatever might happen next. "You decided I shouldn't go to the hospital?" she asked quietly.

"I spoke to the ambulance driver. He told me they would release the other three girls into the custody of their husbands or parents. I didn't think you wanted the hospital to call your folks in the middle of the night. They seemed pretty certain it was a Mickey Finn, no real damage, just knocking you out... and then a headache. I thought it was a good call." His explanation sounded so lame relative to the importance he placed on her response. He wanted to look away from her but could not bring himself to do it.

Becky was looking at him intently. Her look was soft and inquisitive. She looked at him for what seemed like a long time then finally spoke. "I apologize for thinking you had anything to do with this." When he started to say something, she held up her hand. "Wait. I was thinking this morning that even though you can be... menacing and a little scary sometimes, I would never be afraid of you or afraid when I'm with you. And I was right. You always seem to be there when I need you. You're always there for me. You're like my guardian angel."

"No one's ever called me an angel before. I don't think I qualify as an angel. Maybe a devil."

"No, John McConnell, you're my angel. And I thank you once again. I'm really glad you didn't let them take me to the hospital. My dad would have been down here in a panic. So it was a good decision."

They looked at each other for a while, quiet but comfortable without talking. John, not knowing what else to say, finally broke their silence. "You know, it's three o'clock in the morning. I can drive you home now, or you can go back to sleep here, and I'll take you home in the morning. Whatever you want."

Becky was now completely relaxed and at ease with what had been only a half hour before a horrific experience. She was sleepy and oddly reluctant to leave her benefactor. "I think I'll stay here. I'll sleep on the couch so you can have your own bed back."

"Don't be silly. Just go back to bed. I'll see you in the morning."

Becky stood up. Walking over to him, she reached up and touched the red line on his cheek, their eyes locked together. "Good night, John. Thank you again." She smiled when she saw him blush. Her finger trailed along his cheek and down his neck as she brought her hand down. "G'night."

"Good night, Becky."

Becky closed the door behind her. Her emotions were flooding over her again, almost to the point of tears. Tears of relief? Joy? She wasn't quite sure. She made her way to the bed in the darkened room, pulled up the covers, and nestled her head down into the pillow. With her first breath the scent of John McConnell filled her senses. A hint of Old Spice and an aroma that had to be…him. She breathed it in, savoring the sensation, the recognition of something she…liked? Appreciated? She knew the word that danced in the back of her mind but was too overwhelming to specify. Loved? These thoughts jockeyed for dominance in her dreams as her eyes closed, and she fell into a deep, peaceful sleep.

John didn't sleep much the rest of the night. He was caught up in this girl, this woman, and all of the coincidences that had brought her here tonight. How much she meant to him, without him really knowing her at all. Around five o'clock, with all chance for sleep gone, he got up, showered, and cleaned up the bathroom, putting his T-shirt in the laundry basket. His next thought was to have breakfast ready for her when she awoke. Besides coffee, the refrigerator held only beer, butter, an old loaf of whole-wheat bread, and half a jar of spaghetti sauce. No gourmet dining in there. At 6:20, John wrote a note. "Gone shopping. Be back by 7:00." Leaving it on the kitchen table, he raced down to the Safeway to get something she might like when she awoke. Not having a clue about her breakfast tastes, he got cream cheese and bagels, three flavors of yogurt, apples, oranges, and bananas and, just to be safe, a box of granola and a quart of fresh, whole milk. "She ought to like something here," he thought. On the way to the checkout counter, he grabbed a jug of cranberry juice and a newspaper. To his relief, she was not yet up when he returned. Ten minutes later, the dining-room table was laid out with all the breakfast choices anyone could desire. "She doesn't seem like the bacon-and-eggs type. Shit! I hope I didn't blow it," he thought as he spread open the morning paper to pass the time until breakfast.

Light from the sun shining through the curtained window caused Becky to stir and come awake, although her eyes remained closed. Events of the previous night replayed themselves, and her eyes opened to a now friendly, comfortable room. Luxuriating in his bed, Becky stretched and lay back to enjoy the last few moments before she knew she must get up. Finally she rose, went into the bathroom, and showered. Her teeth were brushed with a dab of Crest on the tip of her finger and another swig of Scope. She had no makeup; her purse was still down at Joe Powell's apartment. Having zero options, she put on the black cocktail dress and snapped on the silver cross. John's hairbrush was the only thing available that would make her hair remotely presentable, so she used it. John was just putting down the morning paper when she emerged from her cocoon at nine o'clock.

"Good morning, John." He rose to acknowledge her as she entered the living room. "I guess a cocktail dress is a bit much for breakfast." She was suddenly self-conscious of her evening fashion.

"It works for me," he said with a grin. "You look good. How do you feel?"

"I feel fine. Slept like a baby."

"I've got breakfast if you're hungry," he said, motioning to the dining-room table.

Looking at the spread of food, Becky smiled and asked, "Who all is coming? It looks like you're expecting a crowd."

"I didn't know what you liked, so I got a few things this morning. Everything's fresh off the shelf. You hungry?" he asked again.

"If I wasn't before, I am now." The two sat down and ate a long leisurely breakfast recounting the night's events, talking about Judy and Hank, abalone recipes, women's volleyball, and John's work. As they were finishing up their coffee, John asked hopefully, "Do we still have a date tonight?"

"As far as I know, we do. After this breakfast, though, let's make it a late supper," Becky teased. "You'll probably need to get some sleep before then."

"Actually, I had planned to drive up to the coast and look for some dive spots. I've never been up there. Wanted to do a little recon. Study the area so I know where I'm going." He explained his military jargon.

"My brother, Dennis, was Force Recon, Marines Corps. He was in Vietnam in '66 and '67. He lives up north in Crescent City now. Whereabouts were you going to go?"

"Force Recon? Tough bunch. I'd better watch my step around his little sister." John thought about Jennifer and how protective he was. Why should her brother be any different? A marine. Cool. "Hank told me to go to Jenner, a little town at the mouth of the Russian River, and go north. Said it was about two hours to Jenner." John looked at his watch, which told him it was just past eleven. "A little late to do that now and be back by seven."

"It might be fun to drive up and then look for a country restaurant along the coast or on the way back," Becky offered. "I mean, if you want company on the drive up. I know how to get to Jenner."

"Hey! That sounds great. I'll throw my dive box in the truck just in case. We can put what's left of breakfast in a cooler. Let's do it!" he said happily.

"Do you think I should change out of this cocktail dress?"

John laughed. "We'll stop at your place, if you insist. But I think the abalone will crawl right out of the water when they see you lookin' so good." He got a cooler from his bedroom closet, emptied both ice trays into it and packed the breakfast remnants in the ice. Becky cleaned up their dishes, and in five minutes they were out the door. Becky stopped to retrieve her purse from a flustered and embarrassed Joe Powell, who apologized profusely for the night before. She didn't tell him she had been one of the victims. Stories got blown out of proportion, and that was the last thing she needed as a student coach. The dive box, the cooler, and a carryall with sweatshirts and dinner slacks for Becky were lashed down in the back of the truck. John in blue jeans, Becky in shorts, and both in tank tops, the young couple were soon cruising north to the coast. It was a beautiful, sunny afternoon; the Beach Boys were telling the world, "I wish they all could be California girls."

They had taken the Guerneville exit off Highway 101 and were now following the meandering Russian River west to its mouth. It was country driving, slow and relaxing after the freeway. They were in no rush. Suddenly Becky blurted out, "We're coming up on the Korbel Winery! Are you ready for a wine lesson? They have a nice tasting room. Korbel makes wine, brandy, and champagnes. Not bad, either."

"Sounds good to me." John pulled into an almost full parking area that sat in a bowl surrounded by slopes of flowers, trees, and scattered brick buildings. The place felt rich in tradition. You felt like you were going into a shrine rather than a winery. Then again, to some it might have been a shrine. Either way it was a pleasant feeling, the woman at his side making John's experience even better. They wandered for a few minutes, taking in the atmosphere, then entered the tasting room, which was decorated with award ribbons, bottles of wine, several nice oil paintings of the grounds, and assorted wine-associated merchandise. It was crowded, but there was room at the tasting bar for them to squeeze in.

"Rebecca! How on earth are you?" The woman behind the bar almost came over the counter to give her a hug. "You sure are grown up. How are your folks?"

"They're fine, Susan. How're you doing? Looks like a busy day today. Susan, this is John McConnell. John, this is Susan Rafter, an old friend of the family."

"Hi, Rebecca!" Another woman behind the bar at the far end greeted her.

"Hi, Gwen."

John, eyebrows raised, looked at Becky. "You must do a lot of tasting here."

Becky laughed. "My dad is a grape grower. Korbel has been buying his grapes for…gosh, a long time. I used to come over here with him. I even worked here one summer. "Susan," she said, turning back to the bar, "what have you got for us today?" For about an hour, John and Becky tasted different wines and champagnes, swirling, sniffing, and comparing. The women behind the bar would bring over special wines, not available to the general public, adding a little spice to their tasting. Finally, agreeing on one wine and one champagne, Becky went to purchase a bottle of each. John offered to pay but was shooed away.

"Good wine isn't cheap. I wish you'd let me get them," John said.

"Since my dad is a grower, he gets an industry discount. I got these for about half the retail price. Maybe we can have one with dinner. Depends on the restaurant."

Once on the road again, they became part of the flow of tourists, vacationers, hippies, ranchers, and wine tasters enjoying the river and the country. John saw several men fishing and stopped to find out what they were after. "Salmon or steelhead," was the reply. They watched for a while and, damn—a guy a hundred yards downstream hooked up. Ten minutes later, he landed an eleven-pound steelhead, a real beauty. "This place has real possibilities," John said.

"My dad fishes for steelhead. He had one mounted. It's in his den."

Before long they were in Jenner, where the Russian River emptied into the Pacific, and John turned the truck north up the coast. There were steep grassy hills that dropped abruptly down to the water and flat terraces where sheep and cattle grazed. They drove slowly, enjoying the day and each other's company. A sign indicating, SALT POINT STATE PARK, prompted them to turn in and investigate. It was a beautiful place with campsites and showers right on the ocean. Salt Point Cove was a perfect place for divers to enter the water, and on the gravel beach were a dozen or more wet-suited divers starting or finishing their dives. A number of snorkels spouting occasional spray into the air could be seen amid the kelp offshore. They parked, and soon John was talking to a group of divers, asking about abalone and good spots to dive. The consensus seemed to be that the cove was great for sight-seeing or teaching new divers, but had been picked pretty clean of abalone. Too easy. Too many divers. Most divers had SCUBA tanks to go deep at least once over the weekend. Spear a fish or explore. There wasn't anyplace nearby to fill the tanks, so snorkeling was still the most common mode and the only legal way to harvest local abalone. Up the road were some good places, but no one could—or would—specify exactly where.

John and Becky decided to have lunch from their cooler on the grass overlooking the cove, catch some rays, and chat with the divers, hoping to glean more information from them. Families picnicked, and kids played on the beach; Frisbees flew, and a single kite fluttered overhead in the light, offshore breeze. A couple in a double kayak rounded the point and paddled in. The champagne sat in the cooler wresting the last cold from the disappearing ice cubes.

It was almost five o'clock when they hit the road again. Several times they stopped and reconnoitered potential spots, sometimes climbing down rocky slopes, clambering over boulders and poking into tide pools. John was reluctant to suit up and dive, always thinking a better spot would appear just up the road. About five miles from Salt Point they came to a level area that looked almost like an orchard. There were what appeared to be trails worn in the grass leading to the ocean. John pulled over. "Let's take a look. Those rock formations out there look really good." Climbing easily over the low, staked wood fence, they walked to the edge of the trees and grass. A cliff about fifty feet above a narrow rocky beach stopped them but offered a magnificent ocean panorama. The sun was approaching the horizon in the West.

"Maybe we can see the 'green flash,'" said Becky, referring to an almost mythical flash of green that was said to occur under certain atmospheric conditions just as the sun disappeared into its western home.

They stood there only a few minutes before John placed the stamp of approval on the water. "OK. This looks like a great spot. Let's find a way down." He led the way along the top, tentatively looking and then starting down several different paths on the steep incline. "This will be tough with all the gear. I doubt many divers have the hair for that much work." He thought about his Seal training.

"There's a rope." Becky pointed to a one-inch thick rope, firmly anchored into the rock by what looked to be a carabiner, a metal device used in mountaineering. A rough trail zigzagging beneath it indicated the rope was there to assist getting up and down the cliff. Moving over to it, they essentially rappelled down to the end of the rope. The rope, however, ended about ten feet from the bottom, where the rough trail began to level out somewhat in a rough rock and dirt slope to the beach. John scrambled to the beach and turned to help Becky with the last few feet of her descent. Becky let go of the rope and moved cautiously down. Almost to the bottom, her foot planted securely on a rock in the dirt, she got ready for the last push to the gravel beach. Without warning the rock came free of the dirt, sending her down unprepared. John caught her by the waist, her momentum carrying her full into him. He stumbled backward but retained his footing and held her close against his body. Their faces were inches apart. He continued to hold her. She made no effort to disengage herself. For both of them everything was suddenly gone; the ocean, the cliff, the abalone were beyond their awareness. It was just the two of them. The aroma from his pillow came to her.

They stayed like that for about twenty seconds, which seemed like an eternity, when John finally loosened his hold on her and turned to the beach without comment. He moved over to the water, scanning for some sign of abalone, she guessed. Her breathing was shallow and she took several deep breaths to regain her composure. "John, may I ask you a personal question?"

"Sure," he answered, half turning to look at her.

"Why didn't you kiss me just now?"

It was John's turn to take deep breaths, which he did several times before answering. "I didn't want to offend you," he explained lamely.

"I wouldn't be offended. If you kissed me now, I wouldn't be offended." Becky remembered later that her statement didn't at all embarrass her. Her surprise was that it didn't.

John looked at her without expression. Without answering. Then he turned and came to her. His arms went around her and his lips brushed against hers. Her whole body responded, all of her feeling welling up into their kiss. Her hands held his cheeks then slipped around him squeezing gently. Their lips brushed softly at first, then more firmly. They came apart and together again, sensually but not sexually. John's mouth opened, softly, and he kissed her lips and cheeks. They were exploring and discovering each other in a new way, in a gentle and innocent embrace, a warm and honest sharing of feelings. Both were exhilarated in the first display of their mutual affection—for five minutes. How long the kiss would have lasted is a mystery. A wave splashed up over their ankles surprising them, their lips coming apart but their arms still holding on. In the twilight they looked at each other, John somberly, Becky with a soft, radiant smile. As another wave approached, they moved closer to the cliff, holding hands, reluctant to let go. "This is the spot. I've got a good feeling about this place." He smiled and Becky laughed. He kissed her again, what would have been a peck had not Becky's lips followed his when he began to move away. Now it was a kiss born of experience, more firm. A statement more than a question.

Becky started up the cliff first. About halfway up her footing gave way again, her grip on the rope keeping her from falling. Reflexively John's hand went up to catch her, only to have her sit directly on his palm. "Sorry," he said.

"Pushing it a little, aren't we, Mr. McConnell?" She teased

They made it to the top and looked back out over the ocean. This would ever be their place. Moving back across the grass and trees to the truck, their peace was rudely interrupted by a harsh voice from the road. "Is this your truck? You know, you're on private land, you're trespassing. In two minutes I'm calling the sheriff." The voice came from a man in his late twenties but older looking. His hair was long, and he wore an army jacket and camou-flage pants. He had a stick. No, a cane.

"Hey, sorry about that. We didn't see a sign. Thought we'd take a look at the beach. Great place for abalone," John explained.

"Well, it's private. Get going," the man said bitterly.

"Is there any chance of talking with the owners? Maybe we could work a trade. Give them some abs for letting us dive here."

"I'm the owner. And I've heard that bullshit before. I'm calling the sheriff."

"Hey, we're out of here. Didn't mean any offense. It's a beautiful spot."

Becky squeezed John's hand. She was nervous and indicated to John that they should get going. The man looked angry and was ready to call the police.

"You a veteran?" John asked out of the blue.

The man turned, hatred and pain in his face. "Yeah. What's it to you, asshole?" Becky forgot not to be afraid when John was around.

"Me, too. Just got out in January. Did three tours in Nam. You?"

"Who were you with?" the man asked with doubt in his voice.

"Navy. Seal Team One, Bravo Platoon, out of Coronado. Worked out of Rach Soi in the delta."

"No shit. Sorry, miss. I was air cav. We worked with Seals a few times."

"What happened to your foot?"

Becky looked at John, appalled he would be so forward and insensitive to the man's obvious disability.

"Lost it to a mine. Wasn't paying attention and paid the price. Got a prosthetic. Not used to it yet." He held up the cane.

"We apologize again for trespassing. Didn't really know."

"Aw, forget it. A lot of people think it's a picnic area. Leave their trash, bust up the rhododendrons. This and up across the road is a rhododendron farm, we call it Cruz Ranch. We chase 'em all off, because as soon as one gets set up ten more stop."

"I didn't know they grew rhodies here. It must be beautiful when they're all in bloom." Becky was visibly relaxing, now that a bond seemed to have been established between the two men. "How many plants do you have?" As she spoke, it occurred to her how easy it was to be afraid. How many relationships could be lost to that fear?

"Actually, quite a few. Several hundred. We sell mostly wholesale. Nurseries and landscapers. Want to come up and see 'em?"

"Sure," they answered together. "Can we give you a lift in the truck? We want to get it off the road before the tourists take over."

"Yeah. Then we can see them before it gets too dark. By the way, I'm Sam Dorner." He held out his hand as he introduced himself.

"John McConnell." John extended his own hand. "This beautiful woman is Becky." Becky blushed slightly, remembering their kiss only a few moments before, and extended her hand to the air cavalry veteran. They drove up a dirt driveway on the inland side of the highway for about two hundred yards, passing a blue-gray house on the way. A woman came to the door. Dorner waved.

"That's my beautiful woman, Grace. Actually, my wife. She's a good woman. Puts up with a lot of my shit … with this foot and all. Good woman." The truck topped a rise that looked out over a hillside of plants, not neatly laid out like a vineyard, seemingly haphazard. But there were lots of them, two or three feet high. More easily transplantable, Dorner explained. There were no blossoms but the long, dark green leaves set them apart from the natural vegetation. In bloom, the view would be outstanding. Back at the house, Dorner introduced his wife, who immediately invited the couple in for a drink.

"You like sangria? I was going to make a pitcher for us. We'd love the company." It sounded like they didn't get much company. Or maybe couldn't get company to stay long. Loss of limb rehabilitation syndrome maybe. But the woman was charming; eager to have them stay for a while.

"Thank you, Grace. That sounds wonderful." Becky accepted for both of them, her fear dissipated by the beauty of the place, the obvious camaraderie, and the man at her side. Ten minutes later the two couples were sitting on the porch, surprisingly refreshing sangria in hand, watching the last light of the day follow the sun into the horizon. The women talked about the sangria recipe—oranges and fresh mangos; the men, in soft voices, of Vietnam. The two conversations would come together on occasion, when a deer walked up the driveway, and an owl swooped by the porch and into a nearby tree.

"What did you mean about people not coming through with abalone? When you let them park, I mean?" John asked Sam.

"People would promise the world, then drive away without saying thanks, even giving me the finger. Finally I decided, screw it, nobody parks there. Somebody once actually pulled up a rhodie by the roots…and just left it. Didn't even steal it. Just destroyed it. So fuck 'em. Sorry, Becky. But it really pisses me off."

Suddenly John stood up. "You know what? I'm gonna get you abalone right now. Got my gear in the truck. Take me an hour, tops."

Becky looked at him with a quizzical smile. "John, look around. It's dark. How many sangrias did he have?" she asked Grace.

"I know," he answered. "That's why I'll need your help, Becky. Sam, you got a flashlight?" Fifteen minutes later John was in full wet suit, carrying his abalone tube filled with fins, mask, snorkel, and dive light down the driveway. Becky trailed behind him.

"John, are you crazy?" she kept asking, not sure if he was kidding, drunk, or actually crazy. They went down the rope. It was easier the second time, but for John, humping the weight belt and gear, it was anything but easy. At the bottom, John put on the rest of his dive gear. As he pulled on his rubber gloves, he said to Becky, "Blink the flashlight every few minutes so I have a reference point. When I blink back, keep it on, pointing at me. I'll be on my way in."

"John, it's pitch black out there. You can't do this." There was a strong note of concern and worry in her voice. He took her hand, only now realizing how concerned she was.

"Hey, babe," he said softly "I've made hundreds of night dives. This isn't dangerous or crazy… for me. In twenty minutes I'll be back. Promise. If I know you're here, nothing can keep me away." He kissed her softly on the lips. Then on the end of her nose. And then he was in the water and gone. Becky stood alone in the darkness on the gravel beach, fifty feet below the road, a thousand miles from her old world. She would wait here, faithfully, until he returned.

The initial chill of the cold water always woke you up, actually felt good after hiking down to the beach, heating up inside of a full quarter-inch wet suit. Now the wet suit fought off the cold and absorbed the bumps when a wave pushed him against an unseen rock. The wind had picked up a little. There was a slight chop on the surface, adding to the waves building as they approached and broke against the rocky shore. In ten feet of water things settled down. His dive light illuminated the bottom at that depth, telling him that anywhere would be a good place to start. McConnell loved diving and was especially exhilarated by the haunting challenge of a night dive. The sense of aloneness and self-reliance was enhanced by the total black of this alien environment. The beam from his dive light pierced through the darkness, illuminating only a slender shaft of the ocean's vastness. Fish slept. Creatures of the night hunted. What you saw seemed more vivid, colors brighter than you remembered in the daylight. Whatever lurked in the darkness, secretive and perhaps threatening, kept you focused, alert, and humble. Not many people choose to experience the night immersed in the ocean. Fewer still come back a second time.

John's attention was focused entirely on the spot of light moving across the bottom, actually making it easier to locate his prey. Resting on the tube, he would take several deep breaths, scan the bottom from the surface, then flip over and dive down. Along the bottom he would cruise, searching, occasionally waking a fish, which would then flit away into the blackness.

His prey, the abalone, is a single shelled mollusk that grazes on algae growing on the rocks. Its foot allows it to move about, albeit slowly, to find fresh pastures. It scrapes the algae off with a file-like tongue, its radula. The flat abalone iron used to pop them off their rock is needed because, once threatened by wave or predator, the abalone contracts its foot muscle and adheres with suction to its rock with incredible force. Hence the abalone iron. The shell, a reddish pink, hosts plants, sponges, and barnacles, which in turn provide camouflage for the animal. Novice abalone divers can look directly at one and never see it.

John concentrated on boulders and beneath ledges, moving quickly to cover as large an area as possible on each dive. Once a large—eight inches or more—, abalone was spotted, he carefully positioned the iron, then quickly slipped it under the relaxed shell and popped it loose. On occasion two of the mollusks would be together and he got both, juggling them to the surface and into the tube's net. Turning the light off, he rested on the tube, completely at ease, relishing the dark beauty around him, listening to the water. Almost always you heard strange noises, real or imagined, speculating but never sure of their origins. Light from the stars, once your eyes adjusted, created an eerie yet magnificent surrounding. A flash of light from the shore flooded John with images of this woman, now part of his life. The memory of her lips on his, her touch, her radiant smile, prompted him to stay on task, and he dove again down into the blackness.

Becky's eyes were locked on the occasional flashes of light out in the dark abyss. Her experience held no record of what was happening to him out there. Her imagination was not kind in producing images of what might happen. Feelings of anger, fear, impatience, and … confidence at just being here on this beach at this time, both confused and energized her. A light blinked, three … four times. He was coming in. She turned her light on and shone it back at him. After five minutes without seeing anything, Becky began to worry. 'Where is he?"

And suddenly he was there, a black figure rising out of the dark water, his godlike image fading as he stumbled on the slippery rocks and crawled out, struggling with the tube, now heavy with his catch. She waded into the water, helping him drag the tube, taking his fins and mask to free his other hand. Becky didn't know what to say. He had done what seemed impossible to her. He had survived. Inspecting the tube, it was clear he had not only survived but succeeded. The net held a lot of abalone. Eight, which was a tad above the legal limit.

John pulled off his hood and gloves. He looked at Becky and smiled. "I told you I'd come back." She stepped over to him and kissed him on the mouth. He held her with his fingertips, reluctant to get her wet, but relishing the warmth and softness of her lips. His heart, already high from the dive, soared with the sweetness of the moment.

John tied the netting on the tube to the cliff rope. Struggling to the top with his gear, Becky helping with fins and mask, they eventually got the gear up and out to the side of the road. Grace and Sam brought the truck down and loaded it into the back. John and Becky returned to the cliff and hauled the tube and abalone up. At the truck, John proudly announced to Sam and Grace, "There's a limit of abs in there for you." There wasn't much anyone could say. Gratitude hung heavy in the air; the foundation of new friendship was being laid. Grace, happy that her husband was happy, announced that a fresh batch of sangria was waiting. With Sam and John in the back, the girls drove back to the porch, each of them eager to hear the details of John's adventure in the sea.

"I got a few extra. We could cook 'em up for a snack," John offered.

"I've got meat loaf in the oven. Stay and have dinner," Grace suggested.

"We have a bottle of champagne. Always carry one in the truck." Becky continued to build their feast. It would be one of those unplannable, spontaneous evenings, so enjoyable and pleasant, one that would be memorable for a lifetime. Around midnight, it was decided that John and Becky would stay in the guest cottage rather than drive back that night. There were two sets of bunk beds, usually reserved for family gatherings. Becky slept in the bottom of one; John in the bunk across the room. Lying in beds so close, each wanting to be with the other, made for a fitful night's sleep. John, unsure that he was worthy of this woman, continued to nurture thoughts of Vietnam and his possible problem. Becky, more sure every day that this man was the one she had been waiting for, was held in check by traditional, now maybe old-fashioned, values. Wanting to do things properly for both their sakes. Jumping into his bed, invited or otherwise, in a fit of lustful desire was not the wholesome image she wanted him to remember. It had been quite a weekend so far and, despite the concupiscence in their minds, they eventually fell asleep.

According to Sam, they still couldn't park on the road, but had carte blanche to park in their driveway anytime. Spend the night. Whatever. They would always be welcome. Before leaving, John got another limit of abalone, and by one o'clock he and Becky were on the road back home. At a roadside stand advertising 'HAND-CRAFTED JEWELRY' via a cardboard sign hung off the roof of a well-used Volkswagen van, a hippie couple was selling their wares. John pulled over, and they examined the couple's handiwork. Not surprisingly, the people were very talented, the workmanship of high quality. Many during this time of turmoil and change in America opted to forgo traditional lifestyles, preferring to be footloose and free on their own terms. After perusing their display table for a few minutes, John caught sight of a pendant. It was made from an abalone shell cut in the shape of a fish, a rough-ribbed, reddish pink on one side; shimmering iridescent mother-of-pearl on the other. A thin wrap of sterling silver framed the curved body of the fish and attached it to a silver chain. He picked it up and placed it around Becky's neck, clasping it closed from behind her. "To remember this weekend," he whispered in her ear, kissing her neck and nuzzling her hair with his cheek. She turned slightly toward him and tilted her head, offering her neck to his lips, her eyes closed, savoring his touch, clasping the fish in her hand.

Applause and a whistle brought them out of their reverie, the hippie couple with big smiles, acknowledging their moment. "True love," they said, teasing and congratulating them. "Ten percent discount," the man said, knowing the sale had been made. A horn honked as a car passed, a woman waving out the window, smiling as she perhaps saw something from her own past. They all waved back.

Before they left the stand, John gave the artists two abalone shells and declined the offer to share a joint. On the road again, Becky said, "You know, every time we go out, somebody else makes dinner for you. I want to make you a dinner, just the two of us, so I have you all to myself. Want to take a chance?"

"Do I get to pick the wine?"

CHAPTER TEN

San Francisco, California

June 1969

During the drive back, Becky and John set the following Friday as the day she would cook supper for the two of them. To avoid having to invite Charlene and Cathy, they decided to do it at John's apartment, Becky bringing over whatever she needed in the way of pots, pans, and utensils. John's Noritake stoneware would be christened at the dinner. Their relationship was at that exciting stage where almost everything they did was for the first time. Everything was new and interesting. They were learning about each other, likes and dislikes; they were eager to please, discover, and surprise. At one point, Becky made the comment that he was very tactile; that he often communicated with her by touching her. Her hand, her shoulder, his arm around her waist, a nuzzle. And she loved it. When he thought about it, John concluded that he had, in fact, never been tactile. Not until Becky came along. She seemed to stimulate him to want to touch her, to tell her things with a brush of his hand or lips, rather than try to find the words. This may have been due somewhat to the fact that he was telling her things that he would not have said aloud. He didn't talk about his feelings. But they were communicated to Becky nonetheless. The two kissed good-bye late Sunday afternoon, comfortable and secure in their fledgling relationship.

At their regular eight o'clock Monday morning meeting, Lowell Berg announced an emergency job that would require a dive team right away. A ship three hundred miles out of San Francisco had fouled its propeller in gill or cargo netting. Gill nets were long fishing nets . When broken loose they posed a serious threat to marine life and shipping. The ship was dead in the water and in need of assistance. The ship reported that it was not in any immediate danger but would require assistance to remove the netting to free up the prop. Berg Marine had contracted to do the job, and their salvage ship would sail at noon to rendezvous with the disabled vessel. McConnell and Cooper would act as the primary divers on the job with Pete Rowley as surface support and backup. It was estimated they would be back no later than Friday. The rest of the team was selected. Harold Sandstrum would captain the salvage ship and serve as project manager. "Any questions?" Berg asked. None forthcoming, he dismissed the team. "Prepare to sail by 1200 hours."

John immediately called Becky to tell her and make contingency plans for their dinner if necessary. No one was home at Steiner Street so he left a message, hoping her roommates would not lose or forget to relay it. He explained that he would be at sea for the week and told her he would leave a key under the mat in case he was not back by the time she got there. She should go in and make herself at home. He also told her to answer the telephone. He would call her to keep her informed of his arrival or lack thereof. However, barring anything unforeseen, he would be home for dinner. With that done, he packed an overnight bag and met with Hank Cooper in the dive locker to select and load their dive gear onto the salvage ship. He and Hank then got on the radio and spoke to the distressed ship's first officer to get firsthand information on the problem. He reported moderate but rising seas. The ship's safety system had shut down the main shaft before it incurred real damage, but the netting was hard wrapped on the propeller, preventing them from any inspection or work on the shaft itself. They would have to go down, cut the netting loose, and free up the shaft. This would require very sharp cutting tools—possibly a torch, if there was metal anywhere in the netting.

By four o'clock they were through the Golden Gate moving at fifteen knots past the Farallon Islands, through the wildlife refuge. It was a sea lion and elephant seal rookery and a known haunt of great white sharks, which fed on them. Hank and John speculated about the abalone population around the Farallons and the odds of actually seeing a great white in the water. Slim to none was the consensus, but that was the rub. They were there. The navigator estimated their arrival on station at around 1000 hours on Tuesday, which would put them in the water by noon. Since they would not be diving deep, they could spend more time in the water. The decompression tables dictated dive duration and rest time. In a nonemergency situation, the tables would be strictly adhered to. Diving shallow meant long stretches in the water where cold and fatigue would come into play. A marine engineer was also aboard with anticipated spare shaft parts if minor damage had occurred. Now it was just a matter of waiting.

Sunday night Becky was on the phone to her Mom. "I need your recipe for veal parmesan, Mom. And if you could walk me through it, that would be great. You serve that with garlic pasta and a salad, right? I mean I won't need a vegetable, too, will I? Oh! Garlic french bread."

"How many will be at your dinner, Rebecca?" her mother asked.

"Four," Becky responded, not quite ready to broadcast her relationship or feelings yet. And it was always better to have more than not enough. She spoke with her mom for over thirty minutes determining utensils, spices, and other items she would need for her obviously special dinner. Her mom offered to put a set of four linen table napkins, some of the required spices, and whatever else she could think of in a package and mail it off. "If I do it on Monday morning, it should be there by Wednesday or Thursday." Emily Saunders knew better than to press her somewhat headstrong daughter on the details of the occasion. In time she would hear all about it.

"Thanks, Mom. I'll let you know how it turns out." Becky could always count on her parents coming through for her, even beyond her expectations.

She was genuinely grateful for what she had. Her chest tightened when she remembered something John had told her—that his mother had died when he was only eight years old. She couldn't even imagine not having her mother around. Yet he grew up without his. That void was a part of him, made him what he was. Her desire to hold him, to share herself with him, became stronger.

Becky got John's message when she got home Monday night and felt her first pangs of real separation. Even though she might not have seen him until Friday night anyway, now he was gone and she couldn't see him. That availability made all the difference. Thinking about him out at sea made her think about him going into the water that night; her concern, and the relief when he crawled out with his catch. He was not like anyone she had ever known. Maybe her brother a little, but in this case, he didn't count. Coincidentally, she spoke to her brother on Sunday night. Told him she was dating a navy guy; about the abalone they had gotten for dad. "A squid?" He had teased her. "Better a squid than some of the other lightweights you've brought home," he went on. Becky assumed a squid was similar to a Seal and didn't say any more. She did not look forward to introducing John to her brother. Dennis had always looked down on her boyfriends, and she had no reason to think that would change now. But John was different. He would hold his own. She hoped they would get along.

The problem on the drifting ship had been caused by a long section of gill net that had come loose, probably somewhere up in the Bering Sea. It had followed the Humboldt Current south and eventually had been sucked into this propeller; simple bad luck for the owner. The job took longer than expected given the length of line wrapped, a rising sea, and several smaller sharks that were feeding on fish and a turtle caught in the netting. It had been a deathtrap for many creatures on its long journey down the Pacific, an underwater wall of death. The sharks were not necessarily dangerous to the divers, but they bore watching and slowed down the repair process. The propeller, more than six feet across, had twisted the nylon cord deep into crevices and pulled so tight it had almost melted it into a solid piece. It wasn't until Wednesday afternoon that the prop was cleared and the engineers could test the shaft. After repeated tests, the engineers determined the ship could get underway but should not exceed ten knots as a precaution until further, more precise tests could be done in San Francisco dry dock. By noon on Thursday the two ships were headed east, the salvage ship staying close by just in case. Hank and John worked up their company reports and dive journals, took cold showers (the hot water heater had crapped out), and tried to rest. They had been fifteen hours in the cold water. The chill was slow to dissipate. Passing under the Golden Gate at five thirty Friday afternoon, John calculated he would not be finished unloading until seven thirty or eight o'clock and would, therefore, be late for his dinner with Becky. He decided to call via the marine operator in case Becky was already there.

True to her word, Emily's dinner package arrived on Thursday afternoon. It included the linen, a wedge of fresh Parmesan cheese and a hand grater, a pepper mill filled with whole peppercorns, and two crystal champagne glasses. A bottle of Korbel champagne and a bottle of her father's homemade Riesling wine were also tucked in. The two glasses told Becky her mom might have guessed the dinner's purpose. That's OK, she thought. John wouldn't be a secret for long anyway.

Becky arrived at John's apartment at five o'clock on Friday, finding the key, as promised, under the mat. Three trips up and down the stairs got her groceries and cooking paraphernalia into the kitchen. She and Molly Haffner chatted for a few minutes before Becky was able to get busy on the dinner. John had told her about his stoneware, but she had no idea where it was, so she put off setting the dinner table. At five thirty the phone rang, and a marine operator informed Becky she had a call, to please hold while it was put through.

"Hello! Becky? This is John. How you doing? Over."

"Hi. John. I'm fine. How are you?"

"Please indicate you are finished speaking by saying 'over.'" The marine operator coached Becky. "Then I can switch you back to the caller."

"Over." Becky complied.

"Good." came John's voice came from somewhere out in the ocean. "Hey, I'll be a little late. Probably be home about eight thirty. Will that be OK? Over."

"OK. I'll plan dinner for nine or nine thirty... ... ..."Over."

"Sounds great. I can't wait. I'll see you in a few hours. Over."

"Miss you. Bring your appetite. Over."

"See you then, Becky. Out."

After a few moments pause, the marine operator asked. "Ma'am, do you have anything else?"

"No. See you, John. Out. Thank you, operator," she said, unsure of what to do next, not liking it that the machine had made their conversation so impersonal. So distant. "He's at sea," she thought. Somewhere she could never find him. He would have to come back to her.

"You're welcome, ma'am. Good-bye." And the line went dead. Becky held the telephone for a minute and then hung up. Impersonal as the call may have been, he was coming and that thought energized her. Now with more time to prepare, Becky set to work a little more at ease. She would aim to have everything ready to serve at nine fifteen. The champagne would be popped when he walked through the door. The only thing that represented a loose end was setting the table.

Her mom had included a handwritten copy of the veal recipe, which Becky reviewed and then laid on the counter for ready reference.

Emily Saunders's recipe for veal parmesan (four servings)
Ingredients
2 pounds veal medallions
Breadcrumb mix
Fresh crushed herbs (parsley, oregano, a pinch of cilantro, whatever else you like)
10 cloves garlic, minced
2 tablespoons of flour
1 egg
Olive oil

butter

1 pound Mozzarella cheese

1 can tomato sauce, one can (Use homemade seasoned spaghetti sauce if you have it.)

Preparation

Slice veal medallions thin. Gently pound each medallion between wax paper.

Dip medallions in whipped egg (add a little water to egg), then into breadcrumb mixture.

Melt butter and olive oil in frying pan (add minced garlic to taste—not too much, Rebecca).

When pan is lightly smoking, add veal. Cook quickly on both sides until golden brown (maybe one minute per side).

Arrange cooked pieces in oven-proof baking dish.

Pour tomato sauce evenly over the cooked veal till all is coated but not too much. Coarsely grate Mozzarella cheese, sprinkle over the top. Add fresh oregano and/or parsley on top.

Dish is now ready for oven. Bake for 10 to 15 minutes at 350° F.

Garlic Pasta: Prepare pasta according to directions. Slightly undercook so it's a little hard. Drain into colander. In pot, place 1/2 stick butter and 6 to 8 cloves of minced garlic. Leave pot with melted butter and warmed garlic until ready to serve. Then add pasta. Toss pasta until well coated and slightly fried or brown.

Grate fresh Parmesan over veal and pasta at the table. A French baguette is always nice with this.

You can get dish ready beforehand and bake just prior to serving. Good time to clean dishes.

Enjoy, Rebecca. Love, Mom. "

Becky followed the recipe faithfully, smiling at her mother's side notes about gentle pounding and not too much garlic. She prepared a tossed green salad, presliced the French baguette, adding the herb and butter sauce, put it in foil, and cleaned the kitchen.

When all else was prepped and ready, she began to wander around the apartment, looking at things. There were a lot of military-related items: coffee cups that read NAVY, a rather large shell casing, a wide-brimmed, camouflage hat, and a short canoe-like paddle with his name on it. An elaborately carved, stone chess set sat on the coffee table. She went into his bedroom, guiltily at first, then remembering she had already spent the night there. There was a photograph on the wall above the dresser depicting a group of heavily armed soldiers on a boat that bristled with the barrels of guns. She looked for John and found him sitting with his legs over the side, a rifle of some sort across his lap. Beneath the photo, two wooden-handled curved knives or sickles hung, blades crossed. Several spear guns were stacked in the corner.

Back in the dining room, she saw a box with Asian characters sitting on the floor by the walk through hall. It turned out to be the stoneware. Happily she unpacked the set, amazed that he would have a full ten place settings of what must have been expensive dinnerware. An unpredictable man indeed. It was fun setting the table, trying to make it as beautiful as possible. She had forgotten candles but remembered place mats and, together with the linen and crystal glasses her mom had sent, the table presented a look of elegance. An Andy Williams record added to the charm of the setting—a little bit folksy, a little bit romantic. Becky was pleased.

At twenty-five past eight the door opened. He walked in carrying his overnight bag and a bouquet of flowers. "Sorry I'm late. I stopped at Safeway," he said, handing her the flowers. Becky took them, putting them up against her face, inhaling. Her eyes were sparkling, her face radiant.

"They're beautiful. Thank you." As she spoke she moved toward him, and they kissed. A soft greeting that lasted just a bit longer than was necessary. "I want to get these in water and turn on the oven," she said moving into the kitchen. "We'll eat in a half an hour, if that's OK with you. You can relax for a while. And you can open the champagne."

"Wow! It looks great. You've been busy. Hey, if you don't mind, I'm going to take a hot shower. We didn't have any hot water on the ship. I'd like to get clean and warm up. Spent fifteen hours in the water."

"I'll hold off on dinner. Let you settle down." Becky looked at him and thought she could see the outline of a dive mask pinched on his face. "You go ahead and shower. Take your time."

"I'll be out in five minutes. Whenever you're ready is great."

Ten minutes later, John emerged from the bedroom wearing jeans and a fresh white T-shirt and carrying a gray knit pullover shirt. His strong tanned arms contrasted with the snug, white shirt and she could smell his Old Spice.

"Now I'll open that champagne. What shall we drink to? The prettiest girl and the best cook in San Francisco?" The cork popped, ricocheting off the ceiling and bubbling over into a dishtowel. He poured two glasses and held one out to Becky.

"Sounds like you're all warmed up." She smiled. "Let's toast the sea. For bringing you back."

"A little late, but here at last. To the sea." They clinked their glasses together and sipped at the bubbly spirit. The strange thought that he might not return from the sea flitted through his mind, but he smiled, appreciative of the dinner and the thoughtfulness of the woman who had become a part of his new world.

"Sit down." Becky directed, waving John to one of the stools by the kitchen serving counter. "Let me put this in the oven, and I'll give your shoulders a rub. You spent a long time in the water."

John did as directed, never one to pass up a neck massage. He sat and leaned his head forward. His body was hard and tight beneath her hands. She could feel the warmth from the shower through his cotton shirt. The aroma of soap and cologne came to her. As she kneaded his shoulders a feeling came over her, almost a tingling. And a shortness of breath. She remembered wondering what her children would be like; where their father was; what kind of person he would be. Her hands began more to caress than to massage. Without being able to stop herself, she kissed the back of his head and rested her forehead against him; still rubbing his shoulders and arms. John breathed deeply. She felt him exhale and relax to her touch.

Becky was caught up in thoughts of this man, and her body starting to react to the depth and desire of her thoughts. She began to kiss his neck and bite at his earlobe, slowly at first, then with more intensity, with more abandon. Caught up in her passion, unable to stop, she turned his head and kissed him full and hard on the mouth. Her tongue pushed its way in, finding his, licking. Their mouths opened and pressed back together, their tongues exploring, urging them on. Becky's hands grabbed at his chest then went around him, pulling him closer to her. This was a kiss unlike any either had experienced before. It pulled at their spirit; their soul. John stood up, he too helplessly overcome, caught up in her passion. Any thoughts of restraint were overrun, lost to an emotional and physical pleasure fully without precedence in their lives. Their bodies pressed together, moving. Their mouths still joined together, he lifted her off the floor and even closer to him. Becky's legs wrapped around him, their bodies grinding even closer together. Sex was in control, their emotions lost in the maelstrom of their desire. They kissed each other's lips, eyes, cheeks, necks … as if searching for a way into the other's soul. With Becky's face buried in his neck, John carried her to the couch. They half fell, still intertwined, onto the soft cushions, again kissing with passion and even more intimacy. John's hand moved down her leg, found the hem of her dress, and slipped beneath it. His hand caressed the bare skin of her inner leg, moving upward along the inside of her thigh. Her skin was incredibly soft, inviting him to continue. His hand obeyed, gently moving her legs apart. Their kisses became more tender, anticipating a tactile explosion, registering their passage beyond friendship into something more.

Becky, in her mind's eye, saw their coupling; the sweat, the lust permeating everything. Suddenly she pulled away, turning her head, but holding him to keep him from leaving. "Oh God! John. We shouldn't do this. I'm sorry. It's my fault." Her words caught him off guard, caught his attention like a splash of cold water. "This isn't the way it should happen. For us." She kissed him on the forehead. "I didn't mean to lead you on. To tease you. I do want you, but not like this. This isn't the way it should be." Tears came to her eyes as she imagined his frustration; his rage at her…cheapness. Her tears became sobs. A sense of despair rose in her, that she would hurt him, cheat him.

John sat up and helped her up. With her sobs loud in his ears, he gently pulled her to him, holding her, his arms securely around her. They sat for a while, John nuzzling her, soothing her with soft words, both aching at the thought of hurting the other. "Becky. It's all right. It's OK."

She looked up at him, her cheeks wet, her eyes in pain. "I didn't mean to do that. You were so… … … beautiful. It was my fault. It wasn't right. I'm so sorry" she sobbed.

John took her by the shoulders, looking directly into her face. Her eyes were evasive. "Look at me! Becky, look at me." Their eyes met and locked, hers filled with sadness. "Becky. You are incredibly special to me. I know in my heart that one day, you and I will make love. Maybe tomorrow. Next week. Next month. It doesn't matter when. For me, just being with you is enough. Is everything. Kissing you. Holding your hand. Seeing you smile. I'm happy. When the time is right for both of us, it will happen. Trust me, it will happen."

Becky looked at him, understanding what he said, but still hurting and embarrassed by her loss of control. Feeling life come back into her through his words, his compassion, she whispered, "I didn't want it to be…all physical. I mean just sex. It's more." Her tears kept flowing, but the cause was now different. He came to her rescue, as he usually did. Brushing away her tears with the back of his finger, he kissed her cheek, wiping away the last tear with his lips. "Can you forgive me?"

"Of course. You're right. There is more to it." He kissed her tenderly on the lips. They held each other, resting after their physical and emotional ordeal. John thought about his secret, his possible post- Vietnam stress disorder and her right to know. His head came up. "By the way, what is it I smell? Smells awfully good."

"Oh God! The veal!" Becky disentangled herself, jumped up and raced into the kitchen. She whipped open the oven door and, after an examination of its contents, breathed a sigh of relief. "I'll need about five minutes," she said, removing the veal and inserting the garlic bread. The salad was placed on the table. "If you would open the wine." John opened the wine to let it breathe and poured more champagne into the crystal glasses. "My mom sent the glasses down. They're beautiful, aren't they?"

"I thought it was your reflection that made them so beautiful." Becky's eyes moved to the floor then back to his. She smiled and held her glass out. "To you. Just because you're you." Not knowing how to respond, he held out his glass, realizing only now that a part of his decision to leave the navy had come through this woman. Becky brought out the salad, the french bread, and, with a mini flourish, the veal. The freshly grated cheese and the freshly ground pepper enhanced not only the taste but also the ambiance of the dinner. Sipping at the Zinfandel they got at Korbel the previous Sunday, they luxuriated over Becky's first culinary triumph.

"Becky, this is outstanding! Better than abalone. This has to be the best dinner I've ever eaten. I mean it."

Becky blushed demurely. "Thank you. I'm glad you like it. Your dishes helped with the presentation."

"Christ, I could eat this off the floor, and it would be outstanding."

Becky laughed. "I don't think so, but thank you anyway." They ate, talked, and sipped wine. They evaluated the wine, admired the crystal, and praised Emily's recipe. John guessed at the herbs in the sauce. Becky asked if a Seal was like a squid, and John laughed for a full minute before asking where she heard that. He actually looked forward to meeting her brother when she told him, anticipating camaraderie and a little friendly competition. Becky, in turn, asked if he had any brothers or sisters. He told her about Jennifer and her desire to visit California.

Out of the blue, Becky somberly asked, "John, would you like to meet my parents?"

Recognizing the seriousness of her question and its implications, he hesitated for only a split second. "Yes, I would."

Becky smiled gratefully at the confirmation of his sincerity. "What would be the best time for you?"

"You set it up, and I'll be there. Whenever." His eyes were set unwaveringly on hers, that intense look he had that scrutinized her intentions but also opened his to her. She knew he would be there, that he would fight to be there. She nodded, her chest slightly tightened from the joy she felt, trying unsuccessfully to hide her happiness. And not really caring that it was poorly hidden.

"I'll call tomorrow. Maybe next weekend."

Eventually the conversation came back to their near sexual encounter. Apologetically at first. Then with more confidence, with an eagerness to understand what it was they both felt would be right, knowing it would happen, and it would be good. Their growing comfort with each other allowed them to speak more frankly, her more than him. He understood where she was coming from and appreciated and respected her position. In fact, it bought him time to get his own act together. His position, he felt, was a little more obscure and delicate. It was a potential deal killer, a turnoff, something perhaps she could not or would not tolerate. He also knew it had to be brought up. And soon. She, of course, was unaware of his reluctance. Maybe she thought he was shy—or a gentleman. "Is she in for a surprise," he mused uncomfortably.

The ring of the telephone interrupted their discussion, postponing again his confession. It was about ten o'clock. John got up to answer, a questioning look on his face. "Hello. Hi, Cathy. Fine and you? Good. Hang on, I'll get her. It's for you." He said as he handed the phone to Becky.

"Hi, Cath. What's up?" Becky listened for a moment and nodded her head. "Okay Cathy. Thanks for calling. I'll get back to her. Bye." She hung up the phone, looked at her watch, and said to John, "My mom called earlier. She wanted to know if I got the package with the glasses and all. It's not too late to call. Do you mind?"

"Go for it. Tell her everything was great."

Becky dialed the number from memory and waited.. "Hi, Mom. I just got your message. It got here Thursday. I should have called, but I got busy…you know. It was great. Especially the glasses. Does this mean they're mine now or was it lend only?" Becky was quiet, listening for a few moments, her face becoming serious and concerned. "Has he left yet? Tell him to stay there. I'll get the kerosene. No, I'm closer and can be up there in less than two hours. He can get the pots started, and we'll fill when we get there." She listened again. "I'll be fine. I'll bring a friend to protect me. I promise. It's the place we used to stop for lunch? Ask for Alex. OK. I'll get as much as I can. Love ya. See you in a little while. Bye." Becky turned to John who was looking at her intently. "A little family crisis. The Napa Valley weather channel just forecast a possible frost tonight. Not good for the grapes. If it's heavy or extended, it could ruin the whole crop."

"So what do you need to do?"

"We have about two hundred and fifty smudge pots scattered throughout the vineyards. We light them, turn on the propeller fans, and hope that will stay the cold. Problem is, a lot of the pots are low on fuel, kerosene, so Dad was going to have to drive all the way to Oakland to get some tonight. I told him I would. Then he can get the others started. He and Mom." She looked at their dinner table, then at him. "I'm sorry."

"When do we leave?"

"You don't have to go. I'll be up all night."

"You think I would let you go to Oakland on a Friday night alone? Your father would probably kick my ass. You can't even be trusted in Larkspur." He smiled. "Besides I've got to work off the calories."

"You sure? I'm not really leaving you much choice. You don't have to."

"Do we have time to sit here and discuss this?"

"No, we don't." She went over and kissed him. "Thank you. Wear old clothes, the smudge pots are dirty. And pack some clean ones for when we're done." Five minutes later they were walking down the stairs, John wearing a pair of camouflage pants from an old set of camo BDUs (battle dress, utilities.) Becky went to her Mustang.

"If we're going to be hauling kerosene, don't you think we should take the truck? We can tie it down in the back. No fuss, no bother." There was complete logic in his suggestion, so she walked to the truck and got in.

"I'll pay for the gas."

John got in and looked at her. "You don't have to pay for gas. I didn't offer to pay for the veal. That would have been rude. You don't have to pay for gas." He started the truck and they were off. Becky didn't say anything. His curt comments caught her off guard, and she was a little hurt. She sat with her fingers clasped, looking ahead, not sure whether to get mad or apologize, not really wanting to do either.

"I'm sorry, babe. Don't be angry. I guess I feel like I should be going with you. That we, underline we, can help out somehow, and I don't need to be reimbursed for gas. I want to do this for you." It was quiet for a minute. "You know what I mean?" There was a long silence. "Becky?" He was beginning to feel like a real shit. "Now would be a great time to tell her I might be a homicidal maniac." he thought. "I could dump the body in Oakland. Shit!" And then, interrupting his troubling monologue, Becky slid across the seat and cuddled against his side, putting her head on his shoulder. John, having to leave his right hand free to shift gears, gave her knee a gentle squeeze and took her hand in his.

"Yes. I know," she whispered, not feeling a need to say more.

They drove on in comfortable silence until they hit the Bay Bridge. "You'll need to tell me where we're going." Becky was not sure of the route numbers, so she directed by pointing at other cars and turnoffs. They drove for about twenty minutes, their spat forgotten but stretching the making-up part.

Finally Becky pointed. "There. That truck stop." John pulled in past the gas pump and parked in front of a combination café and store. Several big rigs were parked nearby, bathed in the eerie mercury vapor light emanating from posts scattered around the lot. They went in and asked the tired-looking waitress for Alex. A middle-aged man in farmer-john overalls and a red shirt came out. "You the gal lookin' for the kerosene?"

"Yes. My dad spoke to you."

"Yup. Told him I'd hold four cans till midnight. They're five-gallon cans. Three ninety-five a can."

"How many cans you got?" John asked. "Besides the four."

"Got another eight."

"Can we buy some of those?"

"Sure. Told him I'd hold four. You got the money, you can buy more."

"Becky, how many would he need? I mean twenty gallons doesn't seem like much for two hundred and fifty smudge pots."

Becky looked at him and nodded. "Let's get more."

"We'll take ten altogether," John said to the man. "You're a real lifesaver, Alex."

Becky thrust a credit card at Alex and a look at John. "Take it out of this, please. And add two coffees, large." John smiled and backed off, hands held up. Alex took the card and motioned for them to get the coffee from the chrome urn. John started hauling the heavy cans out to the truck.

"You can use that hand truck back against the wall, fella. Be a little easier."

Ten minutes later they were on the road again, fifty gallons of kerosene lashed securely in the truck bed. Their relationship back on track, they talked the rest of the way, reminiscing about their interrupted dinner and making plans to do it again, maybe with Judy and Hank. Becky also explained in detail the problem a frost could bring and how they had to deal with it. How the pots were refueled and lighted. Shortly before midnight, they pulled into a long driveway and parked in front of what John thought was a beautiful, sprawling house. A half-moon provided enough light to just make out the rows of grape vines laid out in perfect geometric lines on the gentle, rolling hills surrounding the house and beyond.

John followed Becky into the house and through to the kitchen. An attractive woman in her midfifties greeted Becky with a hug and a warm smile. "Hi! I really appreciate your doing this, Rebecca. Your father is a little worried and would have been a nervous wreck driving to Oakland and then lighting off. You really saved the day for him." Emily Saunders looked past Becky at John. "Hello, I'm Emily Saunders."

Becky quickly picked up the introduction. "I'm sorry. Mom this is my friend John McConnell. John, this is my mother."

"Mrs. Saunders." John extended his hand and nodded. "Very nice to meet you."

"Well, they're not the best circumstances, but my husband and I appreciate your keeping Rebecca company through Oakland and all. I've got a pot of coffee on. Help yourself. I'll call Dad on his radio, find out where he is." She went into the next room and could be heard using a citizens'-band (CB) radio. A few moments later she was back in the kitchen. "He's in the south vineyard. Said to come on out and bring the kerosene. You two go ahead. I want to make some sandwiches for later. It will be a long night, I'm afraid. I'll be about twenty minutes."

"OK, Mom." Becky turned to John. "Let's go."

Ed Saunders had started lighting off pots. The flame from the pot warmed the vineyard, warding off the potentially damaging frost. It only took a few seconds to light one off but they were widely scattered throughout six separate vineyards. He was halfway finished. With help, the rest would be hot soon, and then they could concentrate on refueling. That would take a while, too. In the distance the CB in his truck squawked, demanding his attention. Again he walked back to the vehicle, annoyed at wasting precious time. "Yes, dear."

"They're on their way. I'll make sandwiches and bring a thermos for you."

"Who's with her? One of those college kids? Maybe the water boy for the girls' volleyball team?" He was frustrated and immediately regretted his pettiness. But some of the guys she brought home would not be much use tonight.

"I don't think he's a water boy, Ed."

"Oh? Why not?"

"He just doesn't look like a water boy. His name is John. Don't be rude. Remember, he went to Oakland with Rebecca, and you should be thankful for that."

"I am. I'll be nice. I'm always nice to her friends. Don't be long with those sandwiches. We need to get lit off." Ed waited by his truck watching for headlights. He reached in and turned his own on, sort of a homing beacon for his daughter. The headlights appeared and soon thereafter the rumbling of a big V-8 engine announced their arrival. A dark truck pulled up behind his and fell quiet. His eye went to the passenger door first when he heard his daughter call out, "Hi, Dad!" His heart always jumped when she came home, energetic and happy; she lit up the whole place. She came over and gave him a hug. Over her shoulder he saw a dark form emerge from the driver's side, move silently to the front of the truck, and stop with only the lower part of his body, in military pants, illuminated by the headlights. Ed could almost feel the presence, his senses sharpening toward this obviously benevolent but disturbing shadow. "Hi, sweetheart," he said to his daughter. "You get to stay up late tonight." He chuckled, recalling how, as a child, when she had done something good she was allowed to stay up later. Becky got the double meaning and laughed.

"Dad, I want you to meet John McConnell." Her head turned toward the shadow. "John, my father." The dark form moved closer, hand extended.

"Nice to meet you, sir." The calm, even voice came from a tall, well-built man whose eyes looked directly into Ed's. The eyes struck Ed immediately. He had seen eyes like that before, in the paratroopers and when his son returned from Vietnam. "Sir" and the pants confirmed military in Ed's first impression. The two men shook hands firmly. A red scar stood out on the young man's left cheek.

"Hello, John. I appreciate your looking after my daughter tonight. I guess you're kind of stuck for the duration."

"Glad I can help. We brought fifty gallons of kerosene. Figured five pots per gallon. Becky's been explaining things to me. Hope that's enough."

"That's great. Thank you…both," he said remembering his daughter. "Now. We have three more fields to light off: north, west, and Chardonnay. Mom and I will do west. You two do north and we'll meet up in Chardonnay to finish up. Then we'll have to start the refueling. That's gonna be the real pain in the ass in the dark, but we have to make sure they don't burn out before morning. I have head flashlights for you in my truck. That should make things a little easier. OK?"

"OK," Becky and John said in unison.

"Wouldn't you know this would happen when Martin and Julie are gone for the weekend. But who the hell knew?" Ed was referring to the couple who worked for him and lived in a cottage on the property. Becky and John got the flashlights, affixed them to their foreheads, and were off to the north vineyard. Becky showed John the smudge pot layout, and, in parallel, they moved rapidly down the rows lighting the wicks with oil-like cans with a small flame at the end of a long spout. An hour later all three fields were lit and the four of them stood in the dark bracing for the next round.

"Let's have a cup of coffee and a snack before we start again. Maybe that will perk us up." Emily suggested with the weight of a wife and mother. No argument. Emily brought out a basket with coffee cups, a thermos, and sandwiches wrapped in wax paper. They all climbed into the rear of Ed's truck, sitting on the sides of the bed as they rested and ate. There was a sense of unity among them, a unity that comes when people are working together unselfishly in crisis. Each was there because they wanted to be. No whining or complaining offered, no thanks asked for. There was small talk; now was not the time for probing questions or deep conversation. The food was good. As John ate his sandwich, he felt Becky's hand on the small of his back. Looking over at her, she gave him a smile, an acknowledgment of her gratitude. Her hand patted him. Neither Emily nor Ed saw the exchange but could not help but notice how comfortable their daughter was with this formidable man. He moved effortlessly in the dark and seemed to watch over her. "No, not a water boy," thought Ed. "She's got a tiger by the tail this time."

'

Ten minutes later, after the coffee and sandwiches had been consumed, Ed Saunders stood up and rallied the troops. "It's easier to work in teams," he explained. "One holds the funnel and relights; the other humps the kerosene and pours. Same teams?" Affirmative nods all around. "Take your time. We're in good shape. We're just reloading. If we see the pots start to go out, then we have to move quickly. Mom and I will start in the north vineyard, you two in the west. They're the lowest and heat rises. John, help me put a few of those cans in my truck. It might save some running around later." Without a word, the young man jumped over the side and walked to his truck. He handed out two cans to Ed and carried another two over himself. Ed handed him a smaller can, much like a watering can with a long spout. "Fill this up. It's lighter and easier to fill the pots." The two men looked at each other for a moment. "You ready, son?"

"Let's go," John replied. With that, the two teams were off. The Saunders watched their daughter move off into the darkness, only the beam from her headlamp visible, and that of her friend's. They exchanged glances, then they, too, started the task of refueling the pots that would protect their livelihood. The temperature was indeed dropping, precluding any thoughts of stopping or delaying. Becky and John quickly learned to avoid looking directly at one another. Doing so brought the beam from the flashlight right into the other's eyes, destroying whatever night vision had built up, making the work that much more tedious. However, after a while they found a rhythm and began to move rapidly through the west field. Finishing up in that vineyard, they went back to the truck, refilled, and drove to the Chardonnay vineyard, calling out to her parents their intention as they drove past. At about four am Becky yawned and rubbed her eyes. John suggested she take a rest, maybe a short nap in the truck. He would continue and wake her in a while. Becky's eyes hardened, any thoughts of sleep immediately gone. They would work together until it was finished. Period.

Somewhere around six thirty in the morning the four of them came together in the Riesling vineyard, the exhausting job completed. A light frost was evident but the smudge pots and propellers seemed to be protecting the plants. There was nothing more they could do. It was time for some sleep.

As they entered the house, Emily asked if anyone was hungry. No takers. She then suggested that Rebecca take a shower first, not using all the hot water. "John, I'll get the guest room ready for you. It will only take me a minute. I'll leave a fresh towel on the bed. You can have the next shower." The two women were gone, leaving Ed Saunders and John standing in the kitchen. John, in his camouflage pants, black smudge on his hands and face, eyes alert and watching even after the all-night effort, brought thoughts of the military back to Ed. They had not spoken since the women left the room, and it was becoming awkward.

Finally Ed extended his hand and said, "John, I really appreciate your help tonight. I don't know if we would have finished on time if I had to run to Oakland myself and then do all this. Thank you." They shook hands again. John was a little embarrassed. He said nothing, but he nodded. He liked this man and was intimidated only by the fact that he was Becky's father. "I think I'll shower in the morning." Ed rolled up his sleeves and washed in the sink. "Think you'll sleep good tonight?" "I'll manage to grab a few Zs. Be interesting to see the fields in the daylight. It's a beautiful home you have."

"I'm sure Rebecca will give you the grand tour. You have any questions, you just ask." Ed said drying his hands and arms then rolling his eyes at the dirt left behind on the once clean towel. "Emily will get on me for this. Oh well." He smiled. "Women are like that."

Emily returned with news that John's room was ready and Rebecca was out of the shower. Putting her arm around John, she began guiding him to his room. "C'mon, I'll show you where you'll sleep." The guest room was done in yellows and blues, with lace curtains and several decorative pillows on the bed. There was a wooden valet next to the bed, a small desk with a teller's lamp, and a screened potbellied stove in the corner next to the window. "Rebecca's out of the shower, so you can go right in. There's your towel." Emily fussed and pointed to the foot of the bed. "John, we appreciate all of your help. You sleep well now, and we'll have a good dinner later. Got everything?"

"I'm fine, Emily. Thank you."

"Good night, then, John." and she closed the door. John showered and was about ready to get into bed when there was a soft knock on the door. He opened the door to find Becky there in a long flannel nightgown. Her hair was still wet, and she smelled clean, though her eyes were tired. John opened the door wide, inviting her in, but she shook her head. "I just wanted to say good night. And thank you again." She leaned in and kissed him on the lips. He moved toward her, put his arms around her, and returned her kiss. Both backed off quickly, this was not the time or place for more than a good-night kiss. "See you in the...afternoon." She smiled. "G'night."

"Good night, Beck. Sleep tight."

John awoke and lay in bed for about ten minutes. Experience told him he would not fall back to sleep, so he got up and dressed in the clean clothes he had brought along. He opened his door and moved to the top of the stairs. He stopped and listened. The house was quiet. He went downstairs into the kitchen, where a pot of coffee was brewing. Taking a mug off a brass hook above the brewer, he poured a cup and wandered out into the living room. A grandfather clock chimed, the arms showing twelve thirty, just past noon. A slow blow over his mug cooled the coffee, and he ventured a sip. A voice from a chair by the window startled him, almost to the point of spilling his drink.

"Hello."

John turned to find an elderly woman, who had apparently been reading by the sunlight through the window, looking up at him with a question mark in her sparkling eyes. "I'm Nell. Emily's mother." She introduced herself then calmly waited to find out who this strange man was.

"Good morning, ma'am. I'm John McConnell. I'm a friend of Becky's."

There was no immediate recognition or response to John's explanation as the lady looked at him quizzically. Then her eyes lit up, and her whole face broke into a smile. "Of course. Rebecca. I haven't heard 'Becky' for such a long time I didn't recognize it. Well I'm Rebecca's grandmother. It's very nice to meet you. No one else is up yet. I put the coffee on. I see you found it. Good."

"Can I get you a cup, ma'am? It's ready."

"No, thank you, I have tea. Sit down. Were you here all night?'

"Yes, ma'am. I came up with Becky...Rebecca...about midnight. We got all the smudge pots filled and lit."

"Good. I was worried. A heavy frost will ruin a grape." The two talked for a while, John asking questions about the vineyards, Grandma Nell recounting her memories of starting the ranch many years ago with her husband. John was fascinated to hear firsthand the history and tradition that surrounded the family, this place, and the Napa Valley. Nell, a wealth of knowledge and a natural storyteller, was enjoying herself talking to this handsome, rapt audience. The story had been unfolding for at least forty-five minutes when John looked over and saw Becky standing in the opening to the kitchen sipping her coffee and listening to her grandmother's story but also watching the two of them so caught up. Now finally spotted, she entered the room, going to her grandmother and giving her a hug and a kiss.

"Hi, Gram. Please don't stop your story. I love hearing it, and I always learn something new." She moved over to John and sat on the floor beside him, resting her arm on his knee. Automatically he put his arm across her back and onto her shoulder. Now the two of them watched her, waiting for the story to continue. Nell was a little flustered, so suddenly and so clearly presented with Rebecca's relationship with this young man, whom she had never met or even heard about before. The two of them complemented one another perfectly, were obviously very much at ease with each other. Maybe this was Rebecca's young man. Perhaps another chapter in the family history was being written today. Nell smiled, collected her thoughts, and continued on, the story now taking on a slightly different tack as Nell recalled her husband, their courtship, and the wonderful life they had shared. This may not have been apparent to the young people sitting in front of her, because for them for the story was still facts and dates and adventures, but the joy of her life's journey, as she spoke, came across.

"Hello, Mother," Emily said as she entered the room about twenty minutes later. "When did you get here? Good morning, John. Rebecca."

"Josh Logan gave me a ride over this morning, about ten. I had a wonderful visit with Mr. McConnell here and was telling my granddaughter a little about how your father courted me fifty years ago."

"About how he chased you until you caught him." Rebecca laughed.

"I think I'll play Shaharazade, telling a little more of the story each time these youngsters come to visit me. Ha. Maybe that will be reason enough for them to stay home. Who wants to listen to an old lady babble about her youth?"

"Grandma Nell! It's really interesting."

'Well it's almost two o'clock. I have to go to the store. John, do you like prime rib?"

John looked up at her with a question in his eyes. "Is that a trick question?" Then he smiled. "Yes, ma'am, I do like prime rib. Very much." He glanced over at Becky and quickly added, "After veal parmesan, it's my favorite." Emily and Becky both smiled at his diplomacy.

"Why don't you show John around while I go to the store?" Emily suggested looking at Rebecca. "Mom, you can come with me, go with the kids, or wait for Ed. He'll be down in a minute."

"Come with us, Gram. You can tell us more about the old days."

"If I get going now, we can have supper at seven. Try not to snack too much."

Nell went with Becky and John. Ed caught up with them, and they surveyed the grapes for damage. It was almost impossible to determine at this point what damage, if any, had been done. That would be told when the wine was finished. But everything looked all right. Nell's story continued, each orchard with its own history and tradition and future. Ed went and got a buckboard, drawn by one of the two horses they still maintained, the other being Becky's paint. They opened a bottle of wine, sipping as they went.

Late in the afternoon Emily came out to join them for a drive around the Chardonnay vineyard, bringing with her a tray of pita chips baked beneath a mixture of mayonnaise, artichoke and grated Parmesan cheese. These did not last long. Emily and Ed held hands on the front seat, apparently having done this before. Nell basked in the full bloom of the courtship around her, her stories bringing her both joy and sadness in the telling.

Supper was served on schedule at seven o'clock, Emily timing the Yorkshire pudding, the spinach soufflé, and the prime rib perfectly. A bottle of reserve Cabernet was opened and poured into Waterford crystal glasses. John could see where Becky got her fine dining training. Ed hoisted his glass. "To the grapes. May we always keep them out of harm's way." Everyone toasted the grapes. Crystal tinkled richly as arms stretched to reach, and eyes searched out all other eyes.

Emily then followed suit, holding up her glass in another toast. "To the Chardonnay vineyard at sunset. May it always remain beautiful and pristine." Again everyone sipped at their wine, each quietly imagining the trysts that must have, in their youth, taken place amongst the grapes. "John," continued Emily, "It's traditional at a special supper for everyone at the table to make a toast. I guess it's our way of saying grace."

"Five or six toasts also loosen things up, and everyone has a more enjoyable evening," Ed added with a chuckle. "That's if they don't fall off their chair first."

Then Grandma Nell held her glass out in front of her. "To Ed and Emily, who carry on the tradition. Who watch over the grapes." A more somber nodding and a slightly longer sip.

"Thank you, Mom. That was sweet." Becky toasted Grandma Nell and Grandpa Frank for starting the vineyards.

Now it was John's turn. All eyes were on him, waiting. "To Becky. For letting me share a moment of this wonderful place with her." Becky pressed her lips together to fight off a tear. She was proud of John and happy that he fit in with the people she loved so much. In fact, everyone smiled, and more than one of the women fought off tears. The rescue of the grapes, the nostalgic storytelling in the buckboard, the very spring in the air made everyone ripe for romance.

As Ed put his glass down, he cast a mischievous eye at his daughter. "Becky." He started slowly. Becky saw what was coming, the shift from Rebecca back to plain old Becky. She gave her father a pleading look, begging him with her eyes not to embarrass her. Not now. Please. Ed never could refuse his little girl and this time was no different. "Our beautiful little girl has grown into a beautiful woman." he finished. Becky blushed red and wished he had done the Rebecca routine.

"Hear! Hear!" came from around the table. Everyone watched not only Becky, but John as well.

Becky recuperated with, "Dad, does this mean we have to do another round of toasts? Can we at least eat a little first?"

"Yes, we can. Ed, you cut the rib. Mom, why don't you start the salad around." Emily put an end to the gaming, to the delight of everyone. Conversation slowed as overflowing plates were set down in front of the hungry group. The women kept up the banter, thoroughly enjoying themselves, while the men plowed into the beef and wiped the yorkshire into the red drippings and gravy. Now the Cabernet came into its own, embellished and embellishing, the wine and beef greater than the sum of their parts.

As the feeding slowed, Ed asked, "So, John, you were in the military, no?"

"Yes, sir. Navy."

"Navy, eh. Get over to Vietnam? My son was there in '67."

"Yes, sir. I did a couple of tours there."

"On a ship?"

"No, not really. I was attached to a Seal team based out of Coronado." Ed saw that John was mildly uncomfortable talking about this.

"Never heard of Seals. Is that something new?"

"Seals grew out of the old UDT units. They do a little more nowadays."

"I remember the UDT guys."

"What's UDT?" Nell asked.

"Underwater Demolition Teams," Ed responded quickly. "They would go in and clear the beaches for the army and marines. They were just getting started back in my day. Pretty tough bunch." He looked at John, who took a mouthful of spinach soufflé.

"Dad was in the paratroopers, John, the 101st Airborne. He was at Bastogne during the Battle of the Bulge." Becky looked at her Dad proudly.

"Nuts," John said. "He really said 'nuts'?" The question was esoteric, but Becky's father had been there. He would understand. John looked at Ed Saunders in a new light—as one who would understand.

"That's what they say. I will say it was sure nice to see old Georgie Patton's boys come clankin' up the road. I was a young staff sergeant then. Is anyone ready for more meat?" The supper went on, culminating with a dessert of fresh sliced fruit topped by a dollop of freshly whipped cream and accompanied by a late-harvest dessert wine. The telephone rang with news that Martin and his wife were back They had heard about the frost and knew there would be work to do.

"We better be going soon, then." Becky surprised them all. "I have a million things to do at home, and you have reinforcements."

"Why not stay the night and get an early start in the morning?" Emily asked.

"No. We'll come up again. Maybe do a little wine tasting. Oh! John, you know what we forgot to bring?" John shrugged and shook his head in the negative. "For Dad. It's in the freezer. We got it with Judy and Hank." Recognition set in, and John nodded.

"What's that?" Ed inquired.

Becky looked at John as if to ask, "Should we tell him?'" John shrugged again.

"John got abalone for you. In the rush I forgot to bring it up. It's in the freezer, so it's OK. He got a full limit for you. I told him how much you like it."

"No kidding? Well I guess that's one of the benefits of having a professional diver around. I look forward to it. Now you two have to hurry back."

By ten o'clock, Becky and John were on the road home. Becky had moved over close to John but was quiet, letting John talk about the vineyards and her family. The drive went by quickly and comfortably. John inquired about why she had to get back tonight. "There's just something I want to do. I'll explain later." That was all he got out of her. The Latin beat of Santana's "Black Magic Woman" perked them up as they entered the city, still alive with Saturday night couples, and singles hoping to become couples. The truck turned into the parking area and slid to a stop in the 303 stall. Becky's Mustang was still in the guest stall. She looked over at John. "May I come up? I still need to clean up a little."

"Of course you can come up. But I can clean up. You cooked. Now take it easy."

They worked together on the few dishes that remained from the night before. Becky still more quiet than usual. When the dishtowel was finally hung up, the kitchen clean, Becky said in an uncharacteristically serious tone. "John. I want to tell you something. Remember last night? We sort of lost it for a minute? Actually I was the one who lost it. And you said that it would happen when the time was right for both of us."

John was looking at her and nodded.

"Well I've thought about that a lot, even though it's only been twenty-four hours. And I want to tell you that I'm ready. I'm comfortable with it. I'm not very comfortable saying this, but I want you to know that's the way I feel." She took a long, deep breath, exhaling slowly, watching him, searching for a reaction. She saw concern and fear fill his face and eyes. Something was not right. This was not the response she expected. Doubts rushed into her mind.

The time had come for John. It was no longer his choice of time and place. He had to tell her about himself... and maybe lose her. He felt sick. "Becky, there are some things you should know about me. About the kind of person I am. Or might be."

"I know what kind of person you are, John. You're a good person. Strong and reliable. Gentle and kind. You're a person I trust."

"But there are things I've done that maybe you wouldn't approve of."

"Like what?" Becky was trying to understand but was failing miserably. Was he married? What could he have done?

"Like in the war."

"Vietnam! Oh God! He hasn't come back yet!" The thought flooded her mind. "He feels guilty about Vietnam."

"Vietnam?" she said aloud.

He looked into her eyes, his pain visible. "Yes." He wanted to say more; to explain, but couldn't find words that didn't sound horrible. "You have a right to know." The powerful feelings of sadness and fear of losing this woman rose up inside him. The mask he had developed to hide such feelings also made its appearance, disguising his face with a facade of both ferocity and calmness, so disconcerting to enemies in battle, now so confusing to this woman before him. He would have liked to cry but couldn't. To tell her, to show her how much he cared for her.

Becky took another deep breath. Her eyes hardened and filled with resolve. "John McConnell, you listen to me. My father was a paratrooper in World War Two. He killed people for his country. My brother was a marine in Vietnam. He killed people because his country asked him to. You went to Vietnam because the country says we have to be there. You killed people, too. It's a shitty war. A lousy thing to have to do. I love my father. I love my brother. I love you. And I won't let this goddamned war stop my love. I think you love me, too. Whatever you are"— she paused for just a moment—"I love you." They looked at each other, Becky's eyes moist with relief, hope and fear. She had said everything she could say. It was his turn. Everything hung in the balance.

John listened to her words. She understood his concern. At least most of it. To hear the words "I love you" from the lips of this woman made his knees go weak. The words made the thought of losing her a nonoption. An untenable concept. Tension and fear began to fall away from him like weights. He reached over, took Becky's head in his hands, and drew her to him, kissing her softly on the mouth. Her arms went around him, squeezing him, their kiss becoming more firm, more passionate. His hand came up the back of her neck, his fingers slipping through her hair pressing her against his mouth. The time, suddenly, was right for both of them, and both recognized the moment and its consequence. The delicious consequence, moving them closer to where they wanted to be physically and emotionally. Neither had been here before, nor would they ever be here again—first love's first journey into the spirit-body of your lover, in its truest sense.

Their kiss was a conduit for all of their feelings: desire, impatience, patience, to please and be pleased, to connect. The conduit flowed both ways, flowing faster as the volume of feelings grew. The rush of happiness caused them each in turn to momentarily close their eyes, to rest passively, receiving, nurturing the pleasure, only to renew their efforts to give back to the other. John reached down behind Becky's knees, picking her up, his lips never leaving hers. Her arms were around his neck, her body against his, tingling, anticipating his touch, tightness in her chest making it difficult to breathe. He carried her into the bedroom and lay down on the bed with her still in his arms. Their bodies pressed together.

Both started to unbutton the other, unsuccessfully in the tangle of nervous hands and fingers. John finally stood up and began to take off his clothes. Becky, in bed, did the same until they were down to their undergarments. There they hesitated, their modesty making them smile at each other. They came together, their bare skin heightening their sensitivity and anticipation. Again they kissed, mouths open, tongues probing gently. John rolled, bringing Becky on top of him. His fingers undid her bra—quite expertly, Becky recalled later—his hands sliding from her back to her sides and finally onto her breasts. Becky rose up slightly allowing him to move his fingers and palms over her and then onto her nipples. The sensation was almost overwhelming, yet nothing like what was to come. He pushed her body up and moved his head down to her chest, taking her nipple into his mouth, gently sucking and licking the hard, red nipple and the soft white flesh beneath it. Becky fed him all that he wanted, moving him back and forth between the two, rubbing them against his face.

His left hand slipped beneath the elastic of her panties and caressed her backside, his finger dragging along the crease between her buttock and thigh. Becky now moved down and began licking and nibbling at his breasts. They began, almost simultaneously, to pull down each other's pants, leaving them fully exposed, fully available. John again drew her on top of him, their now bare bodies generating more heat, the new warmth stimulating their passion and discovery. Becky could feel him, his penis, enlarged and hard, pressing against her. Their bodies slowly began to move against each other, mouths together, hands exploring, caressing. Their hips were now in the vanguard of exploration, each making minute adjustments, signaling and positioning themselves for the other. Becky could feel him hard against her and maneuvered to accommodate him. Then she felt him find her opening. She could feel him throb, pulse. She moved again, and the tip of his erection caressed the length of her, now half buried, both of them enjoying the search for their long-awaited coming together. She half sat up on him, her knees straddling his body. She raised herself, and suddenly he was inside of her. His hands caressed her breasts. His eyes were closed. Both moved their hips back and forth, each movement allowing more penetration. They would withdraw slightly then come back together, a little deeper, a little closer. Natural juices began to flow and, in a single, wonderful moment, the full length of his erection slid inside of her. She moaned then moved to bring the coupling to its deepest and most tantalizing union. His hands on her breasts went to her shoulders and he pulled her down to him. They kissed. Their bodies moving so slowly, savoring the bursts of pleasure their nerve endings sent with each movement. John did not want this to end. Each movement was blissful, each a precursor to an explosion of delight. John let Becky direct the pace and positioning, her climax more difficult to attain, her head now buried into his neck, her body shifting, exploring this wonderful place. His fingers ran through her hair, lightly scratching her back with his nails, mapping the contours of her body in his mind. His lips kissing and nuzzling her neck; her scent stronger and more alluring than ever before.

Becky was mesmerized, lost in the pleasure of him inside of her. Each slight movement of her hips created a powerful, wonderful sensation, beyond anything she had ever encountered before. Time was in slow motion. Then there was nothing but intrinsic pleasure, rising like a tsunami. Her breath was short, her body shaking. Her orgasm was imminent, unstoppable now. She started to move faster, bringing John along with her as part of her being, part of her climax. Taking her lead, John too began now to move, still slowly but with purpose. Becky began to moan, her hands grabbing at his body, squeezing. Her head fell back, her breasts jutting out, magnificent and beautiful, her whole body quivering. John moved faster, in and out, long deliberate strokes, Becky convulsing in ecstasy. John, about to climax, pulled Becky to him, his lips full on her mouth. Realizing his moment had also come, she returned his kiss and John exploded into her, his body now contracting involuntarily with the sensations her touch brought to him. Becky felt his juices warm within her, mixing with hers. The time was right. He was right for her, and she loved him so much. She contracted her muscles, trying to draw him deeper; to tell him she wanted him there. She felt his body shudder and twitch, and she contracted her muscles again, squeezing his shaft, wishing she could see it, touch it.

Their moment sealed, the physical slowly relinquishing its hold on their spirits, calmness, a peace flooded over them, sweat from their lovemaking now cooling them. Looking into each other's eyes, seeing a friend … like no other. A happiness and contentment. They kissed softly, John pulling the cover over their cooling bodies. His hand softly caressed her breast, her eyes closing to enjoy his pleasure as well as her own. "That's why I wanted to come home tonight," she whispered. "To tell you the time was right."

CHAPTER ELEVEN

Chico Correctional Facility, Chico, California.

June 1969

Rodney Harris walked through the gates of the correctional facility and across the simmering pavement to the two men sitting on Harleys. Although it was almost eighty degrees, with the promise of higher temperatures later on, the two men wore black leather pants and leather vests over bare skin. The vests advertised their gang affiliation with the Road Warriors; maybe Hell's Angels wannabes. Rodney—although no one had called him that ever that he could remember—sauntered over and acknowledged the two who had come to get him and take him home. He had spent the last three months locked up for illegal gun possession and possession of cocaine, the offshoot of that run-in with the girl in Larkspur, the cheap-shot artist who brought about his downfall, and the cops' subsequent search of his bike. He had gone over the accounts of that day in his mind a lot in jail and had convinced himself that he would have kicked that guy's ass if not for a lucky, cheap shot. If he ever came across him again, things would turn out differently, of that he was certain.

"Hey Crash. Hotshot. Thanks for comin'." The two men nodded as they examined their buddy for any sign of a bad jail time experience. "Let's get out of this shithole. I'm buyin' the beer," he announced as he swung his leg over the back of Crash's wheels. "Let's get my bike first. I feel like a damn broad sittin' on the back." The three of them laughed as they roared away from their home away from home.

"Not a whole lot of broads in Chico, eh, Boomer?" Crash inquired. "Not any good-lookin' ones, anyway." He laughed, aware of the rampant homosexuality inside the joint. Crash didn't think Boomer would go for that, but in stir anything could happen and, if you were in long enough, it usually did. Tonight would be a howler, with Boomer makin' up for lost time. The plan was to peddle some dope, get some cash, and go raise some hell. They would have to be a little cautious, or it would be slammer time again. Their choppers and clothing advertised their lawlessness anyway, brought attention without them having to do anything. But there were always bars that catered to their ilk and women who were attracted to the bikes, the aura of violence, and the likelihood of a wild party. When you played on the edge you sometimes fell or got knocked off, and then you went to Chico or Lompac or Folsom, or even San Quentin, and paid the price. These men were sort of the counterparts of the love children of the day. Society—the nine-to-five, white-picket-fence, two-point-three children, a puppy, and a hefty mortgage kind of society—just wasn't their cup of tea. They wanted to drink, get laid, fight, and be on the edge. Fuck what everybody else thinks. For many, this was a lifestyle choice and, in their own way, they had a good life. For others, like Rodney Harris, aka Boomer, it was a vent for ignorance, meanness, and an inability to do anything else.

An hour later, the bikes rumbled through the town of Vallejo and into the courtyard of what had once been a cheap motel, now converted to cheap apartments. Chopped Harley Davidsons were the prominent vehicles parked outside, some belonging to visitors and some to residents. If Rodney had a home, this would be it, although he wasn't on a lease or rental agreement. He kept his few things here, threw in some rent money when he was flush, and slept on a bare mattress in apartment number six. Connie, a twenty-six-year-old woman with two children and a drinking problem, also lived in apartment six. She was not Rodney's woman, but she slept with him, and several others, whenever they wanted to get their rocks off. The father of the children was a sort of mystery even to Connie, but this was her way of paying rent and providing some semblance of home and family for several who had nothing else. She worked part time in a supermarket and occasionally hooked when money was tight. She fed and clothed her children, saw they went to school most of the time. and that was good enough. When she saw Boomer on the back of Crash's bike, she knew there would be some rough sex. That was all right with her; she just hoped it wouldn't get out of hand. Put her in the emergency room again. It wouldn't be so bad if it weren't for the kids.

"Hey, Connie, baby." Boomer embraced her with a big hug. He had been enjoying the ride, the noise, the wind in his face. Now the touch of a woman—the soft skin, the scent—set him off, reminding him of his long abstinence from the real McCoy. Trying to be nonchalant, he caressed her arms and back. Joking with the guys and chugging a half a can of beer without even thinking about it, he could feel his loins twitching. He wanted to screw Connie, or anybody, bad. "Where's the kids?"

"In school, where they should be. Good to see you, Boomer. Miss me?" she teased. She was going to get laid, so she might as well take the lead and get some gratitude out of it, so at least she could feel she wasn't being raped. That happened sometimes if you got technical about definitions. She put her hand into Boomer's back pocket and squeezed his buns. "Come on inside. I got somethin' to show ya." Her leer was unmistakable.

Rodney winked at the guys. "This shouldn't take too long. I'll be out in about thirty seconds." Heads nodded, smiles. Hey, a guy just outta stir had to get laid. Some of the guys looked around for their women—or any available woman. Funny how once you started thinking about it, it kinda took control. Connie took the edge off, perhaps enough to keep them out of the slammer.

Later that afternoon, six Road Warriors rolled out of the apartment complex with waves from the women and children, dust and gravel kicked up by the scratching wheels of the big Harleys. and the thunderous noise of six powerful motorcycles all accelerating up to the red line was always guaranteed to catch the attention of passing motorists. who did everything they could to stay out of the way but, deep down, a few of them envied the excitement and adventure of the gang and wished they could ride, just once, on the back of the beast, carefree, not giving a shit about tomorrow. The six represented a little less than half the total membership, although there were always a few squirrels hanging around trying to join up. This contingent was off to a bar, any bar, for drinks and trouble. Not serious trouble, but enough to scare the crap out of some civilians and have something to talk about tomorrow. Nobody would get hurt, discounting of course, broken noses, black eyes, chipped teeth, or cracked knuckles.

Boomer, on the other hand, was the kind who enjoyed inflicting pain for its own sake and didn't know when to stop. Even Crash, the unofficial leader of the Warriors, had had occasion to pull Boomer off some poor bastard trying to protect his girlfriend or family. Crash knew sooner or later Boomer would get into serious trouble and maybe take a few of the members down with him. But that was part of life on the edge. What kept Boomer in line was the fact that the Warriors were all he had, and he knew Crash would kick him out, maybe kill him, if he got too far out of line. On the positive side, everyone knew Boomer was a good man to have with you in a rumble. He would not quit and he could definitely kick ass. Crash thought Boomer to be certifiably crazy, but so were three or four other guys in the gang. Hell, better than a bunch of love-beaded hippies preaching peace, driving around in a piece-of-shit Volkswagen van.

Boomer wanted to head over to Marin, maybe find the asshole who sucker punched him. Crash declined, opting for Oakland, a place a little more tolerant of bikers and a little closer to home. Some of the other members would join them later, and there was more action in Oakland. Boomer acquiesced, maybe subconsciously remembering the man with the eyes who had stood over him waiting for him to get up. As the six cruised north along the highway, enjoying their road celebrity, Boomer patted his saddle-bag, feeling the hardness of a .45 automatic he had tucked away, just in case. "Next time, asshole, you go down," he thought. "Hard."

CHAPTER TWELVE

San Francisco, California

June 1969

Becky and John awoke almost simultaneously, the movements of one silently signaling to the other. They made love again; slowly savoring each other, each reaffirming that this was not a dream but real. For both the aftermath of their sexual union was fulfilling, satisfying, and an immediate realization that what had been missing in their lives before was now theirs. This was what they had both been seeking: an emotional, spiritual caring about their partner that carried beyond the sexual act and into the future. Things had moved quickly over the last few weeks, and they needed to catch up with their emotions, to stabilize and try to define their relationship both to themselves and to one another.

Love, whether the puppy love of teenagers or a mature love rooted in years of sharing, seems wonderful and eternal. But it isn't always so. Thus, in conversation, the two lovers spoke with a long-range sense of permanence that only time would prove correct. For now, life was incredibly full and happy; the future bright. They showered together, still touching and nuzzling one another, waiting impatiently, with as much graciousness as they could muster, for hormones to regenerate John's capacity for lovemaking. He made a pot of coffee and offered to make crepes; a thin pancake sprinkled with cinnamon and sugar then rolled up and served with, perhaps, a dollop of whipped cream. They talked, more straightforward now, learning about these two individuals who were now a couple.

"Your folks are really nice. I can see why you go up there as often as you do," John said blowing over the top of his navy coffee cup. Becky nodded in agreement, smiling as she thought of her dad's parting aside to her. "He seems like a fine young man. You bring him home anytime."

"Well, I look forward to meeting your folks and Jennifer. Too bad they're so far away," Becky responded, really looking forward to meeting and befriending John's sister. "Didn't you say she might come out for the summer? That would be fun. How old is she again?"

"Fourteen. And I said she wanted to come out, not that she was coming. I don't know if I could handle her for a summer."

"Chicken." Becky laughed. "She'd spend more time with me than with you."

The telephone rang. John answered to Hank Cooper on the other end. The two men spoke briefly, John turning to Becky after a few moments. "Hank says hello. Judy wants to talk to you."

Becky took the receiver. "Hello, Judy? How are you? Yes, I do spend a lot of time here," she said laughing, looking over at John. "These navy guys are pretty fast operators. They seem real nice, but they are slick. I don't think we have any plans for breakfast." Becky looked over at John, shrugging her shoulders in a question about his feelings on brunch with the Coopers.

"Whatever you want is fine," he whispered in response.

"OK, Judy. We'll see you in a bit. Can I bring anything? OK. Bye." Becky came back to the table, sat down, and sipped her cup of coffee. "They want us to come over for coffee and homemade jelly donuts. She sounded excited. Maybe they found their dream house. Anyway, they have to be at her folks' at two, so we won't be all day. OK?" She made a little-girl face, smiling, looking for something from John that the decision was all right.

"I was hoping to keep you in bed all day." Head down, he looked up with raised eyebrows and a forlorn face with just the hint of a smile.

Becky broke into a full grin. "I was hoping you would, too. Now I'll have to be content with a jelly donut."

They dressed and headed out for the twenty-minute drive to their friends. Becky asked John to stop at a florist so she could pick up a small bouquet of flowers. Always bring a small gift when you visit, Becky's mother had taught her. It shows you care. Without question John found a florist and pulled the truck into a parking spot half a block away. He accompanied her into the shop, watching her as she talked with the clerk, and perused the colorful bunches of cut flowers. Somehow Becky seemed different. More attractive; more graceful; more confident. "Maybe," thought John, "it's me that's different. Maybe I'm seeing things more clearly. God, she is beautiful." The flowers selected and paid for, they moved back out onto the sidewalk and toward the truck. John leaned over and whispered something he had not yet verbalized to Becky yet. "I love you." Becky's eyes opened wider, and she looked into his eyes as they walked. Her face broke into a broad smile. "I know you do, John." She took his hand, squeezing it. "I know you do," she repeated. Another couple, walking toward them, smiled as if to acknowledge their contribution to the love permeating the San Francisco air. The couples nodded at each other and went on.

There were hugs and handshakes all around, Hank and Judy radiating as much joy as Becky and John. This atmosphere of open joy was so foreign to John that it was almost like a dream of a strange and distant land. He himself was incredibly happy and recognized that he was a part of this group; whatever he might be contributing, it was coming back to him threefold. "This must be the 'world' we talked about in Nam," he thought. "This is why we fight."

"I lied about the homemade jelly donuts," Judy explained with a giggle. "But we wanted to see you. Hank did get some at the bakery so it was just a white lie. The flowers are beautiful. Thank you." She hugged both of them, ostensibly for the flowers, but there was more to the embrace than simple thanks.

"Well, you guys are sure up to something," Becky noted. "Either that or you've been eating groovy brownies. Whatever it is, tell us." Becky could feel their excitement. It made you feel happy when your friends were happy, so the whole group was lifting off on a wonderful natural high. "We think it's a house. You found your dream house. Are we right?"

"Here. Get some coffee and a donut and come in and sit down. No, it's not a house." They shuffled around the kitchen, Hank pouring coffee while Judy doled out mounds of white powdered sugar covered pastry with a blotch of red filling on the end of each one. Judy kept looking up at Becky and grinning, like someone who had a secret that would knock your socks off and could barely contain herself. Hank apologized to John for not offering a beer, but it was, after all, just a little early. Seated finally in the small but brightly lighted living room, Judy took center stage. She looked at Hank, who sat beside her on the arm of the easy chair. "Do you want to tell them?" Hank smiled and rolled his eyes slightly, shaking his head. "No, dear, you tell them." He looked over at John and shrugged his shoulders, suggesting there was no way in the world he could reveal the news and still remain married. Judy looked at Becky then at John and back to Becky. She took a deep breath. "Hank and I are going to have a baby. We found out on Thursday."

There was a moment of silence, everyone watching everyone else for reaction. Becky was the first to respond. "Ooh, Judy! That's wonderful. That's fantastic!" The two women stood and hugged, tears welling in their eyes.

"Hank, you old snake. That's what happens when you shoot live bullets, man. Congratulations, buddy. You're gonna be a poppa. Damn, that's great." The two men shook hands and finally switched off and hugged the women, who were both radiant. The talk of boy or girl, due date, did their parents know, a new urgency about a house, and work went on for about an hour. Coffee was warmed up; back slaps and hugs continued as the donuts disappeared. "Judy will be a good mother," thought Becky. "You can almost see a sense of responsibility growing. A maturity evolving." Thoughts of family snuck in and out of Becky's mind as she talked with her friend. A glance at John fanned these thoughts to the point that Judy said, "Becky. Did you hear me? We were talking breast-feeding."

"I'm sorry. My mind was wandering. What about breast-feeding?"

"You were thinking about babies, weren't you?" Judy said softly. Becky nodded, her eyes telling the story. "You know, women don't start thinking about babies like that until they have a sense of who the father is going to be. You and John have come together, haven't you? It's written all over both of you. You guys make a great couple. And here I am, all wrapped up in me."

"No, Judy. The baby is wonderful. It's the best. You and Hank are a couple of steps ahead of us. Maybe I see a little of John and me in you guys. I hope we can be as happy as you."

"Well someday, when we both have a bunch of kids running around tearing things up, we'll remember today. We'll watch our men go under for abalone, we'll still worry about them, and we'll do the same for each of our kids. Worry and enjoy. Come on. Give me a hug." The two women embraced again, their bond, their friendship strengthening.

On the way back to the apartment, John and Becky were subdued in their conversation, each thinking about the future, fantasizing about all the possibilities and the growing importance of the person sitting next to them. "Have you ever thought about children, John?" Becky asked.

"Not really. Not until now. I like kids. I guess it would be nice to have a few."

"A few?"

"Well it would be nice to have brothers and sisters, wouldn't it? I mean from the kid's perspective. It might be more difficult for the parents, but you'd have all these built-in buddies. Lot's of activity. What do you think?"

Becky hesitated. "I was thinking about a child. I mean, having a child. The process of carrying and delivering and holding your own child. What that would be like? I wasn't thinking about a whole family. But I guess it would be nice to have a bunch of them." Judy's words about a bunch of kids came back to her. "Their parents would have to be patient. Maybe give up some things. My folks would go nuts with grandchildren! Can you see them up there?"

John looked away from the road to the woman beside him. He wanted to pull to the side of the street and make the whole family right now. Before it all disappeared. Put the kids in the back of the truck with a dog, maybe a beagle, a cooler of soda pop, and a bag of chips. They could all drive to Stinson Beach and build sand castles, surf cast for salmon, and beachcomb for washed-up treasures. Instead he caught Becky's eye and, without words, exchanged thoughts with her. They would still have to struggle with the words and the timing as they discovered of one another, but the end result flashed between them, becoming a silent, guiding goal. "I love this woman. I would kill for her." His old fear now surfaced as an ally. A tool at his disposal to defend and protect her. Her family. Their family. He didn't think it would ever come to that, but it was there, in case. He chuckled to himself as he thought about perspective and how it turned evil into good and vice versa.

Becky's voice broke into his thoughts, bringing reality delightfully back to him. "Don't you think my folks would spoil them silly?" She smiled at him. "Can you see my dad riding them around in the buckboard all over the vineyards?" She looked at him again, waiting for a response but getting none. His face held that implacable, impossible to read look she had seen before. A dangerous look. Confusing to her. Then he looked over at her, and his eyes opened to her. She felt, more than saw, a rush of feeling pour from him. The concept of children, their children, their family filled her, and she knew it would happen one day. She had found her soul mate, the father of her children, the man she would share her life with. He had just told her. Someday he would say the words, but they almost didn't matter. At that moment, she knew that her path was his path.

They pulled into the 303 parking stall. John turned off the ignition, and they both sat there. John reached over and gently pulled her to him. They kissed with all of the magic that new love can bring to two people. Their spirits were melding. In the apartment they came together again to make love, to get closer, to give to the other, fed by this new aspect in their relationship, a gift from the Coopers.

Shortly after one o'clock, Becky decided to run to the supermarket in preparation for dinner. "Any preference?" she asked. "How about a chef's salad? It's light, healthy, and easy."

"Sounds great. Would you get some beer? Budweiser. And let me give you some money."

"That's OK. I'll get it."

"You know, we need to talk about this. You don't have to buy all the food. You're on a tighter budget than I am. We need to figure out how we'll work it. OK?"

"OK. You pick up my birth-control pills and feminine-hygiene products next time you go to the store. That'll about balance it out." They both laughed. John remembering the embarrassment the first time he bought a rubber at the drugstore and then laughing even more. "You know what I mean. Don't mess with me, woman."

Becky had gone a little wild at the store. getting two six packs, fruit, hard bread, and cheese, all the makings for the salad, and eggs and bacon and cereal for breakfast. As she struggled getting the groceries out of the Mustang, a motorcycle rumbled into the parking area and into an empty spot not marked with parking stripes. Two men in colored T-shirts and blue denim jeans dismounted and looked around. Spotting Becky, they walked over. Both men looked hard, almost scary, but the one in front smiled as he approached. "You look like you could use some help with those packages, ma'am. Be my pleasure to give you a hand."

"I think I can manage. But thank you."

"Be no problem at all. My buddy and I are from out of town. Here to visit an old friend. He's somewhere in these apartments. If you have a sister or a good-lookin' roommate, maybe we could all go out and have dinner. See San Francisco."

Becky saw the close-trimmed haircuts and close shaves on the two men. The look reminded her of John when she first met him. "Who are you looking for? What apartment?"

"John McConnell. Apartment 303. He's a good guy. I'm Dave. This is Jack. We're up from Coronado. Down by San Diego."

"These guys are some of his navy buddies," Becky thought to herself. She smiled, almost laughed before saying, "You know, maybe you can help me with this stuff. It'll save me a trip. And I do have a roommate. Follow me." The three of them went up the steps, Constanza turning back to wink at Jack Thompson, who nodded in the affirmative. Once again he was amazed at Constanza's ability to come up with the women. And this one was for sure a fox. They got to the third level and went left to the end apartment. As Becky's hand went for the doorknob, Constanza noticed the 303 on the door. "Ooh, great!" He exclaimed. "This is 303. McConnell's place. Then you must be Becky."

Becky smiled and nodded. "Gotcha."

Thompson burst into laughter as Constanza's dilemma loomed up.

Constanza moaned, "Oh, boy. I haven't seen McConnell in four months, and the first thing I do is hit on his girl. Oh, this ought to be fun."

Becky, laughing along with Thompson, gave Constanza a break. "Dave, I won't tell if you won't. Deal?" she said, holding out her hand. Dave shook her hand, nodding. And suddenly the door opened from the inside, and McConnell was there. "We have guests, John."

After hearty handshakes and greetings, four beers were popped and the three men started talking story. How's Retino? How's Friendly's leg? Jack, how's your eardrum? When is the platoon going out again? John's emotions were on a roller-coaster ride this day, and he recognized it. Between his finding of Becky the night before, the morning with Hank and Judy, and now these comrades from his old world, it was a fantastic journey bringing old and new lives together. He was glad Becky could meet his friends and they her. He didn't realize how proud of her he was. And he didn't realize how much he missed his comrades-in-arms, and the action they had been through together, and how clear the memories were.

"What brings you guys this far north?" John asked, curious about his friends' arrival.

"We're up here on a bullshit career counseling school at Treasure Island. Oops. Pardon my French, Becky."

"Hey, John. You know Friendly's retiring. His leg hasn't really healed up right, so he's taking a 50 percent disability and getting out with twenty years. He just announced it, so you'll be getting an invitation to the retirement party," Jack Thompson related. "Maybe we could have our retirement parties together."

"How bad is his leg?"

"Probably be fine for a civilian. But he'd be draggin' it along on patrol in the U Minh."

"Where do we find all these great-lookin' San Francisco women I've been hearin' about?" Constanza, ever on the prowl, queried. "You guys got any suggestions?"

"I could call my roomies. See if they're free." Becky could see Cathy and the man called Jack as a good pair. "I'll give them a call. Where do you want to go? John, any suggestions?"

John looked up, eyebrows raised. "How about we go over to Sausalito. Maybe the turtle races at Zack's or the Cat N Fiddle. That whole town pops on Sunday afternoon. And I hear there are sometimes some nice ladies around." He winked at Constanza. "They hang around after church for a few beers."

Dave Constanza smiled and looked up at Becky. "Sausalito it is, ma'am."

Several minutes later Becky was back with the news. "Cathy will be ready in fifteen minutes. We can pick her up on the way. Charlene wasn't home. Maybe she went to church over there this morning, and we'll meet her in the bar." She looked at John with mock indignation.

"OK. Let's go!" John said as he stood. "We'll take my truck."

"Why don't I follow you so we'll have extra wheels if we need them," Jack suggested. "You never know." he added sheepishly.

They knocked down their beers and bustled out the door and down the steps to the parking lot. "I borrowed a motorcycle from a buddy of mine at the base. I'll follow you but give me directions just in case," Jack suggested to John. The two of them walked over to the bike, John explaining how to get over the Golden Gate and down to Sausalito. "OK. Got it. I'll follow you anyway. Hey, John. I think you owe me a beer."

John looked over. "How's that, Jack?"

"Remember when we would sit and talk? You were worried that you would never find a good woman who would accept you and your black, murderous heart? I told you then that you would. And it looks like I was right. That good advice ought to be worth at least a beer, my friend."

"Then I would owe you a truck load of beer, Jack," John quietly agreed. "She is the best thing that ever happened to me. My whole life is different. You were right." Jack slapped his friend on the shoulder and mounted the bike. "Now we got to find one for me!" Thompson laughed. "But I'm better lookin', so it should be a lot easier." And he jumped on the starter bringing thunder to their ears.

They pulled up in front of 311 Steiner Street to find Cathy waiting outside. She wore dark slacks, a white blouse, and a brocade vest that gave her a classy but casual look. The motorcycle pulled up behind John's truck with a roar. Becky made introductions and, before Constanza could make a move, suggested Cathy ride with Jack, in case he lost the truck in traffic. Cathy knew the way to Sausalito. Jack reminded Becky a little of John, quiet but strong. Reliable. She thought for a moment of the horrible things these three men must have been through together and how powerful their bond must be. How they all deserved to be nurtured.

"Let's go!" John called out.

"Cold beer!" Thompson urged.

"Hooyah!" yelled Constanza.

"Hooyah!" Again all around.

The truck took off while Cathy was getting on the back of the bike. Jack showed her where to put her feet and the best place to hold on, which was around his waist. As soon as her arms were around him, Cathy said "Ready!" The 1000 cc machine squealed slightly and zipped away toward the Sausalito playground. It was a sunny afternoon, and the Golden Gate was the Yellow Brick Road, a pathway to Oz or Camelot, part of the San

Francisco oasis of mellow fun and revelry. Wind blowing through their hair, Jack and Cathy pulled along side of the others, smiling and waving. Simon and Garfunkel's "Mrs. Robinson" poured out of the truck's window as the group cruised three hundred feet above the potato patch and the sailboats snoozing along in the light wind. This afternoon was for speed and new friendships; for a brew and strutting your stuff on wooden decks jutting out over the sun-drenched saltwater of San Francisco Bay.

They arrived, struggled to find a Bridgeway Avenue parking spot, and gathered at the front door of Zack's, a landmark Sausalito tavern. The place was packed, but there was always room for a few more. Especially if a couple of good-looking women were part of the group. Much of the crowd's attention was focused on six turtles in the middle of a race across the floor to a finish line five feet away. You could drink at least one beer without missing the finish. The large outside deck was crowded, too, but not as bad as the inside with the races on. They managed to find room for the two girls to sit at the bench against the deck rail. The noise level was higher than usual from the race area, but outside the sun seemed to tone down the noise, and couples and groups huddled and talked and enjoyed the afternoon oblivious to the turtles hurtling toward the finish. Several pairs or threesomes of girls sat talking, looking around and waiting for Sir Galahad to arrive and sweep them off their feet. Finding guys in Sausalito was not a problem. Finding one that wasn't 100 percent interested in getting into your pants before the end of the evening was more difficult. Constanza stood by the railing surveying the crowd like an eagle on a perch surveying a field of cottontails. He wore a huge smile. Jack, on the other hand, seemed more interested in Cathy. John ordered three bottles of beer and two glasses of Chablis from one of the harried waitresses. This was a good place to be for this group. Each with their own agenda and the means to make it happen.

Sunday was Sausalito's early night and, except for a few dozen diehards, people were on their way home by seven thirty. Jack and Dave returned to Treasure Island, Dave with several telephone numbers. On the way home, Cathy informed Becky that she would be having dinner with Jack on Monday. "These Seals are slippery, Cathy. Be advised." Becky cautioned with a wink at John.

The following week was eventful, as Becky and John dealt with the everyday activities of life only now doing it as a confirmed couple. They spent more time thinking and talking about the future and, without coming right out and saying it, focused on that future as a couple. At work, Lowell Berg approached John and brought up the subject of education. "Any thoughts on what you want to do yet?" The question took John by surprise. His attention had been focused almost exclusively on Becky. But thoughts of kids and family quickly reminded John that a degree would be a good thing. He responded saying he definitely wanted to go for it but hadn't come up with a major yet. Berg suggested they have lunch on Thursday and discuss it some more. Right on!

This then became the subject of discussion over dinner and beyond, Becky serving as a sounding board for John's thoughts, contributing much with her knowledge of college degrees, requirements, and study loads. She genuinely wanted John to be doing something he enjoyed. Volleyball now took up more time than Becky wanted to spend on it, but the team was coming along nicely, and they had a shot at finishing first or second in their conference. Wanting to spend time with John made her more conscious of planning her other tasks so that the time they had would be quality time. As luck would have it, there was a tournament this coming weekend that required her to spend Friday and Saturday nights in the dormitory at Berkeley with the team. She could have come home after the girls were tucked in, but staying was the right thing to do.

Ed Saunders called to tell Becky that Dennis was building a deck onto his house in Crescent City in three weeks, and he and Emily would be going up to help out. Becky was invited, and if her new friend wanted to help, he would be more than welcome. Becky recognized her father's attempt to provide an opportunity for John and Dennis to meet. Dennis would never of his own volition have invited one of Becky's boyfriends or dates to his home to do anything. Although still apprehensive about her brother's attitude toward whomever she brought home, she wanted them to meet and, good or bad, have that hurdle behind them. John naturally agreed to go up and help out, recognizing that this was a worrisome meeting for Becky. A Force Recon marine with time served in Nam was, in his eyes, a brother-in-arms. and he actually looked forward to meeting Dennis, believing that, unless he was a total asshole, they would become friends.

Finally Hank Cooper called wanting to set up an abalone dive/camping weekend up at Salt Point. It was settled on two weeks out. They would leave Saturday around noon and make a late afternoon dive Saturday and morning dives on Sunday. John called Sam Dorner, who was delighted. He insisted they stay at the ranch. Becky suggested they swing by the wine country on the way home, taste a little, and then go to her folks' house for early supper. Everyone thought that was a great idea, and Emily was delighted to accommodate. Life was full and busy and happy. Becky had essentially moved into John's apartment, but she was too embarrassed to tell her parents of the move. so she kept the Steiner Street apartment and had Cathy and Charlene cover for her.

With Becky at her volleyball for the weekend, John worked late Friday and most of Saturday at Berg Marine. Lunch Thursday with Lowell had been interesting and informative. He suggested John go for an engineering degree but to also focus on project management, planning, and communication elements. "So much time and resources are lost because of poor communication. And most engineers have difficulty talking with nonengineers. They believe the blueprints say it all. The degree is important, but your technical expertise will come from the field and training from manufacturers and vendors. The ability to pull it all together is what makes you a valuable commodity. If you want to do it, John, then let's do it. I'll back you." Berg had recognized a change in the young Seal and had discovered there was a woman in his life. He was glad the young man was leaving the war behind him and getting on with life. John seemed to have a knack for this work and could move up the ladder in the business, which would ultimately be good for Berg Marine.

The USF volleyball team did OK—but not great—tying for second with Stanford and losing to Cal. Becky had to fight the urge to suit up and play, her competitive nature urging her to action. She arrived home Sunday afternoon to find John waiting with fresh strawberries and a bottle of champagne. Becky threw her overnight bag on the chair and fell into his arms. They kissed, and she laid her head on his chest, breathing deeply, feeling his arms around her. "I missed you," she said.

"Me, too."

Their sexual arousal was overpowered by their desire simply to touch, talk, and be together. Overpowered for the moment, of course. They sipped the champagne and talked about their weekends and the upcoming dive weekend. "Can I go in the water with you?" Becky asked as she nibbled on a bright red strawberry. "It must be wonderful. I'd like to at least see that world you enjoy so much. Maybe you can show me how find abalone."

"Absolutely! I have most of the stuff you'd need in the dive locker at work. We'll probably need to rent a wet suit. That's no problem. Great idea. We can bring an extra tank. If the ab dive goes OK, maybe we'll take you down for a spin through the kelp. It's really beautiful."

The week went by quickly. An invitation to Bob Friendly's retirement ceremony and reception arrived in the mail the card reading, "John McConnell and guest." The recent time spent with Constanza and Thompson had stirred John's memories, and he wanted to go. Becky agreed. Ultimately they decided to go down together, John thinking he and Lou Retino could protect his lady from the predictably rowdy Seals. The event would prove momentous for both John and Becky.

At noon on Saturday, the gray truck took off for the north coast, John and the two women in the cab. while Hank lounged on sleeping bags in the back, wedged in amongst the dive bags, air bottles, and coolers. Grace and Sam would be waiting, eager to see their newfound friends and the new couple they were bringing. As usual it was a fine day, warm but not hot in these dog days of Northern California summer. John got off the freeway as soon as he could, preferring the winding but infinitely more interesting country back roads. They stopped at a makeshift roadside stand for fresh corn and fruit, and Becky bought a bouquet of mixed flowers for Grace. Turkey vultures glided on the thermals looking for roadkill or other carrion. Red-tailed hawks cruised the air in search of moving prey. A doe and a smaller pair of first-year whitetails stood anxiously at the side of the road waiting to cross or scamper back into the security of the forest behind them. A bobcat was spotted off in the distance. Maybe it was a house cat, but bobcats were more exciting to see, so they all agreed that's what it was. The truck rolled up the Dorners' driveway at three o'clock. Hugs, handshakes, and introductions went on for several minutes before John politely indicated there were abalone waiting and a cold beer waiting for them right after that.

The ocean was flat, perfect for a novice diver's first venture out. They suited up at the top of the cliff, weight belts secured around their waists, hoods, gloves, and miscellaneous gear tucked into the dive tubes. Between the excitement of her first dive and the struggle to wriggle into the quarter- inch-thick rubber wet suit, Becky was very close to overheating when she reached the bottom of the cliff. "Just relax, babe. We'll get the rest of your gear on, and then we'll sit in the water for a few minutes. Trust me, you will cool down. It'll be great." John could see both excitement and fear in her eyes, the latter fueled by the rising body heat. Soon, however, they were in the near-fifty-degree water, cooling down. With her mask and snorkel on, Becky cruised along facedown in about eighteen inches of water and was stunned by the diversity and abundance of intertidal life filling every niche. With John on one side and Hank on the other, Becky finally waved to Judy and Grace on the cliff, rolled over, and was off on her first underwater adventure. Visibility was about thirty feet, intermittently blocked by gently waving leaves of brown kelp, holding fast to the rocky bottom but always reaching for the surface. Swimming through the kelp was a matter of moving slowly and easily while it parted to allow you through. Occasionally a plume hooked on a tank or leg-strapped dive knife, which then required unlooping. Thrashing around in kelp was not a good idea because then more things got tangled, and it took more patience to untangle. In about fifteen feet of water, John signaled that he was going down. Hank, too, now moved off, and Becky was floating on her tube alone, face in the water, watching her loved one kick down and move gracefully along the bottom. He suddenly stopped, working at something and then shot to the surface with an abalone in his hand. John spit out his mouthpiece and said, "For you, my dear. Now it's your turn." He dropped the mollusk into his dive tube then looked at Becky. "OK. Take a few deep breaths. When you're ready, lie on the surface, take a deep breath, and throw your fins up behind you. Your head will go down. and when your fins hit the water, kick down to the bottom. We'll practice a few times. OK?" Becky nodded. Then she let go of the float and in a moment was headed down, John moving with her. Becky was an athlete and always ready to meet a challenge. Any fears she might have had disappeared when she got into the fantastic new world below the surface, John hovering close by. Soon they were swimming along the bottom together, John pointing out abalone then popping them off. Then he handed her the abalone iron. It was her turn. Resting on the surface for a few minutes between dives, they would talk. John mostly listened to Becky tell him about the wonderful things she was seeing. John hunched over to kiss her, but their masks banged together, making it impossible to obtain a good lip-lock. Becky laughed. "We'll take care of that later. At least I know you've never kissed anybody while you were diving. That's a comfort."

"You've never seen Sean Connery and Ursula Andress in *Doctor No*."

The next trip to the bottom uncovered no abalone. On the second dive, Becky veered away pointing. John looked and nodded. Becky had found her own ab and, after a botched first effort, managed to dislodge it then kick to the surface. "I got it!" she yelled holding up her prize. "I got it!" Becky was into it. A natural athlete, she had the strength, coordination, and now the confidence to be comfortable and have fun in and under the water. Over the next thirty minutes, she found two more abalone, not bad for a novice diver. "I love it, John. Can you teach me more?" she implored. "Did you see the seal? It came right up to me. Scared me at first. But I knew you were there. What kind was it?"

"A little harbor seal. Almost as cute as you. Hey we need one more ab to limit out. Hank and I think you should get it."

"Darn right." Becky hung onto her tube and took several deep breaths, building up her oxygen supply. Then she slipped off her tube, kicked hard up, and flipped over, kicking down to the bottom fifteen feet below. John and Hank followed her, hovering and weaving amongst the kelp, both impressed with her newfound ability. Four dives later a luckless abalone was discovered, captured, and secured. The trio headed back to the shore, where Becky basked in the wonderment and praise of the group. After an arduous trek to the top of the cliff with all hands pitching in where they could, they packed their gear up to the house. The seafood was prepared, fueled by sangria, Chablis, and cold beer. While the others were cleaning and rinsing the salt off the dive gear, Grace and Judy, under Grace's direction, created a bowlful of ceviche by dicing the meat of one abalone, combining it with chopped green onion, tomato, and a touch of ginger, then douching the whole bowl in lime juice. The citric acid in the juice cooked the ingredients. It was served to the dive crew as a nutritious snack, not unlike Hawaiian poke. Like any new and unusual food, it was tried tentatively and, for the most part, happily accepted. Hank wasn't partial to the raw fish, lime juice be damned. He settled for ham and cheese on crackers.

The six people blended together into what seemed to be a perfectly compatible mix, each contributing to the fast moving conversation, each with a unique perspective but attuned to the audience. Babies were a hot topic, as was diving. Becky's SCUBA foray the following day was the focus of that subject. Home improvement projects, wine tasting, and various ways to prepare abalone also shared time. Hank told the group he had once ground abalone up like hamburger, added ground bacon for fat, and cooked it up like a meat loaf. It actually sounded great. Sam, encouraged by John, talked about his foot, how he lost it, and how he was beginning to get used to moving around with a prosthetic. This was, Grace noted, the first time he spoke about it with people other than her or his doctors and, it seemed to her, that he spoke with less anger and bitterness than he had since his arrival home. His audience was curious, honest, and encouraging. At sunset they all went out to search for the elusive green flash. thought by some to be a mythical tale, by others an errant ray of light through an atmospheric prism. No green flash tonight, but it was an opportunity for each couple to watch the sunset, hold hands, and perhaps steal a kiss. The sautéed abalone dinner was a great success. Grace's salad and homemade dressing getting accolades and requests for the recipe from the women. By eleven o'clock, the promise of an early start and a busy day tomorrow prompted them to adjourn. Each couple moved to their respective bedding areas. Hank and Judy got the guest cabin, Judy's 'condition' giving her special treatment despite her protests; John and Becky set up a tent in the yard.

Having zipped their sleeping bags together and settled in, Becky and John lay quietly, Becky's head resting on his arm. They reflected on the day's events. "It was really beautiful under the water. And exciting to find the abalone. Thank you for taking me."

"You did great. And it was my pleasure. You'll like tomorrow when we SCUBA. You don't have to pop up and down. You become part of it. And you'll have time to see a lot more. Hey, you want to make a night dive?" John kidded.

"Smarty." Becky nudged him in the ribs. They were quiet for a while, resting, calming themselves before dropping off to sleep. "John, do you still think about Vietnam? I mean, does it still bother you?" Becky asked softly. "I know it's something you had to deal with that night...our first night together. Is it all right now?"

John didn't respond right away. Finally he spoke, motivated by what he felt was the strength of their relationship and a desire to clarify for both of them the fears that almost kept him from finding this place, this woman. "My biggest fear was that I had become something I didn't really want to be, and maybe I enjoyed that a little too much. An overly efficient soldier whose primary directive was to kill the enemy, who wasn't always easy to identify. I thought it could keep me from finding my way back home, back to the world. Keep me from finding a good woman, having a family. Then

I met you, and it wasn't theoretical anymore. It was real. If you found out about what I might be, would you even want to talk to me, never mind be with me for a lifetime? Would you run away? I was scared. Afraid I would lose you but, in fairness to you, I felt I had to tell you. I couldn't bring myself to tell you and couldn't move forward to court you. I was sort of trapped. I fell in love with you but was afraid to tell you. Then I was afraid I would look like a mad dog and lose you anyway. You reached in and pulled the fear out. Tossed it aside. I guess Vietnam will always be a part of me, just like being a Seal will always be a part of me. But it's not the only part. Yes, I'm OK."

He brought his arm up rolling Becky on top of him, hugging her and nuzzling her neck. He held her as if he was holding life itself. Becky closed her eyes. Her heart soared; a smile welled up from her chest, making her more beautiful than ever. She almost laughed aloud, her happiness so great. Their lips came together somewhere between gently and roughly, their spirits mingling. John's hands slipped under her nightshirt, moved up, and cupped her breasts while they kissed. Becky lifted slightly to give him room to fondle her. Five minutes of foreplay later, they were locked together moving toward a climax. John burst inside of her, surely pleasurable on its own physical merit, but now far more so. It was a sharing of himself with this special woman. They clung together not wanting it to end, finally falling asleep still wrapped together body and soul, flesh and spirit.

Judy and Hank also settled in. They too talked quietly about the day's activity, enjoying the memories, happy with their new friends and their lives in general. Hank made tentative advances ready to back off at the first sign of discomfort from Judy. Understanding her husband's caution, his unwillingness to do anything that might be injurious to her or their baby, Judy took the lead, became the aggressor. She encouraged him, guided him, and urged him on. After all, she wasn't even three months pregnant. The nice thing was that her breasts were supersensitive, and his hands felt wonderful as they caressed and squeezed, her nipples hardening to his touch. Their lovemaking was different from John and Becky's. They were farther down love's path. They had a little less romance, a little more companionship, and a slightly different balance of emotion. Not better or worse, just farther down the road of love, still a terrific place to be.

Grace and Sam were also thinking about the day. Sam had decided several days before to skip the trip to St. Helena for wine tasting and dinner at the Saunders'. Grace had not been surprised at her husband's reclusiveness and reluctance to go public. She was disappointed but understanding. As they lay together, she spoke to her wounded warrior. "They are really great people. All of them. I like Judy a lot. She always has a smile. Hank, too. And Becky and John are tops. Do you think you'll really dive with him one day?"

"Anything is possible, babe. Yeah, they are all good people."

"Are you sure you don't want to go with them tomorrow? It sounds like fun." She hesitated, reluctant to challenge his decision to stay home but sure it was a mistake, especially after this wonderful day. "I know they'll all be there for you. We can always leave early. We'll have to go out sometime, Sam. Now just seems like a good time." Grace held her breath, expecting her husband to roll over and tell her he didn't want to talk about it. That had been the pattern since he arrived home from Vietnam. She understood, but it was difficult for her as well as for him.

"Maybe we could go."

Grace's heart jumped. She wanted to yell with joy, to run out and tell everyone. But she lay quiet; waiting. "I don't think I should wear my camis or Army clothes. Do you still have that stuff you got for me? The slacks and yellow shirt? That would be better, don't you think?"

Grace's throat was choked up. She almost didn't, couldn't, answer. "Yes, I still have them. I think they'd be fine, Sam. Just fine." A tear rolled across her face. Her husband, the man she loved, was coming back to her. She moved over to him and kissed him then rested her head on his chest. Sam patted her head, sensing her feelings, knowing how badly she wanted to go. Knowing how badly she needed to get out into the world again. His decision to go, however frightening it was for him, was prompted not only by these new friends and the comfort they afforded him, but by a developing concern that he might lose his woman because of his fears to get on with his own life, one foot or two. Sam and Grace also made love that night. Their relationship, too, was different once again from the others'. They were even farther down life's road, theirs a rocky road, and they had rediscovered one another; reaffirmed their battered union and coming out perhaps stronger because of their adversity.

At around one o'clock, the moon rose bright, muting the magnificence of the stars but casting its own pale brilliance over the shoreline and its coastal forest. As the three couples slept, each at peace with their life, a small herd of white-tailed deer passed through the front yard only a few feet from the tent; a pair of raccoons sniffed around the trash cans, and an owl pounced on a small, nocturnal mammal. Moonbeams ricocheted off the gently rolling ocean, and far offshore a gray whale blew.

By ten o'clock on Saturday a second limit of abalone was retrieved, and the group drove down the coast to Salt Point Cove for Becky's first venture beneath the sea with SCUBA. Both John and Hank coached her on procedures and underwater hand signs. Becky, eager to go, listened attentively but urged them to get into the water. Forty minutes later they emerged. Becky was totally hooked on the sport. The men were impressed with her initial skill and agreed that she should get certified and join the ranks of underwater explorers and adventurers. Showers, a quick pack up, and a lunch of submarine sandwiches preceded the drive to St. Helena and the wineries of the Napa Valley. By three thirty, they had tasted at Christian Brothers, Mondavi, and St. Clement wineries and were feeling even more mellow than before. Right around four o'clock, Becky, driving the gray pickup with Judy and Hank, and Sam, in his black Camaro with Grace and John, turned into the Saunders's long driveway and on up to the house. On the porch sat Emily and Ed together with Cathy Ventura and Jack Thompson. After hearty greetings and complex introductions were completed, Cathy explained that Jack had come up for the weekend and, trying to locate Becky and John, they had been invited by Emily to join the gang for dinner. "You were right about these Seals, Rebecca. They're slick, and they move fast," said Cathy with a wink at Jack.

"We were just having a glass of wine," explained Emily, "Would anyone like to join us?"

Only Judy declined, having to watch her diet because of the baby. The more usual separation of a group like this into men and women's sections, each pursuing different lines of conversation, did not happen. Each couple was tuned into their partner and in turn into the group, such that everyone was interested in everything that was said.

"Dad! Guess what I got for you today? I mean I got them with my own hands." Becky shot a glance at John and Hank and smiled. "The guys helped a little, but I actually caught them."

Ed Saunders looked at his daughter then at the men. He shrugged. "I give up. What did you get?"

"A limit of abalone! Five! Well, actually four. But big ones." Her eyes shone with pride, and the whole group clapped and cheered.

"She was great. A natural. The next guy to become an ab diver is Sam," John informed them. "If a girl can do it, then so can air cav." There was a brief silence. Those knowing about Sam's foot were a little shocked; those unaware were at a loss to understand. Sam turned red at being suddenly thrust into the spotlight. He knew John had said it to bring attention to his foot and put Sam's fears to rest. Deep down he knew it wasn't intended to be malicious, but it sure was uncomfortable. John went on to explain Sam's situation and several ideas he had to rig up a dive fin for Sam's leg. The group now threw out additional suggestions and words of encouragement, each, to a man, indicating they wanted to be there for the first dive.

"The air cavalry is kind of an offshoot of the paratroopers," Ed Saunders offered. "I know he'll do it. Hell, maybe I'll make a dive, too. Sam, you keep me posted. I'll go out with you."

Sam didn't respond except for a nod. Grace at first thought the worst, that his anger was rising, and there might be a scene. When she looked, however, she saw a glistening in his eye and realized he was emotionally choked up at the support and acceptance that surrounded him. Ed saw it, too, and immediately offered to give a tour of the vineyards. He would hitch up the buckboard for Sam and the women; the rest would have to hoof it. John elected to stay back and help Emily with dinner preparations. Before he and Cathy started to the barn with the others, Jack Thompson put his hand on John's shoulder and squeezed. The two looked at each other just for a moment, and John nodded. Becky reluctantly went off to help with the tour. A bottle of chilled white wine was put in a cooler and loaded onto the buckboard.

"I can manage fine, John, if you want to go," said Emily, releasing John from kitchen patrol.

"That's OK, Emily. I'll give you a hand. You've got a crowd tonight. And whatever you're cooking, it smells great."

"Thank you. I thought a roast turkey would be good and, actually, it's pretty easy. We'll have stuffing, mashed potatoes with gravy, fresh green beans, and cranberry."

"It's like Thanksgiving. I haven't had a home-cooked Thanksgiving dinner for probably four years. This is great. And I appreciate your including Sam and Jack. I know it means a lot to them, too."

"It's our pleasure, John. Besides you brought abalone, and Ed will be in heaven when we cook that up. Well, I've got the table set. Everything is pretty much on hold until they get back. If we keep an eye on the buckboard, we can go into action when it gets back to the barn. Then we'll be ready to serve by the time they get here and wash up."

"You give the word."

"We can sit on the back step and have a glass of wine. As a matter of fact, let's do that, and then we'll carve the turkey. You know how to carve?"

"I've carved them before, but I don't think I did it the right way. Navy guys aren't particular about how things look. Just how they taste."

"I'll show you. There's not much to it. The main thing is to think about how you put it on the serving platter and cut accordingly. Hold out your glass, John." Emily filled John's wineglass and then her own, and the two sat watching the vineyards, the buckboard in the distance, and the shadows lengthening in the late afternoon coolness.

"You have a pretty terrific daughter, Emily, if you don't mind me saying it."

Emily looked over at the young man whose fierce eyes seemed to have softened as he spoke of her Rebecca. "Yes, John, I do. And I don't mind you saying that at all."

They made comfortable small talk until the buckboard reappeared on the top of the rolling hill, then returned to the kitchen, where Emily began the final preparations for supper. John focused intently on the twenty-two-pound turkey, Emily occasionally offering words of encouragement or advice. As John was nearing completion, Becky burst into the kitchen. "Dad is so into his tours. He ought to open them to the public. And Sam thinks he can fix the old tractor. It wouldn't start and has been sitting for almost a year. Wouldn't that be great?" She moved over to John, placed her arm around his waist, and leaned her chin on his shoulder as she examined his carving work. The motion was, on the surface, very casual, but there was an intimacy to it, a deep level of comfort, which was not lost on Emily. Her daughter clearly had strong feelings for this man and, just as clearly, he for her. He held his hands, moist with turkey juice, up and away from Becky. "I don't want to get this all over you. Be careful."

"Be careful? It might be fun!" Becky teased and poking him in the ribs playfully. John pulled away halfheartedly, a slight smile on his face. They looked at each other, and Emily thought for a moment they would kiss right there in the kitchen. Instead John looked up at her and appeared to blush slightly. Without saying a word he reaffirmed to Emily what a terrific daughter she had and how much he cared about her. Emily, in turn, was happily taken aback by the suddenness with which Becky had apparently found her man, and the kind of man he was or appeared to be. Strong, reliable, and caring. She thought of her young paratrooper, so tough and hard in the beginning.

The others began streaming into the kitchen asking what they could do to help. In minutes the food was on the table, wine poured, everyone waiting to observe whatever protocol their hosts would initiate. Emily looked at Ed and advised, "Dear, I think we'll just say grace tonight." indicating toasts all around would have everyone on their heels, indeed if they weren't already. Ed and Emily placed their hands, palms up on the table, and everyone joined hands for grace. Head bowed, Ed began. "Heavenly Father, bless this food we are about to receive; bless all these wonderful young people; continue to keep them safe and happy. And bless our vineyards, for 'in vino veritas.' Amen." Most chorused the amen and again politely waited for some word to start. Emily opened the floodgates. "Help yourself. Don't be shy. There's plenty more in the kitchen."

Ed Saunders looked out over the table, quietly registering his daughter's new friends. How the profile had changed so dramatically. How she had matured so quickly. And how his wait for that special boyfriend had seemingly come to an end. John was clearly special in her eyes and indeed in his own. Ed had done some research on the Seals and was surprised and impressed with their elite military reputation. He thought about his son, Dennis, and thought the meeting of the two young men would be interesting and fun to observe. Seals, married couples, air cav veterans, divers, and pregnant women replaced the volleyball team and the graduate students. With Vietnam becoming thick in the air, today's youth had to grow up fast, make hard decisions early and live, or die, with consequences that were too severe for their youthful inexperience. He loved these young people. Each one of them. They were men and women. His sweet Rebecca was among them, safe, he mused, in the hands of this ... Seal.

CHAPTER THIRTEEN

Crescent City, California

August 1969

Shadows from the tall trees nearby fell across the concrete foundation as Dennis Saunders stood on the scrub lawn in his backyard surveying the project that was bringing his family and friends over to help out this weekend. The lumber was stacked along the side of the house; plywood, fasteners, and roofing material were tucked in next to the wood. There were three guys coming over to help, not counting Rebecca's friend. The women would keep the food flowing. He looked forward to seeing his parents and welcomed his dad's advice on the remodeling task he had undertaken. Two fairly large bedrooms and a bathroom would be added to the house, each bedroom having its own sliding glass door to the backyard patio. His plan was to return to school at Humboldt State using the GI Bill. and the rental of the two rooms to help finance his education. Currently he was making decent money as a redwood logger, but he would need the extra income when he started school. The return to school was mostly his wife and his mom's idea. He wasn't overly enthusiastic about it but was willing to give it a try, recognizing its future potential. He saw his sister's near obsession with school, sports, and the college crowd as a negative; but he quietly admired her graduation from Cal and postgraduate work at USF.

Dennis was not quite as tall as John McConnell, but he weighed in at about twenty pounds heavier. His close-cropped, sandy-brown hair topped a square face with slightly jutting jaw and a longish mustache. He was solidly built, and his tendency toward being a redneck was ameliorated by the fact that his mother was a class act, and his family upbringing simply overwhelmed any element of crudeness in his personality. Dennis could kick ass down in San Francisco's Tenderloin district or comfortably slide into a white shirt and tie for drinks at the Top of the Mark before the theater. After his yearlong tour with Marine Force Recon in Vietnam, he enjoyed working as a logger, being in the woods around rough-cut, honest working people. His marriage to Cheryl, his high-school sweetheart, had made his return to the world easier. Cheryl, his family, and the relative seclusion of the forest eased him gently back into society. Dennis was very straightforward. If he didn't like you or agree with you, he told you. He knew his sister did not hold this quality of his in high regard, but she did bring home a bunch of wimpy guys and really couldn't expect much enthusiasm from him. He thought with some puzzlement about the new boyfriend she was bringing up this weekend, not able to comprehend exactly why she would want to bring him here, of all places, unless she was moderately serious about the guy. To his knowledge, Rebecca had never really fallen for anyone; the guys she dated were just that: dates. Well, his dad seemed to think this guy was OK, so he would try to be nice, but if he got in the way…

For John and Becky, Monday morning brought the wonderful weekend crashing back to earth: work, school, and everyday chores. They were settling into a living-together relationship, spending virtually all of their free time together; talking, sharing, learning habits and idiosyncrasies, but also giving each other space to take time alone when necessary. Both respected individuality and independence. As a result, their relationship as a couple was coalescing nicely around a core of love and mutual respect.

On Tuesday evening, John not yet home from work, Becky sat at the dining-room table studying her master's thesis draft, marking the rough work with blue pencil as she corrected and improved the ever-growing body of knowledge that would represent her contribution to the education system's future. Papers and reference books cluttered the table, a few spilling over onto the floor. She was entirely engrossed when the telephone rang loudly in the quiet apartment. The telephone had not yet become hers and still drew within her a momentarily uncomfortable sense that she was trespassing on his turf. She thought of John on the stairs of her apartment the night they met; how incredibly uncomfortable he must have been. On the third ring, she answered. There was a long pause on the other end. Finally the voice of a woman—no, a girl—asked, "Hello. Is John McConnell there?"

Certainly Becky trusted her man but an involuntarily feeling of discomfort welled up in her chest just for a moment before she confidently responded, "I'm sorry he's not. May I take a message for him? I do expect him shortly."

"Um, yes. This is his sister, Jennifer. Could you tell him I called?"

"Jennifer! Of course I'll tell him. I'm Becky. I guess you could say I'm John's girlfriend. He's told me about you. It's nice to finally talk to you." Becky bubbled out happily. She had thought about Jennifer, about having a sister, and what that would be like.

"He's told us about you, too. I mean that there's a girl he like and her name was Becky. John doesn't talk much. At least not to me."

Becky laughed into the receiver. "I've been there, Jennifer. I know exactly what you mean. He is the strong silent type. But he's quite a guy, isn't he?"

"Yeah. He's pretty cool."

"Is there any message I can give him? Or anything I can help you with?"

"Well, when John came home at Christmas, he said that maybe I could come out to California to visit. We live in Florida. I was calling to see if, um, well, if I could do that. I know he's busy and all but, well, I thought maybe I could. My folks say it's OK with them, if it's OK with John."

"I think that would be wonderful," Becky responded without hesitation. "I would love to meet you, and there are all kinds of things to do. When could you come?"

"Well I was thinking either Christmas break or spring break. Spring break is in March. That's the only time I can get out of school."

"Either time would be fine, but Christmas would be better for me. I'm still in school myself, so I'll be off then, too. While John is working, we can play."

The two girls talked for twenty minutes, setting a foundation for friendship in the future and plotting how they would talk John into a visit. Becky promised to have John call back ASAP, allowing for the three-hour time difference. When Becky hung up the phone she was excited at the prospect of Jennifer's visit and extending her relationship with John by meeting his family. She began thinking about things a fourteen-year-old would like to do, recognizing that just spending time with her brother would be the coolest. Nonetheless, a list started to form, and a genuine enthusiasm for the visit was germinated.

The door had hardly closed behind him when John was hit with both barrels of Becky's announcement that Jennifer would be spending the Christmas holidays with them. Would he please call his sister to finalize the dates? He sensed that he was being manipulated, but he couldn't bring himself to rain on the girls' parade, given the sparkle in Becky's eyes and the growing importance of family in his life. He made the call without objection. A hug and a kiss while he waited for the telephone in Florida to be picked up confirmed it was a sound decision.

The two of them lay in bed, the lights out, discussing Jennifer, her trip, and the preparations required to make it memorable. John was delighted at Becky's enthusiasm. It was infectious to the point where he found himself actually looking forward to Jennifer's arrival. He watched as Becky went on, her voice animated, about taking Jennifer shopping, visiting her parents, a football game at Cal. Reaching over, he rolled her into his arms and kissed her on the mouth. Their bodies moved together, the talk replaced by more tactile communication. As they were making love, John found himself completely caught up in the physical pleasure but, at the same time, he felt an almost out-of-body sense as he observed their two bodies embracing on the bed. The experience generated a lingering rush of emotion he had never experienced before. A feeling for this other human being; a sense of…love?

An almost physical ingestion of her spirit brought on a sense of peace that almost overshadowed the very powerful physical pleasure he was at that very moment enjoying. The emotional or spiritual experience confirmed without reservation his love for this woman and his commitment to her well-being and happiness for as long as he lived.

After they had climaxed John didn't speak but continued to hold her, breathing deeply, his muscles still tensed as though she might somehow slip away in the night. "Are you all right, John?" she asked softly.

He didn't answer right away as he tried to find the words that might explain what had just happened to him. No definable explanation came to him. His response was, simply "I'm fine. I love you, that's all."

"Well, that's a good thing." Becky whispered into his ear. She was beginning to understand that on the subject of love and loving, the few words John actually said represented a myriad of thoughts and feelings condensed down into a very basic and clear message. She loved hearing those distilled words, perhaps because they weren't carelessly or often spoken. She squeezed him, rested her head on his chest, and went to sleep.

Emily and Ed had arrived at their son's home on Friday afternoon. With them they brought a large leg of lamb, baked goods and, of course, a generous supply of wine to supplement Dennis's larder to feed his volunteer help. The two men examined the blueprints for the remodel, laying out the procedures they would follow in the morning when the workers arrived. Dennis explained the skills each of his three buddies had. One was a part-time roofer, and the others had rudimentary carpentry skills. When asked how he planned to use Rebecca's friend, Dennis proposed he hump lumber and roofing materials to the real workers.

Ed Saunders, curious about this new military unit, the Navy Seals, had done a little more research on just what it was they did. His stint as a paratrooper stimulated his curiosity and the fact that his daughter was involved with one heightened that curiosity. Besides, the quiet young man had made an impression on him. His research told him that Seals were an elite commando-type force, experts with a wide range of weapons, SCUBA, hand-to-hand combat. and counter insurgency training. Best of all in Ed's mind was that they were all jump qualified, some doing high-altitude free falls and helicopter rappelling. Spending time in Vietnam as a Seal explained to Ed the quiet confidence of the young man whose eyes had undoubtedly seen close combat. He was much like Dennis in that sense. Ed actually looked forward to watching his son meet Rebecca's beau, who was so differ-ent from anyone she had ever brought home before. He deliberately didn't say anything to Dennis except that he thought Rebecca's friend had some electrical background. "Does that mean he can't hump lumber?" Dennis retorted with that "another pussy" tone in his voice. Ed smiled, enjoying already the prospect of what he perceived was to come.

Becky and John pulled up in front of the house about nine fifteen, the driveway already filled with pickup trucks and Ed's Ford station wagon. They'd left San Francisco at five thirty, stopping only for coffee and an English muffin in Eureka. Becky hauled out a grocery bag full of chips, dips, and two sourdough breads. John carried a case of Budweiser, a twenty-ounce hammer, and a nail pouch he had purchased for the occasion. Cheryl and Emily came out front to greet them. The men were around back, the buzz of a table saw and the pounding of hammers attesting to the fact they were already at work. A few moments later, the four of them came out the back door ready to make introductions.

"Hello, sweet sister. How're you doin'?" Dennis said as he moved away from the saw to give his sister a hug. Ed Saunders moved over to shake John's hand and welcome him.

"Hi, Dennis. Boy, you've really got things going here. But it'll be huge when you're finished." Becky observed as she took in the scope of her broth-er's remodeling project.

"Hey, guys. This is my sister, Rebecca. This is Red, Pete, and Sonny," Dennis said introducing the three men with a wave of his hand.

"Dennis, this my friend John McConnell. John, my brother Dennis." Both men stepped forward to shake hands. If Dennis had any feeling about the other man, it did not show in his face. Dennis turned and reintroduced his buddies, each of them stepping forward to shake the newcomer's hand. "You ready to hump a little lumber, John?"

"Whatever you need. I'm here to help." John fell into the routine and quickly had lumber stacked up on the slab where two teams were building the framed walls that would soon be raised. Dennis required a third pile by the table saw as he cut window and doorframes, headers and bracing for each of the teams. There were two sets of plans, one for the teams and one for the saw man. Roof trusses had been cut and partially put together earlier. John moved among the three workstations providing the required lengths of wood usually before it was asked for. The group, except for Red, worked smoothly. Red was not able to read blueprints and had to be told regularly what and where to nail. He was, however, eager and enthusiastic and kept them all chuckling. Dennis watched John surreptitiously, unable to find fault in his willingness or ability to contribute to the project. And he knew immediately that the guy was not the least bit intimidated by his own rough, domineering attitude. The guy was polite and obviously here to work, but clearly as an equal.

The work groove was interrupted by a call to lunch by the women. Dennis knew they had to have lunch but groused internally at having to pause when things were rolling along so well. Emily quietly let Cheryl take the lead role serving the meal. This was her domain, and she deserved to be in the limelight for what was a wonderful barbecue of hamburgers and hotdogs with every condiment you could think of, including sautéed onions, honey mustard, and a sharp, English cheddar cheese. Potato salad, Jell-O fruit mold, a variety of chips, and an assortment of sweet and kosher dill pickles were also squeezed onto the serving table. Such a fine, full lunch was dangerous to offer men scheduled to work until dark. Nonetheless, it was a pleasant break appreciated by everyone. At one fifteen Dennis finally rallied the crew back to their stations, and within thirty minutes the groove had been reestablished.

The sun was high in the sky, and the long-sleeved shirts that warded off the coolness of the morning were shed, leaving the men in T-shirts or tank tops. The internal walls were raised and braced; the exterior walls almost ready to go. As John walked past with an armful of cut lumber, Dennis, almost without looking up, inquired, "How did you get that scar on your arm?"

John looked over at him, then down at his arm. "Took a bullet there. It went right through."

Again without looking at him, Dennis continued his inquiry. "What kind of bullet?"

"AK-47."

"Where?"

"In the arm." John smiled, knowing that was not the answer he wanted.

Dennis looked directly at John. He didn't verbalize the question again.

"Nam."

"I figured Nam. Where in Nam? I thought you were an oceangoing squid?"

"In the delta. Rach Soi on the Cai Lon River."

"What were you? PBRs?"

"Bravo Platoon, Seal Team One. Did three tours there."

Dennis was still looking at him, digesting this somewhat startling information. "You work the U Minh?"

"A few times."

Dennis looked down at the board he was cutting, ran it through the blade and put the wood on a pile destined for the west wall. He reached down and turned the machine off. John had begun to continue on with his load. "Hey!" Dennis said, quietly but firmly. John stopped and turned, his eyes hard, ready for potential shit. "Why the fuck doesn't anyone tell me my sister is going out with a Seal? She brings home all these assholes, then all of a sudden she moves to the other end of the spectrum and finds a goddamned Seal. I worked with you guys a couple of times. After Recon, you guys are top drawer." Dennis extended his hand. The two men shook hands for the second time, this time a camaraderie flowing through, Dennis even taking hold of John's elbow. Both men looked over at Ed, who was wiping a tear from his eye. They thought he was wiping away tears of laughter. But he wasn't.

"You knew, Dad. Didn't you?" Dennis didn't like being duped but saw the humor in the situation. He turned to John. "You knew, too. That shit about 'in the arm.'"

John smiled and shrugged. "I figured. I had you at an advantage. Your sister and parents are very proud that you were a marine. And very happy you made it home. They told me about you. And after she talked with you, Becky asked me if a squid was the same as a Seal. After I stopped laughing, I thought this might happen when we met."

Dennis laughed, slapped John on the shoulder, and moved toward the house. He false punched his father's ribs as he went by on his way inside. Becky was setting the table for dinner when Dennis entered the room and approached her. His eyes were intense but with a touch of mirth as he walked up to and into her space. "Next time you bring a guy home who's a navy Seal, you tell me right away. OK?"

Becky looked up at her brother, slowly assimilating what he was saying; finally realizing her brother was not mad but smiling at her. "I won't be bringing any other guys home, Dennis." moisture welling up in her eyes as she looked directly into his. Dennis, comprehending the significance of what his sister was saying, put his arms around her and hugged her softly.

"If he gives you any trouble you tell me. OK?"

"OK, Den."

Dennis stepped back, squeezed her arms in approval, and started back outside. In the doorway he stopped and turned back to her. "And what is this crap about 'Becky'? After all the whining about 'It's Rebecca,' now we're back to Becky? Let's get this squared away." He smiled and went outside.

Dinner was a tribute to the women, and the women basked in the compliments of their mates. Sonny's wife arrived with two freshly baked apple pies. Emily's leg of lamb was the hub around which the meal unfolded. After working hard all day and now enjoying the effects of the first few cold Budweisers and the banquet of food, the tired men mellowed quickly, melting into sofas and easy chairs. Becky proudly told the story of her aba-lone exploits and first venture into the underwater world. Cheryl, an accomplished potter, served the food almost exclusively on her work, proudly showing off her wares and her skill with a kiln. It was really beautiful pottery and in step with the growing move to self-sufficiency in the younger generation, especially those in the more rural areas. Talk of elk hunting in the fall caught John's interest. A planning meeting was put on the calendar in mid-September to scout and set up the necessary logistics.

The following day was even more productive. The three rooms were completely framed out, the roof trusses with plywood sheathing were in place, and Romex wire, with the help of Cheryl wiggling through the overhead crawl space, had been pulled back through to the main breaker box. Dennis felt they had accomplished much more than he had anticipated and embraced each of his volunteer crew with heartfelt thanks. To John he said, "We'll see you in September, if not before, to plan out that hunt. There's lot's of elk around here. And the meat hits the barbecue pretty good."

"If you get down to San Francisco, you and Cheryl can stay with us," John responded.

Dennis's eyebrow arched. "Oh? Rebecca's not on Steiner Street anymore?" He smiled as he watched both Becky and John turn red with embarrassment and fear that Emily or Ed might have overheard. They hadn't. "Well, thanks for the invitation. Maybe we can have some of that abalone, eh? Gee, guys. Cat got your tongue?" He laughed as he stepped between them, putting his arms simultaneously around them both. "John, you're not really a social studies professor at the university are you?" His infectious laughter caused Becky and John to regain their breath and composure and laugh along with him.

"Dennis, it's not what you think. I really like your sister. She's very special."

"Oh! You mean you're not sleeping together?" John blushed again, this time a rush of anger contributing to the color in his face. Dennis's arm tightened on his shoulder, and he burst into full laughter. "It's OK, young man.

At ease. This is the Age of Aquarius." Becky punched her brother moderately hard in his chest as a smile broke over her face. Quickly the three of them were laughing again.

"Don't tell Mom, Dennis. I have to figure out the best way to tell her."

"Mum's the word…Becky. Becky. I like that." He laughed again.

Dennis watched as his sister and her friend pulled away from the house waving out the Mustang's windows. John was a totally unexpected reversal in her choice of men. He had often thought about holiday dinners and family gatherings and having to put up with some asshole he didn't even like for thirty years. He actually liked John. His history as a Seal naturally worked to his advantage, but he was a good guy. Reliable, willing to get sweaty for a friend, tough. And his sister obviously liked him. He thought about her words yesterday about not bringing any more guys home. It sounded like she meant it. He waved. Oddly, he thought about who his best friend might be at this moment. John's name kept rolling through his mind. But that was silly. He had only just met the guy.

After long conversations, it was decided that John would take one or two classes at Cal in the fall semester. He could pick up remaining required GE courses and maybe take some engineering or marine geology prerequisites. He would talk to Lowell Berg about time off during the day if necessary, and how he could make up the time in the evening or on the weekend. The next major event in their busy schedule would be the trip to Coronado for Bob Friendly's retirement ceremony. Becky was looking forward to the trip, curious about seeing where John used to live and meeting more of those strange but fascinating men he had spent so much of his life with. She knew John welcomed her along, but she also recognized that she was trespassing in a man's domain and in a very close, very private society. Her thoughts were to keep a low profile and give John as much space as he wanted during their visit.

They left immediately after work on Friday, figuring to drive straight through to San Diego. but get a motel room that night and arrive at the

Coronado base in time for the ceremony at one o'clock. John had made arrangements for them to stay Saturday night at guest quarters on the base. It was a given that there would be a huge party after the ceremony. Actually there would be two parties. One would be for friends and family mixing in with the Seals. This would be dress uniform, a table of hors d'oeuvres, nonalcoholic punch, and a no-host bar. This was where parents, wives, girlfriends, and children could formally mingle with officers and other dignitaries, pay their respects, and still have a good time. The party would gradually grow more and more boisterous until, after most of the normal people had said their farewells, the party would move to the EM club where the hell-raising would begin in earnest. The latter was where the Seals paid tribute to one of their own in their unique pedal-to-the-metal fashion. John thought he could touch base with some of his closer buddies on Saturday morning before the ceremony, and then he and Becky would meet everyone at the official ceremony and party. About the EM club party, he still hadn't made up his mind. If Becky was to be the only woman, there was no way. Someone would surely get killed. But other wives and girlfriends would probably be there. He would have to wait and see.

It was eleven thirty when they checked into the Orange Grove Motel. They showered and watched the late news before hitting the sack. There was a segment on the news about a woman, somehow involved with a motorcycle group or gang, who had been killed after falling off a bike at high speed. Bruises acquired prior to the accident raised questions about whether she fell off the bike or was pushed. Her name was Connie Meister. She left two young children behind. Sometime around midnight, just before he fell asleep, John moved his hand to brush Becky's cheek gently with his fingers. The momentary physical contact filled his senses: the smoothness of her skin, her warmth, the delicious smell of her hair, and all of the things about her he had stored in his memory; her smile, the sound of her voice, the goodness of her heart. He let the feelings and the thoughts wash over and through him. Then he closed his eyes and drifted off to sleep.

At nine thirty the following morning, the marine sentry at the gate reviewed the guest list for Friendly's ceremony, found McConnell's name, and gave him a guest pass. John drove to the administration office to check in and see who was around. A very junior clerk whom John didn't recognize was alone in the office. The clerk told John the duty officer, Ensign Hugo, was making rounds but could be paged if necessary. On a weekend, particularly a weekend where a major retirement ceremony was scheduled, the most junior people were usually allocated the duty. They in turn usually had the least idea about where people were and what was going on, excluding, of course, the primary military functions of the day. John elected to scout around and see who was around. He explained to the young seaman at the desk who he was, and asked him to find out what quarters had been arranged for them and to check he and Becky in.

"Beck. You wait here. I want to run over to ops and see who's around. This defender of freedom," he said, indicating the young yeoman, "will tell you where we'll be staying. I'll be back in five minutes. OK?" With a wink at the slightly off-balance clerk, he left the office.

"OK." Becky was still taking in the incredible number of warships in the harbor, the massive amount of military hardware staged for loading, and the men in battle dress uniform who seemed to be everywhere. Guards at the gate with sidearms. This was truly a different world from the Cal campus and the carefree, permissive life in San Francisco. She watched John exit and thought about him slipping back into his old life of adventure with these men. As she observed all these things the word that kept coming to her mind was "consequences." That these people were dealing with very real, very scary consequences. The consequences of war. There was a fascination about being involved in something so powerful. So meaningful. Not that war was meaningful. But death sure was. Was her hold on him that strong?

John had only been gone a few minutes when a man in summer white uniform entered the office. The clerk sat up straight in his chair and said, "Sir!"

"Hello, Reilly. At ease." The man wore double silver bars on his collar. He had dark hair and swarthy, tanned skin. There were several small scars and many weather lines on his face. Becky thought him to be quite handsome in a rough way, almost a poster for a battle-hardened leader who shot up the enemy and led his men on to victory. When he saw Becky he stopped, removing his cover as he did so. "Ma'am. Are you being helped?"

Becky looked up at him, a little taken aback. "Yes, I am. Thank you. I'm waiting for John McConnell. He should be back any moment."

"So. John's here. It'll be good to see him. I'm Lou Retino. John and I worked together. Welcome to Coronado." He smiled warmly extending his hand to Becky.

"Hello. I'm Rebecca Saunders. John has mentioned your name. It's nice to be able to put a face with it." The two were shaking hands as John reentered the room.

"Hello, Lou. How's it goin'?" John smiled as he moved forward to shake his old CO's hand. "You guys getting by without me?"

"Always helps to get rid of deadwood." They shook hands warmly. "How's it going up at Berg Marine?"

"Good. He's a pretty good guy. Looks like I'm going back to school, too. Engineering. Hey, you've met Becky?'

"Yes, I have. And now I understand why you went up to San Francisco." Retino turned back to Becky. "My wife, Susan, will be here around noon. I'm sure she'd love to meet you, too. As a matter of fact, we may be coming up to San Francisco around Christmastime. To visit with Lowell. He's my daughter's godfather, you know. Maybe we can get together."

"That would be great," Becky responded, thinking to herself about how different these people were from most of her school friends. Not better or worse. Just different.

"John, I have a million things to do. I'll have Reilly here show you to your quarters and, if you want, take you over to the Exchange if you want to shop at our bargain prices. And I think there's a side boys practice at eleven o'clock in the gear warehouse. Thompson, Constanza, Blackley, and Mako are over there now. Rebecca, as soon as my wife gets here, we'll find you. Friendly's parents are here, too. You ladies may have to escort them during the ceremony." Retino turned to the yeoman at the desk. "Reilly. Take care of these people. Get Slewinsky over here to cover the office." Looking back at John and Rebecca, he said, "Among other things, I've got to wear full dress whites this afternoon. Not my favorite thing to do." He went into his office, shuffled through some papers, and headed out with a slight bow toward Becky and a pat on the shoulder for John. "See you later."

Around noon, as Becky was just finishing the final touches to the summer dress she would wear to the ceremony, there was a knock on the door of the barrack-like quarters they would call home tonight. John had gone off to practice something, and she would meet him at the ceremony. Becky opened the wooden door to find an attractive woman, fortyish, standing there and extending her hand. "I hope you're Rebecca. Hi. I'm Susan Retino, your guide for the afternoon and possibly part of the evening. One can never tell with these guys, my husband included."

Becky took the woman's hand and smiled. "I'm Rebecca. I hope I won't be in the way. I appreciate your looking after me. This is quite a place. And all these men. They're everywhere."

Susan laughed. "Yes, they are. And your John is one of the best. I'm so happy to see he's made his way back. From Vietnam and the Seals, I mean. A lot of them don't. Or else it takes a while. Anyway, if you're ready, we can get going. Lou asked me to look after Bob's parents, get them to the ceremony. So we'll have a little company."

"If there's anything I can do to help, please just ask. I'll be ready in just a second. Come in." Becky went into the bathroom to give her makeup one last inspection. Then she grabbed her purse and looked at Susan. "Ready."

The two women drove off base to a rather nice motel on a bluff overlooking the ocean to pick up the senior Friendlys. They were nice people, very proud of their son. They seemed a little nervous about the ceremony, not really sure what would be asked of them or what they should do. Susan had a knack for putting people at ease and, at Duane Friendly's insistence, the four of them had a cup of coffee as they chatted and looked out over the ocean.

"We're from Iowa. I never did understand how Bob got so involved with the ocean and all this underwater stuff," Mrs. Friendly confided to the group.

"I just made my first SCUBA dive about a week ago," Becky explained, "and it is absolutely fascinating. I can't wait to do it again. The ocean does have a way of grabbing hold of you."

They arrived at the grassy area where the ceremonial platform had been set up. In the distance, navy ships tugged relentlessly against their moorings, eager to be free to join in battle. Replenishment vehicles moved up and down the piers, and military people not involved with Friendly's retirement went about the business of war. Susan delivered the older couple to their son, who stood at the end of a red carpet that bisected two rows of folding chairs on its way to the stage platform. There were forty or fifty people already sitting or milling around the chairs. A group of maybe twenty-five members of the United States Navy Band were tuning their instruments, making that series of disjointed musical sounds that always seemed to precede a concert. The two women took seats near the front on the inboard side closest to the red carpet. They sat and talked for the fifteen minutes. before the band started playing a march, and everyone moved to the seats. Susan waved and greeted several other women as they waited. Becky waved to Dave Constanza and Jack Thompson, who sat across the aisle with a crowd of other young, obviously military men.

Finally the music stopped and things got quiet. From out of nowhere, a small formation of eight men—two rows of four—began a slow march toward the red carpet. These were side boys, sort of an honor guard; in this case, each side boy was a friend, comrade, or someone otherwise special in Bob Friendly's navy career. Traditionally, Susan explained, they would have worn dress white uniforms but, at Bob's request, they wore Tiger striped camouflage battle dress utilities. Friendly had asked for permission for them to wear scruffy uniforms, with grenades and ammo bandoliers and possibly sweatbands, in keeping with normal Seal operating garb. The request was denied; the concession to tradition was that the utilities were clean, boots gloss shined, and trouser cuffs tucked into the boot tops. His wish that the side boys all wear face paint was granted so the side boys were now 'men with green faces,' each with a .45 automatic (sans ammunition) strapped to one hip and a KA-BAR knife to the other. They made an impressive slow-march entry. They moved up, taking position four on either side of the red carpet, finally turning smartly toward the center and coming to attention. The band struck up again, and several high-ranking officers, including two admirals and two captains, moved along the carpet, through the guests and side boys, to the platform. Bob, his parents, and several men in civilian clothes followed them. Friendly's limp was not pronounced, but it was noticeable.

"Aren't Mr. Retino and John going to be here?" Becky asked, not seeing either man in attendance.

"They're both part of the ceremony. Look at the last side boy on the left." Becky studied the countenance under the camouflage to find John's face, very stern, glaring intently straight ahead. Even though she knew better, his face was frightening, the paint, the uniform, and the sidearms adding to the persona of the entire group. "That's Master Chief Andy Ryan in the front; Joel Curtis, another chief who retired last year; Jim Emory, who flew in from Little Creek for the ceremony. There are several faces I don't recognize, but they're all special people to Bob. I think John is, or was, the most junior guy. That's why he's last in line. It goes according to rank."

"Where's Mr. Retino?"

"Lou? He's delivering the flag. That's something they do at the end. It's actually quite touching. You'll enjoy it."

The band played the "Star Spangled Banner," and a navy captain took the microphone to begin the testimonials. Each of the officers on the platform gave glowing accounts of Bob Friendly's exploits over the years, liberally sprinkling their narratives with anecdotes of Bob's wilder side, particularly as a youngster. Many had known Bob for twenty years. Several gifts were presented and the US Navy presented a Certificate of

Appreciation to Friendly's mother. Mr. Friendly, with a tear in his eye, told the audience how proud he and his wife were of their son. Bob came over to give them both a big hug. The audience applauded. Friendly then gave a short speech, extolling his career with the navy, UDT, and the Seals, the close friends he had made, and his entire military family. In closing he looked back at one of the admirals. "I'm still a little ticked off about being restricted to quarters that time in Panama. A little machine-gun fire on the golf course makes the game more exciting, and the Javelina was delicious." The admiral laughed and shook his head as he rolled his eyes skyward. "Thank you all for coming." Bob concluded his speech and took his seat.

"There is one more presentation to make," the captain announced. "Chief Friendly, front and center, please." As Bob arrived at center stage, a cherry '57 Chevy, chrome gleaming against the immaculate metallic-red paint job, cruised up and parked near the end of the red carpet.

Susan leaned over to whisper in Becky's ear. "That's Bob's car. Not the one he drives but the one he works on and takes to auto shows. It's his pride and joy. It's sort of a symbol of his time off base and one of the things he'll do in his retirement." Lou Retino, in full dress whites, exited the car and approached the red carpet. In his extended hands he carried a folded American flag. Arriving at the carpet's edge, he stopped at rigid attention. At some unobservable signal, the side boys simultaneously took a step forward and maneuvered into a single line facing the platform. Andy Ryan directed an about-face, which brought John McConnell and Retino face-to-face. John, with exaggerated slowness, saluted the flag and then extended his arms to receive it from Retino. Lou then returned the salute. John made a smart about-face to receive a salute from the seventh side boy, who in turn took the flag and received a salute from John. As the flag was passed forward, the poem "Old Glory" was recited over the public address system. The solemnity with which the flag was passed forward, together with the moving words describing our flag, brought moisture to the eyes and a tightness in the chest of all in attendance.

The salutes continued, and the flag was passed through the line of side boys until it was delivered to Bob Friendly, who was then saluted by the entire line of friends and comrades. The side boys then returned to their double row formation along the carpet while Friendly, now holding the flag under his left arm, stood for a long moment as if deliberating what he should do next. Finally he turned and walked to where his father was seated. Bending over he placed the flag on his father's lap, straightened, and saluted. The senior, tears streaming down his face, nodded to his son. Then a bosun's whistle piped Bob off the stage. "Senior Chief Friendly, departing." The ceremony was officially concluded, and Bob returned to receive salutes and handshakes from the departing officers.

When the platform was cleared of dignitaries, the band played "Anchors Aweigh," the side boys marched off, and the crowd gathered around Bob and his parents to wish him well. To the left of the platform, an outdoor bar had been set up, and several tables of appetizers and finger food were uncovered. About fifteen minutes later, John, in civilian slacks and a light-blue golf shirt, arrived to join them. Becky was introduced to so many people that there was no hope of remembering them all. Bob Friendly put his arm around her when John introduced them. "So this is the gal that won old Johnny Boy's heart. Welcome to Coronado, my dear. You're beau is a good man. You be sure to take good care of him."

"I will," Becky responded not really sure what else she could say. Dave and Jack gave her hugs and pecks on the cheek, Dave looking over at John with mock innocence. Behind them was almost a line of tough young men waiting to be introduced to their old comrade's woman. To a man, they were polite and gentlemanly, respecting the fact that she was spoken for by one of their own. Becky thought with a chuckle what life would be like in San Francisco if this group came up for a visit. She saw her volleyball girls as innocent lambs.

By 1630 the high-ranking officers, most of the civilians, children, relatives and such had made their departure. This phase of the partying started closing down as the Seals, both officers and enlisted, accompanied by about ten wives or girlfriends, moved over to the EM Club to continue the reminiscing, storytelling, and companionship. Bob opened the bar, all drinks on him. The women tended to sit together in twos and threes mixed in among the men. Becky, Susan, and three others sat talking and watching and listening. "I'm always fascinated listening to their stories. And I always hear something new, some incredible predicament or situation these guys got into that scares the hell out of me. Of course, it's after the fact, and they're sitting in front of you, alive and laughing about it. Lou always plays it down, but the wives eventually hear about it. Worry comes with the territory. Becky, you're the lucky one. He's finished with Vietnam."

"Vietnam scares me. Andy thinks it's going to go on for a while despite what MacNamara says. The casualties are mounting fast. A lot faster than we know." Marjorie Ryan spoke with the authority of her husband. It was quiet among the women as this bit of information was digested.

There was a tinkle of glass as Bob Friendly stood tapping on his glass of beer. "Attention. Can I have your attention." Bob looked serious. The room quieted down. "I'd like to propose a toast to fallen comrades," he said holding up his glass. "I got word late this morning that Bosun Jackson was killed on Thursday. It was a routine sampan check. Couple of VC hidden below came out firing. Like all our comrades, he was a good man." He downed his beer, and everyone in the room followed his lead. Most of the men in that room had worked with Chief Bosun Mate Jackson in Vietnam. His loss was a significant dent in the notion that we were over there just toying with the Vietnamese until we decided to kick ass and go home. "Let's get a few pitchers of beer out here," Friendly instructed the bartender. "Somebody slip a quarter in that jukebox. And none of that Beatles shit!" The clear, mellow sound of John Denver's "Country Road" came joyously out of the machine taking minds off the lousy news of Jackson's demise. If nothing else, Seals don't dwell on bad news, at least not publicly, and the party resumed its happy track.

Fifteen minutes later, as the crowd grew more intoxicated with both drink and fellowship, Lou Retino stood and tapped his glass for attention.

It took a little longer, but the noise eventually diminished. "About a month ago a commendation medal was officially posted. I've been sitting on it, waiting for the right time to present it. Now seems like a good time." Lou took some official papers from a folder on the table and read. "The United States Navy hereby awards the Silver Star to Second Class petty officer John Reilly McConnell, for bravery under fire when, on 12 July 1969, while on a reconnaissance patrol with members of Bravo Platoon, Seal Team One, in the U Minh Forest area south of Saigon in the Republic of Vietnam, the patrol came under fire from a vastly superior enemy force of NVA regulars. The seven-man patrol held back the enemy as they called in for air support and artillery fire. One member of the patrol was killed and several, including McConnell, were seriously wounded. Despite his own wounds, he carried one wounded member of the patrol to a helicopter then went back into the midst of the enemy to recover another wounded comrade. Upon reaching the evacuation helicopter with his second comrade, McConnell collapsed with wounds to his arm and stomach." Retino paused. He looked up at the men. Waving his hand in a casual manner, he said, "It goes on, but you get the idea. He was pulled unconscious into the helo as it took off. I know he was out cold, because I pulled him in. John..." he said as he held out a small velvet box in the direction of the nonplussed young man sitting two tables away.

Becky had tears rolling down her face as she watched John. Susan gently squeezed her arm. The talk of death reverberated in their minds as this harrowing experience was added to the montage. Becky's emotion was as much from fear of almost having lost him, as it was her pride in his courage. John finally got up amid cheers and yells and slaps on the back. He took the package from Retino. "I didn't know you pulled me in, Lou. Thanks." Retino nodded as they shook hands.

Quietly Bob Friendly had the bartender set up about fifty shots of Jim Beam along the bar. "Everybody grab a shot here. You too, ladies," he called. When everyone had his or her glass, he lifted his in a toast. "To John McConnell. And just for the record, my ass was one of the ones he pulled

257

out." And he downed the amber liquid in one throw. Cheers went up, and drinks went down.

"Here we go," Susan said to Becky with a smile. "I think this will be a mellow night. But it won't be quiet or early."

Jack Thompson had come up alongside John, putting his arm around his shoulder. "I was the other comrade this guy dragged out. I already bought him a Heineken. But there'll be a round of drinks for everyone tomorrow at 0500. On me." Another roar went up amid shouts of "Speech! Speech!"

Finally McConnell, his shot glass replenished, stood up on a chair and looked out over the crowd. Still somewhat choked up, he tried several times to speak but stopped each time. A glance at his shot glass gave him a short-term respite as he then slowly emptied the contents and licked his lips. "We all know that everyone here would have done the same thing, given the opportunity. Even Constanza." He smiled over at Dave. "Every man in this room is magnificent; one hell of a soldier... and my friend. We should all have one of these." He held up the box. Cheers went up. "You guys are all special." John stopped for a moment to have his glass refilled. He seemed to have a thought and paused for a moment to sort it out. "I'll tell you what I would like from you guys. When I have my babies... my children, I want every member of the team to be an honorary godfather. To watch over them. Cover their back trail." A roar went up again.

"You got it, John."

"We'll be there for them, buddy!"

"How many you plan on having?"

"Hey, John! Does their mother know about this yet?"

A lot of eyes were on Becky, sitting almost in a trance, the other women huddling about her protectively. On the chair, John looked momentarily puzzled. "Hold on a minute, guys. I better check on this." He turned toward Becky, locking on her eyes across the room. She could see deep into his eyes, feel his presence, and knew they were communicating. "Becky, will you marry me?"

The question was like an explosion. All eyes were on her, but she saw only John. Would she marry him? The words were like nectar. Of course she would marry him. But she sat in stunned silence. "If not him, how about me?" a voice came from the back. Finally she smiled a radiant smile and said, "Yes, John. I will."

The room erupted into applause, yells, and whistles.

"Can we all be godfathers?" a voice asked.

Becky looked around the room at Constanza, Thompson, Friendly, Blackley, McDaniels, Andy Ryan, Lou Retino, and the others. "I would be honored to have you gentlemen be godfathers to our babies." Another roar went up. The room was an oasis that occasionally in our lives we are blessed to experience. Everyone was happy. Everyone was smiling and feeling good and telling people about it. The women were all crying happy tears, hugging Becky.

Marjorie Ryan, a tear rolling down her cheek, went to the bar. "Keep that goddamned whiskey away from the women and bring a bottle of white wine with stemmed glasses to our table," she told the barman. She would take charge of the women now, keep them safe and protected from what was sure to be a crazy night. She caught her husband's eye. He smiled and winked at her. For him that was a lot, and the tear on her cheek was replenished.

By eleven o'clock the women were gone. Susan drove Becky back to their quarters. The men would party long into the night, and it wouldn't do for a wife to be passed out behind the bar. Some of the men would be passed out. Most would have a serious hangover in the morning. But under the circumstances tonight, that would be all right. As it was, the women had finished off three bottles of wine before leaving and were pleasantly sloshed themselves. Retino had shore patrol standing by to provide rides for the women and any sailor who might need assistance. A retirement party was considered a legitimate excuse to party, raise a little Cain, and get shitfaced. Becky couldn't sleep right away, despite all the alcohol. Mrs. John McConnell! It was unbelievable. Waves of happiness washed over her. She saw John standing there in a tuxedo, the minister smiling, her dad waiting to walk her down the aisle. "The wondering is over." She smiled to herself. "This will be my life. We will make our world together." Judy and her baby came into her mind. Judy would be happy for her.

There was noise at the door. Knocking and scuffing. Looking at the portable clock on the night table and ascertaining it was two thirty in the morning, Becky asked who it was. Lou Retino answered. When she opened the door Lou, Bob Friendly, and Andy Ryan held John about an inch off the floor. His head flopped as they moved him inside. "He's sound asleep, ma'am," Ryan explained. "Asleep may not be the right word. But you understand." The men laid their fellow Seal onto one of the twin beds, Bob removing John's shoes. They stood awkwardly for a moment, wondering if there was any more they could do, then moved to the door. Retino handed her the small velvet box. "Good night," they said and closed the door behind them. Becky watched them so gently take care of her man, aware that the three men were indeed warriors, men whose lives were filled with danger, violence, death, sorrow, pain. And yet they could be so tender and kind and caring. "Yes," she thought, "They can be godfathers. They would watch her children's back trail."

She thought of her brother and wished he could have been here. He was like these men. A loud snore or grunt brought her attention back to John. She took off his shirt and pants and sighed, running her fingers over his hair. She leaned over kissing him on the temple. There was no reaction. "I must be losing my charm," she mused. At three thirty in the morning, she was still sitting on his bed watching him, thinking about the evening. Lt. Retino's words about John in Vietnam, about his being shot, and shooting the enemy ran through her mind; the medal in the velvet case was testament to his courage and to the depth of feeling he had for these men. She found it hard to imagine a world so dangerous; so violent; so different from her own. So different from their own now. Her eyes finally started to close involuntarily, so she moved into her bed and quickly nodded off to sleep.

Becky was showering when John awoke around noon. His head throbbed painfully, the memories of the night before fuzzy. He remembered the Silver Star, his proposal to Becky, and a lot of backslapping. He did not remember coming home or getting into bed. He thought he might puke and wished Becky would hurry out of the shower.

When she emerged from the bathroom, John was sitting on the bed, his head in his hands and his elbows on his knees. She went to him and gently massaged his temples. He stood up quickly and went into the bathroom without saying a word. The sounds of his retching at least clarified why he wasn't talking. She listened as he brushed his teeth and showered. He finally emerged with a towel wrapped around his waist looking for fresh underwear and clean clothes. "How're you doing, partner?" Becky inquired.

"I've been better. I feel like ten pounds of crap in a five-pound bag. My apologies if I embarrassed you last night. I don't even remember coming home. I've never been that drunk. Jesus."

"Maybe you're just out of practice."

"Maybe. We probably need to talk about some things, but if it can wait until we get home, I would sure appreciate it. I can barely think, never mind talk coherently."

"Sure." Becky responded. She was not sure what to think. Not sure what he remembered or what he wanted to remember. She didn't doubt his love for her for a moment,, but last night had hit both of them like a sledgehammer. "He just needs time to sort things out and put things in order in his own mind. God! I hope he remembers proposing. Of course he does," she thought. "I'll sure remind him if he doesn't."

"Are you OK to drive?" he asked.

"Yes. I'll drive. You take it easy." They stopped at the admin office. Only the yeoman was there. John left a note for Lou, got some APCs (all-purpose capsules—like aspirin, only stronger), and then they were through the gate and on the road. John fell asleep almost immediately. He woke when they stopped for gas and got coffee. Although he gave Becky a hug and a peck on the cheek as the gas was being pumped, after five minutes on the road he was asleep again.

They hauled their overnight bags up the stairs. It seemed as if they had been away for a month rather than two days. "More coffee?" Becky asked.

"Please." John retrieved his dop kit from the luggage and brushed his teeth again, downing several more APCs in the process. He went into the bedroom returning a few moments later to the stool by the kitchen counter.

"I may have put you on the spot last night," he started. "You really didn't have time to think about it, or much choice, given the crowd support I had. If you want more time to think about it, or if you want to back out, I'll understand. But you should know when I asked you to marry me, I was not drunk or confused or unsure. It all seemed so clear to me at that moment. I love you. We should have kids. We should get married. It's the right thing. They probably wouldn't make very good godfathers, but that seemed like a good idea at the time. Becky, I would like you to be my wife. Forever. Will you marry me?"

"I had all the time I needed to think about it last night. I love you too, John. I would be proud and happy to be your wife. And I think those men would make fabulous godfathers. I think they're all wonderful." She moved into his arms and kissed him, tasting the fresh toothpaste and loving the feel of his arms around her again, his lips on hers.

John fumbled in his pocket. "I didn't anticipate this happening so soon so I don't have a ring for you yet. But my dad sent this when I told him about you. It was my mother's engagement ring. He felt that I should have it." He slipped the diamond ring on Becky's finger and kissed her hand. "If you don't like it we can get another one. It may be too old-fashioned. We'll get one you like."

Becky looked at the sparkling gem on her finger. It was a fairly large diamond surrounded by a ring of smaller diamonds. It was absolutely beautiful. "Diamonds don't go out of fashion, John. I love it. I wouldn't give it up for anything." They kissed again. "You know, John, each week I think 'Wow! What a terrific weekend. This was one in a million. And the very next weekend I say the same thing. What do you have planned for next weekend?" They laughed. And they thought about their future.

CHAPTER FOURTEEN

Big Sur, California

September 1969

The news of Becky and John's engagement was received throughout their circle of family and friends with approval and excitement. The news itself wasn't a big surprise to those who knew them, their feelings for each other were so open and obvious, but the speed with which it happened took most unawares. Some of Becky's friends and family had never met or even heard of John or, at best, had met him only once. Their formal announcement was made at a family dinner in St. Helena over the Labor Day weekend. The Seal community, of course, was in the know from the beginning. Jack Thompson had leaked the news to Cathy Ventura several days after he recovered from the retirement party. But the family was surprised. They were happy to see their daughter so happy, settling in with the man she loved and who, apparently, loved her very much, despite the short time they'd known each other.

John had cornered Ed Saunders alone in the barn soon after their arrival on Saturday morning to ask for his blessing in seeking his daughter's hand in marriage. Initially nervous and making small talk, John finally looked Ed in the eye and straight-out asked permission, swearing to love and care for her forever. At first Ed was taken aback by the request, but he quickly gave his consent with a handshake and a hug for his future son-in-law. Dennis and Cheryl came down from Crescent City for the weekend, and everyone commented on how cheerful and jovial Dennis was. It had been before

Vietnam that anyone could remember Dennis being so outgoing. He took the liberty of breaking out a bottle of his father's thirty-year-old Glenfiddich Scotch to toast the engagement.

At the announcement Ed shook John's hand approvingly as he formally welcomed him to the family. He hugged his daughter, her eyes glistening and radiant. The question of what kind of man she would finally bring home had been answered much to his satisfaction. Emily cried happy tears and hugged them both. Grandma Nell told them they had to come to her house for dinner soon. There was an air of mystery in her voice. Becky proudly displayed her engagement ring and, much to John's embarrassment, showed everyone his Silver Star medal, which prompted a second Glenfiddich toast by Dennis.

The two men shared several more fingers of the quality Scotch, as they talked quietly alone for a while. The bottle would undoubtedly have been completely drained had not John been in such high demand to meet new family members. There was a slide show and 8 mm movies of the Saunders' early years. Becky and Dennis both blushed when shown at ages two and four bathing in the buff in an oak barrel cut in half for use as a kiddies' swimming pool. Ed explained the sacrifice he and Emily had made in unselfishly drinking all that wine just so their kids could have a pool to splash around in. Several old W. C. Fields movie shorts were also aired to laughter and a variety of equally funny imitations. A long telephone call to Florida drew John's side of the family in on the occasion. John spoke to his dad and Jennifer for perhaps five minutes, the latter confirming her Christmas visit. Becky, Emily, and Ed spoke with the McConnells for over an hour. A spring wedding was decided upon. The two families would keep in touch. It was a good weekend.

USF won some volleyball games, and John matriculated at Cal for two classes with Lowell Berg's blessing. They had Judy and Jim over for "homemade jelly donuts" to announce their engagement. Becky concocted Monterey Jack cheese and abalone omelets with bagels and cream cheese in lieu of jelly donuts. The omelets weren't bad. Actually darn good. The stereo brought the sound of the Beatles into their lives, and they went to see *Butch Cassidy and the Sundance Kid.* Becky thought her brother looked like Sundance. John wondered just how much dynamite Butch used on the train's door.

Autumn began to touch the leaves. Kelp washed up onto the beach more frequently. John thought he fell more deeply in love every day but then rationalized that that was an impossibility. Somewhere in mid-September they both realized their weekends were like roller-coaster rides, and it was time to slow down, if only for one weekend. To just spend some time together, regroup, smell the roses. Staying at home would invariably lead to company, so it would have to be a getaway weekend. But where? After discussion over a glass of wine, John's suggestion to drive down to Big Sur on the ocean won the day. After Labor Day the camping crowds would be diminished, the weather not really that cold, and the chances of running into someone they knew slight. They would bring some dive gear to poke around in the water, maybe even spear a fish or two now that, by California Fish and Wildlife edict, the abalone season was officially over. There were a few awkward moments when they had to make excuses for not being avail-able, but both were looking forward to their time alone and were not to be deterred.

On Saturday morning of the third weekend of September, John and the future Mrs. McConnell took off in the gray pickup and headed south on the Pacific Coast Highway toward Carmel, Monterey, and Big Sur. A chill in the morning air brought out sweaters and sweatshirts, but the ascending sun in the east promised a beautiful day. There was no rush. Part of the getaway was the drive itself. The notion that they didn't have to be anywhere until Monday morning was itself a major part of the relaxation process. At Carmel they walked for a while, browsing in the neat shops and getting a soup and sandwich combo for lunch at a sidewalk cafe. The mother of pearl fish pen-dant dangled from a silver thread on Becky's chest, secure and warm and loved. At Monterey, John stopped at a dive shop across from Cannery Row, which had been abandoned when the once-abundant sardines mysteriously disappeared from the offshore waters, to shoot the breeze and perhaps pick up a few pointers on where to dive. Lovers' Cove or Monastery Beach were recommended. The cove was a marine sanctuary, however, so spearfishing was forbidden, but there was good stuff to see. Several local divers suggested places to hunt for lingcod and cabazon. The weather was great for diving, but at this time of year you had to watch more closely for the rogue seasonal wave and the riptide. John could almost see Ed Ricketts of *Between Pacific Tides* fame and immortalized by John Steinbeck's novel *Cannery Row* poking about in the tide pools collecting intertidal specimens.

They chose Monastery Beach for its large and deep kelp beds, prolific intertidal organisms and the chance, albeit not a great chance, to spear a fish for dinner. After another quick refresher lesson on SCUBA procedures, they backed into the water from the sandy beach and, literally moments later, were cruising along the rock/sand bottom at eighty feet. At that depth, the kelp was like a forest of tree trunks beneath a canopy of undulating brown. Sunlight filtering through the water cast moving shadows, dance partners to the leaves of kelp windblown on the surface. Bright orange garibaldi, California's glorious state fish, darted about with impunity from John's spear. Becky's eyes widened when John pointed to her depth gauge reading of eighty feet. Putting his thumb and forefinger together he told her everything was all right. He extended his arms palms up and floated in a 360-degree circle, a foot off the bottom. Giving a thumbs-up, his eyes said, "Isn't this great?" Becky nodded, smiling through her mouthpiece, her confidence restored by John's presence and obvious skill in this environment. Still, eighty feet is eighty feet and something to be aware of.

Their black swim fins propelled them leisurely through the forest of kelp; looking, poking, exploring. A tug on John's fin drew his attention. Becky had spotted a fish, a lingcod, lying perfectly camouflaged on a yellow, green, and red sponge-and-algae-covered rocky outcropping. John brought up his double-banded Arbolete spear gun, circled to the rear of the fish, and approached from behind. John came in about six feet off the bottom but with his arm extended, the barbed tip on the end of the four foot long spear gun was only a few inches off the bottom. The tip came slowly to the neck of the fish and suddenly exploded. The fish lunged violently off the bottom, jerking the line and the gun in John's hand. John went hand over hand down the nylon line to the spear shaft and the prey. The fish was pretty large, ten or eleven pounds, and thrashed with surprising force. Once John had the spear in hand, however, the thrashing was contained to the shaft and slowly subsided. Removing the fish from the spear, John pulled out a cloth rice bag, stuck the fish in head first, and tucked the end of the bag under his weight belt. Becky silently applauded and rubbed her stomach. John gave another thumbs-up to Becky and then a signal to begin moving back toward the beach and the surface.

"John, that was beautiful! The kelp and those orange fish! And what were those things that looked sort of like abalone?"

"Chitons. Some of them get pretty big but you can't eat them. Hey, good eye on that lingcod. I completely missed him."

"He moved after you passed over him. I just saw him move, or I would have gone right by, too. I think he would have dragged me away. He really pulled on the gun."

"Well, thanks to your sharp eye, we have fresh fish for dinner."

After getting their gear off, John cleaned the fish right on the beach drawing a small flock of seagulls. He threw bits of the entrails into the air to watch their aerial acrobatics. They changed in the truck, throwing the salt-laden dive gear into the back bed until a fresh water hose could be found. Becky ran into a small grocery store for additional food supplies announcing that the menu was sautéed filet of lingcod, macaroni and cheese, and green salad with italian dressing. A bottle of Chablis thoughtfully brought from home would complement the meal. The next hour was spent searching for a suitable campground, preferably one with a view of the ocean. In the end it wasn't perfect, but it was getting late. It did have a view of the ocean, if you walked a hundred yards or so, and they were getting hungry.

Becky began preparations for dinner while John rigged up the tent, collected wood for a campfire, and hosed off the dive gear. The two-burner

Coleman camp stove popped on to heat water for the macaroni. Becky tried to calculate the meal's timing, so she could have everything ready at the same time. Across the way, a pickup truck with a full-size camper fitted onto the bed was the only other vehicle parked in the campground. A couple, maybe in their late forties, walked over to where John was washing the dive gear and introduced themselves. The three talked while John continued to hose. The man then helped John hang the gear over the back of the truck and on nearby branches. When they all approached Becky, John introduced her to Rose and Ira Hampton. The Hamptons were traveling from Las Vegas to Portland to visit relatives. The trip was as much, they explained, to see and touch the ocean, as it was to visit relatives. The desert was wonderful, but they needed an annual dose of salt air and water as far as the eye could see. Rose offered to bring over the tortilla chips and salsa they were about to have. Becky countered with an invitation to share their freshly caught lingcod. The two women began to pool their grocery resources, and a much-expanded garden salad and garlic french bread were added to the menu. Conversation was fast and interesting. Rose was a blackjack dealer at the Sands Hotel, and Ira worked for security at the Desert Inn. Questions and stories went on until eleven o'clock, when everyone decided it was time to hit the sack. Breakfast of coffee, fruit, and donuts would happen whenever they woke up.

John zipped their sleeping bags together. Snuggling into the oversize bag, they cuddled and talked about the day. "Rose and Ira are neat people," Becky commented. "It would be fun to visit them in Las Vegas some day. You know, John, for someone who's sort of…quiet, you always seem to meet people. It's a quality about you."

"I had a hell of a time meeting you. So it doesn't work all the time."

"You know what I mean. Anyway, they're nice. It must be crazy living in Vegas. I mean everything being open twenty-four hours a day, the gambling, entertainment."

"He sure had some interesting stories. I guess when there's that much money someplace, there will always be people who think they can win it or steal it. And some probably do. Those are the stories we don't hear about."

"You know, I've never really spent time in the desert. It would be fun to explore a real desert. Cactus and scorpions."

"And sidewinders. But yeah, it would. Let's put that on the calendar. Maybe in 1973, we could squeeze it in. Good night, babe."

"Good night, John." Becky rolled over to kiss John goodnight. Their kiss lingered just a moment too long. The delay changed it from a good-night kiss to something more passionate. As the passion grew, John's hand slipped beneath Becky's T-shirt. His hand caressed her breast; his fingertip made tiny circles on her nipple. The kiss was now way beyond good night. Her hand slid under his boxers, sliding down until she felt his now swelling member. She caressed it, encouraging it to grow; succeeding. John slipped her shirt off and took her breast into his mouth. Becky continued to massage him, finally stopping only to pull his shorts down and off. His erection was complete. She rolled on top of him, her pubic hair soft and inviting against him. Their bodies moving together, rubbing, feeling; their kiss uninterrupted; their tongues intertwined. Soon Becky reached down to guide John into her. Her wetness allowed him to slide deep into her without delay. Their kiss now became more delicate, orchestrated by subtle movements of their bodies. John's hands gripped her buttocks, rocking her on him. His fingers moved up and down on her back, scratching gently. Becky's hands held John's head, caressing his cheeks and temple. They moved slowly, both wanting to prolong the moment. "I love you, John."

"I love you, too." The exchange prompted more vigorous movement, a greater eagerness to please. Their movement joined in a rhythm with more purpose. By unspoken mutual consent they rolled over, John on top now, moving steadily. There was no thought of sex or lust. It was sharing; love. Just before he came, John kissed Becky, holding the kiss as he poured into her, as he gave her part of himself. Becky, on the verge of orgasm, whispered, "Don't stop. Keep going." John obliged until he felt her body contract hard several times, then slowly relax, almost going limp. She moaned softly while John kept moving until, without his consent, he slipped out of her, spent. Rolling his weight off to lie next to her, he kissed her cheek and neck while she lay with her eyes closed. His hand began again to gently caress her breasts. They lay together quietly for several minutes. "I'm so happy, John. I'm almost afraid I'm too happy. That it won't last. That it's a dream. I do love you."

"The sleeping bag is all wet. That tells you it's not a dream." He laughed. More seriously he said, "I know how you feel, Beck. But we won't let it end. Ever. I promise." He kissed her gently on the lips and lay back. Becky nestled her head on his shoulder, his arm around her. Each thought similar thoughts and dreamed of their life to come.

After the Hamptons took off, reiterating their invitation to visit, they hiked down a fairly steep trail to a small rocky beach wedged in between two granite outcroppings. Wet suits and snorkel gear allowed them to explore offshore and try, unsuccessfully, to get close to a pair of sea otters frolicking in a nearby kelp bed. The remnants of a campfire and a broken surfboard on the beach spoke of activity. They poked around the cobblestone beach discovering seashells, a fascinating piece of driftwood that looked like a sperm whale, and an old bottle, alas without a message inside. Lugging the driftwood back up the hill to become a memento of the trip and a neat decorative part of their apartment, they returned to the campsite and packed up. The warmth of the sun dictated T-shirts for the leisurely drive back. It was early in the day that so time was not an issue. They were wide open to explore and seize on any adventure that might present itself. Perhaps not consciously, they were building a foundation of experiences as a couple, as a team. Not too far up the road was what appeared to be a unique restaurant or tavern, or both set up on a hill on the ocean side of the road among madrone and wind-sculpted Monterrey cypress. The use of whole tree trunks in its construction gave it a wonderfully natural and timeless look. It was called Nepenthe's.

Back in Oakland the jukebox blared acid rock, ivory balls on the pool table clicked, and smoke hung heavy from the ceiling. Dozens of men in black leather, dirty T-shirts, and heavy boots vied for the unattached women and some of the attached women. Fights were common but seldom interrupted the action for long. It was Saturday night in Oakland and it was party time. Suddenly a whistle blew, drawing everyone's attention to the bartender. "Two black-and-whites outside. Shuck your shit or go out the back. I don't want trouble inside." Joints and small bags of marijuana hit the floor to be ground into the worn wood. Several people, who probably had more than they wanted to throw away, moved quickly out the back door. At least two guns were hidden away, hopefully to be retrieved later. About a dozen moved out the front door to see what had prompted the unsolicited visit of four cops.

"Who owns this bike?" A large uniformed officer asked the crowd.

"I do. So what?" came the response as one of the crowd stepped forward.

"Ah. Mr. Harris. Nice to see you again. Unfortunately you have a broken rearview mirror. See? It's cracked. That's a no-no. I'm gonna have to issue you a citation."

"What bullshit! You guys are just busting my ass." Boomer moved forward threateningly.

The officer looked across the street where two additional police cruisers were parked. "However you want to play it, Boomer. I think we have enough juice to take you down, if that's what you want."

"Back off, Boomer," shouted several voices from the crowd.

Reluctantly Boomer accepted his citation, body search, and general humiliation. Then the officer tipped his cap and said, "Have a nice day, Mr. Harris." Back inside, it was Crash who was really pissed off. Not at the cops, but at Boomer. Since Connie had "fallen off" his bike, the cops had hounded Boomer and, by association, all of the gang members. Crash, like the police, suspected that Boomer had killed her, but there was no evidence to support that suspicion. Boomer stuck to his story that she'd simply fallen off at sixty miles an hour. As a result of these suspicions, the police kept up a regular check on Boomer, hoping that something would happen to give them a lead, or someone in the gang or close to it would come forward with information voluntarily, or in exchange for immunity from another minor offense. It was getting to be a real pain in the ass.

After the police had gone, the bartender suggested to Boomer and his fellow gang members that it might be better if they didn't come around for a while. It was bad for business when cops showed up, and the cops seemed to be all over Boomer. Most other customers applauded the suggestion. Crash took a final bottle of beer, downed it in one chugalug, and announced to his gang and the crowd generally, "Tomorrow I'm heading to LA. Staying here is bullshit. Maybe we'll come back when things cool down." Looking at the bartender, he said, "Sorry for the trouble. We're out of here." and he went out the door, leaving the rest of the gang to decide what they were going to do. All followed, as did the two police cruisers when they pulled out of the tavern's parking lot. It was late afternoon on Sunday before six members of the gang pulled up stakes and headed with Crash to the Pacific Coast Highway for a hassle-free drive to Los Angeles. Boomer opted to come along. Crash was torn between kicking his dangerous ass out of the gang and the unwritten law of all gangs to support their own. There were some in the gang who thought Boomer was the cat's ass. Tough and good to have around when there was trouble. Crash wondered how people could be so fucked up. In the end, Boomer was allowed to come along.

Nepenthe was more an experience than an expensive lunch. It was a California landmark that would stay with you. The view was spectacular; the food good, the building open and wonderful. The parking area held Cadillacs and VW bugs; vans and campers, motorcycles and family station wagons. The place was a product of the sixties—mellow, the owners making their own dream come true while giving an experience to travelers who elected to drive the winding coast road, rather than blast up through the fumes and heat of Interstate 5. Becky and John spent almost two hours over lunch, touring the grounds, and browsing the small gift shop. They could see to the horizon and down the coast for miles. Hawks, flying perhaps a thousand feet over the water, hung in the air only a short distance off the deck where they ate. Mockingbirds and chipmunks in the nearby trees demanded food, occasionally venturing to the railing to snatch a crumb or carrot slice set out to draw them closer. Reluctant to leave, by four o'clock the lovers were once again on their way, watching a distant offshore rain squall move like the shadow of a predator through the sun lit waves to the west.

They had been driving for about twenty minutes when John saw the troop of motorcycles coming down the opposite side of the single-lane highway. They moved gracefully, each tilting in turn with every rise and curve, like a centipede. John watched them close and finally begin to pass. As he watched the riders, his eyes locked on to eyes he had seen before. The man in the tavern in Larkspur! The man who had given Becky such a hard time. Their eyes held for a split second that seemed like an eternity then disappeared as fast as a blink. John felt a rush, the once-familiar sense of fear, anticipation, and exhilaration that mixed together before a combat mission. His eyes went to the rearview mirror, hoping to see the motorcycles grow smaller and finally disappear into the blacktop. To his alarm and dismay, one bike blinked brake lights. Then another.

John put his foot to the floor, the truck surging forward pushing them back against the seats. Becky looked over questioningly, seeing the look of concern on John's face. "What is it? What happened?"

"Remember that guy in Larkspur? The biker in the Blue Fox? The day you took me to San Francisco General? That was him just went by. We looked right at each other. I think they're turning around." The truck squealed around a curve. "We have to find a place to lose them or fight. I don't think that guy was too happy getting hauled off to jail that day. He'll want revenge on me. And he'll want you. Listen. You do exactly what I tell you. There's no time for questions. Just trust me."

"Oh God, John. There were a bunch of them. What will you do?"

"There were seven of them. I have to get you safe first. Then I can work on them."

Becky twisted around and looked out the truck's rear window. "There's no one behind us. Maybe they're not coming." And then they appeared from behind a curve, like a serpent, black and malevolent. "They're com-ing." Becky's heart tightened.

John saw them a mile or two back. He was doing seventy, looking for something, he wasn't sure what. "I'm going to stop. When I tell you, jump out fast and hide. Just hide yourself. Don't let them see you, no matter what. Let them deal with me. OK? You understand?"

"I can't leave you alone. I can't do that, John." Tears were rolling down her face.

"You have to. It's the only way we'll get out of this. You have to trust me." He screeched around yet another sharp curve, almost going off the road. Ahead he saw a campground sign to the left and cut hard. He braked, barely negotiating the entrance turn. He tore down a hundred-foot road that ter-minated in a one-way loop to the right. He hit the brake again and yelled to Becky. "Get out! Hide in those bushes on the left. Crawl away as far as you can. Don't show yourself until you hear me call or the cops come. *Do it!*"

The minute she was clear of the truck, he hit the accelerator, laid rubber to the loop, and squealed right. He saw Becky dive into the bushes and disap-pear in the undergrowth a second before he made the turn. At the end of the loop he pulled into a campsite-parking lane, reached under the seat for the KA-BAR—he had given up carrying the .45 in the truck—and melted into the bushes that provided some privacy to individual campsites. With Becky safe for the moment, he stopped, drawing a deep breath. His hands could almost feel the old shotgun he'd carried in Vietnam. His psyche was changing, reverting back, steeling itself for what he might have to do to protect his beloved. There was no fear. No bile in his throat. No queasiness for the violence he anticipated. He moved to a cluster of trees that edged a horse corral. The position gave him a view of both the bushes where Becky lay hidden and the road.

Boomer's eyes had opened wide as he looked into the eyes of the man who had conquered him that day in the bar. All of the stories he had told of being sucker punched and tricked flooded back to him, convincing him that the next time, this time, would be different. That this time he would emerge victorious. Vindicated. Yelling to Crash, he braked and pulled off onto the shoulder. Seeing Boomer fall out of formation, the rest of the bikers braked and swung around to see what had happened.

He was obviously excited, yelling as veins in his thick neck stood out. "The son of a bitch who sucker punched me. He just drove by. I'm gonna get that bastard. Come on!" Without waiting, he twisted the accelerator handle, spraying dirt and gravel behind him, leaving Crash and the others little choice but to follow. The sight of the truck far ahead spurred Boomer on. The powerful Harley quickly gained speed and closed ground. Obviously the truck had accelerated also and periodically was lost to sight as the road curved and dipped. Each time Boomer and the gang came round a curve, the truck was there, a little closer, losing ground to the faster bikes.

Boomer raced a hundred feet or more ahead of the others. As he came around the latest curve, the truck was not in sight on the long straightaway before him. He braked, assuming correctly that the truck had turned off. There was only one place to turn, into the campground just as you came out of the curve. Boomer was turning around as the rest came thundering and squealing around the bend. He waved to the turnoff. Lefty, leading the pack because he rode dangerously fast, saw the signal. He began to brake at the same time he started his turn. Speed dictated the turn ratio, and Lefty's speed far exceeded what was possible. His bike slid across the highway sideways, banged into a large barrier rock, and smashed against the corral corner post. Lefty's foot was broken against the rock and his body caught between the tumbling bike and the stout post. The others went past the turnoff, slowed, and circled back to the wreck. Boomer drove right by Lefty down the entrance road in search of the gray truck. Soon after he made the right turn he saw the quarry sitting in a campsite-parking stall. Empty.

Crash pulled over to tend to Lefty, who was not in good shape. He waved at Gomez, who carried a first aid kit on long trips. "Bring the kit! Charlie. You stay at the entrance in case the son of a bitch tries to come back out. The rest of you go in and help Boomer." The two men pulled Lefty from between the motorcycle and the fence post and applied pressure bandages to any place that was bleeding. Lefty was conscious but in pain and going into shock. "Get a sleeping bag." Crash directed Gomez. "Quick!" He raised the injured man's feet and covered him with the cheap sleeping bag Gomez brought over. "Get another bag. This piece of shit is like a dishrag."

The campground was small. The individual campsites, six in all, were relatively close together. They were afforded some privacy by the madrone and other brush planted around each one. Even in such close quarters, one could avoid detection by stealth and prudent movement. John moved toward the corral and began to belly in Becky's direction. He watched Boomer go past. Then he saw Lefty go into the post. He saw Boomer motor recklessly up to the truck. Moving like the point man on a combat patrol, he made for the row of stacked hay and a shed that provided cover for the horses in the corner of the corral.

Hotshot and Waco stopped at the entrance, watching as Crash and Gomez tended to Lefty. At Crash's command, they proceeded down the road in pursuit of Boomer. Waco continued straight, going against the one-way sign. Hotshot saw Boomer at the end of the loop. He moved toward him but stopped when Boomer waved him back. Stacking his bike, Hotshot removed a billy club from his saddlebag and began to search on foot for somebody. The campground seemed deserted, so he figured anything that moved would be fair game. With Boomer ahead of him and Waco gone the other way, Hotshot decided to look behind the stacked hay. He moved silently, gripping the club tightly in his hand. This would not be Hotshot's first fight. He, like Boomer, had a penchant for finding trouble. He reveled in it. As he cleared the shrubbery lining the road, he saw the hay bales and, some distance across the corral, Crash and Gomez working on Lefty.

Peering carefully around the hay bales, he froze. The pale blue of a t-shirt caught his eye. A man lay prone at the edge of the shed watching Crash and the road. The man was about twenty feet in front of him. At the sound of Charlie impatiently revving his Harley, Hotshot decided the noise would cover his movement and keep his prey's attention. He began to quietly close the distance, his club ready to come down hard on this turd.

Across the road, Becky also watched events unfold. Any hope that everything would work out peacefully was dashed when Lefty went into the post and blood was on the ground. As she watched from her concealment in the bushes, she saw one of the bikers come into the corral. It looked like he was sneaking up on something. She raised her head for a better view, looking for whatever or whomever he was sneaking up on. And saw John looking over in her direction. Noise from a motorcycle filled her ears. She remembered John's instructions. In a second the man would be on him. She saw a stick raised behind John and knew he had to be warned. She stood and yelled across the road, "John! Behind you!"

Hotshot brought the billy club down hard, but at the last moment his target rolled to the side. The club hit the corral dirt. A hand grabbed Hotshot's collar and jerked his face into the ground and the billy club. A tooth broke. The side of his head exploded and, as he lolled off into unconsciousness, he felt a pain in his chest. He gasped for air.

Charlie and Crash both saw the girl stand up and yell. Charlie was off his bike and on her in a moment. Crash looked around seeking to locate whomever she had been yelling at. The shrubbery screened his view of the lower portion of the area, but he could see no one standing in the corral or on the road. As he moved over to Charlie and the girl, he instructed Gomez to watch Lefty. The girl glared at Charlie, who held her firmly by the wrist. Her eyes, angry and intense, flashed on Crash as he approached. His first impression was that this was a classy lady, good-looking and ready to fight. "Who are you?" was all he could think of to say.

"I'm trying to mind my own business. Who are you? What do you want?" Her voice was feisty.

"I don't really know," Crash thought to himself. Things were moving fast, and Boomer was in control. If he has a beef with this guy, then it needs to be resolved. "Take her up the road to one of the campsites," he commanded Charlie. "I'm gonna see what the hell is happening."

John's first thought when he saw Becky stand up was anger. Anger that she would be their captive. Anger that he would be more restricted in his actions. Then he realized she was trying to warn him of something. He rolled quickly onto his side narrowly avoiding a vicious blow, which landed instead in the dirt where he had been. His left hand grabbed the man wielding the stick and yanked him into the ground. The man was slightly off balance, so he came down easily and with a thud as his face landed on the club. John followed with a hard blow to the man's temple and, rolling him up slightly, another blow to the center of his chest. He then bellied quickly to the edge of the haystacks and looked back to see what was happening to Becky.

Knowing he had only a few moments before they would be searching the corral area for him, he scurried to the edge of the road, saw no one, and ran across keeping bent low. He heard Boomer yelling, his voice coming from some distance to his right. In the corner of his eye, he saw a movement, another biker on the road in front of him. Waco stood alongside his bike scanning the bushes on either side of the road. John came up fast behind him. He threw a forearm across the man's neck and dragged him on his heels to the far side of the road and into the thicker bushes there.

Fifteen feet into the undergrowth, John threw the man to the ground bringing the sharp, black steel of his KA-BAR against the man's throat. The man's eyes went wide and, for a moment, he knew what dying would be like. Several moments passed, and he was still alive. His eyes focused on a face with steel-blue eyes that looked directly into his own, telling him that he could easily still die. Waco had little choice but to wait. Without any instructions he knew that if he struggled or tried to shout, he would be dead.

Finally, the man spoke, softly and without excitement or anxiety. "I have no quarrel with you. But if you are on his side, then you are the enemy. Do you want to live?"

Waco nodded.

"Will you give me your word of honor that you're out of it? No matter what, you won't come after the girl or me? Word of honor."

Waco could hardly believe his ears. The steel of the knife still firm against him, he whispered hoarsely, "What girl?"

Realizing the man didn't even know about Becky, John said simply, "Any girl you see here. Your word of honor. I need to know your answer now."

The offer was his life for stepping out of the fight. All he had to say was yes. The thought of this stranger offering to give him his life and trusting him to keep his word hit Waco's somewhat dusty and tarnished principles. The man was willing to trust him with his own life as well. Waco knew Boomer, Crash, Charlie, Gomez, and Hotshot still presented a formidable challenge to this guy. It was still five against one. "I'm out of it," he finally said. "You got my word."

"Just so you know, if I come across you again, there won't be any talking." As suddenly as the man had appeared, he was gone. Into the bushes and gone.

Waco lay on the ground for a few moments, reviewing what had just happened and what he should do. "I break every law in California and don't lose a minute's sleep over it," he thought. "But this is different. This is between that guy and me. He gave me my life, so I owe him. That's it. Fuck Boomer." He got up slowly, walked back toward the road and sat down on a picnic table, his feet on the bench, his eyes on his motorcycle. Waco figured he would catch some shit for his position, but what the hell, better catching shit for a while than catching dirt in your face as they covered you up for good. A shout from across the road caught his attention.

Boomer had heard the commotion and doubled back toward the beginning of the loop. He saw the girl and whooped as he ran over to where Charlie held her. His eyes widened when he recognized the girl from the bar. He'd wanted her then and, by God, he wanted her now. Just as soon as the pain-in-the-ass boyfriend was taken care of. "Holy shit. Look who we got here. Hello, little darlin'. You miss me?" Boomer took hold of Becky's left arm, glancing threateningly at Charlie, who released his hold on the girl's right arm. "Get everybody down to the truck. My guess is that he'll come out to save his girlfriend. From a fate worse than death I might add," he said, smiling lecherously at Becky. With that he half ran back to the truck, dragging Becky along behind.

281

As Crash came up to Charlie a moment later, he was told of Boomer's instructions. Crash looked around seeing Hotshot's bike in the middle of the road. Boomer was moving down the road, with the girl toward the truck. "Find Hotshot and get down to the truck. I'll get Waco." Crash then moved in a crouch down the left fork of the Y while Charlie began the search for the missing Hotshot. The sight of Waco sitting on the picnic table puzzled Crash. What the hell was he doing? "Waco! Follow me. We got his girl down the end."

"Waco is solid," thought Crash as he moved past the picnic table. But Waco wasn't getting up to follow. He just sat there looking at Crash. "C'mon, Wac," he said again over his shoulder. Still no response. Crash stopped. Waco was looking at him. He seemed uninjured. "What's up?"

"I can't, Crash."

Crash walked to the table. The two men stared into each other's eyes, each looking for something. "What do you mean, you can't?" Crash saw resolve in his buddy's eyes. "Talk to me, Waco. What's happening?"

"The guy got me, Crash. He came out of nowhere, dragged me into the bushes, and put a knife to my throat. A big knife. He could have cut my head off."

"But he didn't," Crash answered. "Why not?"

"He said, 'If you give me your word of honor to stay out of it, I'll let you live.' I thought about it for a while and said OK. So I'm out of it, Crash. I'd like to help out, but I gave my word, and he let me live. And there's no doubt in my mind he would have put me away. He's not a pussy. His fucking eyes cut right through you. Anyway, I'm out of it. You still got five guys. I'll go look after Lefty. Free up Gomez."

Most of us still react to ideas like honor and the value of one's promise. Even when we weaken and take the easy way, deep down we still recognize the right way. Certainly the idea of life versus death catches our attention when it hits close to home. Crash looked at Waco, solid Waco, and he understood. He could see in Waco's eyes the experience of narrowly missing death's snare. He had seen the look in Vietnam. He had seen it in Oakland.

Crash put his hand on Waco's shoulder. "You look after Lefty. We'll handle this other shit. You're doin' the right thing." He squeezed Waco's shoulder. He wheeled and trotted off, his boots heavy on the hard packed dirt road.

McConnell edged back in the direction he had last seen Becky, wanting to take the fight to them rather than simply avoid them. Getting away was not the issue. Getting away with Becky safe was. John watched as Charlie grabbed her and another man ran over. Becky was brought to the fork. where he saw Boomer come running up. Boomer took her back down to the truck at the end of the loop. The other two men split up, one going left toward the man he'd just left, the other to Hotshot's bike. Of the seven bikers, two, possibly three, were out of it, leaving four to deal with. One was nursing the accident victim; another was down by the truck; a third gone around the loop toward the man he just left. The fourth was now isolated between himself and the truck. He would have to be next. John saw Gomez still busy tending to the crash victim. He ran low across the road back toward the man he had left unconscious in the corral. He crawled to the edge of the hay bales and checked Gomez again. From only a few feet away, he heard his quarry call. "Hotshot. Where the hell are you, man? Hotshot?"

"Around here. Come here, quick." was the excited response. Charlie, relieved he had located the missing Hotshot, came around the end of the hay bales to receive a full fist hard into the middle of his face followed by an explosion in the back of his head. Charlie was out cold before he hit the ground. Checking Gomez once again, John moved quickly through the bushes toward the end of the loop.

Boomer's voice rang out. "Come on, big shot. I've got your woman here. I'm gonna have a little fun." John watched as Boomer roughly grabbed at Becky's breasts, rubbing his palms callously against her. When she resisted, Boomer slapped her across the face. Becky's head spun, but she recovered to slap Boomer hard in the face with her free hand.

Boomer's rage exploded. He jerked Becky's arm violently, a loud popping emanating from her shoulder as it dislocated. Becky tried weakly to slap him again but was thrown down, the arm hanging from her dislocated shoulder smacking onto the edge of a picnic table and cracking. Her head spun as she drifted in and out of consciousness. John watched, horrified, almost rushing in to help her. Boomer, however, yanked a .45 automatic from his waist belt, held it high, and yelled again. "Come on, you prick! There won't be anything left of your girlfriend. Where's your big balls now?" Saliva dribbled down Boomer's chin. His eyes were red with rage.

"Over here, you lump a shit!"

Boomer whirled to the voice taunting him. The .45 cocked and ready, he moved toward the voice in the bushes. His prey was tricky, but Boomer was ready for him. There was no question that he would kill the bastard, although he wished the creep could be alive to watch him screw his woman. Boomer's senses were as alert as they had ever been. Instinctively he knew that life and death were the prizes. He moved a branch aside. There to the left was a blue shirt. The son of a bitch was running away.

John knew he had little time. Becky was injured, how badly he could only guess. Still concealed in the bushes, he moved closer. Suddenly he peeled off his shirt, looking for a suitable bush to hang it on. It would be his decoy to draw fire from the .45 and bring Boomer closer.

Boomer was yelling again. Taunting him. Hoping to draw him out into the open, into his gun sight. Lying on the ground close to the hanging tee shirt John responded. "Over here you lump a shit!" He then bellied slowly back from the shirt, crouching, coiling behind the shrubs, counting on the shirt to catch and hold Boomer's attention. Boomer wasted no time coming. John's eyes alternated between Boomer's eyes and the .45. He caught the precise moment Boomers eyes fixed on the shirt and the gun came up to bear on the shirt. John saw hate and fear mixed in with rage and knew his options were disappearing. This man would stop at nothing to hurt him and Becky. If not now, then later. If left alive, he would shadow them forever. That was not a viable option for John. His chest was tight. He was back in the U Minh. Back in combat. The bushes exploded with thunderous gunfire, the shirt flapped sharply when the heavy, soft-lead bullets ripped it apart. As John moved toward the gun, he heard a laugh that at first sent a shock of fear through him. An excited maybe crazy laugh. The fear turned to focused determination. There would only be one opportunity. Becky's life hung in the balance.

John's left hand grabbed Boomer's right wrist, his gun hand. He pushed the wrist upward, the gun barrel skyward. The arm jerked as the automatic roared again. With his right hand, John brought the KA-BAR hard up under the rib cage, the long, darkened steel blade driving up into the heart. The force of John's body behind the thrust brought Boomer off his heels. The top of John's fist held fast against the lowest rib. The deadly tip tore at the thick walls of the black heart. John felt the man slowly go limp but held the body upright with the knife. He twisted the grip once and then lowered it out of its target, the body following it and falling to the ground.

John took a deep breath. Boomer was dead. His thoughts turned immediately to Becky and he ran to her. Falling to his knees, he lifted her head onto his lap and caressed her hair. Her eyes flickered open. When her vision focused, she recognized John. "John. You're all right? Oh John, I was so frightened."

"You're all right now, love. Everything's gonna be all right." He kissed her on the forehead. Becky's arm lay at an awkward angle. "We're going to get you patched up."

A voice behind him brought the nightmare back to life. "I hope everything's gonna be all right." John turned to the voice. Another man in black leather pants stood about six feet away, Boomer's .45 in his hand. Crash looked at the man on his knees trying to comfort his injured woman. The man had lost, but he radiated defiance and danger. Crash now understood what Waco had been talking about. The man's eyes were intense. And fierce. "You did a number on old Boomer. A permanent number."

"He didn't leave me much choice."

"No. I guess he didn't. He was like that." Crash looked around and realized he was alone. "I know about Waco. That you let him go. He stayed out of it, by the way. Just so you know. You kill any of the others?" Crash asked, thinking about his own losses and how capably this man had dealt with the significant violence thrust upon him. His men were not weak or unseasoned fighters.

"There are two over by the hay bales. They should be OK. Headaches, maybe. Your guy by the post took care of himself." McConnell paused. "That's good about Waco."

"Who are you?"

"I'm just a guy trying to protect his woman. From that." John nodded toward the bushes where Boomer's body lay. The two men looked at one another. Both were quiet for several minutes. Becky moaned quietly. John saw strength in the other man. and realized he had little chance to do anything with Becky in his lap and the .45 pointed in his direction. He thought that, brief though it might have been, Becky had been a gift, and the last few months a blessing. He caressed her hair again and returned his gaze to the man with the gun.

The gun slowly lowered. Crash released the hammer and pushed on the safety. "I think that everyone who was supposed to die here today is dead. I think it's over. We both have wounded to attend to." He looked into John's eyes. "Agreed?"

"Agreed." John felt a weight lift from his shoulders and his heart. He took Becky into his arms, stood up, and carried her to the passenger side of the truck.

Carefully he sat her on the seat then took two towels from a bag in the truck's bed, made a rough splint and sling for her forearm, then secured the whole arm to her body.

Crash started to walk away but stopped and looked back over his shoulder. "One question. Where did you learn this stuff? They don't teach what you did here in San Francisco."

John kissed Becky again on the forehead. Gently he closed the door and finally acknowledged Crash's question. "Navy. Seal Team One. Three tours."

Crash nodded. "I figured something like that. I was Army. Special Forces. You work the delta?"

"Yeah. Out of Rach Soi."

"Who knows? We may have walked through the same rice paddy. Anyway, Boomer got what he deserved. I'll square it with the police. Good luck to you."

"I owe you for this. I appreciate it." John walked to the driver's side and opened the door. Before he got in, he looked over the truck at Crash. "And good luck to you." With that, John got in, turned over the engine, and drove slowly around the loop to the highway. Waco raised his hand in a small wave as the truck passed. John nodded and gave a thumbs-up in return. Waco signaled Gomez to let the truck go by. At the intersection to the highway, John stopped. Then he turned north, his attention now focused on getting medical help for Becky. Glancing over to check on her, he found her awake, watching him, and smiling.

"My guardian angel at work again." The towel wrapped around her body made her appear small and a little helpless, but her smile was like the sun lighting up the whole world. After the grim business they were leaving behind, her words and smile made it all seem acceptable. Made it right. "Are you all right, John? I mean…" She hesitated. "I mean…inside?"

He reached over and patted her knee. "Yes." He smiled back at her. "If you're all right, then so am I."

"Let's go home, John." She leaned over, wincing slightly when her arm throbbed. and kissed him softly on the lips. "Let's go home."

Crash stood over the now groaning forms of his cohorts lying along-side the hay bales. The whine of the gray truck as it shifted gears and gained speed caught his attention. He watched as it moved up the coast and out of his life. "The guy has made it back. He's come home. Back to the world," Crash thought. "And I'm still trying to find my way back. Maybe this is my world."

"The guy sucker punched me, Crash," Hotshot complained as he held his chest, still gasping somewhat for a full breath of air.

"Shut up!" As he looked down at Hotshot, it came to Crash that this was not the world he wanted to be in. Not the people he really wanted to be with. He needed to continue the search for his world. Or maybe start working to make a world he wanted. The sound of the gray truck faded away. Crash stood in the corral, thinking about the mess he had to clean up as he waited for the police. He would remember the man with eyes of fire and the woman who loved him. And maybe he, too, would make his way back to the world.

BIOGRAPHY

L arry Chime was raised in New Jersey. He attended St. Peter's College earning a BS degree in Bus. Admin. Upon graduation he joined the Navy, was appointed to Officer Candidate School in Newport, RI, and was commissioned an Ensign in 1965. He served aboard the USS Lake Champlain (CVS-39), the last of the Essex class carriers. He then served aboard the USS Okinawa (LPH-3) an amphibious assault carrier and deployed to Vietnam for most of 1967. After his military service Chime moved to the San Francisco Bay area, went back to school, and earned a Masters degree in marine biology from Sonoma State University. He lived in California until 1977 when he moved to Hawaii where he met and married his wife, Patti. Together there they raised four sons; Jason, Jonathan, Andrew and Christopher. Larry and his wife currently reside in Panama City Beach, FL where Larry still works part time as a Team Leader at the Navy Base marina. They have four grandchildren.

Made in the USA
Columbia, SC
09 July 2023

19919886R00178